NINE LIVES

John F Hope

With illustrations by

Julie Hope

A Cato9tails Production

By the same authors:

CHRISTMAS CAROLS FOR CATS
NURSERY RHYMES FOR CATS
CHRISTMAS CRACKERS FOR CATS

Copyright © 2010 John and Julie Hope

The right of John and Julie Hope to be identified as the Authors of the Work has been asserted by them in accordance with the Copyright, Designs and Patents Act 1988.

First published in the United Kingdom by Cato9tails Productions.

Apart from any use permitted under UK copyright law, this publication may only be reproduced, stored, or transmitted, in any form, or by any means, with prior permission in writing of the publishers, or in the case of reprographic production, in accordance with the terms of licenses issued by the Copyright Licensing Agency.

All human characters in this publication are real persons but names have been changed to protect their privacy. All cats in this publication are real cats, but you shouldn't believe everything they say.

Cataloguing in Publication Data is available from the British Library

ISBN: 978-1-907540-22-6

Typeset in Times Roman 12 by AnchorPrint Group Limited,
Leicester, Leicestershire, UK.

Printed and bound in the UK by AnchorPrint Group Limited,
Leicester, Leicestershire, UK.

Cato9tails Productions
info@cato9tails.net

This book is dedicated to the memory of

The Lion
(a.k.a. Old Lady)
and
All the cats we've been blessed to know.

Special thanks are due to family, friends and colleagues for critique, suggestions and encouragement during this production of this book.

John Hope was born in South Africa around the time that police Studebakers prowled the streets of Johannesburg. He trained as an electronics engineer and over the last thirty years has designed electronics for everything from helicopter avionics through research equipment to mine locomotives. For the last thirteen years he has been designing audio equipment for the broadcast industry. And for himself.

Julie Hope was born in Sheffield, Yorkshire and saw Jimi Hendrix live in the Sheffield City Hall. She trained as a furniture designer and illustrator, and her designs may be found in celebrity kitchens and top executive boardrooms. By far her greatest satisfaction comes from drawing cats rummaging in rubbish.

Julie and John have been married for 20 years. They have been writing whimsical prose for longer than they care to remember. Their first three books, *Christmas Carols for Cats*, *Nursery Rhymes for Cats*, and *Festive Feline Limericks* were published by Bantam. *Nine Lives* is their first full-length book, designed as a companion to the cato9tails.net website.

They live in Oxfordshire with their two cats, Sixpence and Choklit-Butch.

GLOSSARY

(For those not familiar with Khat-speak and Khat Lore)

air-shufa	flatulence
appreciation	petting by an human
ayoomfa	human
ayoomfa eating sticks	cutlery
ayoomfa marking sticks	pens
ayoomfapuriks	human children
ayoomfarolê	a human of quality that may be considered an honorary cat
ayoomfawumpus	human's bed
bangstick	gun
bangstick box	gun safe
big flash magic	camera
binidali	the hole of a *binigaus*
binigaus	unspecified burrowing creature.
bizzum	flying insect
bizzumroli	motorcycle
blibble	unspecified inedible internal organ
bloik-bloik	throwing up
blue-head cackacks	Guinea Fowl
booma-skwasha	run over by a car
bouncy	rubber
brushsticks	brooms
bumpity hill	stairs
burning box	oven
cackack	chicken
chirrit	bird
chukkachin	petting a cat by tickling it under the chin
cracklesack	plastic bag
dark roomi	cupboard
digestion	usually refers to an engine or apparatus
door fur	mat
fence box	cage

fence room	caged area such as at a pound or kennels
floor-rumbleroli	low bed truck
fluffpuff flower	dandelion
food room	kitchen
fruka-fruka	sexual intercourse
glorp	unspecified abundance
gone box	kitchen rubbish bin
ground squee	burrowing mouse or mole
gruf	dog
grush	tall grass/bush
guelph	unspecified mammal other than dog or cat
gulpa	goldfish
happi-rumble	purring
happi-water	booze
hissing air slinki	air compressor hose
hopit	rabbit
house of many long walls	supermarket
humvee	unspecified dairy fluid
khouncile	council
kikkarik	lightning
corner krorli	Spider. See also *spinnelly*
kraak	crow
krinckle-krunckle	kneading with forepaws
krorlis	ants, beetles or other crawling insects
lidda	foil lid of yoghurt pot to be licked clean
lollijubber	loose fluffy belly fat
magic night stick	candle
magic rain box	shower
magic rain-slinki	garden hose
magic speakstick	telephone
magic sun	electric light
magic window	television
mujaji	unspecified incomprehensible
mujaji (fire) strings	electric cables
mujaji lord	engineer, scientist, technician, sorcerer etc
mujaji of invisible fire	electricity
mwaa!	insufficiency

oozule	oil, grease etc
paddlefoot-roli	bicycle
pepper play	paperwork, reading, writing
phluffi	fluffy
pink sea slinkis	shrimps, prawns
plokkits	crunchy, dry pellets of cat food; kibble
potta	yoghurt pot to be licked clean
purik	kitten
push-roli	flatbed trolley.
rain-smoke	steam
roli	wheel, moving
roli rainslinki	garden hose spool
roli-board	stretcher, mechanics trolley.
rolibox	shopping trolley
roli-house	caravan or camper
roli-rumble door	automatic roll up garage door
rounds	Coins, washers, discs etc.
rumbleroli	truck, bus, fire engine, space shuttle etc
rumbling potta	kettle
sand plokkits	cat litter
shnoogliwumpus	igloo-type cat bed
screaming wind	vacuum cleaner
seedballs	testicles
shmoo kukri	soft, wet cat food
shreeka-shreeka bizzum	cicada or loud cricket
shufa	excrement
shufa bowl	WC
shufa box	cat litter tray
shufa sheets	toilet paper
shufacation	defecation
shufa-hole	anus
sitzrolis	pram
sitz-softah	comfortable chair or sofa
sitzup	desk chair, stool
skybang	thunder
slidyboxes	drawers
slinki	unspecified reptile

smootha-skin	leather, plastic etc.
smort	dirt, filthy
softah	fabrics - carpets, curtains, etc
spinnelly	Spider. See also *corner krorli*
spitting tin	aerosol can
squee	mouse
stinkiroli	passenger vehicle
surprise rain	automatic sprinkler
Tabithat	God of all cats
tikki	small
tiny cold room	refrigerator
troon	doze
wa	tranquility
wark-wark	cough up a furball
washdoosh box	dishwasher
water slinki	unspecified marine creatures other than fish
wee-woo flashroli	ambulance, also possibly police car, fire engine etc.
whacka-whacka	helicopter
whitecoati	veterinarian
whumpage	power of paw
wizz	urine
Woon	black cat with white paws and bib
woo-woo	wind
wubbis	blanket
wumpus	cat bed (general)
yhat	rat
yowli	tomcat

CHAPTER ONE:
Capture!

It was an outrage! An absolute spitting, hissing outrage! We had been kidnapped from my house in Harvard where I had been innocently enjoying a sunny retirement. Worse still, MyGranni was involved in this conspiracy. She had betrayed us and had I not been confined in that horrid, stinking box, and uh. . Had I any teeth left, I would have bitten her most vexatiously. What I had learned back in Vietnam was correct; you simply cannot trust the *ayoomfas* at all. It stands to reason that any creature that walks on only two legs is bound to use the other two to make mischief! I set up a long, deep growling, of the kind that spikes fear into all animals with soft exposed parts.

My dear companion Butch had also been abducted, but he seemed quite unconcerned about it all.

'What do you think they'll give us for supper?' he asked casually.

'You stupid animal!' How can you think of food at a time like this? Our very lives may be in peril and all you can think about is food. Give me strength!'

'But food is important, Bunni. ' he droned on, 'food will give you strength.'

'Shut up fool!' I snarled at him, 'or I'll whump you back into last week when I get out of here!' I really didn't need his speculating on trivia during this crisis. At least I couldn't see his gormless expression, for MyGranni had bundled him into a big wicker basket with a lid. The two of us sat in our prisons, with MyGranni between us, in the back of the Young Man's blue *stinkiroli*. The Young Man and the Young Man's woman sat in the front of the stinkiroli, singing silly songs to us to try dupe us into believing everything would be fine. The stinkiroli had been in motion for a long time, certainly longer than it would have taken to go see the *whitecoati*. No, this wasn't a whitecoati trip; this was something else.

Only once before had I been in a stinkiroli for such a long time, and I vaguely recalled something similar that had happened back in Vietnam. While in 'Nam I had come across this big white box-like thing that was part stinkiroli, part house. It rolled on rounds like a stinkiroli but it never seemed to move, and was like a house inside, with beds and magic suns and even a white *shufa bowl* for the Ayoomfas to make shufa. This *roli-house* seemed always open and MyGrandad - whom I had long since forgiven for spraying me with water before he knew me properly - would go nap in it in the afternoons. Very sensible he was, my Grandad. He would have made a fine cat indeed. For weeks on end I used to go inside the roli-house every afternoon and nap with MyGrandad. One day when I had I dozed off in this manner, snuggled and making gentle sleepi-rumble against MyGrandad while he made loud sleepi-rumble, the roli-house quietly moved away from Vietnam and when I woke up and got out of it I found myself in Harvard. My Grandad appeared to have slept through the whole incident and I'm convinced of his total innocence in this matter. But I've always had a sneaky suspicion that my move to Harvard was somehow orchestrated by MyGranni and the other ayoomfas, although I could neither fathom how they did it nor prove anything.

My daughter Khalli - a foolish animal if ever there was - had somehow also managed to get to Harvard, although I know not how. MyGranni doted on Khalli, and I could never understand this. I did my best to show MyGranni what a stupid animal was Khalli by thrashing her regularly, but if anything this seemed only to make matters worse and further endear the silly girl to MyGranni. Harvard was a good home, although I missed MyGrandad after he died, and I missed the Young Man after he moved away with his woman. I even missed Khalli when she got sick and died, for with her gone there was nobody I could beat up on. We acquired another addition to the family when MyGranni - for reasons I could never understand - had adopted Butch, a huge black and white tomcat with a very gentle nature. Butch - bless his simple soul - even seemed tolerant to being whumped by me on a regular basis, and we'd all lived quite happily in Harvard - until *this*.

After a long travel of about six naps, the blue stinkiroli stopped and after a lot of typical ayoomfa banging and crashing - for they are such clumsy creatures it pains me, it truly does - we were let out of our boxes inside a big house. A bright, sunny house, Spartan, not cozy like Harvard. And it didn't have the plants growing on the outside walls like Harvard had. It was very wild outside. More open than Vietnam, set in grassland with a few scattered trees. The Ayoomfas called it *Midrand*.

Worse still, there was another cat there. Butch and I had been thrown together with *another animal*. More outrage! She was in her prime, big and fat, and with stocky powerful paws full of *whumpage*. She had placed herself outside the house in front of the little door within a door of the kind that lazy ayoomfas construct so that they can get out of opening and closing the big doors for us, and we may go in and out of the house as we please. I approached the door cautiously.

'Who are you and what are you doing at my house?' I asked suspiciously

'I might well ask the same of you,' she said. My name's Scrap and I didn't get that name for nothing. I've been in The Prison, you know.

'Yes? Well I've been in Vietnam. And I went to Harvard.' I spoke my words carefully, so she wouldn't spot that I had no teeth left.

'Never heard of either place. Probably homes for phraidy cats, I wouldn't be surprised.'

'Yes, well, never mind that now.' As a careful old cat of immense wisdom and experience - and astonishing beauty, of course - I decided to ignore Scrap's mischievous provocation and to pursue a course of conviviality unless events forced me to do otherwise. 'How did you get here?' I asked.

'I was in The Prison for a long time until my Mummy and That Man came and escaped me. Then they brought me here yesterday. Not a bad place, this. The food's good, and I found a job.'

'What kind of job?' I asked suspiciously.

'I'm in charge of this little door within a door and all who would pass must pay me a toll of two big *bizzums*. I particularly like the big green and blue ones with two sets of wings. You can find them outside by the place of water. . . '

'I want to go outside and make *wizz*. Now. And I don't have any bizzums,' I said provocatively.

'I can open an account for you. . . '

I figured that Scrap might have got a little soft in The Prison, and being as portly as she was it wasn't likely her reactions were anything to brag about. Also, I was older and with age comes wisdom, cunning and mastery of deceit. I took a big gamble.

'I've got a much better idea,' I said sweetly, while I stealthily pulled back the door within a door towards me as far as it would go. 'I'm just a sweet little old lady, so why don't I just – and I released the little door - *whumpa whumpa whumpa* – let this door come and wallop you on the head like this until you get the Hell out of my way!' Scrap had not expected that at all and she fell back, dazed and astonished.

'You should know better than to mess with an old lady who wants to wizz,' I said later as I sat on the outside of the door within a door, calmly washing my forepaws as Scrap sat glaring at me from a safe distance, brooding over her loss of face. 'From now on I shall use this door within a door whenever I please, without hindrance. And now that we've established the ground rules, you can call me Bunni. I guess we're going to live together so we might as well get along.'

Life at Midrand was quite pleasant provided one didn't venture too far away from the house. Beyond the area of tidy cut grass and plants that surrounded the house, there was high *grush* that extended for a long, long way. Serious wild grush almost as high as the Young Man's woman and fraught with unexpected danger. Even now I shudder to think what dangers lay within. Wild cats with a desperate, savage glint in their yellow eyes and poison in their bite, ready to rip and kill. Stray *grufs* and unidentified big *guelphs* that could bite one in two, or shoot spikes infected with Tabithat knows what poisons into one's sensitive nose leather; evil slithering *slinkis* that would hiss and terrorise; horrid stinging *bizzums* as big as one's paw; not to mention the perils of bottomless holes and fetid water one could fall into and from where one's pleas for help would not be heard.

On the Morning Sun side and beyond the long grush was a stinkiroli-path; what the ayoomfas call a *road,* and beyond that more long grush as far as they eye could see. On the Afternoon Sun side and beyond the long grush was another house around which roamed two large grufs, whose sole desire in life seemed to be to kill and eat all of us, the Young Man and his woman included. Thank Tabithat these grufs were behind a wire fence and couldn't fulfil their slavering fantasies, but I was still concerned that they might one day become so infused with hatred and bloodlust that they would jump right over the fence. Fortunately, grufs aren't gifted with the degree of amazing athletic prowess that we are and are nearly as clumsy as ayoomfas, so they'd more than likely end up crashing down and painfully entangling themselves on the sharp barbs of the fence without achieving anything other than agony and embarrassment. Evidently their simple minds were just sufficiently large enough to register this possibility and so the likelihood of the grufs jumping the fence and coming to get us was not great. But these were real nasty grufs, so we were all very wary. I had seen grufs exactly like these on MyGranni's *magic window*; they had been helping teams of bad ayoomfas who wore square pots on their heads and who stamped and shouted and made much noise with their *bangsticks*. I remember MyGranni called them *Nasties* and she clearly felt very strongly about them, for she would begin a dark muttering and drink more happi-water from the bottle-that-plays-songs whenever she saw them on the magic window. Personally, I don't blame the Nasties at all for being disgruntled and angry. Collars are a bad enough irritant, having to wear a square pot on one's head must be truly infuriating.

In my younger days I would have handled this entire trauma with consummate ease and without batting a paw, for it was no worse than Vietnam. Easier, in fact, because I'd faced much worse and triumphed. But now as a retired cat who had seen two full paw's pads plus four winters, I was really too old for this *shufa*.

Scrap and I became good friends at Midrand. She had spent a long time in The Prison and had endured hard beginnings, not unlike my own. She never volunteered the reason for her having been in The Prison and we knew better than to ask. Scrap was younger than me; I'd guess her to have been about one full paw of pads plus two winters. She herself had no idea of her age and when asked simply said, 'Young enough to thrash anyone and old enough not to care about it.' A rather nice philosophy, I must admit, but even she was nonetheless sensible enough not to stray too far from the house. She used to spend many afternoons on a big structure with a flat eating surface that the ayoomfas had installed in the sunniest room of the house, and which they called a *tay-bill*. There she would lie fatly on her back, with her four stubby paws sticking up from a great mountain of fluffy flesh. She looked quite ridiculous in this position but seemed not to care a whisker. Placed in the centre of the tay-bill was an object containing some water and flowers. Some kind of ayoomfa's toy, I imagine, although they never seemed to play with it. Often Scrap would lie on the eating surface and lazily roll about with the afternoon sunlight playing on her belly, and sometimes she would roll into the ayoomfa's flower toy which would fall over with a mighty crash and spill water everywhere. Traditional wisdom from Khat Lore suggests that under such circumstances a cat should run away, since the burden of proof of who caused the mayhem lies squarely with the ayoomfas. They could not possibly know which cat had done the deed and therefore could not bring themselves to scold any particular one of us. But Scrap didn't subscribe to this theory.

'I'm beautiful, cuddly, and full of largesse,' she said defiantly. 'The ayoomfas all love me and wouldn't dream of scolding me. I shall simply move to lie on a dry part of this fine tay-bill and wait for them to return, clean up the mess, and make amends for their thoughtlessness in leaving this silly thing where it could be knocked over.'

Amazingly, this ploy never failed and in time the ayoomfas saw fit to substitute a heavier toy which Scrap couldn't knock over.

Scrap had previously been the supervisor of the Young Man's woman and now she became a supervisor of the Young Man as well. As time went by the Young Man grew very fond of Scrap and she took to calling him Daddi. In return the Young Man gave Scrap the new name of *Phat Balune*. I was most amused at Scrap's new name - hee! hee! hee! - but of course I knew better than to tease her about it. I politely feigned indignation on her behalf and told her that we all knew she was not fat, but simply filled with largesse. The Young Man's woman - whom Phat Balune called Mummi - was also a little unhappy about the new name and usually truncated it to simply *Balune*. And somehow the name stuck, sometimes prefixed with *Phat*, other times with *Helium*, and on rare occasions with *Heavus Maximus*, but mostly just Balune. In fact the only ayoomfa that didn't use Scrap's new name was MyGranni, who regularly came to visit us in Midrand. For reasons unknown she addressed Balune variously as *SugarBelle* or *Princess*. Scrap doted on MyGranni, whom she said treated her with 'proper respect for a lady'.

It was the Young Man's duty to feed us most mornings and he quickly established a ritual eating ceremony in which all three of us were required to participate before we could eat. It began with the Young Man making lots of noises of the kind ayoomfas imagine that cats respond to, and all three of us were required to sing and make trilling sounds. Any sounds would do really, as the Young Man didn't understand a single word of *Khat*. We could call him a squee's shufa-hole and he would still be delighted. Once we had sung sufficiently, we each had to allow ourselves to be picked up, cradled in his arms, and squeezed until we made further sounds of joy. I was lucky insofar as Young Man considered me old and delicate and would not usually squeeze me too much, and to reinforce this opinion I took to making *poor old feeble cat* noises when he picked me up; much the same sounds as MyGranni used to make when she had cause to grovel on the floor to fetch something she'd dropped and which had rolled under one of the pointless structures with which the ayoomfas see fit to clutter our houses.

Butch - as was his timid nature - would trot away just out of reach and Young Man soon gave up trying to pick him up during the breakfast ceremony. Poor old Scrap got the worst of it. Being built as she was, she was eminently squeezable, and Young Man would brook no resistance, excuses or reluctance from her. Every day she was lifted up, cradled and squeezed, and she was expected to like it and make convincing sounds of appreciation. Surprisingly, she didn't really mind this much, and from then on the Young Man was the only ayoomfa ever allowed to pick her up, let alone squeeze her, or give her *Full Encapsulation of Face*. Many others tried and went away nursing their wounds.

After the Young Man had completed his molestations, the breakfast ceremony continued with him cleaning our food bowls and refilling them with fresh *shmoo kukri*. A bowl of *plokkits* and another of water was placed in a convenient location for our communal use throughout the day. The sacred principle that cat food bowls and bowl positions are not interchangeable - at least not by ayoomfa serving staff - was sufficiently understood by the Young Man. Scrap always had the pink bowl, I always had the green bowl and Butch had the blue bowl. Scrap's bowl was always the one on the right, mine was on the left and Butch's was in the middle. Young Man would place our bowls in a neat row and watch with benign satisfaction as we started to tuck into our food. Sometimes just to tease us, he'd swap the bowls around and watch gleefully as we feigned outrage and milled around unhappily for a while before voicing our displeasure and sometimes even wandering off in disgust. But I also discovered - the hard way - that with these ayoomfas it was best to eat enthusiastically during the breakfast ceremony, for any reluctance to eat would instantly be interpreted as the onset of serious illness and the culprit would soon be seized, imprisoned, and whisked off in the stinkiroli to see the whitecoati.

The whitecoati in Midrand was not the same kindly young whitecoati that we used to visit when I was staying with MyGranni at Harvard, but a big brusque ayoomfa male who was accustomed to working with massive dumb guelphs of the kind ayoomfas sometimes ride on, and I didn't really think he had either the finesse or skill to deal with more complex and sophisticated creatures such as ourselves. Indeed he wasn't even truly a whitecoati and could only really be described as a *white-spattered-with-blood-coati*.

However, events unfolded which proved that he was indeed a proper practitioner of *whitecoati magic* and also an ayoomfa of good intent and top quality, known in Khat as an *ayoomfarolê*. For some years I had had an annoying little pimple on my nose leather. I have no idea where it came from or why; these things are in the hands of Tabithat. It didn't usually pose a problem for me but sometimes it would become engorged with blood and then I would inadvertently scratch it while washing, causing it to bleed profusely out of all proportion to the size of the scratch. Young Man and his woman were somewhat concerned about it, but were of the sensible opinion that my nose pimple did not warrant the trauma and upset, all the hissing and growling and spitting that was unavoidably associated with my capture and taking me to the whitecoati. Then one day when I scratched it, the nose pimple burst with such vigour that it spurted blood all over the *softahs* where the ayoomfas sit, and the other softahs they had hanging by the windows, and also on the softahs they had lining the floor. It bled all over my face but I'd been asleep when I'd scratched it and so was totally unaware of all the carnage caused by my nose pimple. When I awoke and saw what had happened, I went and hid away under one of the structures in the house because I knew that all ayoomfas are terribly precious about their softahs and I thought my Young Man and his woman would be angry with me for making such a mess. They would know with certainty that it was not Scrap or Butch because I would be the only one bleeding. But I had misjudged them, for when the ayoomfas saw all the blood they were unconcerned at the mess and feared only that I was mortally injured. They begat an undignified panic over my welfare. They didn't know what had happened and imagined I'd been savaged by one of the Nasty Grufs. The Young Man was all set on avenging me by going to kill the grufs with his bangstick, but the woman tends to be more level-headed in a crisis and she pacified him. Then like a clever cat she cunningly followed the trail of blood which led her to my hiding place, and it soon became apparent that all the blood was the result of my insignificant little nose pimple having burst. Young Man was a little disappointed that he hadn't been allowed to go and kill the Nasty Grufs with his bangstick, but both he and the woman were very concerned with my injury and promptly bundled me up in the picnic basket and whisked me off to the whitecoati.

I don't really remember much of what happened at the whitecoati – for some reason I became very sleepy and dozed off, despite trying hard to stay awake and follow proceedings as best I could. When I awoke, I discovered that there had been unknown *whitecoati magic* done and that my nose pimple was gone. Just like that!

Ayoomfas are very devious and have some amazingly clever magics. One such clever ayoomfa magic is the *magic window*. Nearly all ayoomfa houses have one of these fitted. A magic window allows ayoomfas to see in window events that are taking place elsewhere, and the ayoomfas use them to inform and entertain themselves. My Young Man and his woman sometimes sat and watched the magic window at night, and this presented an excellent opportunity for quality lap and snuggle. During the winter nights I would weasel myself right under the outer coverings of the woman like I'd done with MyGrandad and keep both of us warm, but I would always keep my head outside in case of danger and also to see what was happening on the magic window.

It was on the magic window that I saw a place exactly like the place where I had grown up, a wild, wild place with thick grush and many trees, bushes and vines. A truly inhospitable and horrendous place, which surely must be unique. I learned that the ayoomfas called this place Vietnam. I suppose it's just conceivable that there may be more than one of these Vietnam places but the one where I grew up is the only one of any importance to me. The magic window showed Vietnam with hordes of noisy ayoomfas with bits of tree and bush tied on their heads stomping around in the grush shouting pointlessly at each other and making a terrible racket with their bangsticks, while others in *whacka-whackas* flew around the sky like *chirrits*, dropping fires on the grush. They all seemed to be looking for someone called Charlie. I never discovered whether or not they ever found this Charlie, or why they were looking for him, for the magic window showed that the ayoomfas with bits of tree and bush tied on their heads simply left without staying to tidy up the fires and mess they had made.

I don't remember encountering these noisy ayoomfas in *my* Vietnam; I must have been asleep when all this happened. I sleep quite a lot, you know. About the noisiest and messiest thing I ever encountered in Vietnam was a troop of huge white chirrits - all much bigger than me - triply blessed in that could walk on land and sail on water and fly in the sky. They made strange honking sounds when they flew in the sky and hissed and spat at other creatures when they were on land, but at least they didn't start any fires. These enormous chirrits had stupidly become lost and were waddling around my Vietnam as if they lived there! Luckily MyGrandad saw that they were making a great mess of shufa and so chased them away with a *magic rain-slinki*.

The magic window in Midrand was bigger than the one MyGranni had at Harvard, and most of the time its magic was good. But one summer's afternoon there was a serious rain storm with much *kikkarik* and *skybang,* and this somehow harmed the magic in the magic window and made it sick. All the objects seen through the window became short and fat and it was clear something was wrong. The Young Man was very annoyed by this and thought he'd have a look and see if he could heal the sick magic himself. I watched him do this. I often watched him while he worked, and I think my presence had a calming influence on him. Young Man went behind the magic window and took away a covering so that the magic inside was exposed. I was very curious to see if I could find any of the ayoomfas and creatures I'd seen on the magic window still lurking inside - maybe I could get back to Harvard through here? I watched intently and when the Young Man went away for a few winks to make wizz, I snuck myself right inside the back of the magic window and had a good sniff around. But there were no ayoomfas or creatures there. Only a big black bottle-like object surrounded by other strange but colourful magic artefacts that whistled loudly and disturbingly in a way I could hear but which the ayoomfas apparently could not.

When Young Man returned - and of course found me sitting innocently next to the magic window not even contemplating rummaging around inside it - he did something that immediately caused a loud noise like skybang and a smell of bad fire from within the magic window. Even the short fat pictures disappeared and the window was dark and brooding. Personally, I wasn't convinced that my Young Man was properly anointed to work with this particular type of ayoomfa magic, and he must have reached similar conclusions to my own, for he abandoned his attempt at healing the sick magic, which was now much sicker than before he'd started. He lifted up the magic window and took it away in his blue stinkiroli, to see the whitecoati, I suppose. I think it must have been very sick and died at the whitecoati, for the Young Man brought back a different magic window than the one he'd left with; I could tell this because the old one used to smell pleasantly of Butch's tomspray and the new one smelled only of unknown ayoomfas.

*****

CHAPTER TWO:
The World According to Butch

Butch had come to live with us while MyGranni and I had been trying to enjoy the autumn of our lives in peace at sunny Harvard. MyGrandad and my foolish daughter Khalli had long since died and the family was reduced to just an old retired ayoomfa lady and her brown-point Siamese cat supervisor. Loosely brown-point Siamese, very loosely. I suspect I'm more Chinese than Siamese, although I have no accurate information on my ancestry and it's not relevant anyway. But I digress. One day while I was dozing in the sun on a log amongst the flowers I happened to open one eye briefly and saw this enormous black cat with white socks and bib sitting not a few tail lengths from where I slept. He was a very long and fit cat and his enormous head was crowned with ears which had seen many a fight. His big eyes sparkled from yellow to emerald green with a beautiful lustre as he turned his head in different lights. He had broad black nose leather and some of the most impressive hunting whiskers I'd ever seen on a tom cat. All in all he was a magnificent specimen with long legs and big feet full of whumpage. But it must be said that did look somewhat run down, as if he'd been dragged through a hedge by a big gruf.

'Hello old lady,' he said gormlessly.

'Who in the name of Tabithat are you and what are you doing here in *my* garden at Harvard?' I was most indignant. I don't like strangers and to be totally honest I don't really like *anybody*. MyGranni and I would have much preferred it if everyone would mind their own business and leave us alone. MyGranni relied heavily on my opinion of her visitors, and if I didn't take favour to a visiting ayoomfa she never allowed them to visit again. In this way I'd been able to assist the Young Man in ridding himself of the attentions of several young women he'd brought visiting and whom I'd considered unsuitable for various reasons. He hadn't always appreciated my help, and he thought that MyGranni was responsible for spurning his young women. But he was a foolish Young Man while I was a wise old cat and MyGranni understood that very well.

'It's very nice here,' said the big black cat, looking around approvingly.

'Yes it is! What makes you think you can just pitch up here? This is my home!' I was furious.

'The hunting's good here. Plenty of *squees* and *chirrits*.'

Was he simple or what? I was not in a position to get into a fight with a male cat twice my size and a third my age, even if he was only a tenth of my intelligence. For starters I had no teeth left, which put me at a serious disadvantage for eating tidbits, let alone fighting.

'What don't you understand about not being welcome here?,' I hissed, 'Read my snarl: *Go away!*'

'But it's nice here and I want to come and live here with you and that nice old ayoomfa lady,' he said sweetly and simply. 'I want to be a Citizen of this House. How do I become a Citizen of this House?'

What was I to do? I felt certain that MyGranni wouldn't fall for such a naively presumptuous and foolish black cat and I was relieved when she happened to see him and came outside and shooed him away. I thought she was too soft, though. Had MyGrandad been alive he'd have gone after this black and white tomfool with the magic rain-slinki and given him a thorough drenching. The black and white tomfool in question trotted off with no air of either permanence or urgency.

I didn't see him for a few days, during which I sensed that MyGranni had spoken of him to other members of her ayoomfa family. She appeared quite angry at his arrival but everyone she told about him seemed absurdly delighted. Fools! The Young Man in particular, when he came to visit, behaved very childishly and actually went around the house and garden looking for the black and white tomfool and calling him! How could I make him understand that this would only serve to encourage the tomfool and we'd end up with a squatter problem? MyGranni appeared to see my point of view and scolded the Young Man.

Good! Problem solved, I thought.

But it wasn't anywhere near solved. The black and white tomfool continued to visit us and the frequency of his visits increased disturbingly. Worse still, he took to sitting expectantly on the *door fur* by the front door of the house, having spent time grooming so as to make himself appear innocent and fluffy.

'Please help me, I'm hungry,' he trilled at MyGranni whenever she approached the door. 'I haven't eaten in two weeks.'

'Bah!' I scoffed, 'Lying scoundrel! I saw you eat a squee only yesterday behind the stinkiroli. And you even ate one of MyGranni's chirrits the day before that near the high water bowl where they come to drink. You jumped up into the water to catch it and you ate it so fast you almost swallowed it whole, beak, feet, feathers and all. Like a gruf would! Nay, not even a gruf has so little finesse. You should be ashamed of yourself for trying to hoodwink an innocent old ayoomfa lady like that!'

He pointedly ignored me and MyGranni pointedly ignored him. I smiled smugly to myself in satisfaction. But he continued to visit over the following days. The most attention MyGranni would pay him was to shoo him away gently and he would trot off for a little distance and sit on the grass, blinking balefully at her. This was another thing I noticed about him: he never ran, he never walked, he always trotted.

After the ritual of rejection had gone on for about two paws' pads of days I thought I could relax and go on being a Retired Cat, having properly delegated this irksome problem to MyGranni.

The black and white tomfool was not easily discouraged. He tried another approach. Instead of looking fluffy and innocent when he sat on the door fur, he made himself look pathetic. I mean really *pathetic,* by Tabithat! I think he must have deliberately rolled in a thorn bush or provoked a pack of hobo toms with the express object of getting himself beaten up. He looked a total wreck.

'I'm sooooo hungry,' he called to MyGranni, 'and I'm sore. Everywhere is sore. Oh woe is me! A poor starving and sore cat in need of any morsel you can spaaaare!'

I must confess he did look a wreck. I tried to help.

'Go away, fool', I told him firmly, 'Just go away. We have our own problems here; we don't need yours as well.'

MyGranni, being big of heart and with a soul full of immense kindness and love, couldn't bring herself to ignore him any further and began tossing him a few handfuls of plokkits every morning when she saw his pathetic figure outside the door. *My* plokkits, by Tabithat!! *Mine!* The tomfool made a big show of darting after them and gobbling up every single one as if it were the last morsel of food in the whole world. Then he would sit washing himself on the door fur. This ritual continued for a week or so until MyGranni, always neat and tidy, objected to the stray plokkits that he'd lost and left lying around to be crunched underfoot. She began presenting the black and white tomfool with a daily breakfast of shmoo kukri or plokkits in a blue bowl. Immediately after feeding me, she would go open the front door and give him his breakfast. This really caused me a great deal of stress and indigestion because I would feel obliged to interrupt my breakfast and quickly run around to the front of the house to check whether things were under proper control; that MyGranni hadn't favoured him with more food than me. Or nicer food than me.

The Young Man was delighted when he came to visit and saw what was going on. Certainly I would get no support from him! I could tell he was greatly enamoured of the tomfool and wanted to pick him up, but the tomfool always trotted just out of reach. Young Man gave the tomfool a name: *Butch*. Worse still, I could fathom the gist of his ayoomfa chattering insofar as he suggested MyGranni should adopt the tomfool as a companion for me. I needed a companion about as much as I needed *shufa* in my water bowl!

As a toothless old Retired Cat about all I could do against the inevitable infusion of Butch into *my* home was to hiss and spit at him in a lacklustre fashion once a day when I saw him sitting by the door. This began to make me feel guilty because Butch always spoke to me in such a kindly manner and he seemed totally oblivious to insults and nastiness. It was like he had the benign spirit of Tabithat in him. Either that or he was simply too foolish to know when someone was being unkind to him. In any case I stopped mouthing obscenities at him and just sat back and watched events unfold in a familiar and predictable way. It was a long, drawn out process, but not nearly as long and drawn out as the whole paw's winters it had taken *me* to lower my guard and come into MyGranni's previous house in Vietnam. MyGranni is a very patient old ayoomfa lady and she'd proved to me beyond any doubt that she could out-wait any cat.

The front door was left open so Butch could come inside if he wanted. For many days he was too nervous to enter and preferred to sit outside the door while MyGranni and I sat inside freezing our tails off in the late autumn evenings and wishing he'd either go away or come inside. After several days he came inside but he wouldn't go further than the first room of the house. MyGranni then cunningly moved his food bowl inside and placed it next to mine in the warm room where she made the food. Now Butch would have to go further than the front room of the house, or he wouldn't be fed; simple as that. This didn't faze him at all and he simply trotted up to his bowl in its new location and started eating.

'Oh hello, old lady' he would say to me as I glowered at him. 'I've come to live here now.'

'So I see. . .' I said with acid scorn.

'I hope soon to be a Citizen of the House,' he added.

'How very nice for you,' I snarled through clenched gums.

'So where do I sleep? Is that my bed over there?' he asked, indicating my cherished old falling-to-bits bed lined with the pink *wubbis* and many years of my fur. This was simply too much for me to bear. I would not tolerate having my bed given away. I went up to Butch and clobbered him about the head and shoulders with my paws, bracing myself for his retaliation. But it never came. He simply trotted away to where MyGranni was sitting in the next room.

'That grumpy old white cat beat me up,' he complained to her, 'when I tried to share her bed. She won't share her bed so you'll have to get me my own bed.'

MyGranni smiled at him and patted him on the head. For an ayoomfa, MyGranni was quite perceptive, and before long Butch had his own bed. It was a fully enclosed bed with a little opening in front. In Khat we call such a bed a *shnoogliwumpus.* Butch's bed was bigger than mine. It was newer than mine. I wanted it immediately and in a fit of angry defiance I summarily occupied it. Butch didn't seem to mind, he straight away went to sleep in my bed. This was a real outrage and I had no choice but to get out of his bed and go batter him on the head until he left my bed. But then he went back to his bed and I couldn't get him out because the shnoogliwumpus was enclosed and my only means of entry was through the little opening. Butch had faced his rear to the entrance and every time I tried to put my head inside, he would let forth a cloud of noxious brown tom-spray from his bottom. After a few attempts I was so poisoned by the dreadful stink that I gave up.

'This is my shnoogliwumpus, old lady' he protested. 'MyGranni gave it to me because I'm soon to become a Citizen of this House. Please go sleep in your own bed.'

'She's not *your* Granni, she's *MyGranni*' I chided him. And in this house all beds belong to me. I tried to squash him out by sitting on top of the shnoogliwumpus and collapsing it, but he paid no heed to this at all. Eventually I got bored with the silly dispute and went off to sleep in my own bed, which was in any case properly worn in and far more comfortable than the shnoogliwumpus.

One day Butch overslept in his shnoogliwumpus and MyGranni took fiendish and merciless advantage of this. She picked up the shnoogliwumpus complete with Butch inside it, and summarily emptied it out into a basket with a lid, what the ayoomfas call a picnic basket. Then she shut the lid of the basket and went away with it in her stinkiroli. To the whitecoati.

When he returned Butch told me that he'd tried to tell MyGranni and the whitecoati that he was fit and well and had nothing wrong with him, but they paid him no heed. The whitecoati stuck something cold up his bottom - right up his shufa-hole - and prodded and felt him all over, while constantly chattering with MyGranni. He remembered the whitecoati sticking him in the forepaw with a little thorn, but after that he fell asleep. When he awoke he found himself again in the picnic basket and travelling home in the stinkiroli, MyGranni crooning gently as they trundled along. He told me his *seed balls* felt very sore and suspected they may have been stolen, but he had no recollection of this happening. He was very pleased to be home. I told him the whole experience was essential to his becoming a Citizen of the House.

MyGranni became concerned that Butch would be able to find and use the little door within a door that I used to come and go as I pleased, and I found myself being used as an unwilling demonstration dummy for Butch's access training. While Butch looked on with a bemused smile, MyGranni heaved me from outside to inside the house through the little door. Then she went inside through the big door and shoved me back outside through the little door again. I endured this for a few times and then decided she was abusing my good nature and that I had better things to do with my time. The next time she pushed me outside, instead of sitting like a fool waiting for her to come around and push me back inside again, I ran away and climbed up a tree onto the roof of the house, where I sat pretending to be unaware of her trying to coax me down. MyGranni then tried to pick up Butch and heave him in and out through the little door within a door as she'd done with me, but he simply trotted away and sat just out of reach, blinking his benign emerald eyes at her. She very sensibly decided that Butch had absorbed the gist of the instruction and that it would be an embarrassing waste of her time trying to get him to repeat the exercise like some stupid gruf. Later, after she'd gone but while I was still watching, Butch went in and out of the little door within a door several times and then came over to tell me with great satisfaction that he was now a Citizen of the House.

Over the next winter Butch became more relaxed in the house and even allowed MyGranni to pick him up a few times. And once when the Young Man came to visit Harvard, Butch wasn't fast enough to trot away and the Young Man scooped him up and spent a long time happily nuzzling him and squeezing his beefy hind legs. He even gave him *Partial Encapsulation of Face* and I thought Butch would wizz himself, but he lay still in the Young Man's arms and endured the ordeal as bravely he could.

This ritual happened every time the Young Man visited and Butch decided it wasn't too bad and often allowed himself to be scooped up. Not only by Young Man, but also by his woman and by MyGranni. It was this cunning wearing down of his defences by the sly ayoomfas that resulted in Butch being captured with me and taken off to live in Midrand.

*****

Butch had a habit which greatly frustrated the ayoomfas in the Midrand house. He realised that lowering his guard and allowing himself to be picked up had resulted in capture and deportation to Midrand, so every time the Young Man or the Young Woman tried to pick him up for a squeeze and cuddle, he would trot off to just out of their reach, perhaps hoping they would try and chase him so could derive huge amusement by leading them on a merry dance, watching them crash around and maybe even fall over. But they were wise to this ploy and never tried to catch him when he had an obvious advantage.

He made up for this by being fastidiously tidy in his eating habits, something which endeared him greatly to the ayoomfas. Sometimes they would prepare for him the carcass of a big *cackack* - which I learned they called a *chicken* - after having eaten most of it themselves. Butch would know when this was imminent and he'd make himself look very fluffy and sit balefully staring at them as they ate the cackack from their bowls on the tay-bill.

'Please feed me, I've been so good all day and not eaten any chirrits,' he would wheedle. 'I'll let you pick me up if you give me some. I promise.'

The message was quite clear to the ayoomfas even though they didn't understand Khat. Young Man would get one of the big white mats with ayoomfa markings on it and spread it out on the floor in the room where they usually fed us. These mats were the ones the ayoomfas would hold in front of their faces or place on the tay-bill and silently stare at for hours. They called them *noose peppers*. Young Man would place the cackack carcass on a noose pepper and then discretely withdraw so as to allow Butch some privacy while he ate. Butch was very systematic when he ate a cackack carcass. He'd start at one end and relentlessly dismantle it into small pieces. Then he'd take each and every small piece in turn and winkle the meat off it with his supremely agile teeth and claws. What really impressed the ayoomfas was that after he had finished he would methodically collect every single bone fragment, no matter how small, and stack them neatly in a little pile. And true to his word he always went to submit himself for pick-up afterwards. Young Man would lavish him with complements and affection and could not resist giving him Partial Encapsulation of Face. Butch's head was very big and fluffy and even the Young Man could not manage to do *Full* Encapsulation of Face with him like he did with Balune and myself. One of Young Man's friends had really huge top paws and when he came to visit he sometimes managed to give Butch Full Encapsulation of Face. But more often than not Butch would trot away and go sit where it was just a little too much like hard work for any of the ayoomfas to go fetch him.

Young Man's favourite food was big red meats. He particularly liked the huge ones with a bone across the top and down the middle and meat on either side. Sometimes he would prepare these at Midrand during one of the ayoomfa's *fire festivals*, but more often he and the Young Woman would go out in the stinkiroli and eat these big bone-meats somewhere else. They always remembered to bring a bone back for Butch. He could smell it a long way off, no matter how well they tried to conceal it and he would trill insistently and mill around their feet dangerously, harrying them to give him his bone.

'Have you brought my bone?' he would nag. 'I must have my bone. I've been waiting so patiently for it. Please hurry! No, no, do that later - give me my bone first. Come quickly, there's no time to lose. I'll let you tickle my tummy if you hurry. . .'

Inevitably a noose pepper would be produced and the bone would be placed on it. Butch would first walk around it, inspecting it thoroughly and calculating an appropriate plan of attack. Then he'd place it so it was resting on the part of the bone that ran along the top, with the other bone sticking up in the air. He'd place one of his big front paws down firmly on each side of the sticking-up bone to hold it in place and then remorselessly scour it of all edible meat morsels it with his sharp white teeth. When he was finished and the bone was clean and shiny, he would push it over in a grand gesture of victory and go wash himself thoroughly. Before I met Butch I had only ever seen a gruf eat a bone in this way. The ayoomfas were seriously enthralled with him and sometimes used to invite other ayoomfas to the house specifically to witness Butch's bone eating trick. They even used *Big Flash Magic* to make pictures of him eating to help them remember afterwards how it looked.

At Midrand there was an older ayoomfa who visited the house regularly to tidy the plants outside and also to clean parts of the house. This banging and clattering around caused us all an immense disturbance and every time he came to Midrand, this older ayoomfa would use the *screaming wind*. At Harvard MyGranni had also used the screaming wind and I had come to understand that although it was noisy and immensely irritating, it was not used to do us any real harm. The purpose of the screaming wind is unknown to me. All it seems to do is suck up air from one place and blow it out at another place, and make a great noise in doing so. On one occasion I'd seen it suck up one of my toy squees and this seemed to cause a great discomfort with its digestion. The older ayoomfa had to stop the wind screaming and make it cough up the troublesome toy squee.

When the screaming wind was in use I usually went outside and lay in the sun for a nap, after which time the screaming wind had abated and been packed away in its special little room where the *brushsticks* were stored. Butch, however, was mortally terrified of the screaming wind and it caused him profound stress. In all my life I have never seen a cat as foolishly fearful of anything as was Butch of the screaming wind. He found himself a special hiding place that he thought was impregnable to the screaming wind and he'd go and hide in this place the moment he heard the older ayoomfa arrive shortly after breakfast time. Butch would stay hidden in this place all day, until well after the older ayoomfa had left. I must concede it was an ingenious place to hide, although it did cause some difficulties for the Young Man.

In one particular room the Young Man had a tay-bill on which was an object similar to a magic window, but smaller, which I learned the ayoomfas called a *kom-pewter*. It was incredibly boring as it only ever showed ayoomfa markings of the kind that one sees on a noose pepper. In front of the kom-pewter was a strange flat thing with lots of little pads that the Young Man used to strike with his softclaws. It's probably a religious artefact of sorts, for I walked on it once and he became upset and chased me away. Young Man would sit for long whiles using all these mysterious objects to achieve some unknown but probably foolish ayoomfa purpose. Underneath the tay-bill but attached to it was a stack of three *slidyboxes* in which Young Man kept a multitude of ayoomfa marking sticks and other mysterious objects associated with making markings. When Young Man wanted to get something from one of them, he would pull on it and cause it to come sliding out with everything inside it exposed for all to see. Another clever but pointless ayoomfa invention.

By observing carefully how these slidyboxes worked and applying Khat Concealment Knowledge, Butch found a way of getting inside the top one by climbing up the back of them. This slidybox became Butch's special hiding place and sometimes he would sneak into it while Young Man was seated right there thumping on his little pads and studying the markings on his kom-pewter. Such is the power of Khat Concealment Knowledge! And sometimes the Young Man would pull out the slidybox in which Butch was hiding and discover him inside it.

Butch would look up and say, 'Hello, Daddi. It's me, Butch. I'm hiding so you can't find me, Daddi.' He thought he was being terribly clever. *Daddi* indeed!

Young Man was usually very considerate and would greet him with a friendly pat on the head and then push the slidybox back. Butch's special hiding place was likely known to all the ayoomfas in the area, but out of courtesy and respect for his privacy - not to mention his ingenuity in getting into the slidybox - they all pretended not to know about it. With the passing of days the hiding place - and all the Young Man's articles within it - became coated with Butch's hair which caused many problems for the ayoomfas. But so greatly did they love Butch that they simply removed their articles to another place so he would have more room to sleep in the slidybox.

'I wish I was clever like you, said Butch one evening as all three of us were sitting outside the Midrand house while the ayoomfas made a fire festival.

'You could never be clever like me' I said, wondering what badness this was leading up to. I was a wise cat and had learned to distrust all praise since praise is inevitably a precursor to a request, exploitation or sometimes even an attack. Indeed, in my younger days I would pre-empt any consequence of praise by hissing and spitting at other creatures before they even spoke to me. Usually this had the desired effect and drove them away with their sly praise unspent.

'You could teach me,' Butch said. Hearing this, Balune guffawed loudly.

'I wouldn't even know where to begin!' I protested, 'you probably even don't know how to count.'

'Yes I do. I can count up to four paws' pads'

'Fool! Like I said, you don't even know how to count! Okay, so if you think you know how to count then tell me how many flowers are on that bush.' I indicated one of MyGranni's favourite plants which had been deported to Midrand along with several others. Butch looked at the plant and then at his paws. He sat and thought for a long, long while.

'Two paws' pads and three', he said at last.

'Fool! You don't have the slightest idea. How many pads in a paw?'

'Five'

'Wrong! You forgot the little pad at the back - there are *six* pads in a paw! That's why six is the most important number in Khat Counting Knowledge.'

'Six, yes, I see,' Butch said studiously examining his paw and frowning.

'No, wait a moment,' Balune interjected, 'that's not right. Our rear paws have five pads and our front paws have five pads. You can't count the little pad at the back of our forepaws. It doesn't even touch the ground when we walk and we don't have it on our hind paws in any case.'

'Do you mind, please Balune - I'm giving the lesson,' I said testily. 'Clearly you could also listen and benefit from my wisdom and experience. The wise elders that formulated Khat Counting Knowledge many, many generations ago were undecided on whether or not to count the little pad at the back of our forepaws. And they knew that our hind paws don't have the little pad at the back. After much thought the wise elders decided that for the purpose of Khat Counting Knowledge we have *six* pads on every one of our paws. The elders were concerned that when He created us Tabithat might have inadvertently omitted to fit the little rear pad to our hind paws. By not counting it we would be drawing attention to Tabithat's mistake which would cause Him to lose face. Nobody would want that.'

'This is utterly foolish!' Balune scoffed, 'Surely we have gained some savvy through the ages and can now count in a sensible way? Why follow such teachings if we know they are senseless?'

'A wise cat does not scoff at the teachings and traditions of our ancestors. What served them well will serve us well, too.'

'I still think its nonsense. The same sort of nonsense an ayoomfa would invent so they can live in a falling-down old house and do nothing about it. But never mind, carry on, please, we are all ears. Six of them, too, in all likelihood.'

'Now how many pads have you got altogether then, if there are six pads on each paw?' I asked Butch, ignoring Scrap's derision.

Butch looked around himself at all his paws. 'Four paws' pads, like I said.'

'No, that's wrong. Now listen carefully, Khat Counting Knowledge is very clever. That's why I'm so good at it. It works like this: How many paws do you have?'

'Four.' Butch looked at his feet. 'Definitely four.'

'Right. We are making some progress. Now how many forepaws do you have?'

'Two.' Butch studiously lifted each of his front paws in turn.

'Right again. So you have four paws plus two forepaws. That makes six paws altogether. And each paw has six pads, agreed? So you can count up to six paws' pads.'

'I think I'd prefer to remain ignorant of these things,' Balune said, 'my brain's about to explode with all this crazy thinking.' She waddled off to go back inside, shaking her head in disbelief.

'But I still only have four paws. . .' Butch said in great puzzlement.

'Yes I know that. I know that. That's not the point. Khat Counting Knowledge uses *virtual paws* which allow us to transcend the simple, tedious restrictions of the physical world and deal with matters of great complexity. To see if you understand this, tell me once again how many flowers are on that bush?'

Butch sat and contemplated the bush for a very long time and said 'One paws' pads plus three.'

'That's right! I'm pleased with you. Now go away and practice your counting for the next six days, remembering that you can count up to six pads on each of your six virtual paws.'

Butch trotted off to practice and I had several peaceful days. But then his limited knowledge ran out by highsun on the fourth day and he became stuck. He had spent the entire morning sitting in front of a bush which was covered in red berries, trying to count them all. In the early afternoon he gave up and wandered over to me.

'What now? I'm resting in case you hadn't noticed!'

'I was trying to count the red berries on that bush. . .'

'Yes, I saw that. You've been at it since breakfast time.'

'And I got as far as six pads' paws but then there were no more pads or paws left but there were still many red berries left. I didn't know what to do.'

'Yes, evidently. Khat Counting Knowledge allows for this by introducing the concept of *glorp.*'

'Glorp?'

'Yes, glorp. Khat Counting Knowledge is based on the special number six and counting stops when you have six paws worth of six pads each. More than six paws' pads are called simply *glorp*. Glorp represents a number higher than we can be bothered to count. Such numbers do exist - like the berries on that bush - but they are irrelevant to us and therefore we use glorp to represent all these numbers so that we don't waste our valuable time trying to count things that are unimportant. Berries, bizzums, blades of grass. If there are glorp berries on a bush and you hook one with your paw and pull it off, you still have glorp berries on the bush.'

'How do ayoomfas count?' Butch asked. I suspect he was so confused with Khat Counting Knowledge that he'd try any alternative he could find.

'Ayoomfas have two back feet and two front feet, although one should really call them bottom feet and top feet because they walk upright. On each foot they have five softclaws, which are quite useful. So in their terms they can count to four feets' softclaws. How much is that in Khat Counting Knowledge?'

Butch trotted off and spent the remainder of the afternoon sitting in the sun counting on his pads. Around dusk he returned and said, 'Three paws' pads and two.'

'Good boy, that's correct. But ayoomfas have special ayoomfa counting knowledge that enables them to count to more than that. One day long ago I sat watching the Young Man count little round shiny things in the stinkiroli room. I could tell immediately there were glorp of them but Young Man saw fit to waste the entire sunny afternoon he could have spent sitting in the sun by actually counting *every single one* of these round shinies. He made little piles of the round shinies; in each was two feets' softclaws. But here comes the clever bit - when he had two feets' softclaws of the *piles* he then had two feets' softclaws of two feets' softclaws of round shinies. He pushed these all into a big pile and then started again making little piles of two feets' softclaws of round shinies. At that point I lost interest and started to play with the shinies and push them about with my paws. Young Man was upset and chased me away. Ayoomfa counting knowledge allows you to carry on counting like this forever; despite it being utterly futile. They don't have much else worthwhile to do so they spend ludicrous amounts of time counting things.'

'What's for supper?' Butch asked.

*****

CHAPTER THREE:
The Shufa Bowl and other Great Magics

One of the new experiences that Midrand held for both Phat Balune and me was the *Khat Khouncile*. Balune and I had both grown up in the wild where there was no collective organisation of any kind, and the only law recognised was every cat for herself. Butch told me there was a Khat Khouncile near Harvard and that he would deal with it, and I was happy to let him take care of all such things. The Harvard Khat Khouncile fortunately remained unaware that we lived there because whenever Butch happened upon Khouncile Cats he told them vaguely that he lived somewhere else far away with me, his old mother, and we were simply visiting friends in the area. Butch can sometimes be quite astute for one who usually appears to be so foolish.

The first we knew of the Midrand Khat Khouncile was the sudden appearance of a skinny ginger tom with a face like a slinki who one morning walked up to where Balune, Butch and I were basking ourselves outside the house and squinting contentedly into the morning sun.

'Who's in charge here?' He demanded arrogantly. None of us said anything, simply staring at him for some minutes. Eventually Balune asked him, 'Who wants to know?'

'I'm Khouncillor MeanWeasel from the Midrand Khat Khouncile and you have to tell me who's in charge so I can issue proper demand for residents to attend moonly meetings of the Midrand Khat Khouncile.'

'Actually there's nobody here,' said Butch. That was probably pushing credibility a bit, even a slinky-faced mustard coloured cat from the khouncile would see through it.

'Have to? Demand? You're not shy, are you,' Balune growled at the Khouncile Cat. 'Why don't I just come over there and whump the wizz out of you?'

But neither Butch's fantasy nor Balune's threat deterred the Khouncile Khat, who said, 'The Khouncile has heard testimony from several other cats in the area that three cats matching your descriptions are Citizens of this House here. The Khouncile concludes that you live here. Therefore you are all compelled to attend the regular meetings of the Midrand Khat Khouncile which are held on the first sunny morning of each new moon, on the big flat red rock next to the *Khouncile Tree* that you can clearly see on the other side of the valley. That's the one standing alone in the grush with no other trees near it. To these meetings you shall each bring a moonly duty of one *squee*.'

'Why?' I asked.

'It's your duty as residents of this area?'

'What is *duty*? I don't know *duty*. I've never done *duty*? What do I get in return for doing this *duty*?' Balune snapped irritably.

'There's nobody home, so please come back tomorrow,' Butch said helpfully. Everyone ignored him although we actually all agreed with him.

Khouncillor MeanWeasel explained. 'Duties from the residents of the area are used to support the Khouncile members in performing their various tasks in the service of the cat community.

'Such as what?'

'As well as the moonly meetings we hold training school for local *puriks* and weight-loss classes for adult cats. Which you might well consider attending,' he added snidely, looking at Balune.

'She's not fat, she's simply full of largesse,' Butch growled supportively, 'and in any case she's not here.'

'Yes, you cheeky shufa!' Balune snarled menacingly at the Khouncile Khat. 'I should really come over there and give you a torn ear. . .'

'Be cool, Scrap,' I urged, not wanting to see the honourable Khouncillor MeanWeasel limp off with shredded head possibly to come back later with two full paws' pads of his huge fighting friends. 'This may prove interesting indeed. An old and extremely wise cat - such as me - knows there's much to be gained and little to be lost by simply watching, listening and waiting.'

'A wise old lady, you should listen to her. Good, that's settled then. You will all be expected to pay squee duty and attend the next meeting of the Midrand Khat Khouncile, to be held on the first sunny day in the next full moon. . .'

'What if it rains every day for the whole moon?' I asked, determined to throw a shufa in his carefully structured plans.

'No meeting. Only meeting on sunny day.' With that, the Khouncillor MeanWeasel scuttled off.

As Chief Cat in charge of the household I decided we should humour the Midrand Khat Khouncile and attend their meeting, so on the first sunny day of the following new moon we all trooped across the valley to the flat red rock on the opposite hill, carefully carrying our duty squees. It was a long way and my paws got wet as we waded across a small stream at the bottom of the valley and this put me in foul humour. Butch clumsily dropped his squee in the stream and so arrived with no duty.

When we arrived at the flat red rock there were glorp cats already present, sitting on the rock and looking sorry for themselves. Most of them held their duty squee firmly between their jaws, but there were several like Butch who had no squees. Three or four khouncillors - including the slinki-faced Khouncillor MeanWeasel that had come to see us - were walking around and posturing.

'All cats with duty squees will now please place their duty squees in a heap over here,' one of the khouncillors instructed, showing us a convenient pothole in the surface of the red rock. He was one of those long-haired cats with the squashed-in face that always manage to look sour and petulant. All the cats began to do his bidding. Squashed Face's beady eyes inspected each and every duty submitted, mostly without comment or sometimes with a simple nod. When it was Butch's turn he asked, 'Where's your duty squee, black and white cat?'

'I'm sorry, sir,' I don't have one.' Butch stammered. 'I have six puriks to feed and could not find enough squees today to both feed them and pay my khouncile duty. I'm terribly sorry. .'

'What's all this rubbish he's whinging on about now?' Balune whispered to me.

'I have no idea.' I made a hushed reply. Butch was definitely up to something odd.

'The Khat Khouncile of Midrand recognises your difficulties, and this is one of the reasons for duty,' said Squashed Face. He picked up a squee from the pile in the pothole and gave it to Butch. 'Here,' he said, 'take this squee and use it to feed your family.'

'Thank you, Khouncillor,' Butch grabbed the squee gratefully and trotted off to sit on the other side of the flat rock where he thought nobody would pay him further notice.

'Of all the lowly tricks!' Scrap hissed. 'Look, Bunny, he's eating the squee now!' As indeed he was, steadily crunching it with much noise and great concentration.

'I think he's had some previous experience with khounciles that he hasn't told us about. I must admit, it does seem a good way of getting a free lunch, though,' I said, watching the squee's hind legs and tail disappear into Butch's mouth.

'I fail to see the point of this *duty* nonsense,' Scrap said. What's happening is that you and I and these other fools here are simply feeding the khouncile cats and all those in the neighbourhood that are either too useless or too lazy to hunt a squee themselves. I'm no phraidy cat and I won't be bullied! That's the last duty I'll ever bring to this rock!'

The payment of duty done, the khouncile moved onto other business. A flabby Calico called Munchkin who held the title of *Principal Rememberer* had the regular task of remembering everything that had happened at the last meeting and reciting this information on request from the khouncillors. This was so that the khouncile could follow up on decisions it made.

'Last moon,' Munchkin began, 'I remember we discussed whether kittens should wash their front feet or their back feet first. We made a decision on this, but it's slipped my mind for now what it was.'

'Let's move on, then,' Squashed Face nodded agreeably, 'what other matters did we discuss?'

'I remember there was something to do with increasing the duty for *phat cats* to two squees per moon. I think we decided not to do this because it was vetoed by Khouncillor SwellenTummis,' Munchkin reported, indicating towards one of the khouncile cats who was so large as to make Phat Balune appear quite svelte, and who occupied a prize position at the very highest point of the big red rock. He had a big round sun-coloured shiny on a ring around his neck which suggested he was a very important cat indeed, maybe the Chief Cat of the Khouncile even. The mean thought crossed my mind that he may not be important, but could simply be a foolish fat cat who couldn't remember where he lived and perpetually had to be rescued by passing ayoomfas who were able to understand the markings on his big round shiny.

'That's quite correct. A totally unworkable idea. Let's move on. What else did we discuss?' This came from Khouncillor SwellenTummis.

'I'm sorry, but I can't remember what else we discussed,' Munchkin admitted unhappily.

'Oh well, in that case we're done with actions arising from the previous meeting,' said Khouncillor SwellenTummis, 'The khouncile thanks Principal Rememberer Munchkin for remembering most of what happened at the previous meeting. We now ask him to prepare us for the next meeting by listening carefully to what we discuss and decide today. And on behalf of the khouncile I have decided that Principal Rememberer Munchkin be given an extra squee from today's duty pile in return for his dedication to the workings of the khouncile. Well done, cat Munchkin. Now, to today's matters. . .'

'But the fool forgot nearly everything,' Balune whispered to me in indignation, 'Why reward him for being utterly useless?'

'I don't know. Maybe khounciles work like this. Butch seems to understand this khouncile stuff, ask him.' I replied.

Are there any new issues for today?' asked Khouncillor SwellenTummis, looking around.

'Yes!' Butch said quite unexpectedly, raising his forepaw. He had finished crunching his squee - leaving only the green-brown *blibble*, as is proper Khat tradition - and trotted over to sit by us. Balune and I looked on in bewildered amazement as he suddenly spoke as one well versed in khouncile matters.

'We should today decide upon proper disciplinary action to take against cats who fail to attend khouncile meetings. . .' he said.

'You stinking thing!' I hissed at him, 'After all I've done for you - teaching you to count and much more!'

Butch, as always, ignored me.

'A good point, cat,' Khouncillor SwellenTummis nodded approvingly at Butch. 'Whenever new cats appear in the neighbourhood we ask Khouncillor MeanWeasel to visit them and give them proper instruction. But it's true; we don't have a system to follow up on cats which are disobedient.'

Butch was being amazingly pro-active. He raised his forepaw again and said, 'We could send Khouncillor MeanWeasel to go whump them. . .' At this suggestion Khouncillor MeanWeasel looked most alarmed and his ears went back. He raised his paw urgently and said nervously, 'Some of the cats in the area are big and aggressive and it's quite unfair to ask any khouncile member to risk physical harm to themselves in the course of their duties.'

Butch raised his paw again. It was obvious he was a master of khouncile practice and Balune and I watched, amazed.

'I can understand that Khouncillor MeanWeasel doesn't want to be torn to pieces on every second house call,' Butch said seriously, 'so how about we rather give the disobedient cats a punishment in the form of an extra squee duty?'

'Yes that sounds like a fair idea, cat. . .uh . . sorry, I didn't get your name?'

'*Binidali*, Khouncillor, cat *Binidali*,' Butch replied inventively.

'Yes, it is a good plan! On behalf of the Midrand Khat Khouncile I vote we do this. Principal Rememberer Munchkin, please remember this.'

Butch, a.k.a. cat Binidali spoke again, forepaw raise deferentially, 'Khouncillor, how will we go about finding out which cats are present and which cats are absent? For example, how do we know what cats were present at the last meeting and are absent today?' Every cat stopped what they are doing and looked around somewhat helplessly.

Eventually Councillor SwellenTummis said, 'Another valid point, cat Binidali. If we count the cats present today, I'm certain we'll find there are *glorp* of them. But it's equally certain that there were *glorp* of them at the last meeting. And as you well know, cat Binidali, glorp is glorp, so we have no way of counting the absentees unless the absolutely unthinkable occurs and fewer than glorp cats attend a meeting. This is the problem facing your khouncile.'

'Yes, Khouncillor, we need to think about this carefully,' Butch said.

All cats present sat and considered this in silence for a long while, basking in the sun on the red rock, some of then washing their tails, which is known to promote creative thinking. Then cat Binidali spoke again. 'We know that counting the cats won't work. What we need is to appoint someone to remember exactly which cats were present at the last meeting and to check that all those same cats are present at the next meeting.'

Khouncillor SwellenTummis was delighted with this suggestion.

'Well done, cat Binidali! It's good to see a cat that *can think outside the bowl*, as the saying goes. We already have an appointed Principal Rememberer in the form of cat Munchkin. Cat Munchkin, you now have an additional task. As Principal Rememberer you will please remember that in future you are to remember which cats are present at each meeting.'

Cat Munchkin looked very stressed. 'I will do my best, Khouncillor. But I see a problem. I don't know which cat is which or any of their names.'

'Yes that could be a problem. Let us think on that some.'

Time passed. More cats began to wash themselves. Butch raised his paw after a suitable time for thought had elapsed. 'Khouncillors, I think I may have an answer to this. The Principal Rememberer must today ask the name of every cat, and remember them all at the next meeting.'

'Th. . .that's quite a lot to remember,' cat Munchkin said, looking nervous and hunted, 'but naturally I will do my very best. Of course it's a lot more to remember than I was I was remembering before for my two squees per moon. . .'

'Khouncile decides cat Munchkin's stipend shall increase to three squees per moon, obtained as usual from the duty collected. I have every faith in you, cat Munchkin, that you will rise to this challenge in your usual manner. And while we are dealing with such crucial issues, khouncile decides herewith to increase the stipend of all khouncillors to five squees each per meeting. Cat Munchkin, remember that, and start gathering names from all the cats present today. This moon's meeting of the Midrand Khat Khouncile is now declared over. Please give your names to cat Munchkin before you leave.'

Munchkin shuffled amongst the cats, asking their names. After a while, he came to where Balune, Butch and I were sitting.

'Cat, uh, . . . Winipot . . .' he said, addressing Butch.

'Binidali,' Butch corrected him.

'Oh yes, that's right, Winidali. And you are. . .' he asked, turning to us.

'Cat GazumpleTrumple,' I said without hesitation.

'I'm her younger sister, cat ShaggyWaggy,' chipped in Balune.

'I'll do my very best to remember you all,' cat Munchkin said sincerely.

'Of course you will,' I replied sincerely.

By this time most cats had lost interest and had ambled over to watch a group of puriks receive schooling from slinki-faced Khouncillor MeanWeasel. The three of us left quietly and began traipsing down the narrow, winding path through the grush to the bottom of the valley again. 'You seem to know a lot about the workings of the khouncile, eh, Butch?' I said when we paused for a while at a little clearing to wash our ears and reflect on the morning that was.

'Yes, I think it was a good idea of mine.' Butch smiled at us, 'I think now our problem is solved.'

'Absolutely brilliant, Butch. I'm quite sure cat Munchkin will perform his task as Principal Rememberer with his customary diligence and. . .'

'. . . and we'll hear no more from the Midrand Khat Khouncile,' Phat Balune completed. 'What a bunch of greedy interfering busybodies they are! I'm sure the ayoomfas wouldn't put up with nonsense like this.'

Midrand had a special room in front of the house which was very different from the others in that it had a floor and a lid, but no walls. It was part of the house yet outside the house, and it was a very suitable place for the ayoomfas to have *fire festivals*, something we all enjoyed tremendously. Young Man would set up the bowl in which they made the fire - the ayoomfas called it a *bry* - and he would make ayoomfa fire magic. This was the signal for us all to come outside and watch from a safe distance, for at first there was smoke and sparks and flame and it was dangerous to go to close, although the fire magic was very clever and the fire stayed in the bowl and didn't burn up the trees or grush like I'd sometimes see happen when fire happened without the special ayoomfa magic. Then after a while Young Man made more fire magic and the smoke cleared and the flames died down. By that time the Woman would have brought out of the house some wonderfully delicious meats, and the Young Man would place these on a special kind of fence above the fire bowl where they would be immediately and completely spoiled by the fire. I have never understood why ayoomfas felt compelled to always wreck good food by burning it.

This was the right time for Balune and me to move in closer and weave excitedly around Young Man's feet, trilling sounds of want and hunger and being as sociable as we could without actually tripping him up. We had to work fast, for the longer the meats were on the fire bowl, the worse they tasted. Good fortune always smiled on us, for Young Man, charmed by our dusky vocalisations, would cut off some small meatlets and give them to us. Sometimes he ate one or two of them himself, presumably to check whether they were of sufficiently high standard to give to us. He usually just dropped our meatlets nearby on the floor, but on occasion he would expect us to stand up on our hind feet and ask for them and he wouldn't give us anything until we complied with this folly. We had to take great care with these meatlets for they'd been on the fire bowl fence and were often quite hot. No sooner had we picked them up than we'd have to spit them out again and we'd then sit there glaring furiously at the Young Man. He understood our discomfort and took to placing our meatlets to one side where they could cool down first, and this was the most tantalising time for us. We could smell them, we could see them, but we couldn't have them for they were too hot. Young Man - Tabithat bless him - realised I had no teeth and he would sometimes chew the meatlets a little for me so I could manage them better. I was truly growing very fond of the Young Man and his Woman.

While we frolic'd in the warm glow of the fire at dusk, Butch would always sit at a discrete distance, and Young Man would have to either throw him his meatlets or walk over and take them to him. If he threw them, Butch would panic and run away. If he walked over with them, Butch would fear pickup and capture and run away. Young Man - understandably - became irritated with this after a few fire festivals, and would not leave the fire bowl to give any of us meatlets. If we wanted meatlets, we had to come to him and get them. And we had to stand up every time. In reprisal for this unwanted common discipline Balune battered Butch over the head and shoulders and threatened to do so every sunset until he stopped being such a phraidy cat. Only a very stupid or insensible cat would dare defy Balune and so Butch soon came to join us by the fire, although he still sat as far away as he could get away with and his standing up on his hind legs was very half-hearted. Young Man wasn't impressed at all, for even Balune who was fa. . uh, full of largesse, stood up very nicely, although her upright state was a bit precarious and she wobbled about a bit. Young Man appreciated her efforts and took pains not to keep her standing up unnecessarily long.

It was at one such fire festival that Butch wandered off into the long grush in pursuit of a big squee and became lost. I have never encountered *any* cat that got lost, least of all one with splendid hunting whiskers and senses honed as sharp as Butch's were. Not only did he become lost, he became lost within a distance of only six trees from where the rest of us civilised cats were savouring the ayoomfa's fire festival. Everyone could plainly hear him calling. The Young Man repeatedly called him, only to be answered with another of Butch's helpless calls.

'Help me, I'm lost!' he wailed. 'I can't see where I am. Weeeow! I don't know where I am. Weeeow! Please help me, Daddi! It's me, Butch, a Citizen of the House and I'm lost, Weeeow! Please come rescue me!'

'Has he no self respect at all, Bunny?' Balune asked, shaking her head sadly. 'How can a cat so sly in dealing with khouncile parasites and so skilled at hunting, be so stupid as to get lost like this? He'll lose great face and not be able to look either of us in the eye for at least a paws' pads of sunrises. If this had happened to either of us we'd have skulked away and hidden ourselves in shame from all other creatures. For two days at least.'

'Butch is not bothered by convention at all, Scrap. He's not perturbed by insults or chastisement to the slightest degree. Tomorrow morning he'll come trotting along to the breakfast ceremony and say 'Oh hello, ladies' as if nothing had ever happened.'

Like Balune and me the ayoomfas had never heard of a cat getting lost within six trees from its house and they derived much of mirth from Butch's predicament. But they were kind ayoomfas and could not simply do nothing while one of their masters was in distress. The

Woman went into the house and came back with the little magic sun that could be carried around. They inevitably encountered some difficulty with this little movable sun for when it was first activated the light was very dim as if its magic was sickening, and it soon stopped completely. The Woman went inside and came back with some objects which she gave to Young Man, who had meanwhile opened up the back of the little movable sun and removed some very similar objects, which I believe are pre-packed containers full of stored ayoomfa sun magic. He replaced the ones in the little movable sun with the ones brought to him by his Woman and soon the movable sun glowed with a bright light that could be seen from many paws' pads trees away. Young Man then walked towards the long grush, calling for Butch and shining the movable sun in the direction of Butch's plaintive wailings which were growing more agitated and pathetic with each passing moment.

Within a small tree's length of entering the long grush, Young Man came across the panicked and frightened Butch and scooped him up in his arms before he could panic and dart off to become even more lost. Amid much cheering from his Woman, in which even Balune and I joined in, Young Man carefully carried Butch back to where we all waited at the fire festival and put him down.

'What's for supper?' Butch asked.

In our Midrand house there was a *bumpity hill* between the Down House and the Up House where Young Man and his Woman slept at night on their a*yoomfawumpus*. And next to the ayoomfa sleeping room was a smaller room in which they would laboriously wash themselves with water because being ayoomfas, they had small and useless tongues and couldn't wash themselves properly like cats do. The little wash room had many interesting ayoomfa constructions within. There was the *magic rain box*. This was a box made entirely out of windows and when Young Man or his Woman wished to wash themselves they would go inside this windows box and activate a magic which made bubbles and a big rain inside the box only. And it wasn't ordinary rain; it was a special rain which was hot. For some unfathomable reason Butch loved to sip the puddles of warm water in the magic rain box after one or the other of the ayoomfas had finished using it. I thought he was crazy because this rain tasted absolutely terrible, but then what do I know about what goes on in Butch's head?

Butch spent a great deal of time with the ayoomfas in the little washing room. Not only would he drink the water puddles from the magic rain box, but in the mornings he would hasten the delivery of our breakfast by gently biting the Young Man's lower softclaws while he was sitting on the shufa bowl. Young Man would yelp and withdraw his lower softclaws or sometimes cover them with his upper softclaws, and Butch would then saunter off as if he'd lost interest. The Young Man would relax and continue with his shufacation, and the moment his lower softclaws were once again unguarded Butch would go and nibble at them again. Young Man and his Woman thought this was very funny indeed.

Another often-used contraption in the little washroom was the *shufa bowl*. Khat Toilet Technique is to make shufa outside in loose fresh sand, and then to bury it in a superficial manner where ayoomfas can stand on it. The ayoomfas themselves have toilet habits which are quite inscrutable. They quite happily make shufa inside the house, yet if we make shufa inside the house they become enraged and scold us most severely. To make shufa the ayoomfas sit on the shufa bowl in the little washing room - sometimes for ages - and make shufa inside it. Ayoomfa *shufacation* is naturally messy and always necessitates them cleaning themselves up afterwards - not by licking themselves like sophisticated creatures, but with the aid of long white *shufa sheets* that they keep on a roli thing near the shufa bowl. They are totally reliant on these sheets and become most agitated and distressed if there are none available or the sheets run out while they are sitting on the shufa bowl.

For a young cat - a *tikki purik* - it's great fun to pull on the roli of shufa sheets and cause it to go roli roli roli so that the whole string of white sheets piles up all over the floor. A really enterprising tikki purik can grab the end of the string of sheets and run away with it, causing the sheets to follow them all over the house! For an old cat like myself it's far too much like hard work, but it's always great fun to suggest this game to a tikki purik and watch events unfold, if you'll pardon the expression.

The Young Woman also used to make wizz in the shufa bowl, and the Young Man would too, but he usually stood up to make wizz, like a tomcat. When he did this some of the wizz would stray from the shufa bowl and end up on the floor or on top of the shufa bowl. The Young Man would then have to use many white shufa sheets to clean it all up or risk a scolding from his Woman, who clearly held the view that male creatures of any kind should always go make wizz outside. Quite right she is, too.

There is a great magic associated with the shufa bowl. A very great magic indeed. When they have completed making shufa and cleaned themselves with the white sheets, the ayoomfas place them in the shufa bowl on top of the shufa. One would then expect them to scratch sand on top of it all and bury it. But they don't. They activate a powerful rain magic which makes great noise like a waterfall, and the shufa and the white sheets simply disappear without trace! I have no idea where it all goes to, or how it gets there. Many times I've studied the shufa bowl inside and outside very carefully but it concedes no clue to its secrets. All there is inside the shufa bowl is a little water at the bottom. It's quite clean water, for I've seen Butch drink it on occasion when the ayoomfas weren't looking. And it's magic water, because it's always there. It's there before the ayoomfas make shufa, and it's there even after the waterfall magic when all sensible understanding of the world would tell us that the shufa bowl should be full to the brim with a *smort*, stinking mess of shufa and white sheets and water. The great shufa bowl magic is advantageous in that allows the ayoomfas to use the same shufa bowl time and time again without it ever becoming *smort*.

Fortunately Khat Lore allows us to deal with such inexplicable phenomena in much the same way as we deal with unnecessary abundance through the concept of *glorp*. The idea of *mujaji* is used to explain and excuse all magic done by other creatures which is not of direct use to us, and with which we need never concern ourselves.

So according to Khat Lore we need never worry about where the ayoomfa shufa goes, or where the ayoomfas go to hunt the big ground chirrits or the big guelphs that they eat, or what makes a stinkiroli move, or where rain comes from - it's all *mujaji*. Most of the time I'm happy to blithely attribute all these unfathomable things to mujaji, but I must confess I simply can't help wondering now and then how some things work, and especially where the ayoomfa shufa goes and how the water in the shufa bowl is always there. I wonder sometimes whether the ayoomfas know this themselves - perhaps they have their own kind of mujaji to handle things they don't understand?

*****

CHAPTER FOUR:
Born to be Wild

My earliest memory is of being a *tikki purik* in Vietnam. My mother reared me and my siblings in a hidey-space she'd found between some big black logs that were stacked up in an enormous pile as high as a tree. Ayoomfas often came with a very big noisy stinkiroli and took some of these logs away. Then other ayoomfas would come on another big noisy stinkiroli and bring some logs back. This foolish ayoomfa game served no obvious purpose, and I don't know why they didn't just leave the logs where they were in the first place. Fortunately there was always a big enough pile of logs to afford cover and protection for our family, and we kept well out of sight. The ayoomfas had done something special to these logs which gave them a most distinctive smell and made them black. Sometimes I'd seen fences that smelled the same. It wasn't an unpleasant smell, but I would always remember it.

My mother's ayoomfa name was Sarah Bunn and she'd once been a Citizen of a House somewhere, with food, milk, a warm snug schnoogli and even a special round shiny around her neck with ayoomfa markings for her name on it, in case they forgot who she was. She told us that through no fault of her own she'd fallen on hard times and had been forced to live off her wits. My father was called Brooser and had never been a citizen of any house anywhere. I caught sight of him once or twice while I was growing up; he was boasting and jesting with his rowdy and rambunctious friends CigarTail and Jimmy Abbott. I made no attempt to go pester him with demands for recognition or paternal love. It is not our way. Also, Mother said he might kill me.

Vietnam was not all grush, and trees. Here and there were some buildings where the ayoomfas came in the daytime, and after sunrise many of them would arrive in their stinkirolis all at the same time. They would spend the day inside the buildings making markings and doing other foolish things which made noise and fire and bright sparkling lights. Then before sunset they would leave in their stinkirolis all at the same time. My mother told me the ayoomfas called these places *Fat-Trees.* After dark when the ayoomfas were all long gone Mother showed us where we might find scraps of food in the big drums the ayoomfas had inexplicably left unguarded outside these Fat-Trees.

Vietnam had an abundance of squees and Mother taught us to hunt them. But hunting squees was serious hard work compared with the easy pickings to be had from the *Chirrit Rock*. This was a large brown

29

rock not far from the Fat-Trees and it had holes in it which accumulated drinking water and so was a natural oasis for chirrits. Around mid-afternoon every day great flocks of stupid grey chirrits would assemble on the rooftop of a nearby Fat-Tree and sit waiting. As the afternoon wore on they got braver and hungrier and as dusk approached they all flew down to the Chirrit Rock and began milling around expectantly. At this juncture an old ayoomfa man would come out of a building and make chirrit-like sounds to call them. He would scatter special chirrit food around Chirrit Rock and then retreat to observe what happened, never making even the slightest attempt to catch any of them. What happened was always the same: the chirrits milled around and gobbled up all the food. They grew so fat on all this bounty they could barely flap themselves airborne and they grew very careless. It was easy picking for us and I would casually saunter into their midst while they were frantically gobbling the seed the ayoomfa man had strewn around, and just as casually saunter out carrying a fat chirrit in my mouth.

Most times the other chirrits didn't even notice me carry off one of their flock, but occasionally they became panicked and rose into the air in a great flapping cloud, their wings desperately thudding to lift their fat bodies into the air. They would blunder into each other in their quest to fly away, making an awesome noise like a *whacka-whacka,* and then settle out of harms way on the roof of the Fat-Tree again. There was such a glorp of chirrits that they could sustain our predations indefinitely without even noticing it! Chirrit Rock became a legend among all the wild cats in Vietnam and I hunted there for many winters, long after my mother and siblings had gone their separate ways and I was a mother myself.

On one occasion the old ayoomfa man saw me seize one of the fat grey chirrits. I should explain first that Khat Lore laid down by the great blessed Tabithat in The Beginning tells us that if we venture onto another creature's natural hunting territory, we are intruding and must expect fierce opposition. However, if the other creature is actively encouraging the prey but declines to hunt it themselves, then Khat Lore allows us to take the prey with impunity. The old ayoomfa man had evidently not studied Khat Lore as promulgated by Tabithat and was thus a very ignorant animal indeed. For some reason he became enraged and ran clumsily after me, shouting and waving his arms and growing very red in the face. I thought this was quite comical to watch and I didn't dart away with my chirrit as fast as I should have done. Next thing I knew the ayoomfa man was holding a *magic rain slinki* which he pointed at me and I was instantly soaked. I dropped the chirrit and ran away, deeply humiliated.

My two siblings grew up and wandered away to other territory. Vietnam had a substantial stray cat population and competition was rife amongst the toms. CigarTail was driven away after a savage fight with my father, and probably died of his wounds somewhere. This fight began as a silly squabble over who owned Chirrit Rock, despite the fact that there were glorp chirrits and certainly more than enough for everyone to hunt their fill. Sometime thereafter Brooser took fancy to a visiting Burmese queen and left with her, never to be seen again, and later that winter my poor mother died of *booma-skwasha* when she fell asleep under a stinkiroli at one of the Fat-Trees and didn't move away in time.

Jimmy Abbott was still around. He was a massive tom with black and white in roughly equal proportions and the most enormous paws I have ever seen on a cat. Even Tabithat's holy paws - bless them all - could surely not be much bigger. Jimmy Abbott was fairly handsome but in manners, tact and guile he was dreadfully impoverished. Seeing that I was a nubile and - if I say so myself - exceedingly beautiful young queen, Jimmy Abbott naturally wanted to *fruka-fruka* with me and I had little choice but to comply. It is our way. Also, my mother had warned me that a tom would probably beat me up if I refused, and Jimmy Abbott with his big paws had whumpage in abundance.

After he had finished he hung around for a few minutes and we talked some.

'You know, girl,' Jimmy Abbott said. 'There's a house over there with three ayoomfas living in it. An old man, an old woman, and a young man. I've been watching them,' Jimmy Abbott said.

'Yes, I know. The old man feeds the stupid grey chirrits at Chirrit Rock and he wet me with a magic rain slinki. I don't like him. The young man wants to pick me up all the time and comes running after me with outstretched forepaws; I forever have to hide from him. He's a pest and I don't like him either. I don't know much about the old woman.'

'Well, I'm tired of living rough,' Jimmy Abbott declared. 'In this hell where every day can be your last. Sickness, hunger, cold, falling trees and rocks, booma-skwasha, other toms, poisoned food, young ayoomfas with bangsticks - you name it, it's here. I'm going to go to that house and tell them there that I want food, shelter, love, and affection. Then when I'm Citizen of the House I'll come back and fetch you and we can fruka-fruka in comfort rather than on top of this pile of dirty concrete bricks.'

'I wish you luck,' I said, sincerely.

Next morning Jimmy Abbott went and sat outside the door of the house, uttering a plaintive wailing.

'Hey you! Ayoomfas!' he shouted, 'Open this stinking door and let me inside!'

Jimmy was nothing if not blunt. It was fortunate that the old man didn't go to the door, for he would likely have kicked Jimmy into the nearest bush. Instead the young man opened the door to find Jimmy Abbott sitting there.

'I want food.' Jimmy wailed. 'I want to come inside and wash my big feet by the warm place.'

In my concealed observation post I cringed, expecting Jimmy to be summarily kicked in the head, but as I discovered over the years to come, this young man would never fail to welcome any cat that came to his door, no matter what the circumstances. He appeared delighted and welcomed Jimmy inside the house Jimmy strolled in as if he'd always lived there. Young Man gave him something to eat and went to tell the older ayoomfas, who came to see what had happened and who both looked far from pleased.

Jimmy's stay in the ayoomfa house was nothing if not eventful. On the first day he made shufa in the house, calm as you please, expecting there to be 'assistants' to clear it up. 'With three ayoomfas all with little to occupy themselves, you'd think it would be the minimum service they'd provide,' he grumbled to me when they firmly ushered him outside. On the second day he made tomspray on the softahs hanging by the window to 'define territory which was rightfully his'. And on the third day he ate his breakfast too fast and threw it up all over the feet of the old man while he was sitting eating his own breakfast at a tay-bill.

Something clearly had to be done about Jimmy Abbott. Only the young man wanted Jimmy to stay, but he was overruled. The ayoomfas knew that if Jimmy were to be evicted, he'd simply sit shouting at the door for weeks on end and make such a nuisance of himself that they'd eventually relent and let him stay. So after a few days another ayoomfa came and took him away in a box. I was very alarmed. What had happened to him? Perhaps the ayoomfas had killed and eaten him? Or abandoned him somewhere. It did not look good at all. Jimmy had been *disappeared* and I became more suspicious of ayoomfas than ever before. Many moons later I heard tell that Jimmy Abbott had been taken to a house in a faraway wild place and a deal had been struck with him: He could live in the house provided he behaved himself and earned his keep by catching *yhats* and the hissing slinkis that ayoomfas call snakes. I heard also that Jimmy Abbott had served his new family with distinction and been the most effective snake catcher they'd ever seen, he was a Citizen of the House and cherished by all. I'm pleased it worked out for him.

I had a litter of kittens from the fruka-fruka with Jimmy Abbott, and of these Khalli looked the most promising, so I didn't eat her. Which may have been a mistake, for although she grew into an extraordinary beautiful Calico cat, she was also a timid, helpless cat who wanted to be my purik forever. I've often wondered where Khalli came from: Jimmy Abbott certainly didn't want for assertiveness. Did I? We all know from Khat Lore that once a purik is big enough to properly look after itself, it must leave its mother and go to make its own way in the world. But Khalli didn't want to leave the nest when she grew up and she continued to follow me around everywhere. This is not the way of nature and it was my duty as a responsible mother to discourage this and beat her up whenever I saw her. I tried my best with Khalli - I really did - but the trouble with my disciplining her was that it turned into a vicious circle, if you'll pardon the choice of words. The more I hit Khalli, she more she felt she had let me down and the harder she tried to behave like an affectionate purik - rubbing and writhing up against me, making *happi-rumble* and simpering phrases of love and devotion day and night. But it proved futile trying to change her ways and after a while I was simply hitting her from force of habit.

There was no shortage of noisy, boisterous toms in Vietnam. Two new arrivals were PhatNose and LampreyTail - where they'd originally come from only Tabithat knows. They were obsessed with me and I found their constant attentions and the enforced fruka-fruka with both of them very tiresome. Some nights they would sit on the high wall between one of the Fat-Trees and the really thick grush and make discordant, ribald callings for me:

'Hey, Siamese Babe I want to fruka-fruka with you-ooooeeeoooouw. . . Yeeeooooow. . . . . . fruka-fruka fruka-fruka just me-eeeeouw and you-oooouw all night looowng. . .'

It was terribly embarrassing to have these hayseeds wailing to me almost every night but there didn't seem that much I could do about it, bearing in mind their rights under Khat Lore and also what mother had told me. They caused such a terrible cacophony that even the old ayoomfa man in the house, some distance away, heard them. He was really angry at being woken up in the middle of the night and he stormed outside the house.

'Fsssshhhhhhhhh! Shutttttttup! Sssssssssssst! Shhhhhhhhhhhhhhttt!' he shouted angrily. What this was supposed to mean was anyone's guess, but it was clearly directed at my noisy suitors. It caused them both to keep quiet, but they resumed their serenade after allowing just sufficient time for the old man to go back inside and fall asleep again. They thought this was a grand game, a really splendid wheeze. From past experience they knew that it was safe to do this twice, but thereafter the old man would come out with his bangstick and activate it, which some instinct told them was very dangerous.

I really didn't like fruka-fruka with LampreyTail because he always made such a dreadful noise while doing it, and he had rotten teeth which made his breath smell really awful. One day I sat in the sun thinking about this for a long time and I devised a cunning plan using Khat deception knowledge. That evening when I saw PhatNose and LampreyTail, I whispered to PhatNose that I didn't want to fruka-fruka with LampreyTail anymore because I thought he was a *poor quality cat* and his kittens would be stupid and feeble and a waste of my valuable pregnancy. PhatNose responded helpfully by beating the living shufa out of LampreyTail and I was never bothered by him again. PhatNose, however, took it upon himself to double the frequency of his fruka-fruka with me as if to make up for the absent LampreyTail. At least he didn't shriek and wail in my ear and his breath smelled better because his teeth were good.

My next litter contained one adorable black and brindled purik that was clearly the offspring of PhatNose, and two others that I suspected hailed from LampreyTail and which I therefore killed and ate. I didn't like to do this, but Khat Lore makes special provisions for single mothers with limited resources, and I fell fairly and squarely into this category. I called my new tikki purik *MyBaby*. From an early age she was very intelligent and asked numerous questions all day long. I was terribly proud of her and took her along wherever I went to show her off to everyone. PhatNose was hugely impressed with his daughter and even licked her on the top of the head to mark her as his own.

One day at sunset I even took my beautiful purik up to the house to show her off to the ayoomfa family. They, too, were impressed and I sensed that Young Man wanted to pick her up. Old Lady came outside with a bowl of delicious white *humvee* for us to slurp, but I hissed and made explosive spitting at her and went and hid under a nearby bush.

'Do not go drink that while the ayoomfas are watching,' I warned my purik. 'They are evil and mean no good at all. Better you stay under the bush with me and wait until they're gone.' But MyBaby had a rebellious streak from the tip of her fat nose leather to the end of her fluffy tail.

'Nonsense Mother,' she said. They've clearly put the humvee out for us to slurp. I really don't think they mean us any harm.'

'You know nothing!' I snapped at her and cuffed her on the head. 'These evil creatures disappeared Jimmy Abbot! And I was never convinced that CigarTail really went off to die of his wounds. For all I know these ayoomfas minced him up in some dreadful act of mujaji and ate him.'

'But Mother. . .'

And then as if I didn't have enough to handle, Khalli decided to put in an appearance and came along to rub herself against me.

'My Mummi,' she burbled adoringly, 'I luv my Mummi. . .'

'Look, Khalli, whatever it is you want will have to wait. I'm very busy trying to prevent the first decent purik I've ever had from being disappeared by these dangerous ayoomfas. Either go away, or sit down and shut up!'

While I was distracted by Khalli, and before I could do anything to stop her, MyBaby toddled up to the bowl of humvee and started slurping it up, right there in front of the ayoomfas! I put my paws over my face, dreading the inevitable, but nothing happened. Instead of seizing MyBaby, the ayoomfas just stood there making pleasant burbling and watched her feeding. Even Young Man made no move to try pick her up.

'Come back, MyBaby!' I hissed at her. 'They are merely waiting for an opportunity to catch you. They'll eat you and use your pelt to make coverings for their heads in the winter! Come back here and hide under this bush with me where they can't get to us.' But MyBaby was having nothing of it. She was bewitched by the delicious humvee. She slurped up all of it and then - I could scarcely believe my eyes - she trotted up to the Young Man and started rubbing herself against his hind legs.

'MyBaby! Stop that! You are behaving like a complete slut! Come back here where it's safe with me and Kh. . .' I looked round, but Khalli was gone. She'd shambled up to the empty bowl and was making her usual pathetic noises.

'Khalli! Come back! You don't know what you're doing, you poor, simple creature! Come back here with me under this nice safe bush. I promise not to whump you on the head anymore today!'

I looked up to where MyBaby was now allowing the Young Man to chuckle her under the chin. She made not the slightest attempt to scratch or bite him, nor even to flee! What was the point in having litters of puriks if they simply allowed themselves to be seduced and eaten? By Tabithat, if I'd known she was so set on being a food animal I'd have jolly well eaten her myself the day she was born!

Old Lady went into the house and came back outside with a big bottle of humvee. As she walked up to the empty bowl, Khalli at least had the good sense to back off just out of reach. Old ayoomfa lady refilled the bowl to the brim with fresh humvee and withdrew. After a little while Khalli returned to the bowl and began slurping the plapa humvee.'

'You! Bad Khalli cat! Don't you dare drink that plapa humvee!'

Khalli lifted her head from the bowl looked up at me lovingly, droplets of humvee on her white muzzle and whiskers.

'Why not, Mummi? The nice ayoomfa lady put it here for me. . .' she said naively. This was an outrage! My simple wayward daughter had made me lose face in front of the ayoomfas.

'No they did not! That humvee belongs to me. Everything here belongs to me. It's not yours, it's mine. You can't have it!!!' I shrieked.

I darted up to Khalli and whumped her on the head repeatedly until she ran away. Then I ran up to where the ayoomfas were, and keeping a safe distance, hissed and spat vigorously at each of them in turn. They were quite astonished. I could be very frightening in my Vietnam days - perhaps I'd paralysed them with fear? I like to think so. In any case they made no move against me and I cautiously retreated backwards step by step towards the bowl of plapa humvee, always keeping them all in clear view.

'Mother you are embarrassing me,' MyBaby shouted at me. As I backed away, giving my lowest and longest *death to all* growl, I couldn't help noticing that she'd allowed the Young Man to pick her up. She looked up at him and said, 'Nice Young Man, this crazy wild Siamese cat has nothing to do with me. I've never seen her before.'

I was hurt and angry and felt very unloved. My first daughter was a mithering simpleton and my second daughter was a careless tart who'd disowned me. And worst of all the whole family of ayoomfas were amused by what had happened. My loss of face was almost unbearable. I simply could not drink the humvee now. I spat at everyone once again for good measure and ran off into the long grush where I hid away using Khat concealment knowledge.

Later, after dark and after all the ayoomfas had gone inside and MyBaby had returned, I went and slurped up all the humvee. Then I made a special point of fiercely beating both Khalli and MyBaby for being such brats.

MyBaby's defection to the ayoomfas was a turning point in all of our lives.

'It's CocoPop, Mother, she proudly told me.'

'What's CocoPop?'

'My new name. Young Man has named me CocoPop.'

'Great Tabithat! CocoPop indeed! Whatever next!'

'Well, next I expect he'll let me sleep on his ayoomfawumpus. It's only a matter of time. I don't know why you're making such a fuss, Mother. The ayoomfas can easily recognise that I'm a sophisticated young cat brimming with charm and intelligence and it's understandable that they want to please me. Chill, Mother. I'll use my influence to see that they feed us all. Your days of living wild will soon be history and you can now have a bit of rest and comfort for which I'm sure you'll be grateful.'

'Pshoo!' I scoffed. 'You're such a smarty puss. Only eight weeks old and you've got the cheek of your father, you do. Just watch that you don't get disappeared like Jimmy Abbott.' I scowled and turned my back on her. 'I'll eat their food if they give it to me, but I won't ever set foot in their house. Not ever. Not as long as shufa is *smort*, never! Are they planning to feed Khalli as well?'

'Definitely, Mother. Old Lady really likes Khalli.'

'Oh give me strength! That's so unfair!'

*****

CHAPTER FIVE:
Battle and Capitulation

CocoPop was true to her word. Every morning Old Lady would open the door of the house and walk outside with three bowls of food of mouthwatering deliciousness. She would place one in the room with lid but no walls for CocoPop, but of course I wouldn't go there, so she was forced to bring my bowl of food right to the bottom of the garden where I wanted to eat. Old Lady had a strong sense of fair play and if CocoPop were fed and I went hungry it would have violated her moral code, so she humoured me and went to some lengths to place my bowl where *I* wanted it. This was a matter of principle and I could not show weakness or lose face again. I would lead the way, running a few paces ahead of her, turning to hiss and spit at her every so often to ensure she was still following attentively and wasn't up to any trickery. Khalli also wouldn't go and eat in the room with lid but no walls but in her case it was because she was fearful and simpering and there were no principles involved.

Old Lady would hang around for long enough to see that I was eating, and then trot off elsewhere to give food to Khalli. Every day it was the same. Feeding Khalli was very bad of her and I did my utmost to put a stop to this wicked practice. I would quickly gulp down my food - which gave me terrible indigestion - and run after her to find out where she was feeding Khalli, so I could clobber Khalli and eat her food. Old Lady saw this and became very angry with me. She was besotted with Khalli and stayed around to guard her while she ate. Khalli was such an indecisive and fearful cat that waiting for her to get stuck into her grub made me want to bite my own tail in frustration, but the Old Lady had unbelievable patience. She would make soothing noises of encouragement while Khalli stood there with one forepaw raised in a pensive, dithering manner and pondered on whether to eat or whether to just stand there pondering about it some more. I couldn't afford to hang around forever while my own food lay out of sight and totally unguarded against the attentions of skulking LampreyTail or whoever, and the sly Old Lady realized this. I developed a strategy wherein I would quickly run back to my own food to check it hadn't been stolen by anyone, and then run back to see if Khalli was unprotected and clobberable. Back and forth, back and forth I ran, and by the time Khalli and CocoPop had finished their food and Old Lady had gone back into the house, I had eaten hardly anything and I was exhausted!

Old Lady then changed her modus operandi. She refused to feed us in separate places and simply put down a big communal bowl of food on the grass not far from the house, where she could keep watch on all of us while we ate. If I hit Khalli, Old Lady would chase me away and Khalli and CocoPop would simply eat my share of the food. Khalli was nervous about eating with me at first and went through the paw in the air dithering for a while until she too saw that if she didn't get her act together straight away, CocoPop and I would gobble up her share. I was compelled to eat the food together with Khalli and CocoPop or risk embarrassment and loss of face. Clever Old Lady!

This arrangement lasted for a whole turn of seasons and we three cats came to regard the garden of the house as our home. We stopped going to the Fat-Trees and the long grush and we only hunted chirrits and squees during the summer - for entertainment. The Old Man appeared to have forgiven me for stealing one of his vapid grey chirrits from Chirrit Rock and we were all very careful not to let him see us hunting them.

Young Man sometimes left his yellow stinkiroli in our garden when he came home in the late afternoons and the stinkiroli was always warm. I found it a great pleasure to sit and bask on the black *rolis* on this stinkiroli, and also on the front lid which covered the roaring digestion inside. Young Man would always try to pick me up, but I was too fast for him and would run away, spitting. Both Young Man and Old Man seemed to find my spitting hugely amusing and would go out of their way to try getting me to spit by feinting to catch me or pick me up. The more explosively I spat, the more it amused them, and they would mimic my spitting and go off cackling to themselves like hens as if it was the funniest thing they'd ever heard. It became embarrassing after a while and I decided not to spit anymore. I really don't like being laughed at and it didn't seem to do any good anyway as they were clearly not afraid of me at all.

It was around this time that I was given my Ayoomfa name, *Bunni*. I have a strong suspicion that the Old Man and the Young Man christened me this because of the way I ran when I ran away from them. A 'bunni' is what the ayoomfas call a *hopit*; the small jumping guelph with the big floppy ears known in Khat Lore to be good eating. Once again I was being ridiculed and it made me very embarrassed. I decided I would no longer run like a *hopit*. Not that I would just sit there foolishly and let them pick me up, you understand, but rather I would trot away with what I hoped was deliberate dignity, just fast enough for them not to be able to catch me.

CocoPop confidently roamed around the house at will. In the room of the Young Man a window was specially left slightly open for her to go in and out as she pleased. There was a row of small spiky and thorny plants in pots by the window which was directly above the Young Man's ayoomfawumpus. CocoPop hadn't paid much heed to the Khat agility knowledge I'd tried to impart to her when she was a kitten and had turned out to be quite a clumsy little girl. She regularly knocked one or more of these over every time she entered the house. Young Man would be rudely awakened in the middle of the night by a shower of earth and pebbles on his head and he was sometimes stabbed painfully by plant thorns. He wasn't pleased by this at all and CocoPop's special window privileges were summarily revoked. She came to me to complain.

'It's most unfair. I can't help it if they leave stuff where it can be knocked over.'

'Well, you've learned a valuable lesson,' I said smugly, 'which of course I could have told you if you'd bothered to listen to me.'

'What's that, then?'

'The ayoomfas giveth, and the ayoomfas taketh away.'

This was true insofar as they'd taken away her special window but to make up for it they'd prepared a splendid big high-sided *wumpus box* for her to sleep in. They'd lined it with lovely softah and placed it in the room with lid but no walls, just beneath a window so that the sly devils could spy on us from inside the house. It was clear that the ayoomfas intended us *all* to sleep in this box, but of course that were totally out of the question. If I slept in the wumpus box I would lose face. *I* did not need any bed from an ayoomfa! *I* would make my own bed where and when I pleased. As the nights got colder in autumn Khalli had no qualms over cuddling up with CocoPop in the box, but I would deliberately find the most awkward and uncomfortable surface in the whole room with lid but no walls and sleep on it. Just to bring my point across firmly and show them that I was master of my own destiny.

Old Lady noticed this and laughed at me, so I lost face anyway. She called Old Man and Young Man to come look and they also laughed at me, and I lost more face. Some of Young Man's friends were there and they laughed at me, too. Oh this terrible ridicule again! And it got worse. Old Man brought out his big flash magic and it made bright flash at me. I was startled and ran away like a hopit, spitting madly. Oh the embarrassment! The loss of face! I could barely look anyone in the eye. I went to ground and lived wild in the grush for two days to regain my composure, and when I returned I thought it best to avoid further humiliation by condescending to sleep with CocoPop and Khalli in the wumpus box.

In truth I found the wumpus box a luxurious delight and I felt such a fool for not wanting to sleep in it. It was big enough to accommodate the three of us comfortably and the high sides kept out the cold wind. Best of all it faced the sunrise so on wintery mornings the three of us would sit neatly in the box like pips in a fruit, with only our heads protruding over the edge as we basked our faces in the morning sun. The only drawback of the wumpus box was that it was difficult to get out of in a hurry, especially when the three of us were lying fast asleep in an absolute tangle of cat. The ayoomfas quickly discovered this and the Young Man and the Old Man redoubled their efforts to try touch me. Once I was nearly too slow and the Young Man managed to briefly touch me with his softclaw. Needless to say I lost my composure and did my spitting hopit routine that left him laughing at me.

The back door of the house led onto the room with lid but no walls and unless it was very cold Old Lady left it ajar during the day. CocoPop and Khalli used to wander around the house at will, exploring the very bowels of the ayoomfas lair without a care in the world. Like me, Khalli avoided getting picked up, but she seemed quite happy for Old Lady to touch her and stroke her. Old Lady discovered that Khalli's favorite food was egg and she used to prepare special egg tidbits to give her. Khalli went absolutely berserk during these egg feasts and would writhe against Old Lady's feet making a great cacophony of gurgling delight in anticipation of her treats. What a disgraceful toady! I certainly didn't make an unctuous sycophant of myself like that! I used to show Old Lady who was boss when she was giving me treats. I would dart up close to her and whump her on the feet and ankles, sometimes spitting as well. That put her in her place, it did.

When I eventually ventured inside the ayoomfas' house I was extremely wary. The fundamental principle of my caution was never to allow anything or anyone to come between me and the open back door of the house. I could never afford to have my escape route cut off, leaving me trapped inside the house where the ayoomfas might kill and eat me. Or use my pelt to make coverings for their heads in winter. Or disappear me like Jimmy Abbott! Great Tabithat forbid! Because of this principle I had to endure a certain amount of embarrassment when I unfailingly ran like hell out the door, my feet skidding and slipping on the slidy floor surface. This happened whenever the wind slammed a door inside the house or one of the ayoomfas made a loud noise somewhere, or even walked past me in an indefinably suspicious manner. For a long time, nearly a turn of seasons, the sly ayoomfas simply ignored me when I ran away like this. I think they hoped I would eventually be embarrassed by my behaviour and stop running away.

Then Young Man took to sneakily shutting the back door when I was inside the house which gave me a serious panic attack the first time it happened. I begat a pathetic, despairing howl that resounded throughout the house: *Oh Tabithat! Oh No! I'll be captured and disappeared! Or eaten and leftovers fed to Khalli! Oh Tabithat please help a poor, innocent old cat.* It was a truly horrible howl, the likes of which have seldom been heard. It was enough to turn the gut of any creature to jelly. Howling as I ran, I fled blindly into the quietest part of the house and secreted myself away in a dark recess to await whatever terrors fate held in store for me. I waited but nothing happened, the ayoomfas didn't hunt me down. I waited some more, for quite a long time, and then cautiously ventured out of my hiding place back to the room with the slidy floor, where the ayoomfas were simply sitting chattering to each other as if nothing had happened. The back door was wide open. I steeled myself not to show how afraid I was, although I suspected even smelly breath LampreyTail way back in the Fat-Trees could have heard my poor heart thumping in my chest. I told myself firmly: *Don't run, Bunni, don't run. Just walk out slowly as if nothing's happened and you're not frightened.* But I ran. Like a *hopit*. Spitting.

Days passed and many times the Young Man had shut the back door while I was inside and he'd never made any move to chase me. Usually, I'd silently sneak off to half-heartedly hide somewhere in the house, but one of the ayoomfas always opened the door again and I was always able to escape to safety. In fact sometimes I didn't even bother to go outside when the door was opened. I got quite blasé about it all and let my guard down completely, so that when it actually happened I completely failed to see it coming. Young Man had prepared his devilish plan to the last nuance. Unbeknownst to me he'd very quietly closed all the other doors inside the house so I couldn't go to ground anywhere. Then when he closed the back door I suddenly found I had absolutely nowhere to go. It came as such a surprise that I didn't even have time to begat my special gut-turning howl of despair. I crept into a corner and cringed in abject defeat, my eyes squeezed tightly shut, waiting to be captured. Resistance was useless. I was completely trapped and even if I attacked Young Man with my sharp claws and what few teeth I had left, it would only make him angry and I would still be trapped! Young Man was clearly master of this encounter and I deserved to perish because I had thrown caution to the wind and disregarded the vital tenets of Wild Khat Knowledge. I had allowed myself to be captured. My heart was thumping so fast I thought it would jump right out of my chest, I was panting in terror, and I'd unintentionally made a small wizz.

Young Man sat down on the ground near me and I slightly opened one eye. When he was sitting down on the slidy floor he didn't look as big and frightening as he did when he was upright on his hind feet. I risked opening both eyes, but not completely. He was making soft and gentle sounds to me and he put out his forepaw and softly stroked the fur on my back. He did this several times and it felt very good. He stroked the top of my head and the tip of my tail and that also felt good. I had never been touched by an ayoomfa before, and I was surprised at how it felt. In fact had I not been frightened out of my wits I might even have considered setting up a *happi-rumble* like I use to do to calm my kittens when I wanted them to sleep. I began to relax. Then Young Man slowly backed off and opened the back door, leaving me still cowering in the corner feeling more stupid I'd ever felt in all my life. Oh, I'd been such a great, stubborn fool! So many turns of seasons had passed since I'd first seen the ayoomfas in this house and I nearly wept at the thought of all the love and affection I'd let slip by.

* * * * *

CHAPTER SIX:
Associate of the House

I had to control this touchy-feely business, you realise. I could not let the ayoomfas simply do what they pleased with me, when they pleased. Circumstances had to be just right for touchy-feely and I would decide when it was appropriate and when it wasn't. On a purely practical level I decided that Young Man could stroke and touch me whenever he pleased, because this would obviate his need to trap me and corner me. However, I wouldn't let him pick me up. I decided Old Lady would be the first to pick me up and so to provoke this one morning I did a *Khalli Egg Dance* around her feet for such a long time that she felt compelled to bend down and scoop me up in her forepaws. It was an odd feeling, being whisked off my feet and held in space, high above the ground, but it wasn't unpleasant. Holding me carefully, Old Lady then walked to another room in the house to show Young Man and Old Man that she had picked me up. Then she tried to pass me to Young Man as if I were an object and this was way beyond the bounds of the touchy-feely I'd planned for the day. I began to wriggle and she put me down for fear I might scratch her.

My next discovery was *lap*. Lap is what the ayoomfas call jumping up on the ayoomfa while they are seated, in order to nestle on top of their lower legs so they can stroke you and chuckle you under the chin. It's very comfortable and a cat is very hard pushed not to make *happi-rumble* or even to fall asleep. I had seen CocoPop perform lap on all of my ayoomfas, so I knew how it was done and I decided Old Man would be my first for lap. In hindsight this wasn't a wise move because I caught him completely unawares. He had fallen asleep while sitting on his favourite *sitz-softah* and was making a deep sleepi-rumble. A better lap would be hard to find, so I simply jumped on top of him there and then. He woke up with a terrible fright and nearly jumped out of his sitz-softah. This in turn panicked me and I lost control and ran away like a *hopit*. Spitting explosively as I ran. I lost much face.

My new life as a Trainer of Ayoomfas was progressing well, until one day I was re-exploring my old haunts and I happened across PhatNose and a long-haired friend.

'Hello girl,' he said. 'Long time no see. You look in robust health. Where have you been lately?'

'Uh, here and there. I've been around.' The last thing I wanted was to alert PhatNose to the benefits of my new life as a Trainer of Ayoomfas and all the perks to be had as an Associate of the House. *My* house, *my* ayoomfas. Fortunately he didn't seem at all interested in that.

He said, 'This here is my friend Imam Ayatollah Godzbadeh Ampzilla Khomeini III. He has a long and distinguished royal bloodline from a far-away place called Persia. But you can call him Khomeini.

'Hullo, Khomeini. What brings you to this wild place?' In truth I wasn't at all interested in the doings of this long-haired fool but Khat Lore prescribed that I should show due diligence in being polite to strange toms.

'I was a Citizen of a House over the hills, but I ran away from home.'

'Why?'

'The ayoomfas were always messing with me. Washing me, putting pink ribbons in my fur, hanging jangling shinies around my neck, taking me to cat shows, and trying to get me to *fruka-fruka* with spoiled snuffling queens with squashed-in faces.'

'What's a *cat show*?' I asked. It wasn't a Khat word I knew.

'It's the name the ayoomfas give to a tasteless festival of their worship of us. At a cat show the ayoomfas and their stinkirolis are *glorp*, like fleas on a gruf. That alone makes it highly unpleasant. They capture us poor cats and bring us in boxes to the cat show so that other ayoomfas can gawk stupidly at us, fondle us with smelly fingers, and rudely mess with us in ways I will not describe to a decent queen such as yourself. They make loud noises and we are jostled, buffeted and bumped around in a dreadful way and have to sit for hours amongst skinny faced Siamese who wail and whinge about everything all the time - no disrespect to yourself intended, ma'am.'

'None taken, I'm Chinese. Well, mostly Chinese. . . Anyway, Khomeini, it's been nice to meet you but I must be off about my business. . . '

'The reason I brought Khomeini here to see you,' PhatNose interjected forcefully, was that I thought he might like to *fruka-fruka* with you. He told me of his sad experiences and I promised to show him what proper wild pussy is like.'

I smiled thinly. Here we go again, I thought. More puriks to raise. I was just beginning to enjoy my life as a Trainer and looked forward to the day when I would have my very own little door within a door and be able to sleep inside as a fully fledged Citizen of the House. But Khat Lore is Khat Lore.

The room with lid but no walls had a little black fence running around most of its edge, for what purpose I knew not. It wasn't a very high fence and if I stood on my back legs, I could see over the top. It couldn't be to stop the ayoomfas falling out of the room with lid but no walls onto the grush because it wasn't nearly high enough for that. And it wasn't really far for them to fall if they did manage to throw themselves over it. It also couldn't be to stop us getting in and out because it had gaps in it through which any of us could pass, and regularly did. As my pregnancy from Khomeini developed and I began to grow fat in the belly it became more and more difficult to wriggle through the gaps in the fence, especially if I was in a hurry, such as when I was running away from an mischievous ayoomfa intent on picking me up when I didn't feel like it. One day quite near to my time of giving birth, I got stuck in the little fence! I couldn't go forwards and in my blind panic I didn't think of retreating backwards. Trapped again! I began to howl my special horrible howl of despair, and Old Man came outside the house to see what all the fuss was about. At first he laughed at me, but when he saw how upset I was he stopped laughing and made gentle and soothing sounds. He walked around to the other side of the fence and approached me from the front. Instinctively I pulled backwards to get away from him and suddenly I was out of the fence and free! I waddled off in embarrassment and shame, and Old Man went back into the house, shaking his head and laughing quietly. At this rate I would hardly have any face left at all by the time I became a Citizen of the House.

When I was fully Ripe with Purik I didn't really think the ayoomfas could possibly play any useful role in the birth, so I decided to take maternity leave. A wise cat uses Khat Concealment Knowledge and goes to ground in a safe hiding place to give birth and keep the puriks safe until they are old enough to take along without them being either a liability or an embarrassment. And so it was that I retired to the same hidey-hole in the long grush where I had given birth to CocoPop and Khalli and all the others over the years, and I stayed there for days numbering three paws' pads. There was only one purik in this litter and he was truly a beautiful little cat. He had my blue Siamese eyes and the shape of my head and body, but he was covered with a pelt of beautiful long and soft, dark grey fur - quite unlike my own. He didn't walk, he scuttled - like a *spinnelly* scuttles up a wall to its web - so I christened him Spinner. Spinner wanted to know everything about everything and would scuttle along next to me, bumping his little nose against all manner of things in his youthful curiosity. It was charming to watch, but I'd done it all before. Many times. By this time the truth be known I was sick and tired of raising puriks only to have them turn out to be fools or brats, so I decided I would give Spinner to the ayoomfas. I simply went back to the house and re-assumed my rightful Trainer's position in the room with lid but no walls with Spinner at my side, and waited for the ayoomfas to raise their lazy carcasses out of bed and bring us breakfast. Ayoomfas are utterly slothful and seldom wake up before dawn, so missing the best hunting times. Young Man saw us first and was overjoyed that I'd returned from my maternity leave. He was even more delighted that I'd brought him Spinner as present and he immediately set out to catch him and pick him up. Spinner scuttled away, but Young Man was very fast and he caught him and held him in both hands, making all sorts of what I imagine he thought were cat mothering noises, but which actually just sounded silly. He stroked and nuzzled Spinner for a long time and gave him the ayoomfa name *Spyder*.

I spoke earnestly to Young Man in Khat, 'Look, Young Man, I'm growing weary of this perpetual motherhood. You like this purik - he's yours. You can have him. I already taught him how to wizz and shufa like a civilized cat so I don't expect he'll make too much mess. He's a good purik so look after him well and good luck to you.' I turned and walked away and sat with my back to him. Not so far that he'd think I'd abandoned my duties as Trainer, but just far enough to let him know I wasn't going to be possessive about Spyder and that I trusted him with this purik. He didn't understand Khat, but I think he got the message.

Watching them fawn over Spyder anyone would have thought the ayoomfas in the house had given birth to the purik themselves. They cooed. They burbled. They made oooooh sounds and aaaaah sounds. They picked him up. They stroked him. They put him down. They picked him up again. They chuckled him under the chin. They talked to him. They sang to him. They found a whippy leaf for him to play with and played with him until he was so tired he fell asleep where he stood. And they called many other ayoomfas to do likewise. Then after this concentrated bout of delight and affection, they gave him to one of their friends who took him away. I didn't fear for Spyder's safety as it was clear to me that he was simply going to live as a Citizen of Another House somewhere - they all adored him and in any case he was too small for them to want to eat.

Spyder's relocation directly preceded the strange incident with the fence-box. A strange box had appeared in the middle of the lawn near where I liked to sit. It was made of sturdy fence all around except for one end which was open. I have no idea how it came to be there - the ayoomfas seemed to ignore it. I could see through the fence walls that there was nothing inside and since the box made no sound or movement I also ignored it. It remained where it was for a whole paw's pads of days and then a miracle happened. Praise Tabithat! The box grew a bowl inside, full of the most delicious shmoo kukri I had ever smelled. I watched it for a long time and nothing happened, so I cautiously ventured inside it and approached the shmoo kukri. Still nothing happened so I ate the shmoo kukri. This whole mujaji procedure repeated itself the next day. And the next. I never actually saw the bowl of kukri materialise, but it was always there when I awoke from my midmorning nap. I concluded that the fence-box must be a shrine to Tabithat and the shmoo kukri had been placed there by Him for me in appreciation for my devotion in leading the ayoomfas towards enlightenment.

On the fourth day disaster struck. I entered the fence-box as usual and approached the shmoo kukri. But then the floor shifted slightly under my paws and there was a great crash behind me as the fence-box shut its door after me. This was terrible! I was trapped in Tabithat's shrine, possibly forever! I was so distraught that I had no thought of the delicious shmoo kukri but instinctively begat my special horrible howl of despair. The Young Man and the Old Woman quickly came out of the house and approached the fence-box very purposefully and they were joined by another ayoomfa whom I recognised as the Jimmy Abbott Disappearer. Suddenly the sickening truth dawned on me: I had been deceived all along! I had been careless and had fallen prey to a mendacious ayoomfa plot to disappear me! Moreover, if the fence-box really was a shrine placed by Tabithat I was appalled that the ayoomfas could be so blasphemous as to misuse it for their own wicked ends. Was nothing sacred to them? Their evil knew no bounds. I intensified my horrible howl of despair and it clearly distressed the ayoomfas. Young Man and the Jimmy Abbott Disappearer lifted the shrine with me in it onto the back of an open stinkiroli with no lid; they got inside the closed part while Old Lady got onto the back of the stinkiroli and sat next to the shrine, making soothing noises to me. As if I was a complete fool! Traitor! Deceiver! I spat at her and hissed at her until I was hoarse.

The stinkiroli moved rapidly, far faster than any cat I know of could run except perhaps for Tabithat, bless his fast paws. I saw houses, trees, numerous stinkirolis of many colours, ayoomfas, a gruf or two, and even a fat tabby cat, flash by almost quicker than the eye could follow. And I saw strange things I had never seen before. It was frightening to travel this fast. Old Lady placed a covering from her ayoomfawumpus over the shrine so I couldn't see where I was being taken. We covered a great distance, stopping every now and then at places where stinkirolis would congregate for a while before moving on again. I don't know what this was for - I can only guess that the stinkirolis are social things and need to check each other out like cats do by sniffing each other's rear parts. During one such stinkiroli meet an ayoomfa in a stinkiroli next to us was disturbed by my horrible howl of despair, for he spoke to Old Lady and she pulled back the covering on the shrine so the other ayoomfa could see me. They both laughed and then Old Lady pulled the cover back over again.

The ayoomfas carried me howling in the Tabithat shrine into a building in which there was the biggest gruf I'd ever seen, a fat ginger tabby queen and a brightly coloured chirrit, each accompanied by an ayoomfa. The huge gruf was being restrained on a lead around its neck, while the Ginge and the rainbow chirrit were all in fence-boxes similar to my own but much smaller and less robust - what ayoomfas call a *kaij*. They were certainly not shrines. My entrance caused quite a stir.

'Oh look, its the pykie queen of Sheba,' sneered the fat ginger who could certainly do with having her clever orange face ripped off. In my agitated state I'd have been only too happy to oblige. 'We have such a huuuuuge box because we're sooo important,' she said snidely, 'and we make such a looouuuud noise.'

I began my horrible howl again, slightly modified to be a howl of righteous rage rather than despair, since it leads to terrible loss of face to show weakness in front of other cats. The fat Ginge looked nervous and kept quiet.

'Yo, white cat! Why you make dat 'orrible noise, mon?' the big gruf asked, 'You like some kind of wild animal, mon. Dis no need for dat row. Jus' wait your turn like everyone else an' your time gonna come sure as sunrise. Look now, white cat, you been frightening dat boid wiv your nasty noise.' He nodded towards where the rainbow chirrit was cowering in the corner of its fence box and had started to systematically pull out its feathers in fear. Plucking itself to save the ayoomfas the trouble, no doubt. Defeatist chirrit! Collaborator aviator!

'Does it matter? Let the silly chirrit shufa itself for all I care. We're all going to die soon, anyway,' I replied dejectedly and slumped down in my Tabithat shrine in despair. I had no more energy for the horrible howl of righteous rage and so shut it down.

'Yo crazy, mon! Where you been all your life? Nobody come here to *die* - not unless he gonna die anyway. We come here when we sick and the whitecoati makes mujaji so we get better. That way we stay well and we don't die. Hey man, how come you doan' know that? I thought cats were supposed to be clever. . .'

'Some of us are,' the fat Ginge piped up again, acidly.

'Shut up, you orange fool,' I snapped. You don't want to mess with me, believe it. I've lived wild in Vietnam for a paw's pads of winters and I eat pampered fat housecats like you for a snack before breakfast every day.' I spat explosively.

'Yo white cat, you full of anger, mon,' the gruf said, 'You must learn to chill out an' relax some. Dis not a bad place here, dis a good place. You, me, dat other puss, even da stoopid boid, we all gonna be jus' fine once da whitecoati get around to fixin' us. Sometimes my master he bring me here even when I'm not sick, jus' in case like.'

I relaxed somewhat, for although it was easily the biggest gruf I had ever set eyes upon, it had a sad, but kindly face set in an enormous fluffy black and brown head. It was nearly as big as the ayoomfa who was straining hard to keep it still on its leash.

'Master?' I asked.

'My name be Ravenous and I be a Saint Bernard. Dis here my master,' he said proudly. He turned around and with a tongue nearly as big as my whole body, devotedly licked the hand of the ayoomfa who was restraining him.

'Well, lucky you,' I said. Grufs are such slavish toadies.

'I don't have a *master*,' the fat Ginge piped up again, 'I have slaves.' For some reason this upset the big gruf, who started to bark loudly and at length at the Ginge and the rainbow chirrit started a high pitched, piercing shrieking. Then the ayoomfa belonging to the Ginge became upset that Gruf Ravenous was barking at his beloved lord and spoke sharply to Gruf Ravenous's master. In seconds the air was rent asunder with a dreadful cacophony. Not wanting to be left out and lose face, I again wound up my horrible howl of righteous rage.

Suddenly there was total hush. A door opened and a large ayoomfa male in white coverings peered out. This must be the much-vaunted whitecoati. Some communication passed between him and the ayoomfas and Gruf Ravenous then shambled after the whitecoati into the other room, dragging his hapless master after him on the leash like a toy. The door was shut and we all sat in silence.

'Who's a clever bird then? Eeeeeeka Eeeeeeeka Eeeeeeeka Eeekeee. . .'

'Oh shut up you stupid chirrit,' snarled the Ginge.

'Yes, shut up!' For once I was in full agreement with her.

'If I wasn't in this *kaij* I'd jump up there and kill that chirrit,' she said, licking her lips.

'Yes, me too. I'd like to rip it wide open and eat it all, beak, feets, feathers, everything except the *blibble*.'

'Ugh! I can understand the *blibble*, I mean no sane cat will eat the *blibble*, but the feets and the beak? Really?'

'For sure. Best parts of a chirrit,' I said. 'Very crunchy.' This Ginge wasn't such a bad cat after all and we began to swap hunting stories. Ginge told me that when it came to eating chirrits she preferred to kind of 'hollow them out' and then leave the empty husk as a gift for the ayoomfas, her servants. She was quite inexperienced and had never eaten the head of a squee or successfully caught a *hopit*. While we were chewing the fat, so to speak, Gruf Ravenous came out, bade us farewell, and dragged his master home. An ayoomfa woman came in the front door, with two boxes and a cat in each - a silver tabby and a very pretty black and white. These new arrivals were in the throes of an argument over ownership of a toy squee, and they snarled and spat at each other but pointedly ignored everyone else. I decided not to become embroiled in this spoiled children's tiff, and having established a rapport with Ginge, I quizzed her on the whitecoati.

'Gruf Ravenous was right in what he said,' Ginge told me. 'It's best to be nice to the whitecoati. He means well.'

'Shouldn't I attack him just in case?' I asked.

'If you feel you must, but it's really not necessary, Trust me.'

Some while later it was my turn to go into the other room. I had decided to attack the whitecoati just to be on the safe side. Old Lady and the Jimmy Abbott Disappearer lifted me up in my heavy shrine and carried me into the lair of the whitecoati, which held many strange objects and many strange smells. They placed the shrine down carefully on a shiny silver surface. The whitecoati made chatterings with them and looked at my shrine with ill-concealed amusement. Old Lady and the Jimmy Abbott Disappearer were not amused and I could sense they regarded me with respectful caution. They left quite quickly, before whitecoati opened the shrine. Just as well, for I gave it my best and scratched his arms and bit his fingers until he howled with rage and pain. That'll teach you, whitecoati! Nobody laughs at Bunni. I led him on a merry dance chasing me round and round the room, and I knocked over everything that I possibly could so as to frustrate his efforts. Eventually I jumped up on a very high surface which was laden with strange things which all toppled to the floor and shattered. I sat there and looked down at whitecoati, spitting explosively and with my horrible howl of righteous rage wound up to full intensity. Still he came, but with more caution and respect now. To protect his hands from further harm he had found a softah from an ayoomfawumpus and he threw this over me so I couldn't see anything. Ayoomfas always cheat when they can't catch you in honest pursuit. I went berserk in the dark under the softah, but then I felt a little thorn prick me and I fell asleep.

I felt terrible when I awoke. My insides felt like sore, worse even than after fruka-fruka with LampreyTail. Somehow I sensed something was different, but I knew not what it was. In the afternoon Old Lady and the Jimmy Abbott Disappearer came to see me and take me back to Vietnam. Whitecoati had white coverings over both his hands and arms. This time he looked at me cautiously and angrily, while Old Lady and the Jimmy Abbott Disappearer looked upon me with fond amusement.

In Vietnam I never became a Citizen of the House. I could not persuade the ayoomfas to make me a personal door within a door so I could sleep inside and come and go as I pleased, so I remained an Associate of the House. But never mind, the big wumpus box was very comfortable and if I needed more space I would always turf Khalli out into the night.

CocoPop was a restless soul and she began roaming farther and farther afield. Sometimes she would stay away for days on end and then suddenly appear as if nothing out of the ordinary had ever happened.

'Where on earth have you been?' I asked her angrily one day, 'You missed three breakfasts which I was obliged to eat in your place to avoid waste!'

'Sweet little black and brown roller - the world is hers to wander,' she sang the words from a popular Khat tune I'd heard the neighbourhood toms singing lately. I sighed in exasperation and scolded her.

'Why do you teenagers always have to be so cryptic? I'm your mother for Tabithat's sake! You should be able to tell me where you've been for the last three days! Everyone was very worried about you. The ayoomfas were all running around everywhere like panicked cackacks, desperately calling your name for hours. Young Man was beside himself that you weren't here. *Khalli* doesn't wander off for days on end. You should try to be more like her - not too much, though, just a little bit.'

She simply shrugged and turned her back on me. Then she walked off, swaying her bottom, curling her tail and singing to herself:

> *Sweet li'l black and brown roamer*
> *The world is hers to wander*
> *Pad around here, pad around there*
> *The toms they been a-sniffin'*
> *The toms they been a-callin' but they*
> *Can't catch the li'l black and brown roamer. . .*

There was nothing I could do. CocoPop continued to roam for days on end and eventually she didn't come back. I have no idea where she went or what happened to her. I can only hope she landed on her feet and didn't end up spending her best years living wild and living off stolen chirrits and tough, chewy squees like her mother had. The distress of the ayoomfas was terrible to behold. They were most distraught and launched a major search operation to try find CocoPop. At night they wandered far into the wild grush of Vietnam, thrashing about and calling pathetically for CocoPop, their little movable magic suns flashing uselessly around. This fruitless blundering around in the dark continued night after night until Old Man stumbled in a hole and hurt his hind paw, after which all searching in the dark was stopped. In the daylight an equally ridiculous search was held. Young Man and Old Lady got inside Young Man's yellow stinkiroli and Young Man made it roll back and forth along the nearby roads again and again while Old Lady leaned out the window calling for CocoPop. Old Man very sensibly stayed at home with me, nursing his injured foot. I really got quite fed up with them calling her name day and night, rain and shine, as if she were the only cat in the world and without her they would die. They still had me to supervise them - what more could they possibly want?

Khalli and I continued as Associates of the House for a full turn of seasons after CocoPop's disappearance. We became very fond of the ayoomfas and looked upon them as MyGranni, MyGrandad, and Young Man. Then one afternoon they used clever ayoomfa deception knowledge against us and I woke up after *trooning* with MyGrandad in the house-stinkiroli to find I was at Harvard! It was an outrage, as I've mentioned before.

But to my great joy, MyGranni put our wumpus box inside the house in a cosy corner in the room where they fed us. Better still, I discovered there was already a little door within a door and I spent the whole day going in and out of this and relishing my newfound satisfaction as a Citizen of the House. Not just a Citizen of any old house, but a Citizen of Harvard!

*****

CHAPTER SEVEN:
Nine spent, none left

A wise cat like myself knows that it's imperative to rest and relax while you can, for the world is forever changing, usually for the worse. One morning in the *yellow leaf season* that leads into winter, I was dozing outside not too far from the Midrand house. I was blinking into the sun in sublime contentment, when I happened to spot that some distance away there was a hole in the fence between us and the House of the Nasty Grufs. Being a clever cat I was able to see the consequences of this: If there was a hole, then the Nasty Grufs could get through it and come and kill us. So where were they? This was not good. All the hairs on the back of my neck rose up in alarm and I knew I had to get up and quickly go back into the house through our little door within a door. Inside I would be safe. The gruf couldn't possibly fit through our little door, and even if he did somehow smash his way in he'd then have to contend with the Young Man and his bangstick and against this the gruf would fare little better than a shufa in the ayoomfa's shufa bowl.

But I was an old cat and my senses or reactions weren't what they had been a paws' pads winters before. The gruf must have been watching me from some concealed hiding place for a while, for he came running fast and furious and was on top of me in the space of a few breaths, not six trees' distance from the safety of my little door within a door. I wasn't going to make it. I could smell his stinking breath as he gripped me around my middle in the vice of his jaws and sunk his dirty great teeth into my soft sides. I'd always had a bad feeling about the House of the Nasty Grufs and this was my worst nightmare come to life. As the snarling gruf lifted me up in his jaws I knew that this was the end of me, the wise old cat the ayoomfas called *Bunni*, for by my count I'd used up all of my nine lives and was already living on borrowed time.

I'd always imagined that Tabithat would call for me while I was asleep inside the house, or that I'd become sick and the ayoomfas would take me to the whitecoati only to find that Tabithat's need of me was stronger than even the whitecoati's most powerful magic. This is usually how Tabithat chose to take His cats to Him. I'd not really even considered the possibility that I'd meet my demise by being bitten in two by a salivating representative of the House of the Nasty Grufs. It was undignified and if nothing else I would lose face with Butch and Balune. This could *not* possibly be the will of Tabithat! It was a blasphemous outrage and I simply had to get away from this slobbering excuse for an animal!

The gruf held me firmly with his jaws around my fluffy tummy. He was simply too strong for me to wriggle free and I knew that if I tried to do this it would tear me up inside and then I would most definitely die. I could tell that gruf wanted desperately to bark and call his accomplices, for grufs are stupid communal animals. They *have* to operate in teams so their collective intelligence is up to the task of hunting, for individual grufs don't have the wits to accomplish much other than bark up a racket or blindly run after sticks and rolis thrown by their ayoomfas. But this gruf knew that if he opened his mouth to bark out his triumph I would certainly fall out and perhaps get away, so he kept his steely jaws tight around my middle.

When a cat catches a big squee of the large kind that can bite back - called a *yhat* - it grabs the squee around the neck and holds it there. The yhat can't breathe, move it's head or defend itself in any way. It is helpless and it soon dies. The evil gruf was so full of ignorant slavering hatred that it hadn't even properly planned what it was going to do. Perhaps he thought I was a stick? Sticks don't fight back. But I did. My entire upper body was free and although I had no teeth anymore, I had two forepaws' worth of very sharp claws, and I'd been in Vietnam and learned how to effectively use them to defend myself. With as much force as I could muster, I raked one paw into his nose leather, right through to the hollow inside, and ripped it up from top to bottom into a mess of blood and gruf snot. The other paw I hooked into the gruf's evil eye and tore around and around with it while I spat what I hoped would be terrible, venomous poisons into the bloody mess I'd made of his nose leather. There was blood everywhere and the gruf was in terrible pain. So was I, but I felt escape was near so I gathered my last remaining strength and in a frenzy started ripping at the gruf's other eye and began shredding up a nice hole in his ear with my back foot. Nearly totally blinded and it's face in two hells of agony, the gruf let go of me and I tumbled to the ground. The gruf made no further attempt to chase me and ran off.

'Yooooooowwwp! Yooooooowwwwp! Yooooowwwww! Ooooowwww!' it howled in pain and anguish as it blundered blindly in the direction it hoped was home, tail tucked between its legs in shame.

Butch and Balune had witnessed my escape from the safety of the house and were very proud of me.

'I've never seen anything like it. You were magnificent! Not even in The Prison have I seen such bravery. The ayoomfas should give you a bowl of cream for your courage in defending our house. I very much doubt *that* gruf will ever come back. You'd so blinded it that it ran off in entirely the wrong direction. Last we saw it was headed for the stinkiroli path where with any luck it will blunder into a stinkiroli and suffer terminal booma-skwasha!'

'Wicked, evil gruf!' said Butch supportively, emitting a menacing low growl.

'It's no good growling *now*,' Balune said contemptuously, 'the gruf is long gone. *You* ran away and hid in your special hiding place when you saw it come after Bunni!'

Butch ignored this jibe and trotted off to grab a quick snack of plokkits from the communal bowl in the food room.

I took comfort from the words of dear Balune, but I was hurt badly and covered in blood. I managed to stand up and began limping very unsteadily towards the little door within a door, only to realise it was too high for me to jump up to in my injured state. "Whitecoati,' I moaned, 'Need whitecoati.'

'Come now, Bunni! Don't be ridiculous,' Balune scoffed. 'Cat's don't *ask* to be taken to the whitecoati! It's not done. Not even in The Prison.'

'Do. Hurt bad. . . must find Young Man.' I hobbled to the stinkiroli house where I'd earlier seen Young Man lying underneath the stinkiroli fiddling with its *digestion* - the roaring mujaji that causes the stinkiroli to move. He was still there, making snarling angry sounds at the recalcitrant magic, but he heard my distress calls from a long way off and quickly ran outside to help me.

'Whitecoati,' I whimpered. 'Please help me. Caught by the gruf. . .must go to the whitecoati . . . .' and I collapsed at the feet of my Young Man.

Young Man immediately understood what had happened, even though he hadn't seen or heard it happen from where he was lying under the stinkiroli. Young Woman and MyGranni - who happened to be visiting us in Midrand that day - gently bundled me up in a wubbis so that I was like what the ayoomfas call a *sosij role,* and MyGranni sat with me on her lap in the back of her little red stinkiroli while Young Man and his Woman sat in the front and made the magic which made it go to the whitecoati. Whitecoati saw me immediately and I could tell from the tone of his ayoomfa-speaks to Young Man that my injuries were very serious.

Even Butch could have told him that! There was a big tear in my flesh on both sides where the gruf's teeth had punctured me and I hurt something awful. Whitecoati made a thorn prick in my front paw and after a little while some of the soreness went away and I fell asleep.

When I awoke I felt worse, if at all possible. Although the blood had gone and the whitecoati had sealed up my wounds in some magical way, I felt weak and very miserable. I was so stiff I could barely move, so I didn't bother. It looked like I was destined to die from the gruf attack after all, and I saw little point in eating or drinking or otherwise resisting my inexorable demise. But the ayoomfas had other ideas. Young Woman made a special nest for me right next to the great ayoomfawumpus where they slept. She kept me warm and wrapped up like a sosij role and stayed with me nearly all the time, making kind and loving sounds and trying to get me to eat shmoo kukri. At first I couldn't be bothered because I was sure I was going to die and it would therefore be supremely pointless and wasteful to eat, but Young Woman put little bits of the kukri on her softclaw and ever so gently weaselled them into my mouth. And a few days later MyGranni visited me with a bowl of the special white fish that she used to give me at Harvard for treats and which she knew full well was my favourite food of all time. She carefully broke off little bits of fish and fed them to me one by one as I lay in my sosij role. Days went by. Nights went by. And still the ayoomfas tended me. They would not give up. They would not let me die and they nursed me slowly and gently back to a reasonable health. Although I was already very wise I'd learned something important from the gruf attack: I should have trusted the Young Man more than I had; after all I'd known him for well over a paws' pads of winters and I'd slept on his ayoomfawumpus most nights when he'd lived at Harvard. And Balune had been right about the Young Woman, I should have listened to her. Young Man and his Woman truly loved me and would care for me as much as MyGranni had done. They were quality ayoomfarolês like MyGranni and had earned the reward of being admitted to my family as Mummi and Daddi.

I was never quite the same after being half eaten by the beast from the House of the Nasty Grufs. It was always a bit uncomfortable when I walked, especially when the weather became cold, and I tired very easily and spent more time sleeping. It became clear to me that although I'd survived the gruf attack I had run out of lives and was well into borrowed time with Tabithat. Before long Tabithat, praise his pads, would come calling for me. Unlike ayoomfas, who wax distressed and tearful at the mere thought of death, we cats are pragmatic. Khat Lore teaches us not to fear passing from one domain to the other. Although we don't remember it, we've all been back and forth many times in the past and will doubtless make the journey many times again in the future. It has no beginning and no end, and much like the water in the ayoomfas' shufa bowl it goes of forever. It is Tabithat's *mujaji of life.* If I died I might become a Citizen of the Temple of Tabithat, and my fate would be entirely in His holy paws. He might decide I was to return to the physical world within a different body to train some other ayoomfas in the ways of civilisation. Or he might choose to send me back to the earthly world in spirit form, to be a *Phirish* with a specific assignment. Or he might send me to the spirit world of the ayoomfas with which I'd heard there was a special exchange program; I could at least be with MyGrandad then and we could troon together like before. Tabithat loves all cats unreservedly and there are no terms and conditions with Tabithat like there are with Lord SlobberChops, God of the Grufs. Provided we are not downright evil, Tabithat doesn't threaten us or expect us to spend our lives compulsively striving towards some nebulous or unrealistic moral target. In fact Tabithat is quite happy for us to do very little at all. But perhaps the best quality of Tabithat is that he doesn't lose his temper and peevishly wreak havoc on the world like my Daddi says the ayoomfa gods do. Hail Tabithat! Praise his fluffy tail!

In these weeks I ate very little and only ventured outside for shufacation and wizz. I'd found myself a special little patch of sunlight in the room which Mummi and Daddi called *lounj* and in which the magic window was located. There I'd ensconce myself for most of the day, basking in the sunlight and reminiscing about my rich and rewarding life while waiting for Tabithat to come take me.

*****

I thought a lot about my daughter Khalli and how she died at Harvard. I'm sure my MyGranni felt I was to blame for Khalli's death, simply because Khalli coincidentally developed a wound on the side of her head at exactly the same place where I regularly whumped her with my sharp claws extended. Because of Khalli's bashful nature and aversion to ayoomfa lap and pick-me-up, this minor wound went unnoticed by MyGranni for some time and became a major wound. And as is so often the way with these things, Khalli developed a great poisoning sickness which quickly spread throughout her whole body. When MyGranni first noticed the change in Khalli's behaviour she managed to capture her and whisk her off to the *whitecoati*, but even the whitecoati's most powerful spells and healing magic could not drive the poisons out.

It had been less than two winters since MyGrandad died and MyGranni was beside herself with grief when Khalli died. She sobbed and sobbed for hours on end and when she finally stopped sobbing she concluded that I was entirely to blame for Khalli's death and would have to be punished. This was most unfair, for I was innocent. The whole sorry business was entirely Khalli's fault and I was being blamed for it!

MyGranni denied me special privileges for a whole moon of sunsets, adopting a cold, uncaring and merciless attitude towards me. She wouldn't let me have *lap*, she made no effort to feed me the special tidbits I really liked, and she wouldn't prepare for me the special fresh white fish that she used to eat herself. She even stopped mashing up my food with an ayoomfa eating stick to help me eat it easily with my one remaining - and very wobbly - tooth. In fact I was even worried that MyGranni might revoke my Citizenship of the House and make me sleep outside like some wild cat, but her anger stopped short of this and gradually subsided. How could I make her understand that I was simply being a good mother?

We know from Khat Lore that once a purik is big enough to properly look after itself, it must leave its mother and go to make its own way in the world. A grown cat certainly does not hang around its mother forever, behaving like a helpless purik. Well, this was exactly what Khalli did, and it was my duty as a responsible mother to discourage such behaviour. Surely MyGranni would not have liked it if Young Man had stayed living in the house with her for so many winters that he was old with grey head fur? It is not the way of nature. Khalli would have stood no chance of surviving in the wild on her own, and were it not for the timely intervention of the ayoomfas in Vietnam and the comprehensive training I gave them, Khalli would have died many winters before she did. MyGranni should really have been grateful to me.

Tabithat came for me one sunny but cold winter's afternoon as I lay dozing in my special snooze place in Midrand, happily dreaming of the huge flocks of grey chirrits in Vietnam that MyGrandad used to feed at Chirrit Rock. My dream started to fade, like it was slowly sinking behind a cloud, and I heard a deep and comforting happi-rumble like my mother used to make when I was a baby under the log pile. I could even smell that distinctive smell of the logs around me. I had a feeling of rising up into the air and then I could see myself below lying in my special snooze place, with Butch and Phat Balune looking up at me in fond curiosity as I rose ever higher. The happi-rumble intensified until it was so loud I couldn't hear anything else, and the cloud that had obscured my dreams started to obscure my vision of myself and my companions below. The top of my head was being gently washed by a slow tongue, I could feel the warmth of a cat's breath and I was suffused with a great contentment like I had never known before. Then a cat's face started to appear out of the mist and I prepared myself to meet my Lord Tabithat and join Him in everlasting happiness. But as the mist slowly cleared I saw that it was Khalli's face!

Now I knew what had happened - I had died and gone to Hell! Oh Woe! I was not to be embraced by Tabithat, but sentenced to everlasting misery and pain in the House of the Nasty Grufs, with giant slinkis and savage guelphs that would either rip me apart or swallow me whole while Khalli looked on in smug revenge. And this would happen over and over again for the rest of eternity. Oh Misery of Miseries! MyGranni must have been right after all about it being my fault that Khalli died and now I would pay the price through all eternity. I began to cry.

'Don't cry Mother, we love you,' the Khalli face said softly, 'I'm here to guide you through the change.'

'What do *you* know about anything? You're dead. I killed you and now I must be punished. Oh Tabithat, have mercy! Oh great and terrible woe!'

'It was not your fault, Mother. You just did what you thought was best. I still love you, we all love you and we're all here for you.'

'Uh, . .okay.' I said warily. Khalli guiding me anywhere would be an event not to be missed - from what I knew of her I doubt if she could have guided a squee into a hole in the ground even if she practiced all day. Then I had a fleeting terror that the particular Hell that had been concocted for me might feature Khalli mithering around me for evermore - would this be better or worse than a pit full of barking grufs and giant hungry slinkis.

'What happens now?' I asked the Khalli face, 'Will you be staying with me for long?'

'Tabithat wants to see you, praise his fluffy ears. He'll come soon, but I have to go, Mother. I love you so very much, but I do have other duties and responsibilities here, so I can't stay.'

I wondered what duties and responsibilities Tabithat - bless his paws and pray fervently that I've not upset him - would have entrusted to Khalli. Personally I wouldn't have trusted her to make wizz without supervision.

'Mother, you must please wait here. Tabithat will be along very soon.'

What did she think I would do, resurrect myself and wander back down to Midrand? 'Yes, Khalli, I will wait here for Tabithat' I said, somewhat patronisingly. 'I don't suppose I could have a bowl of humvee while I was waiting?'

'Of course, Mother love. It will be so.'

I didn't see her do anything, but a bowl of delicious humvee mysteriously presented itself in front of me and I got lapping into this as if there was no tomorrow, which as I wryly thought at the time, was a distinct possibility. A very splendid bowl of humvee it was, too, for when I had licked it dry and was busy washing my face, it magically refilled itself. Being adverse to waste of any kind, I diligently tried three times to empty the magic bowl of humvee so that it stayed empty, but in the end I gave up. There was no point in making myself sick - Tabithat would hardly be impressed if I threw up on his blessed paws.

It's hard to describe Tabithat. I can at least say that He's punctual, for He didn't keep me waiting around for long. He has the face of all cats and the face of no cats and His face - when you can see it - is constantly changing to the face of other cats. You don't really *see* Tabithat; you rather become aware of Him, that he is about, around, and even inside of you. You can't reach out and touch him, for his physical being is elusive and it seems to dance in and out of mist, although when He wants to touch you, you do feel it most clearly. At one point when I looked down for a moment I saw that I was actually sitting on the heart-shaped pad of one of Tabithat's beautiful and enormous sacred forepaws, but when I looked again it was gone, but I could feel the leather of his pads stroking the top of my head. Tabithat is the embodiment of all the cats who ever lived and all the cats which will ever live.

The happi-rumble subsided and Tabithat spoke.

'Wargi,' he said, using my Special Secret Khat name known only to myself and Him, 'I welcome you here in My House. Your beautiful daughter Khalli told me that you were here. Such a sweet, gentle cat,' He said fondly. I began to worry: *I wonder what else the foolish girl told him.*

'What happens now?' I asked apprehensively. 'Am I to be a Citizen of the House of Tabithat?' I had so many questions. Where was MyGrandad? Will I see my Mother, Sarah Bunn? And what happened to Jimmy Abbott and CigarTail and my daughter CocoPop? Where is my wumpus? And when do we get fed?

'Yes, you're dead. And no, you're not yet a Citizen of the House of Tabithat. I ordered your sleeping wumpus in your favourite tartan softah but I'm told they are out of stock and it won't be delivered for six to eight weeks. So there's no bed for you yet. Those Maine Coons I've got in Facilities aren't the sharpest thorns on the tree - I really should have a word with them, but I don't like to micromanage, you understand. Defeats the whole point of delegating tasks it does. Anyway, I shouldn't bore you with my problems. I've been watching you, Wargi. . .'

Oh no! Woe of woes! He's going to send me to Hell! The drooling grufs and the giant slinkis that look like logs in the water. . . I began to panic.

'It wasn't my fault, Lord, I beg of you. . .'

'What wasn't your fault, Wargi?'

'Uh, everything. Oh and anything. None of it. All of it. I blame Khalli myself.'

'Now, now, stop that nonsense! I'm not going to hurt you. And before you worry yourself into a state of fear, let me reassure you that there is no Hell for cats.'

'There isn't, Lord? No Hell?'

'Be at peace, little Wargi. The Hell of your fears doesn't exist. It simply doesn't make sense. Look at it from a practical viewpoint: An escape-proof place with giant cat-chomping slinkis and boiling vats of fat and slavering guelphs with teeth as long as your tail would require massive input of energy, materials, skills, supervision, and maintenance . . . and it would produce no useful output whatsoever. So what motive can there possibly be for any being to set up such a worthless enterprise?'

'But my mother, Sarah Bunn said that. . .'

'Sure she did. All mothers make up these stories about a dreadful Hell to get their tikki puriks to behave. And the Khat Khounciles jump in on the act and propagate myths of Hell to bully cats into paying their squee duties.'

'What about the *bad cats*, Lord? What happens to them if there's no Hell for cats?'

'Obviously I can't have bad cats living in My House, as I'm sure you'll agree. It would be very disruptive and I'd have to set up a police force of Scottish Wild Cats or something similar to maintain order. Believe me, once you start creating systems and institutions and procedures it soon gets completely out of hand. Much better to keep it simple. Which is why the entry requirements to My House are so stringent, Wargi. If I think a cat has led a bad life, I will simply send them back to the mortal world to learn their lessons again.'

'Am I a bad cat, Lord?'

'Not exactly, Wargi. You're a good cat inasmuch as you've done very well for yourself under very difficult conditions and displayed much of those qualities of initiative and resourcefulness that are the hallmark of a truly great cat. . .

I began to feel good and wholesome again.

' . . . You've raised many fine puriks and you've given great reward and delight to a number of worthy ayoomfas who've grown to love you dearly. . .

I was getting so puffed up with pride I felt I might burst.

'But there is the matter of your treatment of your daughter Khalli . . .'

Oh dear here it comes! He'll send me back to start all over again in the log pile and I'll have to fruka-fruka with LampreyTail again. . .

'I got to thinking about how you were unnecessarily unkind to Khalli, and what a really a sad blemish on your otherwise good and worthy life it is. Were it not for this one badness I would have no hesitation in immediately making you not just an ordinary Citizen, but a *Phello* of the House of Tabithat. So while your bed is being prepared - and also upgraded because it will soon be a Phello's bed - I'm going to give you an opportunity to make amends by giving you a very special task.'

'I am going to send you back to Earth as a *Phirish*, a spirit cat. You will be visible to other cats and will be able to fully communicate with them.'

'What will I look like to other cats, my Lord? Will I have a fluffy tail and pink pads and be beautiful like I was? Will I be in colour?'

'Now that you are a disembodied soul you actually have no form or shape at all except provided at my discretion, so forget about your pink pads. I have to make you appear in a form with which other cats will be comfortable. You will be seen as a transparent image of your former self in a cloud-like shade of grey. You will not be visible to ayoomfas because they have great terror of all things they don't understand and will probably either run away or try kill you. Finally, I am going to enable you with a very special gift: you will be able to understand the speech of the ayoomfas.'

'Thank you, Lord. How will this help me?'

'That is up to you. While your Phello's bed is being prepared I am going to task you with looking after the ayoomfarolês you called Mummi and Daddi. They are heartbroken that you died and I would want these good people always to be in the company of quality cats like yourself and your friends. So I am tasking you to watch over these ayoomfarolês and their cat family. From time to time I will come see how you are doing.'

'What about MyGranni, Lord?'

'She loves you very much. You will see her when you see her. Go now and fulfill your task.'

*****

CHAPTER EIGHT:
New Tricks

So it happened that I found I could ignore the door within a door and walk through the walls if I chose. Or the doors, or windows, or even jump through the roof if I fancied! The only objects I couldn't comfortably pass through were the brown and blue coloured *mujaji strings* that were buried in the walls of the house and which also lay strewn around under the roof. These mujaji strings were some ayoomfa magic that tried to push me away by creating a powerful humming vibration, and I learned to avoid them. Some of them appeared to be associated with the magic suns, and the strings grew more powerful when the ayoomfas activated the magic suns. Many of the ayoomfa objects and constructions tied to the coloured mujaji strings also tried to push me away. The magic window and some of the strange things in the room where Daddi spent a lot of time made a powerful turbulence against me; some of them hummed but others shrieked a cacophony of sound that was most disturbing. These things never behaved so ungraciously before, and neither the ayoomfas nor my friends Balune and Butch appeared to hear this racket at all, so I suppose it must be one of the collateral talents of a Phirish. The most powerful of these strings was big and black and as fat as the base of my tail. It came into the house from outside and was buried in the ground. This was a very powerful mujaji string that didn't like me at all and I took special care to avoid it, especially while playing my new game of chasing *ground squees* and *binigaus* through their tunnels under the ground.

At first I found my ability to pass through objects a great novelty and had enormous fun suddenly appearing and disappearing in front of Phat Balune and Butch. Balune was not impressed by my antics.

'You're supposed to be dead. Go away and be dead properly.'

She scoffed at the explanation that I gave her that I had been tasked with looking after her.

'I don't need any looking after,' she said. 'Especially by a dead cat that plays foolish tricks on me.'

'Oh, you're back,' Butch said simply, 'Mummi will be very pleased to see you. Come let's go ask her to give us our supper,' and he trotted away.

It was alarming at first to have Daddi and Mummi walk right through me because I had forgotten they couldn't see me. It felt odd, too, like a warm flush that came and went. I wonder what they felt, if anything. In the past I used to enjoy sitting where they would trip and fall over me but of course this didn't happen any more. Tabithat giveth and Tabithat taketh away.

Another of Tabithat's little bonus gifts I discovered I had been given was the ability to see living creatures with a surrounding radiance that seemed to reflect their condition and indeed their state of mind. For example, Balune always had a fiery red crown over her head when she was angry, which was quite often because she was easily displeased. Tabithat's gifts don't come with an explanation on how to use them and it took a lot of time and practice before I was able to properly understand what I was seeing.

My newfound understanding of ayoomfa-speak seemed largely a waste of time. It simply reinforced my belief that ayoomfas were foolish creatures that wasted a lot of time on unimportant nonsense. Much of their talk concerned the various objects and constructions that they surrounded themselves with, and since at first I did not understand the purpose of these objects, nor even which objects were which, I could not understand any of the ayoomfas' chatter concerning them. Certainly a great deal of their time and efforts were devoted to things around them. They also spent a lot of time away from home at a place they called *work* which clearly made them unhappy, but both Mummi and Daddi stubbornly persisted in going to this place nearly every day.

I decided to accompany Daddi to his place of work to see what it was all about, so one morning I journeyed there with him in the blue stinkiroli. It took a long time to get to work and there were glorp stinkirolis on the stinkiroli paths and Daddi's stinkiroli was forced to go very slowly and stop many times for other stinkirolis to sniff and go past. Daddi became very angry at this and his radiance became inflamed, red and fiery above his head like Balune's as he shouted at everything around him. He had a mujaji string object in the stinkiroli which made sounds of the kind that ayoomfas make for enjoyment and singing - what they like to call *mewsik* - and he made this mewsik so loud that it made the whole stinkiroli shake like an earthquake. Had I been alive this would have really hurt my ears; sometimes being dead has its advantages.

Work turned out to be what I remember from Vietnam was called a Fat-Tree and it was full of glorp ayoomfas, all jabbering at the same time and drinking a horrid brown plapa that I'd learned they called *kofi*. Disappointingly there were no cats or guelphs at the fat-tree, which was full of boring ayoomfa mujaji objects; in fact it looked like the Fat-Tree was a place where the ayoomfas created these objects. In this place my Daddi was clearly a Mujaji Lord, a great and wise whitecoati of mujaji, for he had deep understanding of many mujaji objects and other ayoomfas frequently came to him for council when one or other mujaji was sick. Sometimes Daddi became angry at the foolishness of these other ayoomfas and called them cross names when they could not hear him. He made many, many markings concerning the magic of the mujaji, both on peppers and also on a special white shiny surface on the wall, like he had in his room at home. Daddi had another kom-pewter at work and it him even angrier than all glorp stinkirolis on the way to work. He spent a great deal of time scolding it, and he frequently told it that it was slow and pathetic and that all the ayoomfas who had made it slow and pathetic were also slow and pathetic. On one occasion all the markings on the kom-pewter's magic window unexpectedly disappeared and the magic window went blue all over. This made Daddi exceptionally angry and he shouted loudly that he was going to hunt down and kill someone called Bill Gates. Possibly this Bill Gates must be some kind of highly prized food animal, for I have heard many ayoomfas express a desire to kill Bill Gates.

Just before the sunset, Daddi would leave the Fat-Tree and go wake up his blue stinkiroli. Then he'd travel back to our house in Midrand, along the same path he had taken in the morning and with the same shouting, anger and red crown of radiant fire.

The work that Mummi went to in the morning was somewhat different. The journey in the stinkiroli was similar - both in the morning and just before sunset - the only difference being that Mummi's stinkiroli was red and she didn't shout as much as Daddi when she was inside it and her radiance was less red and inflamed. This may be because Mummi didn't make such loud mewsik in the stinkiroli.

Wurk for Mummi was in a house, not a Fat-Tree. There were less than a paw's pads of other ayoomfas at this place and the whole atmosphere was of a quieter and calmer nature than that at Daddi's work, probably because Mummi and the ayoomfas there didn't drink so much kofi. I've observed that ayoomfas tend to get excitable when they drink a lot of kofi. Like Daddi, Mummi also called the other ayoomfas cross names when they were not around, especially one particular one called Boss. She spent most of the day making markings on peppers but they were different from the markings Daddi made. Whereas all of Daddi's markings looked like mujaji spells nobody would understand, some of Mummi's markings looked a bit like little houses. This was probably coincidence - obviously the markings couldn't be meant to be real houses, for Mummi would have had to find a very big *pepper* as big as a real house. Perhaps the markings were meant to be little houses for squees, although why anyone would want to make a house for a squee is quite beyond my understanding. The only significant interest factor I could find at Mummi's work was that there was a cat there. She was a big, fluffy, orange queen with beautiful Calico-like markings and she liked to roll about in the sunshine outside the house of Mummi's work. She was an Associate of the House of work, and a Citizen of the House next to it.

I looked carefully at this middle-aged queen as she frolic'd happily without a care in the world. She had one of the most spectacular tails I'd ever seen; it was as wide as her body at the base and tapered only slightly to a great fat bushy end. The orange in her fur began as a medium orange on her head and became progressively darker down her body until the end of her tail was pure black. I introduced myself to this splendid cat.

'Hello, I'm Bunni. What's your name,' I asked by way of introduction.'

'§pina§h.'

'Spinach? What kind of name is that?

'It'§ what my Mummi and Daddi call§ me. I don't know what it mean§.'

I suspect Spinach must have been fed on soft food most of her life or her whitecoati had lost his powers, for most of her teeth had gone. This poverty of tooth caused her to make a great splashing noise when she spoke any words that had a hissing sound in them. I'd never had this problem when I'd been alive, even though I'd also had no teeth in my autumn years.

'Don't you have another name?'

'Only my §ecret Khat name whic§h is Pipuliou§ but I'm not §uppo§ed to §ay it out loud in ca§e you hear me.'

'Yes, yes, one must be discreet, of course. That's my Mummi inside that house,' I said proudly.

'§he plays with me every day,' said Spinach. 'I like your Mummi.'

'That's probably why she comes to this place, to play with you. She can't play with me anymore because I'm dead and she can't see me.'

'Ye§, I can §ee that you're dead. I've never been dead. What'§ it like being dead?'

'Well, let's just say it's very different from being alive. It has a good side and a bad side. On the good side I don't have to worry about being killed. I used to worry greatly about this when I was alive. Also, I don't have to bother about shufa or wizz or feeling cold or getting wet or howling toms with fruka-fruka on their mind, or eating or drinking. On the other hand I used to enjoy eating and drinking, so that's also a bad point. It's fun walking through walls and burrowing underground with no effort, and getting around and about is really cool. One can get to a place simply by thinking about it, but after a while the novelty wears off and it becomes just another thing like walking or washing your paws. I think what I really miss the most is not being able to sit on Mummi's lap or troon with MyGranni.'

'That'§ too §ad, really. I'm §o very §orry for you,' Spinach splashed sympathetically.

'Do you have a Mummi and Daddi?' I asked.

'Ye§. They live in that hou§e with the §hiny §ilver §tinkiroli that'§ §tanding out§ide in the §un. My Mummi and Daddi u§ed to be happy ayoomfa§ and would §pend lot§ of time with me, but lately they're §o bu§y §houting at eac§h other that they §carcely remember to feed me or gruf Bakerloo.'

Had I not been dead I would have been soaked.

I felt very sorry for cat Spinach and her broken home. But being dead, I didn't know what I could do to help her, but I did suggest she keep company with my Mummi whenever it pleased her. Then I wished her well and then went to watch over my Mummi inside the Wurk house.

*****

A full turn of seasons had passed since I'd become a Phirish and I noticed that Butch seemed to be getting a pair of yellow whirlpools on his radiance, towards the back. At first I thought nothing of it but as time went by I noticed he was beginning to lack enthusiasm for his food. This was highly out of character for Butch, especially since he was clearly very hungry. At mealtimes he would shout at Daddi for food but when the food came he would have a mouthful or two and then sadly turn away. Then he'd shout at his Daddi again to highlight his frustration at the injustice of his situation. Daddi was concerned about this and tried his best to get Butch to eat by repeatedly taking him back to his food and patting his sides. What he thought that would help is anyone's guess, for what Butch was telling him in no uncertain terms is that he couldn't eat even though he wanted to. Mummi also tried to coax Butch into eating, with equally poor results. It's a serious disadvantage in life not being fluent in Khat; it really should be taught to all young ayoomfas to properly prepare them for the civilised world. After nearly a week of fruitless coaxing Mummi and Daddi snatched Butch and hustled him away to the whitecoati. This being Midrand, the whitecoati was the one with the spattered coati and I'd always had reservations about him. When I'd been injured by the beast from the House of the Nasty Grufs he'd done quality magic and fixed me, but let's face it, that was not a challenging situation. He didn't have to use any great powers of magic at all to figure out that I had a big hole in my side.

With Butch he had a far greater challenge because he couldn't see what was happening inside the poor cat. I could see the yellow whirlpools in Butch's radiance and knew that these pointed to there being a problem but they gave no hint to the solution. I went along with Mummi, Daddi and Butch in the stinkiroli to the whitecoati to keep abreast of developments. The whitecoati felt Butch all over and squeezed him in many places. Butch was quite amenable to all this. Whitecoati then took out a *tikki mujaji slinki* which had two tiny heads and a tail with a round shiny on it. Whitecoati stuck the two heads of the tikki mujaji slinki into his ears and then used the round shiny on the tail to feel around Butch's tummy. Butch was quite relaxed about all this, too. He was even resigned when whitecoati stuck a thornstick into him and stole some of his blood. Then whitecoati went too far. He got a shiny silver stick and stuck it in Butch's shufa-hole. Butch wasn't happy about this one bit and shouted angrily at the whitecoati.

'Yeooouuuuwrrrrr!!!!' he said.

'Bite him, bite him! Scratch him to shreds!' I encouraged Butch loudly, 'Steal *his* blood!'

'No, he's just doing his best to help me,' Butch said.

'Who told you that nonsense? The Khouncile? For one so big you are such a phraidy cat! I would have bitten him long ago and if I weren't dead I would bite him now!'

Whitecoati didn't do anything else to Butch, which was just as well. He talked to Mummi and Daddi for a long time about what he though the problem could be. I could fathom the gist of this talking was that Butch had a sickness in his *kid-nees*, whatever they were. Whitecoati said he would send the blood he'd stolen from Butch to another whitecoati who would examine it with the help of one or other clever ayoomfa mujaji examining thing and then tell him exactly what was wrong with Butch and what could be done about it. This all sounded very suspicious to me. I'm a wise old cat and I've been washing every part of myself for most of my life and I know my body very well by now. There's nothing that matches the whitecoati's description of kid-nees anywhere on the outside of a cat. I know also that on the inside of a cat there's only a blood-soaked mess of meat and offal, because back when I was a young queen in Vietnam I saw cat SwishTail on the stinkiroli path when he'd burst after suffering booma-skwasha. There was just a bloody mess, nothing that looked like what the whitecoati described as kid-nees.

The whitecoati went on to tell Mummi and Daddi that in the meantime Butch must be given more plant leaves - what he called *vejtibils* - to eat. Particularly the little white grains that are glorp and which the ayoomfas call *rice*. Great moons of Tabithat! Now I knew for certain this whitecoati was not much smarter than a vejtibil himself! Cats eat meat - they simply don't like vejtibils and they especially don't eat rice!

On the way home I told Butch what the whitecoati had proposed. He was quite dismayed. 'I can't keep anything down, let alone plants and this horrible stuff called rice. I wouldn't have been able to eat rice at the best of times.'

'I think Mummi and Daddi will see that this plan is unworkable before long,' I comforted him. 'And the whitecoati that's sniffing the blood that was stolen from you might be brighter than this one - Tabithat knows that wouldn't be difficult.'

That was exactly what happened. At mealtimes Butch refused to eat the rice and cried even more plaintively than before. Mummi and Daddi were in great distress because they didn't know what to do to help him. They, too, were suspicious of the advice of the whitecoati, whom Mummi referred to as Doctor Oaf. After some discussion Daddi suggested they take Butch to the nice whitecoati that he used to go to with MyGranni when we lived at Harvard. I thought this was a good idea and as usual I went along as an invisible observer. It was a long journey to the Harvard whitecoati, but he was definitely a cut above Doctor Oaf. For a start Harvard whitecoati was clean and he clearly liked cats, whereas every cat who'd seen Doctor Oaf could tell that he preferred huge guelphs of the kind ayoomfas ride upon and the other ones they eat, and he was therefore a philistine. Harvard whitecoati talked for a long time with Mummi and Daddi. I think they made him understand that it was unreasonable to try making Butch eat vejtibils and rice, and Harvard whitecoati seemed to appreciate the sense in this. But he told Mummi and Daddi that he thought Doctor Oaf was likely right and that Butch did have something wrong with his kid-knees. Harvard whitecoati had a big white pepper stuck to his wall on which was a picture of a cat which had only insides and no outsides, the poor creature. It must certainly have died in great pain, having neither fur nor skin and having parts of it cut away, too. I felt desperately sorry for this insides-only cat, and hoped that Tabithat would have taken him as a Citizen of His Holy House and restored his outside parts again. Whitecoati showed Mummi on this picture where Butch's kid-knees were and this turned out to be exactly the same place as I was seeing the

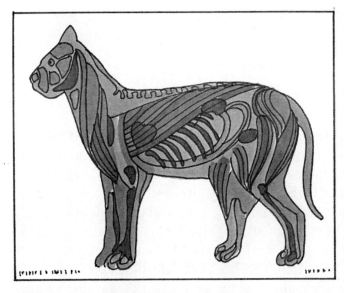

yellow whorls on his radiance. Whitecoati wanted to keep Butch there with him for a few days and try fixing him with a special kind of water magic, to wash out poisons from his body. Butch was frightened about what was in store for him and about being left there away from his family.

'What will happen to me,' he asked.

'Well, the worst that could happen is that you become very sick and die.' I said, 'But then you'll become a Citizen of the House of Tabithat, which is quite fine. So look on the bright side. Oh, and there is no Hell, Tabithat told me personally, so you have nothing to worry about.' I simply didn't have the heart to tell Butch that his kid-knee sickness might cause him to have to slop around as an insides-only cat like the one in whitecoati's picture.

'I hope I don't die,' he said, 'That would make my Daddi and Mummi very, very sad.'

'Yes. That would make us all very sad, my Butch. But you may get well if the water magic works. I'll come and visit you when Mummi and Daddi come back here in a few sunrises.'

When I next saw Butch he appeared a bit livelier and the twin yellow whirls on his radiance had become much paler. Clearly the magic was working. Mummi and Daddi were delighted and took Butch home and made a big fuss of him. MyGranni was there to visit us and she'd made him a special batch of his favourite white fish which smelled very strongly and which she called *stinkfish*. Everyone watched Butch very closely over the next few days and hoped that the Harvard water magic would have resulted in a permanent recovery, but it was not to be. After a few days of eating normally, Butch began to feel sick and stopped eating again, and I could see the yellow whorls growing stronger on his radiance. In less than a paw's pads of sunrises he was thin, his coat had lost its gloss and his eyes had become dull with sickness. He really was feeling very bad.

'I feel so wretched and sick,' he said to Balune and me. 'I think I'm going to die soon.'

Balune and I both nodded sagely at him in agreement. It's not our way to hide these things.

'I'm not afraid to die but I'm really sad. I've been so happy since I've known you both, and I don't want to leave you and my ayoomfas.' He began to cry.

Daddi and Mummi were very miserable and took him back to the Harvard whitecoati, carefully wrapped up like a sosij role in my old pink wubbis, and with me sitting unseen on the shelf by the back window of the stinkiroli. Harvard whitecoati looked very gloomy and shook his head sadly. I understood from what he said to Daddi that that Butch had a very powerful kid-knee sickness that had defeated the best Harvard mujaji. He was very ill and would not survive more than a few days.

'Bunni, will you stay with me when Tabithat comes to fetch me?' Butch asked.

'Yes, Butch. I will be there with you.'

And I was.

*****

CHAPTER NINE:
Spinach

Midrand became a single cat house with two very miserable ayoomfarolês and one fluffy Phat Balune who didn't really mind either way. Balune had become very self-sufficient in prison and she wasn't a sociable cat in any case. She gladly absorbed the overflow of affection from the ayoomfas, considering it no more than her due. I, on the other hand, had nothing to do and was really bored. Being a Phirish I couldn't even have a satisfying wizz or catch a squee and I'd grown tired of teasing Balune by suddenly jumping in front of her with a loud *meeeeoowl* when she was just about to fall asleep. At first this had been huge fun, for she'd all but jump out of her skin and then she'd try to to whump me on the head with her stocky forepaws. Of course she would end up thumping nothing but air and I would float away, laughing at her. After about a moon's sunrises she became inured to my tricks and eventually the best reaction I could get from her was that she'd half open one yellow eye and scowl at me before dozing off again.

'Why don't you ask Tabithat if your bed's ready yet?' she said testily one morning, 'so you can go away and be properly dead instead of hanging around here playing stupid pranks.'

I realised she had a point. Tabithat - bless his inter-pad fluffiness - had been closely monitoring events, for he came to me in a dream one sunny afternoon.'

'Praise Tabithat, Great Lord of All Cats!' I greeted his huge fluffy face as it swam in and out of the mist before me and his powerful happi-rumble shook the ground. 'Does my Lord come to tell me my bed is ready?'

'No, little Wargi. Your bed is not yet ready. Facilities tell me that the special tartan wubbis you wanted has been discontinued, so they can't finish your bed at the moment. They're trying to get hold of some on the grey market.'

I must have looked crestfallen, for Tabithat - bless his fat, fluffy tail - said, 'Be of good cheer, little Wargi. I assure you that you will get your bed exactly as I promised, but you must be patient. In the meantime, I have an important task for you.'

I pricked up my ears and bristled with pride. That Tabithat would entrust me with something important was a great honour, although in truth anything to relieve the boredom would have been welcome.

'There are not enough cats in the house of which you are *Caretaking Phirish*. It is my wish that you obtain some quality cats to bring cheer to these sad ayoomfarolês. So I have decided that cat Pipulious must be made a Citizen of your House. Your task is to make it so.' Having said that, Tabithat vanished.

I made a point of accompanying Mummi to work every day. Most days we would come across Pipulious - aka Spinach - rolling around on that part of the outside that was a path for the stinkirolis. She seemed totally oblivious to the danger of the stinkirolis and never made the slightest move to get out of the way. Ayoomfas like Mummi who came to the house would have to make their stinkiroli stop, get out and carefully move Spinach out of the way, before they could proceed. I felt it my duty to warn her of the danger of stinkirolis.

'You really shouldn't get in the way of the stinkirolis. Have you not heard of *booma-skwasha*? You could easily be killed lying around in their path.'

'That's ridiculou§ non§en§e!' she sloshed at me, 'The §tinkiroli§ alway§ §top for me.' Which was kind of true in a way. I could not persuade her to desist and I prayed to Tabithat to keep her safe. I think he would have, for it would surely be a stupid waste of both his time and mine for him to give me the task of bringing her home only to have her killed in a *booma-skwasha*. But Tabithat works in ways ordinary cats don't understand, so anything could happen. Praise his soft nose leather.

I asked Spinach how she was doing at home.

'Mummi and Daddi §topped §houting at ea§h other.' she said. 'Daddi'§ gone away and I think he'§ living §omewhere el§e. He took gruf Bakerloo with him. I mi§§§ gruf Bakerloo §§§ooo muc§h,' she said unhappily, 'He loved me and u§ed to wa§h me every day with hi§ big tongue.'

I would have thought the washing would be the other way around, but mindful of how my unkindness to Khalli had landed me in my present predicament, I kept these uncharitable thoughts to myself.

'And your Mummi?'

'Mummi'§ not happy. §he trie§ hard to be happy and §he goe§ out a lot with her ayoomfa friend§. §ometimes §he §tays away all night. Othertime§ §he come§ back very, very late and then she's all wobbly. La§t night when §he came home §he was §o wobbly §he fell over my water bowl and made a big me§§. And §he often forget'§ to feed me. But it'§ not too §erious becau§e the kind ayoomfa woman that comes to thi§ hou§e feed§ me §ometime§.'

Aha, I thought, this cat is ripe for Tabithat's plan. I wasted no time in exploiting this.

'The woman you speak of is my Mummi,' I said proudly. She is an *ayoomfarolê* and I know she would like to feed you every day. You really should leave this place and come and live with us in our house in Midrand.'

'What if my Daddi come§ back?'

'He won't. When an ayoomfa man goes away and takes his gruf with him he isn't coming back. Ayoomfa men and grufs are very chummy because their minds work in the same way.' This was something I'd heard Mummi say one day, and it sounded very plausible. Also I'd found that being a Phirish seemed to raise one's credibility. For some reason it seemed expected that a Phirish should *know* things that ordinary cats didn't.

'But I can't leave my Mummi. §he need§ me,' Spinach said sadly.

'If she needs you so much then how come she goes out all night and forgets to feed you? She's probably lapping too much of the ayoomfa *happi-water*.'

'§he only doe§ that becau§e §he'§ §ad that my Daddi left.'

'That's no excuse,' I said firmly. 'Ayoomfas must take their duties seriously and must not inconvenience or mislead the cats in charge of them. She is guilty of Wasting Khat Time, which is not a trivial misdemeanour. Who used to feed you and gruf Bellicose when your Daddi was staying in the house?'

'Gruf Bakerloo,' she corrected. Spinach was evidently a pedant.

'Yes, yes, gruf Bakerloo. I'm §orry. . .I mean sorry. Who used to feed you?'

'My Daddi fed me and gruf Bakerloo when he §tayed here. But it wa§ hopele§§ - ab§olutely hopele§§. He and Mummi would §hout at eac§h other like §quabbling toms. And on§e when §he wouldn't let Daddi §leep in the ayoomfawumpu§, he lapped too muc§h happi-water and fell down a§leep with hi§ head in my bowl of food. I felt §§§oooo §orry for him becau§e when he woke up he looked §ick and he had §hmoo kukri and plokkits in hi§ head-fur.'

By Blessed Tabithat, what an awful house this must be! 'You should come live with us at once!' I urged. 'There's nothing worthwhile left here.'

'But I love§ my Mummi,' said Spinach with great determination, 'and my Daddi. And gruf Bakerloo.'

There was little I could do faced with this sloshing obstinacy. I went home to lay sly plans and plot schemes, hoping that events would follow the course I expected.

They did. All I had to do was wait. Ayoomfas are sociable creatures and don't like to live alone. It's one of their many weaknesses, but this time it worked to my advantage. Within a few moons Mummi Spinach started having a male visitor in the form of a man whom I shall call *Man Horrible*. Man Horrible was thin and wiry and not much bigger than Mummi Spinach. He had no real head fur and he disguised this from Mummi Spinach by covering his head at all times with a piece of someone else's head fur that was made to look like his own. Spinach said he smelled funny; kind of like fruit that's been left in the sun. Not a good specimen at all for Mummi Spinach; their puriks would doubtless be small and puny and smell bad.

Worst of all, Man Horrible didn't like cats. Oh, he *said* he liked cats, but we always know who like us and who don't. We are not stupid like grufs, who will believe anything you tell them. One day I sat and watched Man Horrible when he sat in the lounj of the house while visiting Mummi Spinach, and with Spinach as my '*a§§i§tant*' I subjected him to various tests.

'Now is a good time to go jump on his lap,' I told Spinach, who did so. Man Horrible tensed and his radiance grew fiery red in anger at Spinach, but he didn't do anything. He just sat stiffly with his hands at his sides and his forepaws made into tight balls. No proper welcome, not a good start.

'He should participate more,' I instructed Spinach, 'Kneed your claws into his legs a bit to encourage him to stroke you.' Spinach did this, too. Man Horrible attempted to raise Spinach's kneading claws off his thighs with his hands, but any cat will tell you that this doesn't work. All that happened was that Spinach's claws kneaded his hands instead of his thighs. There was no proper stroking, no *chukkachin*, no top-of-head scratch, it was really a poor show. No possibility of raising a happi-rumble, so he failed our test dismally. After a few minutes Man Horrible made the excuse that he had to go to the room with the shufa bowl, and he firmly picked up Spinach and put her down on the floor.

'And you want to stay in this house with this man?' I said to Spinach.

'Well, I don't really like him. . .'

'What you don't like isn't going to count for a bowl of plokkits here, don't you see, Spinach? Your Mummi is in season and she can't think straight at the moment. Now listen, I'll go watch him in the little room with the shufa bowl. Meanwhile, you begin with his second test. I see that he's left his top outer covering that he took off earlier hanging on the back of the softah. You go pull it off the softah and onto the floor. Then sit on it and wash your paws.' Spinach did this.

In the little room with the shufa bowl Man Horrible didn't make shufa or wizz. He just washed his hands and checked that his Let's Pretend Head Fur was set properly on his head. When he returned to the lounj and found Spinach sitting slobbering on his top covering on the floor, I thought he would explode. His radiance grew bright red and pulsed like a magic sun going on and off quickly. He rudely turned Spinach off his top covering and made a big show of brushing it down with his hands. He even pretended to smile. I don't know what he thought he had to smile about, for he had just failed his test on Khat Property Lore. Khat Property Lore endows a cat who is Citizen of a House full ownership of anything inside the house, in other words *What's mine is mine and what's yours is also mine.*

Man Horrible's second visit to the house fared little better. Naturally I was there to try show Spinach the poor quality of life in store for her if she remained in the house. Man Horrible and Mummi Spinach were standing talking ayoomfa-speak in the room where Spinach was fed. Spinach was sitting on the floor watching him intently, hoping he'd sit down so she could jump on his lap again. He seemed to take pains to avoid this happening.

'Are you going to sit there forever waiting for lap? In your own house?' I taunted Spinach. 'Don't be a phraidy cat, go take what's rightfully yours. Jump on him and climb up his hind leg like it were a tree.' Spinach did this, using her long sharp claws and big pads to maximum advantage.

'Wo$$za wo$$za,' she said gleefully. Man Horrible let out a howl of pain and jumped around trying to swat Spinach off him with a noose pepper as if she were a pesky bizzum. Spinach hung on with great fortitude but eventually she let go when the noose pepper battering became too intense. Mummi Spinach was most concerned, and made many sounds of calm and soothing, but her concern seemed to be directed more at Man Horrible than Spinach. She scooped Spinach up, dumped her unceremoniously outside the house and shut the door on her. Mummi Horrid.

'I love my Mummi sssssssooooooo much,' I mocked Spinach. 'Come on, Spinach, wake up! This is just a taste of what's in store for you if you stay here. Your Mummi is making a new wumpus for herself and now so must you.

The second part of my sly scheme swung into motion. While Spinach was quite happy to further befriend my Mummi, she could not commit herself to leaving home. She took to waiting for my Mummi's stinkiroli to appear after sunrise, walking in front of it and collapsing on the ground in a fluffy, sloshing heap. Mummi had to stop the stinkiroli very promptly to avoid running it over Spinach and making booma-skwasha. She would get out of the stinkiroli and go to Spinach, who would be rolling around on her back in great delight.

'*MWWAAA!*' Spinach would say. Hey! It's me! I'm hungry! Mwawwaa! is an efficient High Density Khat word that encapsulates all of a hail, a greeting and a demand in one word.

Every day my Mummi would pick up Spinach, who made a big effort to pull her flanks in so as to appear thin and hungry. Mummi inspected Spinach all over and I could see that she was thinking of feeding her. For the time being, she simply placed Spinach out of the way of the stinkiroli and had a little game with her which involved rolling Spinach around and rubbing her incredibly fluffy belly until Spinach couldn't contain herself any longer and squealed with glee. Later that day Mummi came out of the work house carrying a bowl of plokkits, which she gave to Spinach. Spinach looked disappointed, but made every effort to crunch the plokkits with her bad teeth. Mummi must have realised she had a problem, for she picked Spinach up again and made her open her mouth so she could see inside. She immediately recoiled from the bad small of Spinach's rotten teeth and put her down again, where she resumed laboriously crunching the plokkits. Mummi went inside the work house and spoke to the other ayoomfas there, all of whom really liked cats and were honoured that Spinach - whom they had named *Timeshare* - had decided to bless them with her part-time presence. It became clear from what they said that they were concerned about her. They had guessed correctly that the ayoomfas in Spinach's house next door were fighting like toms and that the ayoomfa man - Spinach's Daddi - had left. They knew also that he had taken the gruf with him. They didn't yet know about Man Horrible and Spinach's Mummi being in season. Mummi suspected that Spinach was hungry and that she wasn't being fed regularly. All the ayoomfas nodded sagely and agreed that this neglect was a wicked thing indeed and it was decided that it would be right and proper for Mummi to feed Spinach every day. When Mummi explained about Spinach's rotting teeth they all nodded and clucked sympathetically. It was further agreed that Spinach had to be taken to the whitecoati to have her teeth fixed, and that Spinach's Mummi really ought to do this. It was accepted that this was unlikely to happen and that it would be best for *my* Mummi to take Spinach to the whitecoati. Of course this implied - although it was never openly stated - that it would first be necessary to *steal* Spinach, and that Spinach would be taken by Mummi to live in Midrand and she would not be brought back.

One day when the sun was at its highest Mummi came out of the work house and went away for a while in her red stinkiroli. She returned with some shmoo kukri which she gave to the very grateful Spinach to slobber up. I thought it unwise to disclose to Spinach at this time that Mummi was considering *stealing* her and taking her to the whitecoati to have her teeth fixed. Spinach would have been appalled at the idea and immediately made herself unavailable using Khat Concealment Knowledge.

After several days of Mummi feeding Spinach and making quality playtime with her, Mummi got a fence-box from somewhere and put it inside her red stinkiroli before leaving for work. It was a medium sized fence-box with a lid that could open, certainly not as grand as the splendid Tabithat Shrine that I had been locked in so many years ago. I watched and waited throughout the day, expecting the fence box to be placed in the garden with a bowl of delicious shmoo kukri inside it. Spinach would then walk into it and *bang!* - it would shut behind her and she'd be locked inside. Ho! Ho! But it didn't happen this way. The fence box stayed inside the stinkiroli with it's lid open. As the day wore on and the sun went lower in the sky I began to think Mummi had lost interest in stealing Spinach and was intent on taking the empty fence-box back home to Midrand. When it happened it was so quick that it took me - and Spinach - completely by surprise. We had no warning of it for Mummi had not spoken of how or when she was going to steal Spinach, nor had she made any suspicious thought pictures that I could see.

It happened in the blink of an eye. One moment Mummi was playing with Spinach on the ground, and had picked her up, much as usual. Spinach was quite amenable to this as she had often been picked up by Mummi. What she didn't expect was that after cuddling her for a few seconds, Mummi would quickly turn around and dump her in the fence-box and shut the lid. I was amazed. I didn't think ayoomfas with their unstable means of walking on only two feet, and their lack of a tail, could move so quickly without falling over!

Well, you have never heard such a fuss! Even Mummi was not prepared for the spitting, sloshing, shrieking tirade that erupted from the captured Spinach. In fact it was not far short of my own tirade when I'd been in the Tabithat Shrine, except much, much wetter. Spinach was consumed with rage.

'Thi§ i§§ outrageou§!!!' she sprayed, 'You can't §teal me like thi§! Open thi§§ §tinking box§ and let me out at on§§e!!! Mwwrrroooowwrrreeee§§§§§!!!'

'Please be quiet, Spinach,' I cautioned, 'You're making your new Mummi upset.'

'I don't care. §he's not my Mummi. I've been §tolen! I want my Mummi and my Daddi! I want gruf Bakerloo and I'll make a§ muc§h noi§e a§ I want!! Mwwwooooww. . .'

'If you don't shut up I'll see to it that Mummi keeps you locked in this box until you are old and grizzled and all your splash has dried up. Now listen to me: You have not been stolen, you have been what the ayoomfas call *konfiskaytid*. It's not the same as stealing. Ordinary stealing is bad. Konfiskaytid is a special type of stealing that is good. Your Mummi and Daddi were not looking after you properly so you were taken away from them by ayoomfas who will look after you very well.'

'What about gruf Bakerloo? I want gruf Bakerloo,' Spinach snivelled.'

'Forget gruf Bakerloo. There are lots of other grufs. You are going to be citizen of a big house in a place called Midrand where there is already a cat called Phat Balune, except that you mustn't call her that, you must call her Mistress Princess.'

'Mi§§tre§§ Prin§ce§§§?'

'Uh, yes, but on second thoughts maybe it's best if you just call her Balune. She's a nice cat and she won't bully you but you must remember she is the Chief Cat of the House and you must treat her with respect. Also living in the house is your new Mummi - whom I know you really like despite all the spitting just now - and your new Daddi, whom I'm sure you will like. You can't sleep on their ayoomfawumpus but they have prepared you a splendid shnoogliwumpus all of your own. They love all cats and they will feed you the best food they can kill. They will play with you and cuddle you and stroke you until you make so much happi-rumble you'll feel like you're about to burst.' Not to alarm her unduly, I didn't tell her that Balune would probably expel her from her shnoogliwumpus on her first night and within a few days her Daddi would give her *Top of Head*, *Face*, and *Full Encapsulation of Head*. And that her extremely bushy tail would doubtless lead to Tabithat knows what other creative demonstrations of affection from Daddi.

Timeshare was let out of the fence box inside the house in Midrand in the presence of Scrap, aka Phat Balune, who watched the proceedings with cautious interest.

'Hello Mi§§tre§§ Prin§ce§§§, my name'§ Spinac§h, but your Mummi call§ me Time§hare. I've come to be a §itizen of thi§ hou§e.'

Balune wiped her face with a stocky paw. 'Hello,' she said with minimal enthusiasm, then wandered off. This was typical of Balune, who was a cat of few words and not easily provoked into excitement. With Mummi and Daddi watching Timeshare's every move, I escorted her around the house. I showed her where her food would be served at mealtimes, where her water bowl was, where her schnoogli wumpus was, and how to use the door within a door to go in and out the house of which she was now a citizen.

'Thi§ i§ a nic§e hou§e,' said Timeshare. 'I§ gruf Bakerloo coming to live here, too?'

'Yes, but he's been delayed,' I replied expediently.

Over the next few moons Timeshare settled in well and I was proud that I had helped her be konfiskaytid. She and Balune didn't speak much, but then Balune didn't speak much to anyone. They seemed to get along well enough. Mummi and Daddi fed Timeshare on rich shmoo kukri and as she began to fill out and get fluffy one could not help noticing what an extraordinarily beautiful cat she was. She enjoyed the spacious outdoors and the house that was full of light and air. Now and then she would ask wistfully after gruf Bakerloo.

'Bunny, when i§ gruf Bakerloo coming to §tay with u§?'

I spun a variety of imaginative yarns to defuse this, such as:

'Soon. He's been delayed. There was a flood and they have to wait for the water to go down before they can bring him here,' or, 'Later. He went on a long journey with another gruf and a beautiful cat that looks just like me, but he fell down a deep hole and was stuck there for a week before the clever cat that looks like me called your Daddi to come help him out.' Or, 'He was on his way in a boat, but it sank and he had to swim to the side of the flooded river holding onto a log with an ayoomfa purik on it,' or 'He'll be a bit late because his house burned down, and he had to help your Daddi escape the fire.' Much of the material for these tales of glory I garnered from things I had seen happen in the magic window. Magic window Grufs were a kind of special gruf that were always heroes instead of stinking, flea-ridden, yammering fools like all the grufs I've ever come across.

Over time it became a huge game with me to fabricate the biggest load of richly imaginative ludicrous nonsense I could think of to account for gruf Bakerloo's whereabouts. Possibly the best of which was, 'He was just about to leave to come join us when your Daddi was attacked by a an enormous green slinki as long as this house, with sharp, pointed teeth each as big as Balune, and breath of fire and smoke. Gruf Bakerloo bravely fought off this evil slinki and saved your Daddi's life. He's been delayed even further because the ayoomfas are going to give him a reward of a big round shiny on a string to hang around his head.'

Timeshare never seemed to see through these stories and she would glow with pride over the heroic acts of gruf Bakerloo. Balune would simply look at me, raise one eyebrow in disbelief.

'Bunni, you really are a piece of work,' she said, shaking her head slowly.

No sooner had Timeshare settled in and started to enjoy her new life when Mummi whisked her off to the whitecoati to have her teeth fixed. Timeshare, I must say, was very laid back about it all and this time made no protest whatsoever as she was bundled into a basket and taken away in the stinkiroli. She had complete trust that Mummi would bring her back soon and saw no point in making what she would have called a 'fu§§'. I could never relax to such an extent, not even with MyGranni, and I inevitably made a huge 'fu§§' whenever I was taken anywhere.

The New Tooth Timeshare was much easier to understand. She still splashed, but not nearly as much.

'Hello, my friend§,' she said groggily as Mummi opened the basket in the lounj and she came tumbling out, 'You mu§t excu§e me for §tumbling about but I'm very §leepy. I've been away at the whitecoati.'

'What did he do to you?, Balune asked.

'I couldn't §ay. I fell a§leep §oon after I got there, §o I couldn't witne§§ the proçeeding§. My mouth hurt§ a bit.'

At about this time Mummi and Daddi somehow guessed Timeshare's secret name, Pipulious, and started calling her *Pipple*. Tabithat knows what the odds against this were, but they somehow managed beat them. An ayoomfa discovering a cat's secret name is a very serious problem. The cat in question must show sincere contrition for their negligence or indiscretion and humbly ask Tabithat to grant them a new secret name. Needless to say, the Khat khouonciles claimed they were Tabithat's authorised representatives, as it was an easy means of extorting a sizeable bunce from the unfortunate cats in their area, in return for little effort beyond a few well-timed words of mumbo-jumbo. The Midrand Khat Khouncile, for example, offered to facilitate the christening of cat with a new secret name for a duty of two binigaus. Payable in advance. Some cats, like grufs, will believe anything they're told so long as it sounds officious enough, and Pipple was adamant that she be given a new secret name by the Midrand Khat Khouncile.

'Ruleş are ruleş,' she splattered stubbornly. I have to do thiş the proper way. The Khoncileş are Tabithat'ş repreşentativeş and I muşt go şee them for a new şecret name.'

Obtaining the iniquitous duty demanded by the Midrand Khat Khouncile had completely stumped us. I couldn't hunt them as, frustratingly, a Phirish has no substance. It's sometimes a serious disadvantage having no substance, you know. Balune was never an enthusiastic hunter, Pipple even less so, as she was, well, kind of clumsy and a bit slow on her feet. But after some thought I hatched a cunning plan that helped Balune and Pipple easily catch two binigaus. I left them outside the opening of a *binidali* - a binigaus hole - both hidden carefully with Khat Concealment Knowledge behind the little mound of finely turned sand that one usually finds near the mouth of these holes. Then I did my clever Phirish trick of passing silently through the ground until I came to where the binigaus family was sleeping in a little nest of dried grush in an underground chamber. There with my fiercest, nastiest phantom face, I appeared as a snarling and spitting demon right next to the hapless binigaus, suddenly filling their sleeping chamber and waking them up.

'I'm an evil cat come back from the undead to rip you to pieces,' I hissed at them until, propelled by terror, they fled along their tunnel, out into the sunlight and right into the waiting paws of Phat Balune and Pipple. Who says cats can't work in teams?

On the first sunny day of the next moon, Pipple, Balune and I trudged awkwardly with our two binigaus down the hill, across the little stream, and up the other side of the valley towards the big red rock. At least Pipple and Balune trudged awkwardly with the heavy binigaus while I floated along in an advisory capacity. Although not as big as a hopit, a binigaus is nonetheless much bigger than a squee and each carrying a binigaus in their mouth caused Balune and Pipple to walk in a clumsy, swaggering way. The meeting of the Midrand Khat Khouncile had just begun and we arrived just in time to tell the very stressed Khouncile Rememberer who we were.

'Cat FeeblePads,' said Balune, immediately, 'Cat Utoxeter Y. FeeblePads III, to be precise.'

'Uh, . .well, hello. Were you here last week? I don't quite remember. . .' cat Munchkin was hopelessly confused. It had been nearly two full turns of season since we'd last been to a Khouncile meeting and cat Munchkin - who could barely remember his own name - was still the official Khat Rememberer. I was not overly surprised at this because Khouncile staff are seldom selected on the basis of their ability. The unfortunate consequence of this is that useless nincompoops tend to remain in office until they die.

'I'm always present where I'm supposed to be,' Balune replied proudly and ambiguously. Cat Munchkin nodded, smiled politely and turned to Pipple.

'Şome ayoomfaş call me Şpinaşh. Other ayoomfaş call me Timeşhare. My şecret name Pipultouş waş dişcovered by the ayoomfaş that call me Timeşhare. I'm here to get a new şecret name and I've brought two binigauş as duty.'

'I'm a Phirish, just here as an observer,' I said. Even khouncile cats are smart enough to realise that the only laws that could possibly be binding on a Phirish are those of Tabithat - bless his whisker holes - but it's never a bad idea to rub it in. 'As I'm sure you know, I'm already dead so I can do just what I like. Today I like to observe as you grant my friend Timeshare a new secret name.'

In due course the matter of Timeshare's new secret name was processed by the khouncile.

'We will now address the issue of a new secret name for cat Timeshare,' announced Khouncillor MeanWeasel, who had in our absence been promoted to Chief Khouncillor MeanWeasel. I noticed that Khouncillor SwellenTummis was not in attendance, perhaps he had finally burst from gorging himself. 'The Khouncile views the disclosure of a cat's secret name in a very serious light,' MeanWeasel said sternly to Timeshare.

'It waş an aççidental coinçidençe,' said Timeshare in deep embarrassment, 'I'm şo very şorry.'

Chief Khouncillor MeanWeasel licked his paw and wiped his face. 'Is there any witness to substantiate this?'

Phat Balune stepped forward boldly. 'Yeah. It was like she said, your MeanWeaselship. An accidental coincidence. I saw it all happen right in front of my own eyes. First the accident, then the coincidence. Exactly like she said.'

'And you are. . .?'

'Cat ThreeBites ChilliFeathers, your khouncillorship.'

'Alright. Thank you, cat . . uh. . Yes, thank you. I see that the necessary and specified administrative levy of two binigaus has been laid in the usual pothole in the rock that we use for collection. It now only remains for the Khouncile to decide a new secret name for cat Timeshare. Are there any suggestions?'

'*Suggestions*? For a *secret* name?' Balune asked, incredulous.

'Yes, cat, uh. . .what did you say your name was. . ?'

'Cat Hullablokka B. Comestible.'

'Yes, cat. .uh, Combustible, the . . .'

'Comestible, your khouncillorship.' Balune corrected pedantically.

'Yes, sorry, cat Comestible. The Midrand Khat Khouncile strongly believes in the principle of democracy, which is why we have to act transparently in all matters. All cats present have equal voice of suggestion of a new secret name for cat Timeshare. Khouncile will examine all suggestions and choose one that we believe Tabithat will like. That name will be awarded to cat Timeshare.'

But none of the cats present were remotely interested as most had become absorbed by a long procession of extraordinarily huge *krorlis* that had emerged from a hole in the rock and were making their way down the side of the red rock and away into the grush. Cats were fascinated in their study of this seemingly endless procession and more than one reckless individual had attempted to catch one of the krorlis and was nursing their paw where they'd been stung.

'Very well, as there are no suggestions, Khouncile will now decide on a new name for cat Timeshare. And since the other members of Khouncile are otherwise occupied at present, it falls on me to choose a name. Cat Timeshare, your new secret name will be *Potus*. Let's move on to the next issue.'

'Thank you, şir,' said Timeshare.

'What sort of shufa name is *Potus*?' Balune whispered angrily at me. 'I could have given her a better name myself and saved us two binigaus and a long trek! Simply told her that Tabithat had come to me in a dream and told me the name. . .'

I had little doubt of this, but at least Timeshare aka Pipple aka Potus had gone through the motions and would now stop pestering everyone about the loss of her secret name. This was true, but as it turned out it wasn't the end of the story. Some moons later, Pipple came to us in great distress and told us she had *forgotten* her secret name. We reminded her what it was, but then she told us that because we had 'discovered' what it was, her secret name was no longer secret and she'd have to be given another. So would we please come with her to . . .

No!

*****

CHAPTER TEN:
HuffPuff and PennyWhistle

Pipple had a lovely time at Midrand, contentedly grubbing around outside amongst the plants, surprising the bizzums and krorlis. She found herself a favourite bush which received the full morning sun and which had leaves almost the same shade of deep orange as her fur. It afforded her excellent camouflage and she spent a great deal of time dozing under this bush practicing her Khat Concealment Knowledge. She became quite possessive over her special orange bush and even hit Balune once when she found Balune asleep under it. Balune was so surprised she hastily murmured a quick apology and left without further ado.

'I don't fancy being drowned,' she said to me later by way of explaining this unusual submissiveness.

The whitecoati's tooth magic hadn't proved very enduring, and before long Pipple was splashing as much as ever before. None of us really minded, though, as she was a good Citizen of our House. With good food and a loving family around her, Pipple grew sleek and, if possible, even more beautiful. Her fat, *phluffi* tail was truly magnificent. There were now two dishes of cat food in the food room of our house. Pipple, as might be expected from the state of her teeth, ate very messily and scattered bits of food in a wide radius around her bowl. Balune frequently would pick her out over dropping bits of food in the communal water bowl and Daddi and Mummi were forever cleaning up after her. When Pipple had finished eating there was food everywhere so that it looked like it had rained from the sky. I really don't know why she felt it necessary to make such a mess; in my final days I had absolutely no teeth at all and I didn't make anywhere nearly as much mess. Nor did I splosh and splash when I spoke or dribble on Mummi's lap or Daddi's Noose Pepper. But I'd been in 'Nam and I believe that it made me a stronger cat.

We learned a few things from Pipple about which ayoomfa foods were edible and which were not. In general ayoomfas know nothing of proper nutrition and insist on burning every single piece of meat they manage to get hold of. And they eat vast quantities of plant matter as well as other unidentifiable softah stuff that they get from goodness knows where and which it's best to avoid if offered. Balune liked one or two of these funny things which she ate when Mummi gave her titbits during the ayoomfa self-feeding. Once again, being a Phirish put me at a tremendous disadvantage; I could smell the food but I couldn't eat it. Sometimes I wonder if Tabithat did this on purpose or whether he simply overlooked some things along the way.

Pipple introduced us to the ayoomfa foods which she called lidda and potta. Every day after feeding us, Daddi would open the tiny cold room and get himself a little potta of some white stuff that looked like thick humvee. Before he could eat any of this he had to open the potta which he did by pulling off a thin round leaf which covered it. The round leaf had some of the white humvee from inside the potta on it and one day Pipple summarily demanded to have this.

'MWAAA!!' she shouted at Daddi, 'Lidda! Lidda! Lidda!' Daddi took the round leaf and put it on the floor where Pipple immediately began licking the white stuff off it with her big pink tongue. As she licked the round leaf she could not avoid pushing it around the floor making a scraping sound. Eventually she lick-pushed it up against a wall where it couldn't escape and there she licked every drop of the white stuff off it. Balune was fascinated by this and determined to try some and so the next morning she, too, demanded lidda. This presented Daddi with a difficulty because he only ever opened one potta of the white stuff for himself and so he couldn't give them each a whole lidda. But ever mindful of his duty of pleasing us, he tore the one lidda into two pieces and gave Balune and Pipple each half of it. Initially Balune was aggrieved because her piece of lidda was clearly much smaller than Pipple's piece and she went to try steal Pipple's piece and got hit on the head and soundly and wetly spat at for her efforts. She returned to the piece of lidda Daddi had given her and began to lick the white stuff.

'Yuk! Awful! What the hell is this stuff, anyway?'

I explained that I'd heard Mummi and Daddi call it different names. The pottas that Mummi ate usually had coloured stuff inside, while Daddi preferred the white stuff, and Pipple ate whatever she was given.

'It depends,' I explained to Balune, 'My understanding is that if it's coloured it's called yog-git and if it's white it's called yo-gurt.'

'Well it's quite revolting whatever it's called,' she muttered and stalked off in disgust.

Pipple's desire for lidda knew no bounds and it didn't take long for her to figure out that not having a proper slurping tongue, Daddi was unable to get all the yo-gurt out of the potta for himself and he would simply throw the potta in the Gone Box when he'd done the best he could, often leaving valuable slurpables in the potta. The reason for the Gone Box was unknown but its effect was quite clear: anything the ayoomfas put in the Gone Box disappeared and was never seen again. Both Mummi and Daddi spent a great deal of time desperately doing things to the Gone Box, wrapping the stuff inside it, trying to conceal it outside the house in black sacks, but it was all in vain and within a day or two whatever had been inside the Gone Box would be gone forever. Ayoomfas have despairingly poor concealment skills. Had Mummi and Daddi the benefit of superior Khat Concealment Knowledge they would have been better able to properly hide stuff from the Gone Box rather than leave it out in the open where it could easily be seen and stolen. One would almost think they wanted it to be taken.

I once sat up all night until sunrise and watched to see who was stealing our stuff from the Gone Box and I learned that it was a number of ayoomfas who ran alongside an enormous noisy *rumbleroli*, escorted by a number of bizzums. These cheeky scoundrels were blatantly stealing stuff from all the houses in broad daylight! And nobody seemed to be doing anything to stop them! If only I could speak to the ayoomfas, I would have told Daddi what I'd seen and he could have laid in wait for the Gone Box thieves with his bangstick and put an end to this nonsense once and for all.

Pipple worked out that she had to time her request for more yo-gurt very carefully. She had to ask Daddi before he threw the potta in the Gone Box, because once in there, it was as good as gone forever. And she had to do her ritual of lidda-chasing around the floor quicker than Daddi could eat the yo-gurt in the potta. On the other hand, if she was too quick and asked him for more before she'd finished her lidda, he'd simply pick her up and place her firmly in front of the lidda. I am hopeless at this sort of co-ordinated plan. Such things make my head hurt and had I been alive I would have given up and gone outside to catch a squee or a binigaus. Pipple, however, had it down to a fine art. She told me the key to getting it just right was to listen for the particular noise made by the ayoomfa eating stick scraping the bottom of the potta. The moment she heard this special sound she knew that Daddi was about to have his last mouthful of yogurt and the time was just right.

'MWAAA!!'

Daddi could not possibly misunderstand this and after first checking that she'd dutifully finished her lidda, he placed the potta in front of Pipple, who immediately stuck her head in it and began licking up the yo-gurt with great zeal.

'Potta Potta potta,' she gurgled to herself in delight. Potta was good. Potta had more yo-gurt inside than Pipple could have licked off several pads' worth of liddas. Another advantage of potta was that it was heavier than lidda and it didn't need so much chasing around the room. For a long time Pipple had lidda and potta every day.

Then one day Daddi and Mummi stopped eating a small potta every day and instead brought home some enormous pottas from which they would eat a bit each morning. Ayoomfas are civilised like us in this regard, unlike grufs who have no discipline and feel compelled to eat all available food in one sitting even if it makes them sick. When Daddi opened one of these giant pottas he always gave Pipple the enormous lidda, but the down side of the giant pottas was that for a paw's pads of days thereafter Pipple had no lidda or potta at all and she watched tantalised and drooling as Daddi ate some yo-gurt from the big potta and then put it back in the tiny cold room when he was done. But she was rewarded eventually with a giant potta which was well worth waiting for.

The giant potta for Pipple became a regular event at Midrand and she looked forward to it. The top of the potta was was about level with her chest and to reach the yo-gurt at the bottom Pipple had to put her head deep into the giant potta. For some strange reason Daddi and Mummi found this most comical and would stand around watching Pipple with her head in the potta and laughing behind their hands in a futile attempt to conceal their mirth. This provided them with light entertainment for a couple of moons until one day as Pipple was about halfway through her potta, the wind slammed a door shut somewhere in the house. Pipple was startled and jumped up in Big Fright while her head was still in the potta, thereby lifting it off the ground. The potta then slid further down over her head, covering her face so she couldn't see anything. Pipple begat a great panic and went running blindly around the Food Room, blundering into things and trying fruitlessly to wriggle her head out of the potta. Daddi found this spectacle hilarious and was laughing so much he could hardly stand up on his hind legs. Pipple must have been dreadfully embarrassed. Even Mummi found it amusing but luckily kept enough of her wits about her to catch Pipple as she was stumbling around and pull the potta off her head. She made a big show of being sorry for Pipple but later in the day I caught her laughing about it when she thought there was nobody around.

'That wa§ terrible! I was ab§olutely helple§§,' Pipple said after she'd been freed from her potta, her face covered in yo-gurt. 'I couldn't §ee a §ingle thing. Horrid potta! Bad potta!' She trotted off through the door within a door and spent the rest of the morning meticulously washing herself in the sunshine. Daddi laughed on and off about this incident for two days and I'm certain he was looking forward to finishing another giant potta for Pipple. But his glee was thwarted for shortly after this Mummi stopped bringing home the giant pottas and Pipple was very careful not to go anywhere near a potta that was bigger than her head.

*****

One would think that Tabithat would have been satisfied with my efforts in restoring a proper plurality of cats to Midrand, but He is not easily pleased. He came to me one day as I was provocatively snoozing under Pipple's favourite orange bush and said,

'You have done well, Little Wargi, but I have yet more work for you. Just as well, as it turns out, because Facilities are on strike and your bed is still not ready.'

I was very indignant on his behalf. 'You should dismiss them at once, My Lord! Strip them of Citizenship of Your House and smite them into the blackness with your huge paws! You should appoint quality cats who are productive and reliable - what about my friend Butch for example? He was very diligent, even if a little slow at times.'

'Your friend Butch is otherwise occupied teaching in my school and he cannot be spared. I have department called Khat Resources to take care of staffing issues, although between you and me they're a lot of parasites and even more useless than Facilities - if that's at all possible. In any case, Little Wargi, Facilities is my problem and you really shouldn't concern yourself with it. Now listen carefully: Your ayoomfarolês have decided to get another cat and they intend to get this cat from The Prison. But I want them to get two cats at The Prison. Two specific cats: Cat HuffPuff and Cat SaucyPads. This is where you come in, Wargi. I want you to go to The Prison beforehand and forewarn these two cats so that they can prepare themselves to be the chosen ones when your ayoomfarolês visit.'

'When will this happen, My Lord?'

'There is no time like the present, Little Wargi,' Tabithat said.

Without further ado or even allowing me time to compose myself or find out how I was to get to The Prison, He transported me there. Tabithat seldom gave one much advance warning of his plans and sometimes I could not help wondering why he saw fit to leave everything until the last possible moment like this. It was very unsettling and somewhat stressful. Cats do not like too much change.

I found myself in a room with about two paw's pads of cats, each in a fence-room. The fence-rooms were of comfortable size and they did have windows, but they were high up and the cats could not look outside. Each cat had their own bowls of plokkits and water, and a box of some strange stones like plokkits in which some of them had made shufa and scattered about. I had heard talk about these boxes from Balune, who called them shufa-boxes. Evidently none of this luxury was of much comfort to the cats in The Prison for they were all either wailing and moaning as if it was the end of the world, or shouting angrily to be let out.

'Grrrrrrreeowwwww! Open this door! You have no right. . .' snarled one.

'I'll tear you to pieces if you don't let me out at once. Ewoowwwwwrrrrrl. . .' threatened another.

'Oh woe is meeeooorrrrlll. . .' lamented yet another.

My appearance brought no cheer to them.

'Look - it's a Phirish! The sign of death. We're finished! Tabithat we implore you to please have mercy on us poor cats! Owwwrrrlll!' They covered their faces with their paws and wailed in despair.

'Oh be quiet you fools!' I snapped impatiently at them. You're such a bunch of whining phraidy cats. You've all got food and water and a snug bed which is more than some poor cats I know! And the ayoomfas here mean you no harm. Now when I was in Vietnam. . . but no, never mind that now. I'm looking for cat HuffPuff and cat SaucyPads.'

'YesYesYes! HuffPuff - that's me! A scraggly tawny tabby cat of about two winters stuck his paw in the air and waved it about. He was a big fellow and like all Tabby cats he had the magnificent Tabithat emblem on his head and a band of fluffy stripes on his chest. Evidently he'd had quite a difficult life for he was quite thin and his hind legs looked slightly awkward as if he'd once perhaps been injured in a booma-skwasha event. His fur was coarse and his tail was miserably pathetic and reminded me of a slinki. His teeth were good but there was a cloud of noxious stink surrounding him as if he'd recently made *air-shufa*. Why Tabithat should choose this unmannered, rundown specimen of a tabby to live with my nice clean ayoomfarolês in *my house* was beyond my comprehension, but I had to honour the wishes of my wise Lord, bless his sharp white teeth.

'Cat SaucyPads, where are you?'

In the fence-box alongside that of cat HuffPuff, a black and white cat put her paw in the air. She was a young cat in reasonable condition, about the same age as HuffPuff, and she was very reminiscent of Butch. She didn't say anything but wore a smug expression of superiority which I instantly found annoying. Had I not been a Phirish I would have quickly swiped the expression off her face.

'Good. Now listen carefully: This applies to you, cat HuffPuff and also to you, cat SaucyPads. The rest of you mind your own business. Cat HuffPuff and cat SaucyPads, it is Tabithat's will that you should become Citizens of my House in Midrand. Before long two ayoomfas will come here looking for a cat. . .'

'YesYesYes! Let's go go go. I'm ready. I'm ready . . ' HuffPuff chattered, his eyes bright with excitement.

'Shut up and listen. These ayoomfas - and they are ayoomfarolês and so of very high quality - do not know you and it is not yet certain that they'll choose you to become Citizens of my House. When they come here it is up to you two to make yourself appear lovable, intelligent, friendly, and well-behaved; in fact all the things that I'm quite sure you are not.

'And all you other cats - listen up. Yes, you, the big moaner, you too. This is Tabithat's will and I have been sent by Him to ensure that His will is done. Now it's not his will that any of you go live in my house; he's got other plans and other houses in mind for you. It's your job to ensure that you *aren't* chosen by the two ayoomfas that are coming, and I'll leave it to you how you go about making yourself unattractive. If someone really doesn't have an idea what to do, they can ask me for advice.

'But I want to get out of here. . .' someone whined.

'If you do as I've asked, Tabithat will see to it that you do, but if you disobey His wishes, he will surely see to it that you stay here until you die,' then really rubbing it in, 'And then you'll go to Hell.' I hoped this was plausible but in truth I had no idea of what Tabithat's plans were for these other cats. From what I knew of Tabithat he was a kind and loving Lord and would surely not allow any cat to suffer needless discomfort? Or would he? I found the lack of control he was able to wield in His own House somewhat disconcerting. The Maine Coons in Facilities, for example. He should smite them from His House for being so sloppy and insolent in the matter of my bed. And the parasites in Khat Resources – what about them? I say Tabithat should get rid of them at once. Phat Balune told me she once had parasites when in The Prison and they had caused her serious itching and discomfort. But I was a simple Phirish with a job to do and so put these weighty issues out of my mind. In any case, the other cats seemed to take the message very seriously for they made not a sound further.

'YesYesYes. WhenWhenWhen? Are they here? Are they coming? HeyHeyHey?' HuffPuff chattered. He could barely contain his excitement. 'I PromisePromisePromise,' he chirped.

'I will be here to tell you when they come,' I said, 'You must wait patiently.'

We didn't have to wait long. Within the time of two naps I heard the voices of my Mummi and Daddi as they talked to the warden of The Prison. The cats had done me proud in preparation and had made a terrible mess. Many of them had made shufa in their plokkits and in their water, while others had scratched all the *sand-plokkits* and shufa out of their shufa-boxes and then gone rolled around in this mess. A few of them had even made wizz on each other through the sides of their fence rooms. Several of them were pretending to fight savagely and were hissing and swearing rudely at each other. The stench was appalling! As my Mummi and Daddi walked into the room, several cats began to howl in a most ear-shattering and offensive manner, and with claws outstretched and teeth bared they flung themselves in orchestrated fury against the front of the fence-rooms towards Mummi and Daddi. Clearly the warden was most shocked at this unprecedented explosion of bad behaviour and he was taking pains to tell Mummi that it was most unusual. He opened the fence room of a ginger tabby queen whom he thought would be suitable for Mummi and Daddi and reached inside to pick her up. The ginger tabby immediately spat at him and scratched him. Warden quickly withdrew his softclaw and shut the door of the fence room.

It was the setup to end all setups and I was afraid that the ayoomfas would see through it all. The only cats whose fence rooms were clean, who hadn't rolled in their shufa, and who were sitting neatly, looking fluffy and adorable, blinking benignly, and affectionately rubbing their heads against the front of their fence boxes, were, wait for it. . . .HuffPuff and SaucyPads! Even an ayoomfa could not fail to see the comparative quality of these cats! Mummi and Daddi were immediately attracted to them and began giving them chukkachin through the front of the fence room. In between demonstrating their appreciation with the loudest happi-rumble they could muster, HuffPuff and SaucyPads also made a big show of being friends inseparable by licking each other through the sides of their adjacent fence rooms. The big challenge still lay ahead - Mummi and Daddi had set out to get one cat, but it was Tabithat's will that they should have two. Probably because she reminded them of Butch, they decided to take cat SaucyPads and she obligingly allowed the warden to open her fence room, lift her out and let Mummi hold her. Not a trace of her smug, superior expression remained - she looked as innocent as a tikki purik. This was the cue for HuffPuff to stand up in his fencebox, begin scrabbling desperately at the door and make a series of sad, mournful whimpers that could not fail to attract the attention of the three ayoomfas. The warden quickly took advantage of this opportunity and looked sad and resigned. He explained to Mummi and Daddy that SaucyPads and HuffPuff were inseparable friends and it would be ever so sad if they were parted. I was quite impressed - so the warden could ham it up as well as the cats! Mummi and Daddi were helpless in the face of this co-ordinated exploitation of their feelings and agreed to take both HuffPuff and SaucyPads to go home with them. Phew! That was touch and go. Had it not been for the warden we might have been in trouble. HuffPuff was lifted from his fence room by the Warden and he and SaucyPads were placed together in the picnic basket that Mummi and Daddi had brought with them, and the ayoomfas turned to leave. Then a strange thing happened. The warden stared right at me, smiled, and winked very deliberately at me! I was quite shocked. Tabithat had explicitly told me that ayoomfas could not see me, yet this one evidently could. Worse still, he not only had discovered my plan of manipulating my ayoomfarolês but had made himself an active party to it! I felt exposed and naked and so begat a flurry of washing myself to make up lost face.

In time I came across one or two other ayoomfas who could see me, but they were very few and far in between.

Cat HuffPuff made himself at home immediately he was released from the box in the Midrand house.

'YesYesYes. Whezza Food? Whezza Food? Whezza Food,' he chattered, simultaneously releasing an audible air-shufa that left a noxious cloud of stink in his wake.

'Who is this oaf?' Balune asked disparagingly.

'Balune, Pipple, this is cat HuffPuff and this is cat SaucyPads,' I explained. 'Cats HuffPuff and SaucyPads, this is cat Pipple and this is cat Balune'. She's in charge here and you'd be wise to remember that.

'YesYesYes Hello Pipple. Whezza Food, Balune?'

Balune turned her back on him and wandered off, flicking her tail in disdain.

Pipple, however, was delighted. 'Lotşa new Çitişen§ of the Houşe - how §plendid!' she said.

HuffPuff had some bad habits which nearly cost him his Citizenship of the House. On his first day he made the cardinal mistake of making a shufa inside the house. Mummi was furious and was of a mind to take him back to The Prison. Daddi was also displeased but he had taken a liking to HuffPuff probably because HuffPuff was the only tomcat - what we call a *yowli* in Khat - amongst a whole lot of queens and Daddi needed moral support for his gender. He persuaded Mummi to give HuffPuff another chance and I had a stern word with HuffPuff over the precarious state of his citizenship, following which he never, ever made shufa, wizz, or *bloik-bloik* inside the house again. Even when he'd accidentally been locked in one of the *dark roomis* all day, the little dark rooms the ayoomfas call *kubbids*, he'd shoot out of the door within a door like lightning and let it all out on the first patch of grush he found. Often this was right outside the house, forcing the other cats to carefully step around it as they went through the door within a door. Balune would have words with him over this and he'd be sent out to bury it.

Like Balune and myself, HuffPuff had led a difficult life. He'd been abandoned as a tikki purik and had to eke out his survival on the streets, along with other feral cats much bigger than him and who had no hesitation of whumping him senseless or biting him when he was unfortunate enough to encounter them. In the long run he was richer for the experience, as his fighting skills were honed to a level that was truly awesome to witness. HuffPuff knew how to fight to the death and win and in combat and Phat Balune was seriously outclassed. After watching him dispatch an intruding yowli one night Balune warmed to him somewhat.

'That was very impressive, HuffPuff,' Balune said regally, 'Of course I could have done it as well if not better myself, but you thoughtfully saved me the trouble. If you had leadership and organisational skills I would retire today and let you take over as Chief Cat of the House.'

One other street skill which HuffPuff had was not so beneficial to the household - the ayoomfarolês didn't find it very useful at all. It concerned the Gone Box.

On the first night of HuffPuff's residency he told us, 'Thez food in that box. YesYesYes, lotsa lotsa food. You jus' gotta gettit out. I'll show you how. Requires skills . . .eh Balune? Watch HuffPuff and learn. . .'

HuffPuff summarily jumped up on the Gone Box, holding onto the side of it in a way that made it rock unsteadily and then come crashing down on its side. Immediately he was inside it, rootling around and frenziedly foraging for edibles. Anything he found that met his - not very high, it must be said - standards for nutritional value was chucked out and strewn across the floor of the Food Room. Anything that got in the way of his rootling was also chucked out and strewn across the floor. He made a terrible mess and when Daddi came to feed us at sunrise, he was not pleased. He spent some time restoring order to the Food Room and he told HuffPuff that he was not pleased. Naturally HuffPuff didn't understand what Daddi was saying and ran excitedly back and forth between his legs saying, 'Lotsa Lotsa food! HuffPuff happi with food, Daddi. Sorry couldn't eat it all. Lotsa food. Glorp food!'

What he didn't expect was that Daddi would then present him with his very own bowl of delicious shmoo kukri. Too bad he was full, but HuffPuff held the street cat view that every piece of food you came across could well be your last for days, and should therefore be eaten. He was bloated and uncomfortable after breakfast but he could certainly afford to fill out a bit and the food was all put to good use.

This ritual with the Gone Box carried on for quite a long time. Every night, HuffPuff would overturn the Gone Box and scatter its contents over the floor of the Food Room, before eating whatever took his fancy. Every sunrise, Daddi would sigh in exasperation, patiently pick up everything and put it all back in the Gone Box. After about four paws' pads of sunrises, it dawned on HuffPuff that he didn't actually have to get his own food.

Balune told him this, 'You don't have to fetch the food yourself,' Citizens of this House have ayoomfa staff to feed them.

'YesYesYes but maybe they decide they don't wanta feed us no more?' Having lived on the street HuffPuff tended to be suspicious and wasn't used to being a Citizen of a House. In fact he wasn't even used to the idea of a house, period.

'Mummi and Daddi are ayoomfa*rolês*. They would never deliberately not feed us. And they know that if they accidentally forgot to feed us we would punish them and they wouldn't quickly forget again.'

HuffPuff had some difficulty getting used to this, but his attacks on the Gone Box diminished over time and after a while the only occasion on which he reverted to his street habits was when he smelled that there was a cackack carcass inside the Gone Box. HuffPuff never could resist a cackack carcass, but unlike Butch, who used to eat extremely tidily and leave the bones in a neat little pile on the noose pepper Mummi and Daddi provided, HuffPuff found it necessary to render the cackack carcass asunder and consume different parts of it in different rooms of the house. He made no effort to pick up the bones, and Mummi and Daddi sometimes got cross when they stood on bits of cackack bone that HuffPuff had abandoned in the lounj, in the Food Room, in the room where they slept, and even in the room with the magic rain box and the shufa bowl.

HuffPuff told us that his street name - HuffPuff - came about because of his habit of making air-shufa and sighing loudly at the same time, a habit which Balune was determined to discourage.

'If you want to make shufa go outside and get it over with and please stay outside until you're quite sure it's finished. We don't want you hanging around inside poisoning us with your toxic gas. A responsible cat doesn't do that kind of thing.'

HuffPuff and SaucyPads were named *Humphrey* and *PennyWhistle* by the ayoomfarolês. It seriously amused them to call her PennyWhistle and make whistling sounds as they spoke this name so that it came out *PennyWhisssssuuuiiillle*. To be quite honest, PennyWhistle was a useless cat. She was totally uninterested in any of our household and we all got the feeling she thought she was doing us a favour by living in our house. Unlike Humphrey and Pipple who were both tremendously affectionate to the ayoomfarolês, PennyWhistle barely tolerated being picked up and given any kind of cuddle, even chukkachin, which few cats can resist. Top of Head, Face, Full Encapsulation of Head, Huggitty-Bumpity and other forms of *appreciation* were quite out of the question. She didn't even deign to come and join us on the phluffi blue sitz-softah when we all snuggled up with Mummi and Daddi and studied the Magic Window. PennyWhistle had her own agenda.

'Please don't think that I don't like any of you,' she told Balune one day, 'or that I don't appreciate your wonderful ayoomfarolês. It's just that I don't belong here and I don't want to become too attached to any of you.'

'Why don't you belong here? What nonsense is this? Bunni tells me that you were specifically chosen by Tabithat to live here. Bunni went to Harvard. And she's a Phirish. So she knows everything.'

'Yes, but I still don't believe I was chosen to live here permanently,' PennyWhistle explained. 'I was chosen so that I could escape from The Prison and find my way home. It's like this, you see. I come from a happy home with two ayoomfas, their two ayoomfapuriks and two big grufs called gruf Curious and gruf Naughtiness. One day I went out on a walk to explore and I became totally lost. For many days I tried to find my way back home but with no success. Eventually I was exhausted, hungry and full of despair and was forced to take shelter with some other rather rough ayoomfas who fed me for a few days. I had intended to resume my search for home once I regained my strength but the ayoomfas took me to The Prison, where I stayed for two whole moons. Now that I'm free I can start again to find out where I am and how I could find my way back to my lost home with gruf Curious and gruf Naughtiness.'

Phat Balune was not sympathetic at all.

'Are you trying to make me cry or what?' she said. 'This sounds too much like a story I would see through the magic window. You must be crazy to want to be a Citizen of a House with ayoomfapuriks who pull your tail and not one, but *two* stinking grufs to slaver on you and chase you up a tree! No, you should stay a Citizen of my House - it's a quality place where the chosen elite of cats can relax and forget the dangers of the world around them. We don't even attend khouncile meetings. Most cats would give half their whiskers to stay here for just a week!'

PennyWhistle was not convinced. Every day she would go wander far and wide, but she came back in the evenings, tired and dispirited.

Having seen Humphrey's Gone Box game Pipple instigated a new game of her own. Mummi and Daddi had provided us with many new toys to play with but mostly we spurned them because cats are highly creative and we prefer to create our own toys from whatever suitable ayoomfa constructions and objects are at hand.

In the lounj at Midrand was a big blue sitz-softah that was irresistibly phluffi and textured just right for cats to exercise their claws. Pipple discovered this and at random times she would rush up to the blue softah and climb up the back of it, scratching furiously on it for all she was worth.

'Wozz§a Wozz§a!' she said, hugely excited, as she dragged her way up the back of the blue sitz-softah. 'Look at clever me!' She was delighted when Mummi and Daddi would join in the game with shouting and clapping of forepaws, and sometimes - if they became sufficiently excited - they would even throw small objects at her. I tried to tell her that they were not really joining in her game of Wozza Wozza and were - for some unknown selfish reason - in fact trying discourage her from climbing up the back of the phluffi blue sitz-softah. Pipple refused to believe me.

'Non§en§e! I know they love thi§ game!' she said stubbornly. 'I'm not §elfis§h. Wozz§a Wozz§a i§ for everyone!'

Humphrey also started to play Wozza Wozza and with the two of them working on it, they managed to pull the covering away from the back of the blue sitz-softah, leaving a small hole. Pipple exercised this small hole until it became big enough for her to climb inside the back of the blue sitz-softah, where there was a little cosy dark room. Wozza Wozza became most exciting with two cats playing! Pipple would hide inside the sitz-softah and scratch it from the inside, while Humphrey would chase her around and scratch it from the outside. One day Humphrey and Balune and even PennyWhistle all climbed through the hole into the blue sitz-softah's cosy dark room and had huge fun all scratching from the inside together. When Daddi saw this he rather unkindly put an end to the game. He chased my friends out of the blue softah and then fetched some little black thorns and a special hitting stick which he used to fasten down the loose covering on the back of the softah so that the hole was gone. This was a great disappointment to Pipple and she was forced to start all over again to make a new hole. This became a good game in itself, one in which Mummi and Daddi were properly able to participate. Daddi would fasten down the back of the sitz-softah, sometimes with sticky stuff, sometimes with the small black thorns, sometimes with thin strings, and sometimes with all three of these things. But within a paw's pads of days Pipple would have made a hole in it and she'd be inside the softah scratching around and pretending to be a crazy wild cat.

The game with the Wozza Wozza Hole went on for several turns of season until one day the whole of the back covering came completely apart from the blue sitz-softah and Wozza Wozza was no fun anymore because there was no cosy dark room to hide in.

Even Mummi and Daddi didn't like it like that, and before long a man in a rumbleroli of the kind that is open at the back came and took the big blue phluffi sitz-softah away. He left some chairs made of hard shiny and black smootha-skin in its place. They were no fun at all.

*****

CHAPTER ELEVEN:
Trick or Treat

Shortly after Humphrey and PennyWhistle came to live with us they were whisked away to the whitecoati for an overnight stay that left them both quite sore for a few days. Humphrey had a theory that the whitecoati had stolen his *seedballs* but he couldn't prove anything because he'd fallen asleep and so hadn't seen what the whitecoati had done. What is there about the whitecoati that always makes us so sleepy? Notwithstanding the possible theft of his seedballs Humphrey decided to go courting Phat Balune, whom he thought very splendid and matronly. He'd already not started off too well with Balune and he decided to improve his standing by bringing her a gift of a cackack bone he'd found in the Gone Box.

'Oh, it's you. What do you want?' Balune was not terribly enthusiastic.

'It's me, HuffPuff. I brought you this nice bone. Yes I did. I did.'

'It stinks and it's full of horrible krorlis. Take it away.'

'I thought you might like it. . . .'

'You thought wrong. Go away and take your stinking bone with you.'

This plan didn't work as well as Humphrey would have liked. He concluded the quality of his gift was to blame and so decided to obtain for Balune a gift truly worthy of a princess. The opportunity presented itself one morning a few days later when Daddi and Mummi took a dead cackack out of the Tiny Cold Room and left it on a high tay-bill near the magic water bowl in the Food Room. They went away somewhere in the stinkiroli leaving the cackack completely unprotected, which Humphrey did not fail to notice. He jumped up on the high tay-bill and prepared to grab the cackack in his jaws, only to find it was frozen so cold that he couldn't bite into it. He tried licking it all over to warm it up but that only made his tongue hurt from the cold. This made him very cross and he resolved to punish the dead cackack by pushing it off the high surface and it crashed onto the floor of the Food Room like a big stone. He got down from the high surface and sat glaring at the cackack for some time.

'Bad cackack! Very Bad!' he scolded it'

'If you leave it for a while it will get warm,' I told him.

'How long? How long must I leave it? Hey, hey?'

'At least the time of one Big Sleep or two full paws' pads of Naps.'

'That's far too long. . .'

'That's how long it takes. There's nothing anyone can do about it. I don't know why they put all this food in the Tiny Cold Room anyway. I must try find out someday.'

Humphrey sighed loudly to himself, lay down and made himself comfortable next to his captured cackack. He tried to sleep but was too excited. He kept asking me, 'Hey, hey, Bunni - how long now 'till it's soft?' until I became annoyed and floated away to play pranks on Balune who was rolling in the dry grass outside.

As sunset approached I went back inside to where Humphrey had finally fallen asleep with his forepaw protectively over the cackack, which was now fairly soft. I woke him up and he glared at me then went to check his prize.

'Good cackack. Good for a princess,' he muttered. He grasped the cackack in his powerful jaws, and with great difficulty half-carried, half-dragged it through the door within a door outside to where Phat Balune still lay rolling in the dry grass.

'What are you doing with that?' Balune said as Humphrey swaggered up to her, dragging his cackack.

'It's me, HuffPuff. I brought you a present because you are so beautiful.'

'Yes I know that. I know that. Where did you find that cackack? In the Gone Box, I suppose?'

'No, I captured it from the ayoomfas before they had a chance to wreck it.'

'You mean you *stole* it.'

'Uh. . . you could say that. But it's for you.'

'Hmmm. . . Actually it smells very nice. I think I'll try just a little bit. . .Yes, thank you, HuffPuff. You can leave it with me. I'll take care of it. You can go away now.'

Humphrey thought it prudent to leave her in peace to enjoy his fine gift and so trotted back inside the house and gazed with great affection through the window at Phat Balune as she began to tear open the cackack and devour it with great gusto right there in the middle of the grush. She was so engrossed that she didn't even see the blue stinkiroli roll up the path and she didn't see Mummi and Daddi get out of it and run towards her shouting angrily and waving their forepaws in the air.

She thought the scolding she got from Mummi and Daddi for stealing the cackack they had planned to eat for supper was most unfair and she pointedly ignored Humphrey for a whole turn of moon.

Pipple liked to sleep in some very strange places. She preferred high places and would determinedly climb up to the very top of some of the ayoomfa constructions in the house. She was quite a clumsy cat and her striving for high ground often caused a rain of the ayoomfa's possessions to cascade down onto the floor.

'§§sorry. A§§cident' she would splatter to anyone who happened to witness the chaos she caused, managing to look contrite and innocent at the same time.

In the little wash room where the ayoomfas made bubbles and washed themselves with water were many wondrous magic objects. I've already mentioned how the ayoomfas made shufa and wizz in the shufa bowl, but there was also another bowl in the little wash room. It looked very much like a shufa bowl, but it wasn't a shufa bowl. Sometimes Mummi sat on this mystery bowl but I never saw Daddi sit on it. It differed from a shufa bowl in several respects. Neither Mummi nor Daddi ever made shufa or wizz in this mystery bowl - I often smelled it very carefully to check this. Also, it didn't have the magic water that always stayed the same at the bottom. The mystery bowl was usually dry, but Mummi could activate an upside-down rain magic that that caused rain to come from the bottom and fly upwards into the sky! Even understanding the context of ayoomfa-speak as I did, I was never able to fully discover the secrets of the mystery bowl, for I never heard the ayoomfas speak of it. This was odd, for if I had such an amazing mystery bowl with upside-down rain I would boast of it often to whoever would listen to me.

One of Pipple's favourite sleeping places was the mystery bowl. She had no doubts as to its purpose.

'It'§ for u§ to §leep in, §illy,' she explained patiently.

'Then why is it here in the little wash room?' I asked.

'§imply becau§e it'§ §o §unny here in the morning§.'

I pointed out to her that a sleeping place had no use of an upside-down rain magic but she refused to believe me that there was any such magic in the mystery bowl. She had never seen it, she said, so it didn't exist. According to Pipple the mystery bowl was a sleeping place and that was that. She slept in the bowl quite often which greatly amused Mummi and Daddi. The first time they saw her sleeping there they found it so hilarious they could barely stand up from laughing. Daddi got his big flash magic flash and made a picture of Pipple asleep in the mystery bowl. This perplexed me greatly and I was determined to discover the real purpose of the mystery bowl.

Neither Balune nor Humphrey seemed overly concerned about the mystery bowl and my attempts to interest them bore no fruit.

'I've never heard of anything so silly as upside-down rain,' Balune snorted derisively, 'being dead must be affecting your brain, Bunny.' And she wandered off.

'NoNoNo, Bunni. It's just another ayoomfa construction,' Humphrey told me, 'If I can't eat it or make fruka-fruka with it or even make shufa or wizz in it then it's useless to me and I'm not bovvered. Think I'll go have some plokkits. . .' 'Pipple says it's to sleep in,' I offered, trying to keep Humphrey focussed.

'Good. If she's sleeping in it then I can't sleep in it and so it's even less use than I thought. But plokkits are real and useful so I'm gonna go scoff some now.'

I asked PennyWhistle what she thought about it during one of the rare occasions she was actually about the house and not out chasing after Tabithat knows what.

'PennyWhistle, what do you think is the purpose of the mystery bowl in the little wash room - the one with the upside down rain in it?' I asked.

'Never seen no upside down rain,' she said, giving me a look that suggested I was completely crazy. ' You should get some rest, old lady. Have a sleep - you'll feel much better for it.'

Surely I could not be the only cat interested in the mystery bowl? It really bothered me that I - a wise and powerful Phirish who could understand ayoomfa-speak - could not discern its purpose.

I even asked Tabithat when he appeared before me in a dream, as he did occasionally to check on how things were going.

'Oh Lord, what is the purpose of the mystery bowl in the little wash room?' I asked his Blessed Holy Whiskerness.

'Why, little Wargi, it's of no real concern to you.'

'But Lord, I *really want to know*. It worries me so much. . .'

'Ah. . .I must confess that I have no clue as to its purpose, Little Wargi. I'll ask my Special Tabby Investigators Mully and Sculder to find out for you.'

'Oh, thank you, Lord. And Lord. . .?'

'Yes, Little Wargi?'

'Is my bed ready yet?'

'No. Facilities tell me there's a *Health and Safety* issue with it. But they are presently on holiday for the Chinese New Year so nothing can be done for a few weeks.'

MyGranni came to visit us far too infrequently in my view. When we were abducted and first came to Midrand we saw quite a lot of her and Butch and I would rejoice when we saw her little red stinkiroli roll up the path. She always brought us delicious treats to eat and she would let us sleep on her ayoomfawumpus and not chase us away if we make *krinckle-krunckle* with our claws. Now, after several winters, the cats like me that were originally her companions were dead and gone and MyGranni was growing old. She no longer came to see us by herself in the little red stinkiroli; usually Mummi and Daddi would go fetch her in Daddi's blue stinkiroli, she'd stay with us for one or two nights, and they'd take her back again. On one of these visits I took the opportunity to accompany them back to where MyGranni lived. She had moved from Harvard, although I did not think she had been abducted like Butch and myself. MyGranni now lived in a little house which was with lots of other little houses in a big garden. These little houses seemed to be exclusively occupied by old ayoomfas and there were no ayoomfapuriks running around screaming or Young Men racing around on noisy *bizzumrolis* to shatter the peace. It was green and tranquil with babbling waters full of big water slinkis and trees full of the dangling nests of the gently twittering yellow chirrits. In short an ideal environment for older cats to live happily with their ayoomfarolê assistants. However, from what I heard MyGranni say, there were some wicked ayoomfas in some kind of Khouncile of the Houses who wouldn't allow cats to be Citizens of these Houses. Or grufs, but this I can understand - it's not an unreasonable prohibition. MyGranni was understandably disappointed by this, because older ayoomfas derive so much pleasure from serving and honouring their cats. The only animals this wicked Khouncile of Houses would allow was chirrits. Indeed, the chief wickedness of the Khouncile of Houses himself had a fence-box chirrit in his little house, and I went to look.

He was a small, skinny little ayoomfa man of a nervous disposition and he lived in his little house with a nasty fat ayoomfa woman who had a voice like a black *kraak*. So fat was she that two of my Mummi and one of MyGranni could fit inside her and still leave room for Phat Balune. Their chirrit was one of those big cheeky white ones with what looked like a yellow plant thing growing out the top of its head. It was imprisoned in a fence-box placed near where Kraak sat fatly watching the magic window and every now and then she would devotedly croak-whistle some imagined affection at the chirrit, which would respond by erupting in a great tirade of shrieking in what I gathered was rude and obscene chirrit-speak. I felt quite sorry for it, really.

On reflection I decided that if this was how they treated chirrits in this place it was perhaps better that they didn't allow cats. It would be a rotten life being shut up in a fence box all day with fat ayoomfas croaking at you.

I decided to spend the evening with MyGranni and return to Midrand some other time, so I made myself comfortable at the bottom of her bed as she prepared to go to sleep. Suddenly she reached out, smiled at me and tried to pat my head.

'Dear Bunni,' she said, and turned out the light. Had I not been dead already I would certainly have died of Big Fright! MyGranni knew I was there! Could she see me, or did she simply sense my presence in some other way? Should I be pleased or frightened? In the end I decided to be pleased, so I curled up and went to sleep with a loud happi-rumble on MyGranni's bed.

Pipple was a cat full of amazing useful tricks. The most valuable of these was her ability to open doors inside the house. None of us had ever seen this before and we were enthralled every time she demonstrated her Big Door Trick. She couldn't open all doors and she couldn't even always open the same door - circumstances had to be just right for Big Door Trick to work. She could only open a door if it was a *pushme* door with a straight opening stick that stuck out sideways. She couldn't open a *pullme* door at all. She didn't really understand how ayoomfa door magic worked, how a pullme door would change to a pushme door once she was inside the room. This frustrated her Big Door Trick on many occasions and made her cross so that she would splash indignantly at whichever ayoomfas happened to be in the vicinity. At least our door within a door was a proper *pushmepullme* door that could open either way and we didn't have to waste thoughts figuring out how to use it. Also it closed after us, all by itself, which was very considerate.

Pipple had watched the ayoomfas opening pushme doors by pulling the opening stick downwards and pushing on the door. She would have a little run at the door, jump up and hang onto the opening stick with her forepaws until the door became unstuck. Usually the door started to drift open and she would then let go and present herself in the room with a loud 'MWWAA!!'. The door to the sleeping room of Mummi and Daddi was just the right kind of pushme door for Pipple to open, and it was morally appropriate, too. Daddi used to shut the door when he and Mummi went to sleep on their big ayoomfawumpus, which prevented any of the cats getting nicely schnoogli with them and from climbing all over them while they slept. Very rude of them it was. Very inconsiderate. Being a Phirish I had no difficulty with the door but Pipple was not going to put up with this rudeness. One morning, an hour before sunrise, when it was proper time for us to be fed, she chose to do Big Door Trick on the door of Mummi and Daddi's sleeping room. Her first attempt was unsuccessful but it made a noise which woke Mummi and Daddi with Big Fright. Big Fright can be serious - sometimes when we hunt small chirrits or squees, they die of Big Fright before we even get a chance to properly play with them. Mummi and Daddi had clearly not expected anyone to be trying to open the door - they must of thought there were evil ayoomfas in the house, so Daddi got his bangstick ready and stood to one side of the door - ready for whatever badness was lurking on the other side of the door. Then before his eyes, the door swung open and Pipple let go the opening stick.

'MWAAA!!! See! Door open! You must come feed us right now!'

I thought Daddi was going to die from Big Fright right there and then, but luckily he didn't otherwise our breakfast would have been delayed. On the one hand he was pleased that it had been Pipple that had opened the door rather than some evil ayoomfa with bad intent, but on the other hand he was very angry with Pipple for nearly killing him with Big Fright. But after the space of naps their Big Fright subsided and Mummi and Daddi decided Pipple's Big Door Trick was funny. At least funny wouldn't kill them.

Once every paw's pads plus one days the ayoomfas would have a *cracklesack day*, during which they would go away in the stinkiroli and return a nap or two later laden with many cracklesacks containing food and various other ayoomfa objects. They would place all the cracklesacks on the floor and begin taking everything out of them. Most things they put in the boxes on the walls, in the Tiny Cold Room, or in the Dark Roomi where the screaming wind lived and which the ayoomfas called the *Pan-Tree*. Humphrey relished these cracklesack days and would walk amongst the cracklesacks and pounce on them with glee. Sometimes he would get right inside the cracklesacks and rummage around hoping to find some tasty morsel before the ayoomfas had a chance to do stupid things to it and ruin it.

'Whezza food? Whezza food? Whezza food?' he would chant as he scratched around.

One particular cracklesack day Humphrey discovered that that ayoomfas had returned with a gigantic orange sack of our favourite plokkits. It was several times the size of Humphrey, and even Daddi - who is a big ayoomfa - struggled to lift it by himself.

'YesYesYes! Big sack o' food!' Humphrey observed. 'DaddiDaddiDaddi got big sack of food for me! Yay!' He watched in fascination as Daddi put the big sack of plokkits it in the Pan-Tree and very deliberately shut the door. That night when Mummi and DaddiDaddiDaddi were asleep Humphrey spent a long time trying unsuccessfully to scratch his way underneath the Pan-Tree door. But Humphrey was nothing but resourceful and decided to enlist the aid of Pipple.

'Hey Pipple, there's a big sack of delicious plokkits in this room. Come here and do your Big Door Trick. Then we can both eat as much as we want. YesYesYes!'

'§orry, it won't work. It'§ a pullme door. I know 'co§ I tried it before,' Pipple conceded sadly.

'Yes, but see here where I've been scratching - I can just get my paw underneath the door and hook it in there. While you do your Big Door Trick I can hook my paw under the door and pull it so it comes open. Let's give it a try.'

At that moment Phat Balune appeared and demanded to know what was going on. Humphrey explained that the ayoomfas had deliberately - and vexatiously - concealed the big bag of food in the Pan-Tree and that he and Pipple were scheming to break in and pillage it.

'Normally I'd send you both to bed with your tails between your legs and a thick ear,' Balune said sternly, 'but the fact remains that it's against the recommendations of Khat Lore for ayoomfas to deliberately conceal food from a cat, since once we are Citizens of a House, everything belongs to us. You are fully within your rights to break into this room and take the food. So go ahead. I won't be party to it, for rights or no rights, I find it unwise to anger Mummi or Daddi.'

Humphrey lay stretched out on his side and winkled his paw under the door. Pipple managed to reach the door opening stick by standing on Humphrey's head and she did her Door Trick while Humphrey pulled on the door for all he was worth. Sure enough it clicked open. Not much, but enough for Humphrey to be able to pull it open with his paw. 'YesYesYes! Yay! Clever us!' he cheered.

'Ye§§. Clever u§' Pipple splashed enthusiastically.

Humphrey's path to bliss was strewn with further obstacles. The huge sack of plokkits sat wedged in a corner of the Pan-Tree. It had not yet been opened and was protected by a very tough skin, tougher even than the skin of a binigaus. Humphrey was obsessed with this huge sack and he began to scratch and bite the tough skin at the bottom of the sack with his sharp claws and big strong teeth. Before long he had made a little hole in the sack and could smell and see the plokkits inside. This further increased his motivation and he set upon the sack with renewed vigour, eventually making a hole big enough for him to put his head inside. The hole was on the side of the sack, near the bottom, and would not easily be spotted by an ayoomfa as they are notoriously unobservant. Balune and I watched in admiration as Humphrey ate and ate and ate for a long time but the sack was so big that the plokkits just kept on coming. After a long while he reluctantly pulled himself out of the sack and made loud air shufa.

'Glorp,' he said, looking uncomfortably full as he waddled away, his mission accomplished, 'Glorp plokkits.'

'You must shut the door,' Balune called after him, 'otherwise the ayoomfarolês will know you've been in there.'

'Too full' he said. 'Don't care. Must rest now.'

'Oh all right, I'll shut it!' she said crossly and smacked her large rounded rump against the door, sending it shut with a decisive click. 'Now nobody will ever know.'

This wasn't exactly true. Some days later at our breakfast time, Daddi decided it was time to open the big sack of plokkits he'd been keeping in the Pan-Tree. He opened the door, lifted up the sack and had carried it halfway across the Food Room when he noticed that a great river of plokkits was pouring out of the hole that Humphrey had made and onto the floor. Humphrey was delighted and darted about in a frenzy, chasing and gobbling as many plokkits as he could.

'Wheeeeeee! Plokkits, plokkits, plokkits! Glorp plokkits! Yay!' he enthused. But Daddi was not pleased, and after this he made a point of using a small shiny stick to make special door mujaji which stopped any of us opening the door to the Pan-Tree.

*****

CHAPTER TWELVE:
The Origin of Plokkits

As Citizens of a House with conscientious and reliable servants, my friends and I had an abundance of leisure time at Midrand. Sitting together in the sunshine with tums full and ablutions complete, we had time at hand for philosophical discussions on the major mysteries of our lives, of which the origins of our food was a frequently recurring topic of debate. I had always assumed that Mummi and Daddi went out hunting and pounced on one or other guelph, which they then chopped up and put into various boxes to bring home. There were the hard little round drums with the picture of the black and white Woon cat on it or the somewhat bigger and softer yellow boxes with a picture of a Ginger on it, and various coloured sacks, too. Why Mummi and Daddi would want to put the food into boxes and sacks that angered them because they struggled to get them open, was as big a mystery as how the food inside the boxes and sacks was caught and prepared.

I could understand how shmoo kukri could be made. This was easy and any cat can make shmoo kukri all by himself by eating a squee or a chirrit and then making *bloik-bloik* about half a day later. I'd once seen Butch - who was a very tidy cat - eat shmoo kukri he'd made like this. He told me it tasted even better than it did the first time. Perhaps Mummi and Daddi made our shmoo kukri like this? The kukri which consisted of shredded bits was probably also easy to make. It was exactly the same as that we made ourselves by tearing a squee to bits and so all Mummi and Daddi would have to do is tear apart the guelph they'd caught, either with their teeth or with various ayoomfa sticks made for the purpose. Ayoomfas are clever with sticks - they have a great variety of special sticks tailored for almost every conceivable purpose. The other kukri which was like little blocks of hard shmoo kukri in jelly was horrid - none of us liked it, so we were more interested in not eating it than in where it came from.

Plokkits completely baffled us. Plokkits are hard and crunchy and they smell and taste good, but there is nothing I've ever seen a cat do to a squee, chirrit or binigaus that will make it into plokkits. Phat Balune had a theory about this.

'Before I was in The Prison I was a traveller on the road. I once ate a dead binigaus that I found which caused me to make bloik-bloik. I forgot about it for some days and left the bloik-bloik lying in the sunshine, and when I came back it was hard and dry, not unlike plokkits. I think Mummi and Daddi catch the guelph, shred it into pieces, and let it dry in the sunshine. They keep it covered so bizzums don't spoil it. This is how I think plokkits are made.'

'If this is so then I would expect the size and shape of plokkits to be more varied.' PennyWhistle piped up. She might have been antisocial but it was clear that she was quite astute. 'And why are plokkits different colours? Everything left in the sun goes hard and black. Plokkits come in different colours - the brown ones are like little blocks, the orange ones are like little rounds, and the green and yellow ones are some other shape that presumably means something to ayoomfas and causes them to become excited.'

Balune said, 'The ayoomfas first make shmoo kukri, probably in the way that Bunni described by eating a guelph and then making bloik-bloik some time later. Then they fashion the shmoo kukri they have made into these little shapes and let it dry to become plokkits. When it's dry they make each plokkit the colour they want it. I've seen Mummi colour things on noose peppers using little pots of stinky colour juice and a special colouring stick with fur on the end.'

PennyWhistle was sceptical. 'That would take a very long time indeed . . .' she said, frowning.

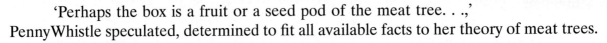

'What else do ayoomfas have to do all day? Between our mealtimes they've the whole day to spend as they wish.' Balune was convinced that her theory was right. PennyWhistle was equally convinced that it was wrong. Her own theory was that plokkits were the berries of special *meat trees* that the ayoomfas had growing somewhere.

'Plokkits come in a box. Yes Yes Yes! In a box,' Humphrey chattered his contribution.

'Perhaps the box is a fruit or a seed pod of the meat tree. . .,' PennyWhistle speculated, determined to fit all available facts to her theory of meat trees.

Pipple couldn't manage plokkits with her poor teeth, so as far as she was concerned, they didn't exist and so it didn't matter where they came from. In short there was no consensus on the origin of plokkits. By popular demand - and because I was an invisible Phirish and very wise - I was given the task of following Mummi and Daddi wherever they went on Cracklesack Day to discover the origin of plokkits.

I prepared for Cracklesack Day by counting the sunrises from the last Cracklesack Day until I reached one paws' pads plus one. I occupied my usual position of invisible travelling companion on the little shelf by the back window of Mummi's red stinkiroli, and in due course Mummi and Daddi climbed inside and woke the stinkiroli into motion. We travelled for a time of about one nap and arrived at a huge construction not unlike a Fat-Tree where there were glorp stinkirolis and glorp ayoomfas. Mummi and Daddi called this place a *shops*. Our stinkiroli came to a halt next to some other stinkirolis which seemed all to be sleeping in neat rows. Daddi grabbed hold of what I will call a *rolibox* and walked inside the shops pushing it along in front of him. The 'shops' was a House of Many Long Walls, and each of these long walls was lined with an amazing glorp of everything one could imagine: softahs that the ayoomfas used to cover themselves, foodstuffs like cackacks, sliced guelphs and vejtibils, noose peppers, and an endless assortment of boxes, little drums, and sacks in a great variety of colours, shapes and sizes containing Tabithat knows what inside. But Mummi and Daddi seemed to know exactly which objects they wanted, even though they could not always see inside the boxes or sacks to identify what was inside them. Some boxes had pictures of things on the outside, but others only had ayoomfa markings on them. I know it sounds ridiculous and is highly unlikely given all we know from Khat Lore, but I suspect that Mummi and Daddi – and possibly other ayoomfas, too - can fathom something from these silly markings.

Between the many long walls were paths on which ayoomfas like my Mummi and Daddi were pushing their roli-boxes and filling them high with all kinds of stuff taken from the long walls. Some ayoomfas were pushing their ayoomfa-puriks along in *sitzrolis* of size grossly disproportionate to the ayoomfapuriks that occupied them. Sometimes these ayoomfapuriks in their sitzrolis completely blocked the paths between the long walls, and I could see from his fiery red radiance that this was making my Daddi very cross. He told my Mummi that he would like to ram them with his rolibox and smash them out of his way. It never ceases to astound me that ayoomfapuriks remain so helpless and useless for so long. A cat purik would have grown up, had tikki puriks itself, grown into an old cat and be well resting in Tabithat's Holy House in the time it takes an ayoomfa purik to be able to hunt for itself!

There was a special place in the House of Long Walls where big guelphs were chopped into pieces by ayoomfas with shiny shrieking mujaji and then put in the little packages that I recognised as the ones Mummi and Daddi often brought home on Cracklesack Day. The guelphs seemed to be dead on arrival, and were complete except for the head and feet. And they were frozen colder than the ice on Mummi's chirrit drinking pool in midwinter! Poor guelphs! I suppose they must have died of Big Cold somewhere and were found by ayoomfas who then brought them to this place, but who couldn't resist snacking on the head and feet along the way. Head of squee is an irresistible delicacy and I imagine the heads of these huge guelphs were similarly tempting for ayoomfas. I thoroughly explored this cold and noisy place in the hopes of seeing how plokkits were made from the frozen guelphs, but there were no plokkits there.

Close to this guelph-slicing place was another place where delicious smelling fish and other water slinkis were cut into small bits and put in glass boxes where ayoomfas could study them as they passed by, sometimes taking one or two of them away with them. The heads - being the tastiest and crunchiest parts of the fish - were clearly too good to simply give away to passing ayoomfas, and the whitecoati ayoomfas who chopped them off were storing these valuable delicacies in a box very similar to our Gone box at home.

Throughout the House of Many Long Walls ayoomfas were helping themselves to this bounty of food and many, many other things that appeared to be placed there purely for their use by some unknown benefactor. One particular long wall contained nothing but food and plokkits for cats, grufs, and chirrits. There were even boxes of food for the little orange fish we call *gulpas*. I have never seen a gulpa myself, but PennyWhistle told me that her original ayoomfas had kept one in a big bowl until she had caught it and eaten it. Most of the food boxes had a picture of an animal on them to help the foolish ayoomfas make the right choice so they didn't end up feeding their hapless grufs on chirrit food. I wonder whether a gruf that ate chirrit food would turn into a chirrit and fly away, wagging its tail and barking furiously? And if a gulpa were given gruf food, would it start barking underwater and make bubbles? There is so much we don't know in this world. But I digress. Boxes and boxes of different plokkits were on this long wall, and I saw Mummi take a box of the ones she knew we liked and put it in the rolibox. Frustratingly I was unable to discover any clue on where plokkits came from or how they were made. Perhaps we are not meant to know this secret? I would have to ask Tabithat.

I watched Mummi and Daddi continue their business of filling up their rolibox. When it was full and could hold no more they trundled it to the front of the House of Many Long Walls where they emptied it one item at a time onto an amazing black tay-bill which moved all by itself and carried the objects past ayoomfas who sat there counting them by pointing a magic counting stick at each object as it passed them. The magic counting sticks made a sound like a squee every time they counted something and with so many ayoomfas counting so many things, there was an unpleasant cacophony of these sounds. Mummi and Daddi packed all the counted objects into cracklesacks and put the full cracklesacks back in the roli-box. The rolibox was then pushed outside to where the stinkirolis were sleeping and they unpacked it yet again, putting all the cracklesacks in the back of the stinkiroli. We all went home again in the stinkiroli, and Mummi and Daddi carried all the cracklesacks into the house. They took everything out of them and packed stuff away in the tiny cold room and in various dark roomis in the Food Room and the Pan-Tree.

What a complete waste of valuable nap time if ever there was! The foolish ayoomfas insist on creating needless work for themselves by making everything more difficult than it needs to be. It's not necessary to count anything, and there is no need for cracklesacks, roliboxes, or squeaking counting sticks. No need for waiting around or endless unpacking and repacking of objects. It's obvious to a wise cat like myself that they should simply take Mummi's red stinkiroli right inside the House of Many Long Walls, load everything into it, go straight home and leave everything in the stinkiroli, only fetching stuff when it was actually needed.

Back at home I felt that I had failed in my mission and I had lost much face. I had not established the origin of plokkits and none of us were any the wiser. In fact the only new snippet of information I brought home was that ayoomfas are scavengers rather than hunters. They don't stalk and kill the big guelphs and the water slinkis they eat, they find them already dead from Big Cold.

*****

At about the time of my fact-finding mission we were plagued by a grey-brown tabby intruder that looked very much like Humphrey, the only significant visual difference being that the newcomer was slightly darker in colour. Pipple's eyesight was not of the best and she started the ball rolling inadvertently one day by inviting the stranger inside the house. 'Come in§ide and have §ome plokkit§,' she said, and the stranger lost no time standing on ceremony. He was a rude, wild, feral cat called Grondus who had evidently never been a Citizen of a House anywhere and he scoffed up everybody's food and then made wizz in the communal water bowl. Phat Balune came to take issue with him and he promptly beat her up and sent her running away to call Humphrey. Any cat that could beat up Phat Balune without thinking twice was truly a serious threat that could only be dealt with by a big, brave yowli like Humphrey. Humphrey was the cat to call in a case like this. Humphrey was totally fearless. He had once chased off a huge black gruf that had parked itself outside the front door of our house. As it transpired from what I heard Mummi and Daddi say to the gruf's master when he came to fetch his gruf, it was only a gentle old deaf gruf that had become lost and so headed for the nearest house. But Humphrey hadn't known this and he bravely marched outside and told it bluntly to go away. The gruf just looked at him. Humphrey yowled and swore and snarled at it. The gruf just looked at him. Humphrey hit it on the nose. The gruf yelped and trotted off to lie down some distance away from the house. Humphrey decided Mummi and Daddi could take it from there and he went back inside to crunch some plokkits with his mission well accomplished.

Unlike the big black gruf the intruding tabby Grondus stood up to Humphrey and a tremendous battle ensued. It began with the usual yowli posturing and bravado, evolved to hysterical screaming and cursing of each other's mothers, and finally ended up as a big cloud of dust in which two vicious cats moved as a furious blur of screaming, growling tabby fur as they tried their best to tear each other to pieces. Daddi heard the screaming and came outside to help, but even he was wary of trying to break apart this awesome fight. When no amount of hissing and shouting and clapping of his forepaws had any effect, Daddi activated the magic rain slinki and from a safe distance he made strong hard rain onto the two fighting yowlis. The fight stopped immediately and Grondus ran away. Daddi allowed Humphrey to go inside the house and rest for a while in order to regain his composure and then went to inspect him for injuries. Humphrey had a wound that required him to be taken to the whitecoati, and this had just about healed when nasty Grondus showed up again and tried to come inside our door within a door. Once again Humphrey went outside to do battle with him. This time it was night and - ayoomfas being the sluggards they are in the dark - Daddi didn't arrive outside in time to offer much help to Humphrey and he'd been in the throes of serious combat with Grondus for quite a while. The belated appearance of reinforcements in the form of Daddi with the magic rain slinki spurred Humphrey into one final push and it was just enough to send Grondus scrambling away hissing obscenities defiantly as he went. Daddi was too late with the magic rain slinki and he succeeded only in wetting the ground where the fight had been. Once again Humphrey had been injured and was taken to the whitecoati the next morning after having been allowed the special solace of spending the rest of the night sleeping on the big ayoomfawumpus with Mummi and Daddi. He was very proud of himself and at breakfast he bragged to Balune of his accomplishments.

'I saw him off, I did. Gave him a proper hiding, YesYesYes I did. He ran away in fear of his life, he did. Oh yes.'

'You look a bit battered yourself, HuffPuff,' Balune observed.

'This is nothing. A mere scratch. A phraidy cat like him couldn't do me much harm. NoNoNo.'

'Nonsense. There's a great big hole in the side of your face big enough for a plokkit to go through. For sure you'll be seeing the whitecoati today. . .'

Humphrey fought the evil Grondus a total of five times and although he always stood his ground and managed - with varying degrees of assistance from Daddi - to defeat his foe in combat, it was becoming a war of attrition and Humphrey was slowly weakening from the repeated wounds and visits to the whitecoati.

Mummi and Daddi decided to take matters into their own hands. They would lay a trap for wicked Grondus, capture him, and take him to some place called Ess Pee Sea Hay, which I think is what ayoomfas call The Prison. What would happen to Grondus thereafter was, of course, unimportant. Mummi came home from work one day with a great big fence-box in the back of her red stinkiroli. I recognised it at once as a Tabithat Shrine similar to the one in which I had been captured many winters before. It was of stout construction from hard shiny and had the same little ramp inside and the same door at one end. I was familiar with the perfidy of these shrines and I had a strong suspicion that this door would shut by special fence-box mujaji the moment a cat had gone inside to worship Tabithat and to eat whatever delicious morsels were inside the shrine. It was clear to me that Mummi and Daddi intended to lay a trap for Grondus and capture him in this Tabithat Shrine. I went at once to warn all my companions to keep away from it. Daddi and Mummi carried the Tabithat Shrine quite far from the house and set it down in the long grush. Mummi brought a deliciously aromatic cackack carcass from the Food Room and placed it carefully on the little platform inside the Tabithat Shrine, and then she and Daddi left the shrine where it was and went inside the house. They anticipated that bad cat Grondus would not be able to resist the cackack carcass and that by the next morning they'd be able to take him away to Ess Pee Sea Hay where he couldn't bother us. It didn't quite work out like that.

The next morning Humphrey was not present for breakfast. Daddi called and called him but he didn't come and Daddi was quite concerned. While Balune and the others were scoffing their food, Daddi went outside in search of Humphrey, calling him repeatedly. After a while he heard a discrete little mewl from the Tabithat Shrine in the long grush. Humphrey was inside it and delighted to see his Daddi. Needless to say the cackack carcass was gone.

'DaddiDaddiDaddi! I found this tasty cackack carcass inside this fence-box and I ate it all. But then I couldn't get out. NoNoNo. I've been here all night. Please let me out, Daddi'

Daddi made fence-box mujaji and released Humphrey who, not content with having demolished an entire cackack carcass on his own during the night, ran immediately to his bowl inside the house and scoffed all the breakfast that had been left for him as if there was no tomorrow. Mummi and Daddi laughed uproariously at him for being caught in the Tabithat Shrine, but Humphrey wasn't an overly sensitive cat and didn't mind a bit of derision in return for a choice cackack carcass. I tried to explain their intentions to him so that it wouldn't happen again. But it did happen again. And again. And again.

'Don't you see that if you go inside that Tabithat Shrine, the door will shut and you won't be able to get out?' I asked him.

'Yes. Every time.'

'So why go inside it then?'

'Because there's cackack carcass inside. Every time. I love to eat a cackack carcass.'

'So you aren't bothered that you might be trapped in the Tabithat Shrine?'

'NoNoNo,' Humphrey scoffed, 'Daddi comes to let me out, y'see. Also every time. Daddi loves me.'

'But the cackack carcass is meant for the wicked cat Grondus.'

'NoNoNo! We don't want that bad cat around here. Mustn't feed him.'

'Mummi and Daddi plan to capture him in the Tabithat Shrine and take him to The Prison.'

'That'll never work. NoNoNo.'

'Why not, Humphrey?'

'Because after I go into the Tabithat Shrine the door closes and I'm inside. Every time. I can't get out and bad cat Grondus can't get inside.'

'Exactly. You shouldn't be inside in the first place.'

'How then must I eat my cackack carcass if I don't go inside? Try not to be foolish, Bunni!'

'You're not supposed to eat the cackack carcass. The plan is for Grondus to eat the cackack carcass so he gets trapped in the Tabithat Shrine.'

'Then it's a bad plan. I won't stand for that cat eating my food. NoNoNo.'

There was no way on earth I could convince Humphrey that his reasoning was flawed, nor could I dissuade him from eating whatever Mummi and Daddi left in the Tabithat Shrine. Eventually the ayoomfas gave up and took the shrine away. As it happened we were never bothered by wicked cat Grondus after his last battle with Humphrey. Perhaps Grondus decided it was too much hard work trying to invade our house? Or perhaps he died of the wounds that Humphrey inflicted, as I don't think he had a Mummi and Daddi to take him to the whitecoati. Sometimes I feel almost sorry for Grondus in a way, but you can't just go invading other cats' houses - it's against Khat Lore and it's simply not tolerated.

*****

CHAPTER THIRTEEN:
Humphrey takes charge

I decided to consult Tabithat on the origin of plokkits as I my own attempts to find out had been completely fruitless and I had lost tremendous face with my friends at Midrand. As if realising this, Lord Tabithat appeared before me in a dream and the familiar deep happi-rumble began to shake my whole body as he appeared in the swirling mist. This time there was a lot of mist and all I saw of his face was one huge green eye which peered at me sternly.

'Hello Little Wargi. I heard you were looking for me'

'Praise be Tabithat, Holy Lord of all whiskered cats, and greatest of phluffi. . .'

'Yes, yes, Wargi. I know who I am. What do you want?'

'Lord Tabithat, my friends and I would like to know where plokkits come from.'

'You mean to say you called me away from important business simply because you want to know where plokkits come from?' Tabithat seemed quite peeved and I decided it was not the time to push my luck and ask after my bed.

'Yes, Lord. Sorry Lord. If my Lord pleases.'

'I have no idea where plokkits come from. My two silver tabby Special Investigators Mully and Sculder have been trying to find this out for glorp winters.'

'What did they discover, Lord?'

'Nothing.' Tabithat sighed in exasperation. 'Mully and Sculder consume endless resources without ever seeming to discover anything at all. And they are easily distracted by almost anything that happens to come along.'

I was shattered. Not even Tabithat's Special Investigators knew the secret of plokkits! And they were silver tabbies, who known to be very resourceful.

'Was there anything else, Wargi?`'

'Uh, no, Lord. So sorry to have disturbed Your Phluffi Excellency. . .'

'While I'm here, I have sad news for you, little Wargi. Your friend Scrap – Phat Balune - is not long for this world. She has the Yellow Sickness inside which is poisoning her and making her eyes muddy. Unfortunately the whitecoati ayoomfas don't have strong enough spells to defeat this poison and I expect I will be meeting Scrap very soon. Since you're still on assignment for me and you don't need it right now, I've provisionally allocated your bed to her. It was delivered today and a truly fine wumpus it is indeed.'

'Whatever you think is best, Lord Tabithat.'

I was quietly seething with indignation. After I'd waited so long for my bed with the special tartan wubbis MyGranni made for me, Tabithat decided on the spur of the moment to give it away! To Phat Balune of all cats. It was an outrage, a complete outrage! I went to where

Balune had been lying quietly all morning under the ayoomfas' big tay-bill. I had to admit, she did look subdued and her eyes were not as bright and clear as they usually were.

'I've just spoken to Phluffi Lord Tabithat in a dream,' I said to Balune.

'Ye-es?' Balune said suspiciously, 'What does His Phluffiship have to say?'

'You are going to die soon. Tabithat has a nice bed ready for you.'

I floated away, still simmering at the injustice of having to sacrifice my fine wubbis.

As the days went by Balune looked ever more lacklustre and I could see from her radiance that the Yellow Sickness was spreading inside of her, carried in her blood. One morning after she reluctantly had a few mouthfuls to eat at breakfast she called Humphrey over for a little talk. I sat nearby and listened in.

'Now Humphrey, I've seen what a big strong yowli you are. . .'

'Yes Yes Yes! Very Big and Strong. Yay for me!'

'Be quiet and listen! I have a sickness inside. It is a Yellow Sickness. Soon Mummi and Daddi will take me to the whitecoati, and I have a strong feeling that I won't be coming back.'

Humphrey looked crestfallen. 'Mummi and Daddi will forget to bring you back from the whitecoati?' he asked in alarm.

'No, HuffPuff. I am going to the whitecoati so he can try to fight the Yellow Sickness. But it's not likely he'll win and I'll probably die while I'm there.'

Humphrey was devastated.

'NoNoNo! It can't be! You're so young!' He added as an afterthought, 'And beautiful!! AndAndAnd. . .full of largesse.'

It was indeed well before her time for Balune had seen no more than nine winters.

'You're so sweet, HuffPuff, and I wish I'd known you for longer. I suspect it was the prison food that wore me down before my time. But it's Tabithat's will that I die now. . .'

'Uh, . . excuse me,' I interrupted. 'It's not Tabithat's will at all. He just can't do anything about it, is all. *And* he doesn't know where plokkits come from.'

Balune looked disappointed. She'd kind of got used to the idea that her dying would be some part of Tabithat's Greater Plan and that in dying she would please Him.

'Yes, well, never mind,' she scowled at me. 'HuffPuff, the reason I am telling you this is because once I'm gone, someone will have to take over as Chief Cat of the House. Bunni doesn't qualify because she's dead and can't really do much except spoil our days. Pipple is too forgetful, so it's obviously between SaucyPads and yourself. So it's really no contest. SaucyPads doesn't even want to live here, let alone be responsible for the entire household and for looking after the ayoomfarolês. Whereas you are a noble yowli of great courage who I know will do his utmost to preserve order and civilisation in my house.'

Humphrey glowed with pride. I could see his radiance sparkle with joy and swell with sadness at the same time. He still harboured a great love for Balune.

'Yes Yes Yes! I won't let you down, Princess Balune, I wont, I won't, and I won't. You can trust me.'

'Of course I do. Would you like to wash the top of my head?'

I thought Humphrey would burst with joy. As gently as he could manage, he began washing Balune's head with his enormous pink tongue. Balune begat a gentle happi-rumble and closed her eyes. Later that day Mummi and Daddi came and gently picked her up, wrapped her in a wubbis, and took her away in the stinkiroli.

The ayoomfarolês were in mourning for a long time after Balune died. Humphrey did his level best to distract and amuse them, and to remind them that life goes on and the living must be cherished. As Chief Cat of the House Humphrey set up a program of Khat Comfort for Mummi and Daddi and everyone was required to show their appreciation each week by hunting a squee, a chirrit or even a binigaus, and donating it to Mummi and Daddi as part of Khat Comfort. Even Pipple, with no teeth at all and little inclination towards violence, was nagged by Humphrey until she eventually managed to catch a small squee which she carried inside in her mouth and placed carefully at Mummi's feet. The squee was very wet, somewhat traumatised, but otherwise unharmed. Mummi picked it up in a small wubbis and took it outside. I didn't see her eat it, but when she returned the squee was gone, so I suppose she must have. PennyWhistle and Humphrey brought in the majority of squees and chirrits and left them in places where Daddi or Mummi would easily find them. Our ayoomfas were obviously overwhelmed with gratitude but they couldn't manage to eat all the squees they were given, so they wrapped each one up carefully in a little wubbis and put it in the Gone Box for later. Needless to say a lot of squees were stolen because of this. To avoid this regrettable waste Humphrey suggested we use Khat Concealment Knowledge and hide a stock of squees, chirrits and binigaus around the house in places we knew were safe from the Gone Box thieves. In roomis for example, under things in the lounj, behind the tiny cold room or other big heavy things in the Food Room, and even behind the shufa bowl in the ayoomfas' little washing room. All very safe hiding places. We did this, but the ayoomfas could always smell when a dead squee had been hidden for a week or so and they would sniff it out and all but tear our house apart to get it so they could hide it themselves in the Gone Box. Some creatures are impossible to help.

Conscious that he might be lacking in leadership and organisational skills, Humphrey had been attending a training course for Chief Cats sponsored by the Midrand Khat Khouncile, and he'd become infused with silly words and sayings that really meant nothing at all. His teacher, a certain old ayoomfa lady the Khat Khouncile had found somewhere to present the course and whom they rewarded with a regular stipend of two freshly caught hopits every moon, was totally smitten by Humphrey's phluffi largesse and ingenuous manner and she plied him with treats during the lessons. The result of all this training was that Humphrey was growing both fat and foolish.

'Mrs Malaprop says we should always try to kill two chirrits in the bush with one stone. . .'

'That's ridiculous! You don't kill a chirrit with a stone! No ways! You just bite their head off!' PennyWhistle retorted. 'What do ayoomfas know about killing chirrits anyway? They just collect thems that have already died of Big Cold. Bunni said it was so. She's a Phirish. She saw it. And you should ask Mrs Malaprop why the foolish ayoomfas tie up the cackacks with string *after* they're dead! Where do they think the cackacks are going to go with no head and their feets cut off? Hey? Hey?'

Under this ruthless pressure Humphrey became flustered. 'Mrs Malaprop hasn't yet said why we need a stone to tie up the cackacks in the bushes,' he said. 'NoNoNo. But she will, oh yes, she will. Soon.'

Mrs Malaprop taught Humphrey to take his duties very seriously and to take pride in his position of Chief Cat of the House. She taught him of the importance of security.

'Mrs Malaprop says security is right at the top of Molotov's Cocktail of Needs,' he told us one day.

'Whatever,' PennyWhistle sighed, 'Do what you have to do. . .'

One of his Humphrey's important tasks was to perform a daily security assessment after breakfast. He felt it necessary to check all of the little dark *roomis* in the Food Room and elsewhere around the house - to make sure there wasn't an intruder lurking inside one of them, he claimed.

'A bad gruf might be hiding in here,' he muttered darkly as he systematically pulled open each of the doors of the roomis that lined the walls of the Food Room. 'Or maybe wicked, wicked Grondus has come back and is lying in ambush inside. You never know, you don't. NoNoNo. Gotta check everywhere. YesYesYes. Everywhere. Mrs Malaprop says to leave no stone uncooked.'

As an added security measure, he left all the doors of the roomis wide open so he could easily see if there was badness skulking within. Daddi didn't like this and would go around after him, shutting all the doors again. A lot of the roomis in the Food Room had pullme doors that Humphrey could open by hooking his claw behind the edge. Other roomis had stronger doors that only ayoomfas could open, sometimes using the little magic shiny sticks. Humphrey would sit patiently outside these roomis - sometimes for the time of many naps - waiting for one of the ayoomfas to come along and open it. When they did, he would dart inside and conduct his security assessment with great fervour. Knowing he was inside, whichever of the ayoomfas had opened the roomi for Humphrey would always leave it open so he could get out when his duties were done. The ayoomfas meant well, but sometimes they made mistakes. Sometimes if one of them had opened the door for Humphrey and left it open, the other one might come along later, wonder why the door was open, and shut it, trapping poor Humphrey inside the roomi! Fortunately we had trained our ayoomfarolês well and they counted us at mealtimes; any absence was noticed and a search begun at once. Humphrey usually managed to draw attention to his accidental incarceration by making a frantic scrabbling that one of the ayoomfas would use to locate and rescue him.

The ayoomfas had many things which worked with the *mujaji of invisible fire*. These included the magic suns, the magic window, the *washdoosh box*, the *rumbling potta*, and many other objects in the Food Room which the ayoomfas used to spoil food.

When I was alive I had examined these things by sniffing them all very thoroughly, which is the only way to properly investigate anything, as is well known. The mujaji of invisible fire makes things look like they are alive, but it's not a proper life as we know it, more like an animated slavery of the living dead.

In the lounj near the Magic Window was a collection of shiny boxes which the ayoomfas used to produce a Great Noise, which the ayoomfas called mewsik.

One of these boxes of the Great Noise consumed bright round shinies about the size of our food bowls. Our ayoomfarolês had an enormous collection of glorp upon glorp of these round shinies. The box of the Great Noise had a hard black tongue and it would stick its tongue out and wait for an ayoomfa place a round shiny on it. The box would withdraw its tongue and eat the round shiny, then reward our ayoomfarolês by making The Great Noise. Sometimes the box didn't like the food it was given and it would spit out the round shiny and wait for Mummi or Daddi to give it another. Others of these living dead boxes didn't seem to eat round shinies at all and would mostly make the sound of ayoomfa talk, possibly because they were malnourished and had not the strength to make The Great Noise.

I learned from watching the magic window that the Great Noise was produced by ayoomfas with long head fur speaking - or even shrieking - in a kind of continuous wail, and simultaneously crashing objects together or blowing into constructions made of pipes that made a noise not unlike the sound made by stinkirolis when they shout at each other. Our ayoomfarolês called the Great Noise *mewsik* and inexplicably, they found it hugely pleasing. Sometimes Mummi or Daddi would clap their forepaws or tap their back feet on the floor while the Great Noise was in progress. When they got really excited they would even contribute to the mewsik themselves so that so that The Great Noise was very loud indeed and disturbed our delicate silky cat ears. When the noise caused us too much discomfort we would follow proper procedure and lodge complaint with the Chief Cat of the House. Humphrey would go right up to Daddi and shout loudly at him and would not leave him alone until Daddi got the message and made the Great Noise softer. Humphrey would stay there shouting at him until it was soft enough for us.

Daddi's love of the Great Noise knew no limits. To my horror, he came home one day with his stinkiroli full of the objects I recognised from watching the magic window as those used by the ayoomfas with long head fur to make the Great Noise. And the things Daddi brought home were those that made the greatest noise of all. There were big round shinies which were either smashed into each other or beaten with sticks. There were round drums which were struck with the same sticks and a very big round drum with no back and a wubbis in it that was placed on the floor, and this one had a special stick all of its own with a big round whumpah ball on the end of it. Daddi sat on a *sitzup* and arranged all these dreadful contraptions around him within striking distance. Then he began to strike them and smash them together in the furious and violent manner I had seen done on the magic window by the ayoomfas with long head fur, but with much worse results. We cats were all so disturbed at Daddi's Great Noise that we all fled the house and sat at the far end of the grush waiting for it to finish. It was far louder and far more unpleasant than any Great Noise that we had heard before. This was unacceptable and we lodged complaint with our Chief Cat of the House.

'We are all Citizens of this House,' Humphrey said indignantly, 'and we cannot allow ourselves to be driven from our homes by this ear-splitting din. NoNoNo, not at all. I have already spoken to the wise Mrs Malaprop about this. Oh, yes.'

We groaned silently.

'I have a plan which could solve the problem of The Great Noise and also help Dorkus Babalegi on his way at the same time. Oh Yes.'

Everyone pricked up their ears and listened. It would be a great plan indeed if we could get rid of Dorkus Babalegi. Strictly speaking, it was Humphrey's job as Chief Cat of the House to dispel unwelcome guests, but Humphrey was a kind cat and he felt sorry for Dorkus Babalegi and didn't have the heart to see him off with tooth and claw like he had done to the evil Grondus and so many others.

I suppose I should explain about Dorkus Babalegi. Dorkus was easily the stupidest and most gormless cat any of us had ever come across. He was a rather shabby tabby who had no home and was pretty useless at looking after himself. At night he slept in the *washdoosh box* in the Food Room of our house and he ate the leftover plokkits and any bits of unappetising sun-dried food we didn't want. During the day he very wisely kept out of sight. Our ayoomfarolês were quite oblivious to his presence; they would have been horrified had they known that Dorkus Babalegi was part-time resident in their *washdoosh box*. This was where they put the flat bowls they ate from but which they were unable to properly lick clean because their ayoomfa tongues were so pathetic. Every now and then they would activate a special cleaning mujaji and the washdoosh box would rumble inside and lick all the flat bowls shiny clean for them. It had swishing-swashing things and also a kind of hot rain inside it, for sometimes when the ayoomfas opened it I could see *rain-smoke.* In between using the washdoosh box, Mummi and Daddi left it with the door open a little bit, and Dorkus Babalegi decided he was going to live inside it. Fortunately, he made sure he was always gone by sunrise when there was a real possibility that he might be accidently trapped inside the washdoosh box when one of the ayoomfarolês happened to make it do the hot rain cleaning rumble. Humphrey had taken pity on Dorkus Babalegi and refused to chase him away. Now Humphrey revealed that by allowing Dorkus to remain a benign squatter, he had acquired a useful tool in the campaign against Daddi's Great Noise. What the ayoomfas would call a *porn*. Pipple was delegated the task of recruiting Dorkus's unwitting participation in the campaign the next morning.

'Hullo Dorku§,' she splattered to him through the slightly open door of the washdoosh box. It was imperative that he be seconded to the operation before sunrise, which was when he usually left the house.

'Doh,' he said, using fully half of his laboriously acquired Khat vocabulary.

'Dorku§, it'§ really not very ni§e in thi§ §§loppy, §§lo§hy, §§htinky and wet plac§e. I've found a plac§e you could §leep that'§ muc§h, nic§er than thi§. It'§ dry, warm and coz§y and you could §tay there all day. Would you like to come with me and §ee thi§ §pecial plac§e?

'Doh?'

'Ye§. Come with me. Walk thi§ way. Follow. Come.' She turned around and led the way, stopping to check now and again that Dorkus Babalegi was still following her. And of course he was, for what yowli could ever resist the lure of the beautiful Pipple with the tail nearly as fat as her body? She pattered her way quietly into the lounj and led Dorkus Babalegi carefully through the forest of shiny sticks and trees that were the tools of Daddi's Great Noise until they reached the very big round drum that sat on its side on the floor; the one with no back and a wubbis in it that had a special stick all of its own with a big round whumpah ball on the end of it.

'See, Dorku§, it'§ nic§e and coz§y in here, like a roomi . . . and it'§ already got a grand wubbi§ in§ide. . . you could probably §leep here all day. . .'

'Doh, yeah!' Dorkus agreed and immediately took up residence on the wubbis inside the big round drum. After she was sure he'd settled in properly, Pipple crept away and went about the important business of waking the ayoomfarolês so they could feed us all. This she did by doing her Big Door Trick again and again, causing the opening stick of Mummi and Daddi's sleeping room door to snap up and down with a loud noise. The door didn't open, for after Daddi's Big Fright he always made use of the shiny magic stick to make sure the door wouldn't open while he and Mummi were sleeping. Nonetheless, Pipple was able to cause a great disturbance which woke them both and strongly reminded them of their sacred duties towards us.

As usual, after feeding everyone Daddi activated the rumbling potta that makes the tea for Mummi and himself. Daddi knew the rumbling potta would take the time of a brief nap to make the tea, and so while it was sighing and burbling to itself he went into the lounj and sat down on his sitzup amid the tools of The Great Noise. Dorkus Babalegi had long since fallen asleep and not being a very alert cat at the best of times, he was blissfully unaware of Daddi's presence. Probably dreaming of vejtibils in the washdoosh box or something equally silly, if I knew Dorkus. Daddi picked up his special sticks and started tickling them on the big shiny rounds. It was clear he was working up to making The Great Noise. The instant Daddi caused the stick with the round whumpah ball to hit the side of the box in which Dorkus was sleeping, Dorkus immediately exploded out of it as if pursued by the Nasty Grufs and landed on Daddi's chest with all claws outstretched and a demented expression on his face. Both Daddi and Dorkus got Very Big Fright. Dorkus spat indignantly at Daddi then fled the house through an open window in the Food Room and we never saw him again. Daddi had to sit still for quite a while to let the Big Fright die down, and I wondered whether he would start up The Great Noise again. But he put down the sticks and went up the stairs carrying the bowls of tea and shaking his head. Daddi didn't make The Great Noise ever again and after some moons an ayoomfa came in a big stinkiroli with no windows except in the front and he took away the sticks and boxes and shiny rounds of The Great Noise.

*****

CHAPTER FOURTEEN:
Tikki Puriks

Midrand was quite a dangerous place for cats who were living rough in the grush and who lacked the protection afforded to Citizens of a House. After every winter came a hot, dry season with great *woo-woo* that lasted until the rains came. No cat likes woo-woo, for we firmly believe that if it blows under your tail it will make you crazy. I don't think the ayoomfas much like woo-woo either, even though they don't have tails and are already crazy. During this season of hot woo-woo there would always come The Big Fire which burned all the long grush. Luckily it didn't burn the house because the grush near the house was short, but Daddi and Mummi nonetheless were very alert to danger during the Big Fire and sometimes they used the magic rain slinki to make rain on the short grush so it wouldn't burn. Sometimes other ayoomfas came to help and would dart around foolishly beating at the Big Fire with wet sacks, when even a simple cat like Dorkus Babalegi could have told them that the wisest course of action would have been to run away. One year when the Big Fire was particularly big and angry, some ayoomfas with strange bowls on their heads came in a huge red rumbleroli which had on it the biggest magic rain slinki any of us had ever seen. I heard Daddi say the red rumbleroli was called Denis. Denis's giant rain slinki was even fatter than Pipple's tail and the ayoomfa holding it had to use all his strength to prevent it escaping and making crazy rain all by itself. The rain from the giant rain slinki had tremendous strength and could easily travel the height of six trees, so the ayoomfa used it to make our house wet with rain so it wouldn't burn down. If only Daddi had had Denis's magic rain slinki like this during the troubles with wicked Grondus - the rain from this slinki would have lifted Grondus right off his feet and tossed him far away into the night.

One year the Big Fire brought us a wonderful present. Across the valley in the long grush lived a pretty black and white wild cat with the name WhiteFootsi Woon. As you probably know, all black and white cats have two names, the second of which is always Woon. WhiteFootsi was an Associate of a nearby house, where a big kindly ayoomfa lady put out food for her, but she chose to live in the long grush and only visit the house to snatch a quick bite to eat in the dead of night. WhiteFootsi came to visit us one night and Humphrey was quite impressed with her - enough even to invite her to come live with us in our house, but WhiteFootsi wanted to remain a Free Cat. She wittered on about freedom and independence and natural way of life and puriks growing up to be real cats yada yada yada and so on until we were all bored and falling asleep. She came to visit us now and again but we didn't see her very often.

On the afternoon of the Big Fire, Pipple was asleep inside the house and Humphrey, PennyWhistle and I were sitting in the room with lid but no walls, watching the fire burn and the ayoomfas flap about like agitated cackacks. Suddenly, out of the smoke and grush appeared WhiteFootsi Woon with a squeaking tikki purik in her mouth.

'Help me, please!' she cried, 'The grush is burning and I have to get my puriks to safety. I've taken three of them to the Khouncile's big red rock where they'll be safe for the time being. I'm missing one but I think he died in the fire. Please look after this little one while I go look for him. . .'

Of course we agreed to do this and we watched as WhiteFootsi stashed her purik in a small tree nearby and then ran off again into the grush. A few minutes later she returned carrying another tikki purik which looked somewhat the worse for wear from the Big Fire. His eye was injured and his tiny ears were actually smoking! 'Found him,' WhiteFootsi said triumphantly as she stashed the smoking purik in the tree with its brother.

'I must go to my other three now before they panic and run off somewhere,' she said. 'Please look after my two little boys until tomorrow morning.' Then she was gone again.

Humphrey guarded the Woon puriks in the tree until the Big Fire was over and the ayoomfas had regained their sensibilities and resumed their normal duties. By which time the two puriks in the tree were very hungry and were kicking up a loud noise.

'Me hungry. Want food. . .Want Mummi. . .' one of them mewled.

'. . Yes, and water. .' added the other. His ears had stopped smoking and he seemed largely uninjured, if a little bit singed and bedraggled.

Mummi and Daddi heard the commotion and came outside looking very concerned. They followed the sound of plaintive mewling to the tree, which was only as tall as they were themselves, and they soon discovered the bedraggled purik. Daddi lifted him out the tree in his forepaws and the purik spat and hissed furiously at him. The other purik which was slightly larger and had a white smudge on his chin, nearly went crazy.

'Hey! Hey!!! That's my brother! What are you doing with my brother? Leave him alone!' he shrieked at Mummi and Daddi with all the ferocity his little person could muster. 'Get away from my brother! Leave my brother alone! Go get your own brother!' This fiercely protective display of sibling devotion served only to divert the ayoomfarolês' attention to him and they sought to lift him out of the tree as well. He gave them quite a run-around but it was inevitable he'd be caught, since he couldn't climb down from the tree and run away as WhiteFootsi Woon hadn't yet trained him in Khat Tree Navigation, a difficult art that some cats never master at all. It was only a matter of time before both he and his beloved brother were each firmly clasped in an ayoomfa forepaw and on their way into the house.

Mummi and Daddi were very selfish over their newly acquired puriks. They named them *Bibble* and *Bobble* and hid them in the little washing room next to their sleeping room in the Up House. Mummi made little walls by tearing apart some old boxes and these served to stop the puriks hiding in places where the ayoomfas with their great clumsy hands couldn't reach them. The puriks were fed regularly on delicious smelling white fish and the door to the little washing room was kept firmly closed. The ayoomfarolês wouldn't let any of the other cats come and inspect the puriks, but about me they could do nothing. For lo, it is easier for an ayoomfa to catch a binigaus underground at night than it is to contain a Phirish. Pipple lived in a happy little world of her own with sunshine and butterflies and was totally oblivious to much of anything outside of it, but Humphrey was simply bursting with curiosity to know what was going on behind the closed door. He all but chewed a hole in it.

Much to Humphrey's acute embarrassment, two days after the tikki puriks had been left in his care, WhiteFootsi Woon came and asked to have them back.

'Where are my tikki puriks?' she demanded to know.

'They are. . uh, unavailable right now. .' Humphrey said, feeling very foolish.

'What do you mean they are *unavailable*? I left them right here in this tree and asked you to look after them. They are not in the tree now and they're too tikki to have climbed down by themselves - so what happened to them?' Whitefootsi was most displeased. Humphrey was seriously losing face and he began earnestly washing his forepaws as a distraction, but WhiteFootsi was not to be fobbed off.

'They are unavailable because they are uh. . .elsewhere,' he muttered. 'Yes, uh. . . elsewhere.'

'Stop washing and listen to me, HuffPuff! You will tell me immediately where my tikki puriks are!'

'Uh . . . actually. . . well, it's a long story. . .'

'You will tell me right now where they are, HuffPuff!' WhiteFootsi snapped.

'The ayoomfarolês *stole* them,' Humphrey said as casually as he could, while pretending to be intently studying the brown pads on his paw.

'How could you let this happen? I ask you to do a simple thing like look after two tikki puriks and you allow them to be stolen! You are really a stupid, useless yowli!'

Humphrey flattened his ears and glared at her and for a moment WhiteFootsi feared she had gone too far and Humphrey would attack her, for Khat Lore mandates that yowlis - and especially Chief Cats of a House - are to be respected at all times and certainly never insulted in this manner. However, Humphrey felt very foolish over the two tikki puriks and he thought it an inappropriate moment to start asserting his yowli rights.

'I'm very sorry,' he said, 'but there was really nothing I could do. NoNoNo, nothing at all,' he explained, and began washing his face. 'My Mummi and Daddi came and took the puriks out the tree.'

'You should have attacked them!'

'NoNoNo! Lord Tabithat, no! I am Chief Cat of this house. I would never attack Mummi or Daddi! Khat Lore forbids us to abuse our ayoomfa servants! Surely you know that? After all, we are civilised creatures, not savage grufs. I'd bring you your puriks now if I could, but the ayoomfarolês have hidden them away from us. And I'm not really a useless yowli, it's just that in this matter my paws were tied with a ha'penny worth of tar. . .'

'What the. . !!?'

'Mrs Malaprop says that. . .'

'Never mind Mrs Malaprop,' WhiteFootsi interrupted angrily. 'Here's how it's going to be: if you don't return my tikki puriks to me by sunrise tomorrow, you'll simply have to raise them yourself.' With that she turned around and stalked off. Humphrey looked around nervously to check if anyone had witnessed his humiliation, then went inside to resume his efforts at chewing the door to the little washing room.

Bibble and Bobble were giving the ayoomfarolês a difficult time. Despite Mummi's best efforts at containing them, Bobble once managed to squirm into a small recess behind the shufa bowl and get seriously stuck there. So stuck indeed that Daddi had to take the top boxie part off the shufa bowl to get him out. Daddi was very cross and got very red in the face. On another occasion Bibble - encouraged by myself of course - made an excellent game with the roli of white shufa papers and pulled them all over the little washing room. This time Mummi got red in the face. After this incident the ayoomfarolês decided it was preferable to let the puriks out the little washing room and let them roam freely around the sleeping room. This was great fun for the puriks as there were numerous places for them to explore. One such place was a fascinating dark roomi inside the big platform that supported the ayoomfawumpus. Both puriks squeezed through a narrow gap and had a good romp inside this roomi, which was full of dust and had several spinnelies and krorlis living in it. After a while they tired of being there and wanted to get out again, but found they couldn't. Or thought they couldn't, which for a purik amounts to the same thing. It was dark inside the roomi and they were being tickled by the thin strings made by the spinnelies and they begat an insistent panicked mewling. Mummi and Daddi had to take apart all the various softahs which made up their ayoomfawumpus and then Daddi had to completely upturn the big, heavy platform itself so Mummi could reach in and rescue Bibble and Bobble. Both Mummi and Daddi got red in the face that time.

After about half a moon the ayoomfas relaxed these restrictions and opened the door to their sleeping room so that the tikki puriks could go down the bumpity hill into the Down House and meet everyone else. They were quite nervous at first and walked slowly down the bumpity hill, looking warily about them on each tentative step. For better or worse, Humphrey was the first cat they saw.

'You young tikki mischiefs have caused me a lot of trouble!' he said sternly. So you better behave yourselves if you live here. I'm Chief Cat of the House and I'll be watching you' He half-heartedly spat at them and then walked off. The second cat they saw was PennyWhistle. She took one horrified look at them and trotted away. She didn't return for three days.

At least Pipple was pleased - if a little surprised - to see them.

'Look, my beautiful puriks! Tabith§at has §eriou§ly ble§§ed me!' she exclaimed in rapturous delight. 'I don't remember giving bir§th to you, but I'm getting quite forgetful nowaday§. You mu§t be my purik§ becau§e there'§ no other queen cat here. I'm §o plea§ed to §ee you. Let me §how you around. . .'

Missus Pipple Foster as the ayoomfarolês began to call her, diligently showed the tikki puriks how to get out of the little door within a door and where they could safely make wizz and shufa without running the risk of the ayoomfarolês shouting at them. She showed them where the Food Room was, and where it was highly likely they'd be fed in future. She showed them where her bed was in the hopes they'd come and cuddle up with her in the nights. And she gave them a long list of things they shouldn't do because it would make the ayoomfarolês get red in the face and shout at them. Motherhood and Pipple were clearly made for each other. As you may have gathered parenting wasn't one of my strong points, but that was in 'Nam and staying alive had higher priority. It's some, but not much, consolation that my daughter Khalli was ten times more useless a mother than I. I seem to remember the one and only time she had puriks they were so disappointed in their mother that they left in disgust and were subsequently adopted by a nearby family of cackacks.

One day, about a moon after she'd left them in the tree, WhiteFootsi Woon saw her puriks playing contentedly in the sunshine under the watchful but dozy eye of Pipple. She came over and said icily,

'Good! I see you've found my puriks at long last. I'll have them back now, thank you.' I noticed she only had one of her three other puriks with her. Pipple smiled benignly and got up to go speak with her but Humphrey intercepted her first and approached her menacingly with his ears flat, making a low, nasty growl.

'These are no longer your puriks, WhiteFootsi. They belong to us now and I have taught them Khat Lore. Just because you're feeling bad that you've only one purik left doesn't mean you can come and steal ours. NoNoNo! This is *my* family and I will protect them with sharp tooth and claw. Oh YesYesYes!'

'Ye§, you §hould §ee hi§ §harp white tee§th!' said Pipple in enthusiastic support, 'He can bite a big binigau§§§ clean in half§§§. . .'

'It's true, I chipped in, 'And I'm a Phirish that can haunt you so that you don't get a wink of sleep ever again in your life. You will be so exhausted you will be begging me to let you die!' We cats can be terribly melodramatic in the heat of anger. Much of it is bravado and bluster and I probably would have got bored with haunting WhiteFootsi after two days at most.

Then to WhiteFootsi's astonishment the smaller purik called Bibble suddenly tottled bravely up to her and hissed, 'You listen here: My uncle HuffPuff is a direct descendant of Poyk, the first ever tabby cat. He has massive paws with long, sharp claws, and he will tear you to pieces. Then your pieces will creep away and die. And I'm going to be big and strong just like my uncle HuffPuff! So you just better go away and leave me and my bruvver alone.' Faced with this WhiteFootsi Woon simply turned and trotted away. The battle for custody of the puriks was over.

Bibble and Bobble - known collectively to the ayoomfas as the Bibbly-Bobblies - had caused a great disturbance while resident in the little washroom upstairs and could definitely not be allowed to spend the nights there unsupervised. Nor could they spend the nights in the ayoomfa sleeping room romping all over the ayoomfawumpus while the ayoomfarolês were sleeping on it. Fortunately, near the bottom of the bumpity hill was another little washroom that was very seldom used by anybody except MyGranni when she came to stay with us. The little room had a door which could be closed to contain the puriks inside so they didn't scamper around our house making mischief during the hours of darkness.

Mummi prepared a very cozy bed for the Bibbly-Bobblies in this little room, along with a bowl of water, two bowls of food and a shufa box full of sand-plokkits in which it was hoped they would make shufa when they felt the need. They were also given a variety of nice toys that were rather presumptuously borrowed from Humphrey and PennyWhistle, who indignantly lamented their loss of their toys notwithstanding that they seldom played with them. PennyWhistle was only at home for one day out of every paw's pads but she nevertheless insisted she needed all her toys to be at hand all day, every day. The Bibbly-Bobblies mostly ignored the toys because it was more fun scratching the sand-plokkits out of the shufa box and all over the floor.

The daily routine of Bibble and Bobble began with them squeaking, mewling and whining in a pathetic manner from well before daybreak in a futile attempt to hasten the arrival of Daddi or Mummi with their breakfast. It took them a long time to realise that ayoomfas only like to rise long after the sun has risen and warmed the ground and they will steadfastly resist any attempts to change this habit. Long after dawn, Mummi or Daddi would wobble slowly and reluctantly down the bumpity hill and open the door of the little room, whereupon the Bibbly-Bobblies would shoot out and dart about in a frenzy of excitement, ripping and tearing at any softahs they could see. They would hurriedly gobble down their breakfast and then rip and tear and scratch and claw some more. Once every four days or so, Bobble - whose digestion was very delicate - would become ill from too much romping and rolling and he'd make *bloik-bloik* on the softah that covers most of the floor inside our house. The ayoomfarolês became very displeased about this but in truth there was little they could do other than clean it up with a stinky white powdery stuff that came out of a *spitting tin*. By mid-morning the tempo of the romping would slow from a frenzy to a dawdle and Humphrey would heave a sigh of relief and herd the puriks into their beds to go sleep. Sometimes it required all of his powers of persuasion.

'You puriks must now go and practice sleeping. . .'

'Why Uncle HuffPuff?' Bibble interrupted.

'Because when you are grown into big cats you will need to sleep a lot. So it's very important that you practice sleeping now. . .'

'Butmybruvversaystheresagametoplayandohlookwhat'shappeningovertherel etsgo seeandisitfoodorisitatoy. . .' The puriks had very little focus.

'NoNoNo! I am your Godfather and you must go to sleep right now or I will bang your heads together and bite your tails.'

Enforced rest. If the ayoomfarolês were at home they would shut the door of the little room for a few long naps to further enforce the rest.

The afternoons were less hectic and the Bibbly-Bobblies usually woke from their enforced rest in a quieter and more reflective frame of mind. They were encouraged to go outside and explore in the warm sunshine, and Humphrey always kept a watchful eye on them to make sure they didn't wander too far and get into danger. By sunset they would be so tired and sleepy that it was sometimes difficult to get them inside the house in good order. Bobble tended to simply fall over and go to sleep wherever he was and when he didn't appear for supper, Daddi would have to go outside, find him, and carry him inside. Bibble always provided useful assistance by shrieking to Daddi at the top of his voice, 'You must come fetch my brother - he's too tired to walk inside! Come fetch him right away. He's over here! No, not there, silly, here! Here, by me, under this bush. Are you deaf or what? Hurry!'

Once the Bibbly-Bobblies has been brought inside and had enjoyed a snack they were allowed to sit on the sitz-softah in the lounj with Humphrey and be told a bedtime story. Humphrey had a vast repository of suitable bedtime stories, all of which were decidedly tabby-centric. Pipple also liked to listen in on the bedtime tales but she seldom stayed awake for the whole story. Telling stories to his adopted puriks was very good for Humphrey's health because he de-stressed as he told them and so forgot his numerous concerns about the Gone Box, security checks, wicked Grondus and food. As he unwound he became rested, calm and avuncular.

'Uncle HuffPuff, tell us again how the tabby cats got their stripes.'

'Ah, YesYesYes,' Humphrey began, 'to know this we must go back in time a long, long time. Longer even than Phirish Bunni is old. Longer even than ayoomfas have known how to walk on their hind legs. . .'

'A long, long looonnng time ago,' Bibble observed sagely, nodding his little head with the white chin smudge.

Humphrey continued, 'Back to the time of the very first cat ever, whose name was Poyk. Poyk wasn't born from his mummy like you and your brother, because he had no mummy.'

'Poor Poyk,' said Bibble sadly and sniffed.

'Yes, but this was only because Poyk was the first cat in the world, y'see,' Humphrey said quickly to avoid having both Bibbly-Bobblies in tears and wailing in sympathy for poor, motherless Poyk. 'Poyk hatched from an enormous brown speckled egg. Because Poyk was bigger than any guelph that ever lived, his egg was as big as our house, maybe even bigger.'

'Wow! How did the huuuggge egg get there, Uncle HuffPuff?'

NoNoNo, I'm not going there, Humphrey said to himself. 'The story doesn't say,' he said firmly. 'Poyk had been inside his egg for five long winters and when it was the right time, he pushed against the inside of it with his powerful forepaws.

The huge egg creaked and groaned but it was simply no match for Poyk's immense strength and before long it cracked and splintered in two. Oh Yes! And so Poyk, the first tabby cat - and also the very first cat of all cats in the whole world - was born. Praise be to Poyk!'

'Hooray!! Yay for Poyk!' the Bibbly-Bobblies cheered in unison.

'Now remember that this was long ago and the trees and plants were much bigger than they are today. There were enormous tall trees and plants everywhere and thick green grush much taller than Mummi and Daddi. For many winters Poyk's egg had lain undisturbed in the long grush under a huge tree which had enormous green, leafy fronds with slits in them. Not unlike the plant that grows in the brown potta in our lounj, but much bigger than that. Much, much bigger!'

'As big as the house, Uncle HuffPuff?'

'Bigger, much bigger. The egg was as big as our house and the big tree was as high as the clouds and next to it the egg looked quite tikki.'

'Wow, that's sooo big!' Bibble was always in awe at the scale of things in Humphrey's tales and his eyes grew big and round in amazement.

'Oh YesYes. Poyk climbed out of his egg, stretched and yawned. Then he lay down. It was very pleasant and peaceful under the giant leaves of the tree and the sun shone through the gaps in the leaves. Poyk lifted his head, sniffed the fresh air and greeted the warm sun. It was so peaceful that he dozed off for the whole summer and the sunlight shining through the gaps in the big leaves bleached his warm brown fur into the beautiful shaded stripes that all tabbies have today. Like mine, for example. Oh yes. And even today, wandering tabby singers have a little song they sing about Poyk's stripes:

'Poyk sat and smiled toward the sun
The reign of the tabby had begun
And there he sat for one whole year
Until his stripes they did appear.'

'Yay! Poyk!' the puriks cheered. 'Uncle HuffPuff, how did the other cats come to be?'

'Which other cats?'

'Cats that are not tabby cats. Like Auntie Pipple and me and my brother.'

'Ah well, that also concerns Poyk. Oh yes.' In Humphrey's stories most things did. 'Poyk was feeling lonely and in need of company. He thought about this for many winters until one day he had a marvellous idea while he was sitting on top of a mountain idly blowing the fluffpuffs off a *fluffpuff flower*.'

'What's a fluffpuff flower, Uncle HuffPuff?'

'It's a plant that has a pretty yellow flower in the spring. When the flower is old it changes to a round ball of fluff which is easily blown away in the wind or by passing cats or other guelphs. I suppose you'll see one later in the season; they come up all over around here.'

'Now Poyk watched the fluffpuffs blow away and sink softly to the ground and he noticed that wherever they had fallen, a new fluffpuff flower grew the following spring. And Poyk had a marvellous idea. Oh yes. At sunrise the next day he cleaned his fur very thoroughly - in fact he didn't stop washing the whole day, not even for lunch or a nap. He washed and he washed and then he washed some more. He washed until the sun was nearly set. And then he waited. Yes, he waited. Soon his tummy started to rumble, his chest began to heave and he began to *wark-wark*. Then out of his mouth came the most enormous furball anyone had ever seen.

'How big, Uncle HuffPuff? As big as this. . .?' Bibble had already spread his tiny forepaws wide in expectation.

'The story doesn't say. All we know is that it was the biggest furball that anyone had ever seen. It fell out of Poyk's' mouth and rolled down the rocky mountainside, bumping and bouncing along, and as it gathered speed, bits of it came off and got left behind. Poyk sat and watched it until it reached the bottom of the hill and fell in the river, where it turned into a big fish. This was the first fish ever. And during the night another amazing thing happened: All the bits that had come off Poyk's giant rolling furball grew into other cats. Little cats, big cats - although none as big as Poyk, of course - black and white Woon cats like you and your brother, beautiful orange cats like your Auntie Pipple, ginger cats, white cats, long hairs, short hairs, grumpy greys and Chinese cats like your dead auntie Bunni.

'And big fat blue cats, Uncle HuffPuff?'

'Uh, . .no.'

'But Uncle HuffPuff, I was watching the magic window with Mummi yesterday and I saw this big fat blue cat sitting on a sitz-softah. It was making ayoomfa speaks with a brown gruf. . .'

'We'll talk more about that another day. Now it's time for you to go to sleep so you can grow big and strong.'

*****

118

CHAPTER FIFTEEN:
Return of an old friend

PennyWhistle came back from a long wander one night in a great state of excitement. She was filthy, and spattered with black stinky *oozule* like that which is found under stinkirolis and she had some white powdery substance in her fur. She'd been away for five days, so it was hardly surprising that she was a bit unkempt. She was very hungry and went straightaway to gobble up everyone's leftover food. Even when she was away, Daddi still put food out for her; usually Humphrey ate it under the pretext of avoiding waste. Humphrey was growing quite fat from all these good intentions. After PennyWhistle had eaten her fill and given herself a most thorough wash from tip of nose to tip of tail, she told us her news. She could hardly contain her excitement.

'I found it! Found it at last!' she said, 'I found my old home, with gruf Curious and gruf Naughtiness and my old ayoomfa family.'

'Where?' Humphrey asked.

'It's quite far, nearly three day's journey. You have to go right down to the bottom of the valley, over the stream, and then you have to cross a big, noisy, road that's full of stinkirolis and rumblerolis at all times of day and night. It's actually two roads with a bit of grush between them, and they sit on a kind of long hill about as high as a tree. The stinkirolis come so fast and so often that it's impossible for a cat to cross to the other side without suffering booma-skwasha. I saw lots of unlucky cats which had been booma-skwasha'd on that horrid stinkiroli path. I wasn't going to take a chance, so I walked alongside the big road until I found a long round hole that went through the ground and under the big road from one side to the other. I think the ayoomfas have put it there so that dirty, smelly water can run from one side of the big road to the other. Why they should want to do this, I don't know.'

'Ayoomfas always want to move stuff from where it is to somewhere else,' Humphrey observed, 'They're never happy with the way things are.'

PennyWhistle continued, 'There's a lot of mud and smelly oozule in the long round hole and I got quite dirty, but I made it safely to the other side. From there it's at least another day's walk up the other hill to my old home. There are lots of houses close together and lots of stinkirolis, grufs, and other hazards, which made my journey up the hill take longer than it should have. But I got there in the end.'

'Was your family pleased to see you?' Humphrey asked.

'Yes. They were all delighted to see me. Gruf Curious washed me all over with his huge wet tongue and gruf Naughtiness was so excited he stayed up all night barking.'

'How thoughtful of gruf Naughtiness,' I observed dryly.

'Yes. He told me the ayoomfapuriks had been very sad when I disappeared, fearing I had come to some harm.'

'Why'§ he called gruf Curiou§?' Pipple asked.

'Because he's curious about everything he sees. He likes to ride with the ayoomfas in the stinkiroli with his head sticking out the window, looking at everything as he goes by and barking happily.'

'I would get bored with that in a very few winks,' I said. 'There's nothing much out there but ayoomfas and stinkirolis and more ayoomfas and more stinkirolis. The only place that's free of ayoomfas and their accursed stinkirolis is a place they call the *sea*. Apparently it's just an immense glorpness of water, like a big river that goes on forever.'

That §ound§ even more boring, Pipple said.

'YesYesYes, never mind that now,' Humphrey said, trying to keep the conversation focussed, 'So what happens now, PennyWhistle? Are you going away to live there with gruf Furious. .'

'Curious.'

'Whatever. Or are you going to stay here in our house? As Chief Cat of the House I need to know who I can expect to find living here so I don't attack someone by mistake in the night.'

'Perhap§ §he should commute,' Pipple suggested helpfully.

'She would be on the road five days out of seven.' Humphrey said.

'I must return to my proper home,' PennyWhistle said, 'I've not been unhappy here and your ayoomfa staff have been most kind and trustworthy, but it's not my true home and I miss my family. Especially gruf Curious.'

Humphrey was showing his scorn by washing himself while PennyWhistle spoke to him.

'Really, PennyWhistle!' Mummi and Daddi will be most disappointed,' I chastised her. 'They've gone out of their way to make you feel at home and this is how you thank them! I hope you'll at least have the decency to properly say farewell to them and not just slink off in the night.'

'I'll try, Bunni.'

I must say she did make a good effort. After eating here breakfast she went to commune with Daddi while he sat in the lounj drinking his morning tea. He was quite amazed at her sudden friendliness and eagerly seized the opportunity to give her Face, Full Encapsulation of Head, Chukkachin and Bellyscratch. PennyWhistle set up a loud happi-rumble in vocal appreciation – something she had never done before. After what she thought was an appropriate time, she got up and headed for the little door within a door. Just before she left she turned and looked at Daddi and he looked at her.

'You're leaving for good now, aren't you?' he said kindly. I translated this for PennyWhistle. Somehow Daddi realised what was happening. Her ever longer absences had been a source of concern to the ayoomfas over the past moons and they suspected she might have found another home. 'I'm sorry if you have to leave us, little *PennyWhisssooollle*, but I suppose if you must you must,' Daddi said sadly, 'Wherever you go, go with our love and take care.'

PennyWhistle – SaucyPads – made a little chirrup of appreciation and then she was gone through the little door within a door. We never saw her again.

The Bibbly-Bobblies grew very quickly into fine, healthy young yowlis with a great zest for life. By the time they were four moons old their individual natures began to assert themselves.

Bibble chirruped and mewled and squeaked at just about anything, and was clearly the smarter of the two. He was also lavishly affectionate and doted on his ayoomfa Mummi. She renamed him *Sixpence*. Unusually for a yowli he displayed no interest whatever in hunting. He had tiny prancing paws and curly decorative whiskers - Mummi called them *theatrical* whiskers - and with the white smudge on his face he looked just like the black and white cat whose picture was on the tins of shmoo kukri. Originally the bigger of the two, Sixpence was soon overtaken in size by his brother Bobble, who the ayoomfas had renamed *Choklit*. Choklit was clearly going to grow into a very large cat, maybe even bigger than Humphrey, who thanks to his anti-waste campaign had grown very big indeed. We liked these new names and so adopted them ourselves - just as well, I suppose, for over the next few turns of season Choklit was variously called *Oompah, Le Gouffre, Bosephus, Butch, Simply Large, Largely Simple,* and Daddi occasionally referred to him as *The Palendromic Cat.* Sixpence remained either Sixpence, or *Six Dee.* A cat's name has to be easily callable by an ayoomfa assistant, so they can stick their head out the window and call us when it's supper time: Choklit! Choklit! Suppertime! Most non-callable names - like *The Palendromic Cat* were abandoned after a short while because the ayoomfas felt foolish shouting them out the window.

Choklit was the complete opposite of Sixpence: he was an enthusiastic hunter with magnificent long, thick, straight whiskers and enormous fat paws, but he wasn't the brightest cat around. He was of a terribly nervous disposition, having been traumatized in the Big Fire. He didn't like being picked up and fondled by the ayoomfas and would run away when they tried to pick him up. Mere mention of the word *FIRE* would send him scarpering away in a panic. Humphrey and Sixpence used to tease him about this. Humphrey would casually saunter past him and then stop and suddenly yell *FIRE!* at the top of his voice. Choklit would shoot up into the air and his little legs would already be running furiously by the time he hit the ground again. Humphrey thought this was very funny and he'd ask Sixpence in mock sincerity, 'What happened here, Sixpence?'

'He ran, Uncle HuffPuff.'

'Where did he run, Sixpence?'

'Away.'

'What did he run away from, Sixpence?'

'He ran away from *FIRE!*'

Then they would both launch into boisterous song followed by raucous cackling.

> *Run around with tail on fire*
> *Up a tree but flame go higher*
> *Run in circles 'till he's dizzy*
> *Chokalitzy make a wizzi*
> *Not as brave as you and me*
> *Chikka chikka chooma chee*

There's no accounting for what some cats find amusing. Or some ayoomfas. Even Daddi got into the act sometimes and the game was so well understood that it mattered not that Humphrey couldn't understand ayoomfa-speak and Daddi couldn't speak a work of Khat. I guess it must be a 'male thing'. Daddi would try to pick up Choklit, who would deftly run away. Daddi would then turn to Humphrey and ask, 'What happened here, Humphrey?

'He ran, Daddi.'

'Where did he run, Humphrey?'

'Away, Daddi.'

'What from, Humphrey?'

'He ran away from MAN!'

The inevitable singing would follow and sometimes Daddi would pick up Humphrey and do a little jig.

> *Phraidy phraidy scared of lady*
> *Off he ran scared of man*
> *Choklit phraidy every day*
> *It's always best to run away*

Then Daddi would walk off chuckling to himself. Male creatures are such fools.

Just before the Bibbly-Bobblies had seen a full turn of seasons they were bundled off to the whitecoati for an overnight stay. When they returned the following day they could not remember what happened because they had fallen asleep, but both of them noticed that their seedballs felt very tender indeed.

'The whitecoati has stolen your seedballs,' Uncle Humphrey explained. 'He stole mine, too. Oh YesYesYes.'

'Why, Uncle HuffPuff?' Sixpence asked groggily

'I don't know. Perhaps the ayoomfas eat them as a delicacy? Maybe they collect them as treasures? Maybe they put our cat seed balls into grufs in the hopes that better seedballs will make grufs smarter and less objectionable? I really cannot say. It's one of life's great mysteries.'

At around this time Mummi adopted a moonly ritual of sprinkling smelly white powder on all the cats' fur and rubbing it in with her hands. I have no idea why she did this and like Humphrey with the seedballs, I could merely speculate. Sixpence, Humphrey and Pipple were able to endure the minor discomfort of the powdering through the distraction of watching Choklit's attempts to flee being thwarted by Daddi while Mummi wielded the Powder.

'What happened here, Sixpence?'

'POWDER!'

'What did Choklit do, Sixpence?'

'He ran.'

'Where did he run to, Sixpence?'

'Nowhere, Uncle HuffPuff.'

Why's that, Sixpence?'

'Because Daddi held him down. Hooray! Yay for Daddi!'

Cheers, whistling and the inevitable song.

> *Daddi will come*
> *And powder your bum*
> *He'll sprinkle your tail*
> *And make-a you wail*
> *You get such a fright*
> *From powder so white*

'What do you boys find so hilarious?' I asked them one day.

'He ran away from POWDER!' Sixpence tittered and they both packed up giggling again.

'Humphrey!' I scolded him, 'You are supposed to be setting a good example to the young boys, not encouraging them to be silly.' But it was no use - they were too far gone.

That summer Mummi and Daddi allowed other ayoomfas to come into the house and change the softah that covers most of the floor inside our house. There was nothing wrong with the old softah of course, but as has been mentioned before ayoomfas are seldom content with their lot. The ayoomfas who changed the floor softah caused a tremendous disturbance to our daily rituals by moving things around and making a lot of noise and hitting things with special hitting sticks. Pipple went outside to sleep under her favourite bush, Humphrey was out on perimeter patrol, and the Bibbly Bobblies had taken refuge in the stinkiroli room as this was the only place where they could find a quiet, cool place to nap without being pestered by teams of ayoomfas moving things around. Sixpence found a box of oozule-spattered softahs to sleep in and Choklit crawled underneath Daddi's blue stinkiroli and then up into a dark place inside it, in between the two rounds near the front. This was not a wise move, for this place is truly a very dangerous place for a cat to be. The hot roaring beast that is the digestion of the stinkiroli and which makes it move lives in this dark place. There are things which move so fast they cannot be seen, and other things that hiss and blow, and yet other things that get as hot as the sun. The steaming, green life blood of the stinkiroli runs around in fat water slinkis in this place, and it's really not a sensible place for a little cat to sleep. Choklit thought it was safe because the roaring beast was obviously asleep, so he found a little shelf inside the dark place and dozed off there.

Daddi decided to go out somewhere in the stinkiroli and Choklit suddenly found the roaring beast awakening right next to him. It shook and it trembled and it roared its fury at him. Something round and red in the front began to spin around on a kind of endless track so fast that Choklit could see it only as a blur. Poor Choklit, already of nervous disposition, was as terrified as any cat had ever been and convinced he'd fallen straight into Hell. Pipple had told him about Hell in order to get him to go to sleep one night when he was being naughty and despite my assurances that Tabithat himself had told me Hell didn't exist, Choklit preferred to believe that it did. He always liked to think the plokkits bowl was half empty when it was actually half full and the events of the morning now convinced him he'd been right to believe in Hell. The stinkiroli began to move and Choklit covered his frightened little head with his forepaws thinking *if I can't see it, it can't see me.* But it soon became apparent that this was unwise, for he needed both his forepaws to hold himself from falling off the narrow ledge. The stinkiroli was moving along the bumpy, sandy path that led from the house up to the big grey road with the white stripes on it and Choklit could see sand and rocks and occasional tufts of grush passing beneath him. Instinctively he felt he had get out of this place - and quickly - but the stinkiroli was shaking on the bumpy path and there was a fat round stick that was turning round and round just below him and he feared that if he jumped he would surely hit the spinning stick and be hurt. His little heart was beating so fast he thought it would explode out of his chest and he felt afraid like he'd never been afraid. He so badly wanted to run away, but there was really no place he could run to. He thought wryly how mercilessly Sixpence and Humphrey would tease him if he ever got out of this mess. They'd make up a full paw's pads of new songs about him.

I wafted up into the air and followed the stinkiroli as it trundled along. Daddi was completely oblivious to the plight of poor Choklit in the dark place of the stinkiroli's digestion. The stinkiroli slowed down nearly to a stop at the point where the sandy bumpity path joined the big stinkiroli path, and I willed Choklit to jump off then. He nearly did at that time, but he was just not quick enough and the stinkiroli began to move again, this time on the big grey road with the white stripes on it. It was much smoother than the bumpity path and Choklit felt that at least he wasn't as likely to be shaken off his ledge. But the beast beside him was roaring louder and louder and the stinkiroli was going faster and faster along the big path. The spinning stick was spinning at a furious rate below and the red thing on the endless track in front was blowing a great hot wind at Choklit. To make matters worse the ledge on which he was sitting and clinging onto was becoming uncomfortably warm. The stinkiroli was going so fast that if he did try to jump he might well fall in the path of one of the big black rounds and suffer terminal *booma-skwasha*. I had to make Daddi stop the stinkiroli before Choklit hurt himself. But Daddi couldn't see me or hear me, of this I was certain. I cried for the help of Tabithat like never before.

'Oh please Lord Tabithat, help me get Daddi to stop this stinkiroli before poor little Choklit is killed! If he could see me he would surely stop. I know you think I'm a pest with my difficult questions and all but I really need your help right now!'

I decided to try anyway as I had nothing to lose. The worst that could happen is that Daddi didn't see me and the stinkiroli would pass through me with no effect. I willed myself into the dark place of the stinkiroli where poor little Choklit was sitting in a little pool of wizz, eyes screwed shut, panting in terror and clinging onto the ledge. The whirring red thing on the endless track was blowing so strongly at him and the ledge was getting so hot that Choklit was in real danger of losing his grip. He mewled pathetically at me and I soothed him as much as I could and told him I was going to try with Tabithat's help to get Daddi to stop the stinkiroli. I urged him to hang on just a tiny bit longer then I floated up through the cover of that noisy dark place and sat on top of it on the outside, right in front of the front window of the big blue stinkiroli. I could see Daddi right in front of me. He held onto the stinkiroli's big round leash with one forepaw and had his other forepaw out the window, tapping on the roof of the stinkiroli. I don't know whether or not he saw me but suddenly he looked very startled the stinkiroli slowed down quickly with a loud shrieking noise and I heard an unmistakable *thunk* as Choklit was thrown off his ledge and fell against the spinning stick before tumbling to the hard grey road below. Fortunately none of the stinkiroli's big rounds rolled over him so he didn't suffer *booma-skwasha,* only some *booma without skwasha.*

Daddi had stopped the stinkiroli on the sandy, stony side part of the road and he saw that Choklit was now in even bigger danger. He was lying all alone in the middle of the big grey road with the white stripes and we didn't know if he was hurt or not. What we did know was that a big yellow snorting rumbleroli was rapidly approaching and would certainly roll over him. It was easily the biggest rumbleroli I had ever seen. It had a silver smoke pipe big enough for a small cat to walk in that belched out sooty black smoke and made gurgling noises from the rumbleroli's digestion. Daddi ran bravely down the road shouting and waving his forepaws in the air to make the big yellow rumbleroli stop. Luckily the ayoomfa inside it saw him from a long way off - Daddi didn't have my problem that ayoomfas couldn't see him - and slowed his rumbleroli to a hissing and grunting halt several trees' distance away from where Choklit lay dazed and confused and very vulnerable in the middle of the big grey road with white stripes. As we approached Choklit we saw that there was no obvious sign of injury from the booma without skwasha, and he groggily stood up on his little feet. He was clearly dazed and didn't know what had happened to him, but when he saw *MAN!* running towards him shouting and waving his forepaws about, his eyes darted from side to side while his dazed mind tried to decide whether he should run away, and if so, where to. There was long grush on both sides of the road, but now other stinkirolis were coming along it in the opposite direction and Daddi couldn't possibly stop them all.

'Please, Choklit' said Daddi, as he approached Choklit as calmly as he could. 'Don't run away now. Just this once. If you run away you will be killed. I'm going to pick you up and get you out of the road. Let me pick you up. Please, my boy.'

I translated for Choklit and urged him to be still. He braced to dart away but I gave him a stern look and said firmly, 'No! Do as I say! Keep still.'

Daddi picked Choklit up and took him inside the blue stinkiroli. He briefly examined him for serious injuries and found none, although Choklit was clearly very dazed and confused. Daddi put him on the front seat of the stinkiroli, turned it around and rolled home again. He called Mummi and explained what had happened, and they took Choklit inside the house and made a big fuss of him while they examined him from head to tail. He had had a very lucky escape although he'd had a nasty bang on the head and we didn't know if or how this would affect him in the longer term. Sixpence and Humphrey came to see what was going on.

'What happened to my bruvver?' Sixpence clamoured in alarm.

'*ROAD!*' Choklit mewled pathetically, '*ROAD!*'

'He suffered serious booma-without-skwasha on the big grey road with white stripes.' I explained and watched Choklit as Sixpence and Humphrey licked his head and the ayoomfas made a big fuss of him. There was something eerily familiar about Choklit which I'd never noticed until now. Suddenly, he looked up and when his shiny blue-green eyes met mine I knew exactly what it was that was so familiar.

'Hullo, Old Lady,' he said, 'we meet again.'

'Butch?'

'Yes, it's me, Butch. I'm back!'

'How? Why? Tabithat told me you were in his workshop.'

'I was. But I got bored just making beds all the time and I missed you. I asked Tabithat if I could come back for a while and he arranged for this to take place. I had to wait for just the right moment. Choklit fell out of the stinkiroli's digestion box and gave his head a hard knock against something. He had a *little death* for a few seconds and that's when I seized the moment to inhabit his body.'

'So where is Choklit now?'

'Oh he's here with me, too. There was plenty of spare space in his head, it wasn't very full. We're all part of the same cat, now. When he woke up and found me there with him he had a bit of a panic and I had to really work hard just to stop him running away foolishly into the path of the stinkirolis or into the long grush. But he's calmed down now because he's back home and he's safe.'

'What should I call you?' I asked. 'Choklit? Butch? Choklit-Butch?'

'I don't mind, old lady. Whatever pleases you at the time. Now what's for supper?' I watched in astonishment as Choklit. . .Butch. . . trotted off to the Food Room and soon I heard the familiar crunching of plokkits.

I never did find out whether Daddi saw me or not when I sat on the front lid of his stinkiroli that day, as he never made any mention of it to anybody. Humphrey and Sixpence changed their attitude to Choklit after *ROAD!* It was understood by all that Choklit had been magnificently brave through a dreadful ordeal and Humphrey declared him to be a *Hero* of *the House.* They even resisted the urge to sing about *MAN!* and *POWDER!* or call him a phraidy cat when he trotted away from Daddi. The presence of Butch in Choklit went a long way to stop him from being so foolish and fearful. *ROAD!* had made him into a better cat.

*****

CHAPTER SIXTEEN:
Shufa happens

Sometime after *ROAD!* an event took place which had a major impact on all of our lives. Pipple, Humphrey, and the two black and white Woon boys had become nicely settled in sunny Midrand and I was simply waiting patiently for a bed to become available in Tabithat's House in the Sky. The ayoomfarolês, however, were not nicely settled at all.

From what I could understand Midrand, Harvard and Vietnam were all parts of a bigger place which the ayoomfas called *Sowf Efrika*. There was a great glorpness of very bad ayoomfas - Mummi called them *criminals* and Daddi called them *scumbags* - around in Sowf Efrika at that time. These scumbags could be likened to cats like the wicked Grondus, who simply enter someone's house and start eating the food, making themselves at home and bullying the cats they found there. Like Grondus the scumbags had no respect for Khat Lore and went around stealing everything they could get their forepaws on and hurting and killing anything or anybody who happened to get in their way. For the ayoomfarolês it was like Humphrey having to contend with six cats like evil Grondus every day and it was wearing them down. Our house had big fence gates on all the doors and all the windows and we'd been lucky up to that point not to have had any bad experiences with scumbags. Of course Humphrey said confidently that he could deal with any eventuality and protect us, but we all knew that this was just big speaks from the Chief Cat of the House who didn't want to lose face.

One night Mummi and Daddi went out. This itself was bad, and we took pains to actively discourage them from going out. After all it was totally unnecessary for them to go out - they had food in store and they had all of us to keep them company and to play with, so what more could they possibly want? I fail to see why they felt the compulsion to go out. Despite our disapproval they continued to go out from time to time and we usually punished them with a conspicuous bloik-bloik when they returned. But I digress - Mummi and Daddi went out in Mummi's little red stinkiroli at about sunset. They'd been gone for a good few naps and it was fully dark when one of the Woon boys noticed several ayoomfas prowling around outside our house, some of them carrying big sticks made of hard stuff. They stopped and peered into each window as they crept around the house. Pipple went around and gathered up Humphrey and the Woons and we sat in the dark watching the ayoomfas outside.

'I'll take care of this,' Humphrey said, bravely but nervously.

'Please don't, Humphrey,' I urged him, 'There are four of them and I've heard Mummi and Daddi talk about ayoomfa scumbags like these. They'll not hesitate to kill you if you stand in their way. They would even kill Daddi or Mummi if they tried to stop them.'

'But Daddi is big and he has a bangstick . . .' Humphrey protested in disbelief.

'So do the kriminils. Mummi says they often have very sharp shiny sticks which are called *nives* and which can cut meat easily. Mummi has some of these in the Food Room which she uses to cut up cackacks, fish, and water slinkis. But the scumbags don't use their nives to cut up cackacks and water slinkis - the scumbags use them to cut up other ayoomfas. These scumbags will kill any cat who stands in their way, no matter how brave he is. Please don't go to them, Humphrey. If you get killed who will help raise the Woon boys and teach them the finer points of Khat Lore? Who will be Chief Cat of the House and ward off other cats like the evil Grondus? No, it's a bad idea to confront them. I have a much better plan.

'What? *You* try and stop them?'

'No. My plan is we all run away out of the little door within a door and hide in the long grush outside until these scumbags have gone.'

'It i§ a good plan,' said Pipple, nodding wetly and wisely.

'Yay! Let's all run away!' cheered Choklit-Butch with great enthusiasm. 'All run away! Run away from *SCUMBAGS!* Run away, run away!' He was delighted that at last some of his ideas had found favour. 'Come, Uncle HuffPuff, come Sixpence. . . come Auntie Pipple. . . I say we should all run away at once. Follow me; I'm Hero of the House. . .'

We did just that.

We all sat in the dark, in the long grush and watched the scumbags at work. There were four of them and they all wore dark covering softahs. One of the stick-carriers stuck his hard stick under the *roli-rumble door* of the stinkiroli room and split it open wide enough for him to crawl inside. Once inside the stinkiroli room he could go anywhere he liked in the house. Another scumbag stuck his hard stick in one of the big fence gates that covered the window-door of the room where Balune's big basking tay-bill stood. The fence gate creaked and groaned as it fought the scumbag's hard stick, but it soon sprang open with a loud bang and before long all the scumbags were inside our house. Outrage! And they smelled horrible, which polluted our house and was further outrage.

I kept a wary hover as I entered the house, which was probably totally unnecessary. Even if they were from that small group of ayoomfas who could see me - what could they possibly do to me? Even if I stayed motionless in front of them and they set upon me with everything they had, what could they achieve? I was a disembodied apparition and quite immune to all their hatred. I guess that for a Phirish the fact that nobody can do anything to you goes quite far to make up for the fact that you can't do anything yourself to anything or anyone. However I didn't want to provoke them unnecessarily and cause them to wax spiteful and make Big Fire in the house or do shufa on the floor or anything like that.

Two of the scumbags had pulled the mujaji fire strings out the back of the magic window and most of Daddi's boxes of the Great Noise. Daddi would be very sad about this because I'd learned that he'd made many of these boxes of the Great Noise himself, and it had taken him a long time. Daddi must have carefully crafted every aspect of the invisible fire mujaji inside these boxes so that the Great Noise was as loud and terrible and cacophonic as it was possible for a Great Noise to be. The third scumbag had collected other stuff they wanted to steal, such as the box with all Mummi and Daddi's shiny eating sticks, and then he and the fourth one had gone up the bumpity hill to the Up House. They found the roomi in the sleeping room where the bangsticks were kept hidden behind the ayoomfa body coverings. The bangsticks were kept in a special *bangstick box* all of their own; it was very heavy and made of strong hard stuff and could not easily be opened unless one had the special magic shiny stick that opened it. The bangstick box was so powerful and strong that I think it could even survive booma-skwasha from a big rumbleroli, or resist attack by several vicious grufs. The scumbags clearly knew this and with the help of their big sticks of hard stuff they simply tore it unopened out of its hole in the wall, leaving mess and dust everywhere and a hole in the side of Mummi's roomi which would make her very cross.

The scumbags collected all the things they wanted to steal and loaded the stuff into Daddi's blue stinkiroli, and they found its set of shiny jingling starting sticks hanging up where he always kept it. Their stealing Daddi's blue stinkiroli would undoubtedly make him terribly furious, because I had watched him build it himself while we were at Harvard and he used to spend many naps washing it with water and bubbles and doing unknown things to its digestion. In fact Mummi said afterwards that their stealing Daddi's blue stinkiroli would save him a lot of time that he would otherwise have spent washing it with water and bubbles and tinkering with its digestion. But Daddi didn't see this as a good thing. Scumbags one to four got into the blue stinkiroli and rolled off up the dusty, bumpy track leading to the big grey road with white stripes, known forever as Choklit's *ROAD!* At the top of the track they turned onto the big grey road and rolled away.

I went back to my friends hiding in the grush and briefly told them what had happened. They were outraged and agreed that I should follow the scumbags and see where they went, so a few winks later I was sitting brazenly in my usual place on the back window ledge of the blue stinkiroli as it rolled along with the four scumbags inside, all chattering to each other and laughing. Although they spoke a different ayoomfaspeaks to Mummi and Daddi and I could not understand it, I sensed they were all very pleased with what they had accomplished during their stealing spree. They were sweaty and dirty and were making Daddi's nice blue stinkiroli filthy and stinky inside. Ayoomfas in general do not smell nice like cats do, but these four scumbags smelled really terrible, like sour bloik-bloik and oozule. If Daddi ever got his stinkiroli back again he would have to wash it with water and bubbles for a whole day to get it clean, and he might even have to use the magic white stuff from the spitting tin that he uses to clean up Choklit's bloik-bloik.

The stinkiroli left the part of Midrand I knew and headed east, and for a while there were few houses to be seen. After the time of a nap or two it turned into a place where other ayoomfas lived, but it was unlike any I'd come across. All the roads were dusty and bumpy, much like the sandy track from our house to Choklit's *ROAD!* And instead of proper houses with walls, windows, doors and a lid, there were ragged constructions made from all manner of box, mud, stones, bits of stinkiroli, noose peppers, bits of big cracklesacks, and sometimes even bits of the big blue and white flat boards with ayoomfa markings on them that one sees alongside the roads. The lids of these dwellings were mostly held down with rocks, so they wouldn't blow away in the woo-woo. I could see no magic suns in this place, certainly none along the rough tracks that passed for roads. And judging from the foul smell of the place, there were not that many shufa bowls that worked properly, or maybe the ayoomfas living in this place hadn't yet mastered the proper use of their special water magic. I saw dirty little ayoomfapuriks running around, some of them without any covering softahs. I saw a man make shufa on the side of the track, without even bothering to scrape out a hole. I saw an old woman have her cracklesack ripped from her arms by two young ayoomfas who ran away with it, after kicking her own to the ground with their hind feet. It was not surprising that the four scumbags came from here, as this dreadful place was clearly a fertile breeding ground for all kinds of badness. The civilizing effect of Khat Lore was completely absent here. But why did these ayoomfas live in this disgusting place when others lived peacefully in the clean bright houses of Midrand and had magic suns to light their way and cats to serve? What made it happen one way or the other? I suppose these ayoomfas were the equivalent of the lean and hungry cats that eked out a living from the Gone Bags left outside, or hunted from the wilds - a life of which I'd had some experience in Vietnam and narrowly escaped thanks to MyGranni. I began to feel quite sorry for the ayoomfas in this awful place, but then it occurred to me that even lean and hungry cats make the effort cover up their shufa, so I decided wouldn't waste further pity on these ayoomfas.

My four scumbags stopped the blue stinkiroli behind a dwelling with mud walls and a lid made from wrinkly hard sheet and held down with rocks. It had no door at all, just a flapping sheet of shiny softah hanging down over the opening where the door should be. They carried all my Daddi's boxes of the Great Noise, our magic window, the bangstick box, and our box of shiny eating sticks into their house and then set about drinking happy-water from tins and loudly cheering their success.

The scumbags had no magic suns in their house. All they had was a *magic night stick*. The magic night stick is a clever ayoomfa device, although not often used in our house. Daddi launches a frantic scrabble in the dark to find one when the magic of the magic suns is broken. He makes a small fire on the top of the magic night stick and this burns for a long time, making a small light so he and Mummi don't fall and hurt themselves in the dark. The magic night stick becomes shorter as the night wears on and it sacrifices itself to make light for the ayoomfas. A very noble object indeed.

Their not having any magic suns means the scumbags wouldn't get far trying to work all my Daddi's boxes of the Great Noise, because these needed the mujaji of invisible fire to make them work, and it's the same mujaji which makes the magic suns work. But their lack of foresight or facilities seemed not to trouble them. One of them was trying to open the bangstick box, with no success. His friends then attacked it with huge, heavy beating sticks and even an amazing kind of mujaji fire slinki which made a small, roaring blue-white fire, the like of which I'd never seen before. It had two enormous round tins, which I assumed held all the stored fire, and the fire came out of the end of a long slinki and was very hot. I wondered why there were two tins of stored fire. Perhaps one tin stored the blue part of the fire and the other tin stored the white part? In any event all this clever mujaji came to nought and was a waste of time. The scumbags did not succeed in opening my Daddi's all-powerful bangstick box. All they managed to do was make a lot of unpleasant noise and a stinking smoke, and one of them somehow burned his hind paw on the magic fire slinki and jumped around shouting and spitting angrily on one leg while rubbing his wound. Good! Hooray!

Daddi's powerful bangstick box proved stronger than them and after a while the scumbags gave up trying to open it. They then spent the time of several long naps raucously laughing, celebrating, drinking happi-water and breathing smoke from little white sticks which they set on fire and put in their mouths. Eventually they stumbled into the house and collapsed asleep on softahs on the floor, leaving my Daddi's blue stinkiroli outside their mud house, gleaming incongruously in the moonlight.

Silence at last. I heard a cat mewl unhappily somewhere in the distance and pitied the poor creature for living here. I was enraged at the acts of these criminals and terribly frustrated because it was clear there was absolutely nothing I could do to avenge the insult to my ayoomfarolês. But I derived some sense of justice from the fact that the four sleeping scumbags would continue to live in this shufahole of an ayoomfa settlement, while I could simply float back to my house in Midrand, which had Mummi and Daddi and magic suns in all the many rooms.

*****

The invasion of the scumbags left Mummi permanently outraged and Daddi smarting over the theft of his blue stinkiroli and his various Boxes of the Great Noise. Although all the cats felt very sorry for him it was generally considered that there was a greater level of peace and *wa* in our house without the Boxes of the Great Noise. Mummi and Daddi had many serious ayoomfa-talks about the badness caused by criminals in Sowf Efrika and what they could do about this. They began to hatch a conspiracy which revolved around the idea of them leaving Sowf Efrika and going to some place called Brittin, which I gathered was far away, over the sea. At first I was very alarmed that they were plotting to abandon us, but it soon became clear that the plan was to capture us and take us to Brittin, too. I reported the gist of the conspiracy to my companions.

'Mummi and Daddi are planning to go to a place far away over the sea.'

'They should run away,' said Choklit. 'It's best.'

'A Hero of the House should never run away,' Humphrey admonished him sternly.

'What about us?' Sixpence asked worriedly, 'Who is going to feed us and look after our house? We can't stay here without our ayoomfas!'

'Nonsense! I did just fine without them before and I'll do just fine without them again. YesYesYes! Bunni knows this is true. She also had to look after herself. If they want to betray us and run away, let them. . .'

Choklit blinked impassively and said, 'Yes. Run away. It's best.'

Humphrey was very cross.

'NoNoNo! Why should we run away? This is our house and we can stay here by ourselves if they desert us.'

'Actually, the ayoomfarolês are not planning to leave us here,' I explained. 'They love us greatly and would never do that. They intend to capture us and take us away with them to Brittin.'

'Yes. All run away. It's best. .' Choklit said.

'Oh shut up, you fool!' Humphrey snapped at him, 'You're like a silly bizzum trying to get out of a window! By Tabithat, Bunni, this is heaping outrage upon outrage! So we have a choice of being abandoned in our house or being kidnapped and taken away from our house. I'm not sure which is worse.'

'Actually, we don't have that choice. Mummi and Daddi *will* capture us and take us to Brittin.'

'Supposing, just supposing, mind you, for it's not going to happen, but supposing we agree to let ourselves be captured, how will they get us to this Brittin place? You said it was far away over the sea.'

'They say we will fly there,' I said, sadly aware that this would illicit a great deal of scorn and controversy.

'No, no §illy Bunni! C§hirrit§ fly in the §ky, but cat§ can't fly. I tried my§elf a long time ago but I kept falling down in the grus§h. It §imply doe§n't work,' Pipple said, chuckling. This triggered Sixpence into uproarious laughter.

'Yay! Fly like a chirrit! Wheee whooo. . .' he sang, standing upright on his hind legs and paddling the air with his little forepaws.

'YesYesYes, don't be silly.' Humphrey was in no mood for jokes.

'We don't actually fly ourselves. Ayoomfas will put us in boxes. . .'

'Not boxes! NoNoNo! I hate boxes!' Humphrey spat in fear and disgust. 'I knew this was all a bad idea. . .'

'Box§e§ are very, very bad. . .'

'Run away.' Choklit said mechanically.

'Please stop saying that, Butch,' I told him, 'It's not at all helpful. I know you're just pretending to be stupid so that nobody will know you're inside there. Anyone who can outwit the Khat Khouncile is no fool.'

But the idea of boxes had not been well received at all. Humphrey was growling to himself in anger, Pipple was splattering sibilant protests to all in spitting distance and little Sixpence was panting in distress. I struggled to make myself heard above the indignant clamour.

'No listen! Please listen to me! The boxes are big and comfortable, with softah wubbis and plenty of food and water.'

'What sort of food?' Humphrey asked. The magic word had piqued his curiosity.

'There'll cackack carcass for sure,' I said, hoping this would appease him. 'And lots of plokkits. It works like this: Ayoomfas saw the chirrits fly and they also wanted to fly, but they found they couldn't. Like Pipple, they probably tried and found they just fell down in the grush.'

'Ye§§h. I . . .'

'Later, Pipple. So they made these big hard shiny constructions that look like chirrits and these things can fly with ayoomfas inside them. The ayoomfa name for them is *error plain*. You must have seen them in the sky over Midrand sometimes?

They make a loud roaring noise like the sound of a great glorpness of shufa bowls all making their water magic at the same time. The ayoomfas and the boxes with cats inside them go inside the error plain and the error plain flies to Brittin.'

'This is utter nonsense! I've seen those hard shiny chirrit things flying about and when I look up at them they are only about the size of a big bizzum. Not even as big as my paw! It's not possible to fit an ayoomfa inside them.'

'No, trust me. It can be done. I saw a picture on a noose pepper of one of these error plains on the ground with some ayoomfas standing next to it and it was much, much bigger than them. One could easily fit glorp ayoomfas and glorp boxes inside and maybe even some stinkirolis as well.'

'Maybe they were very tiny ayoomfa§ in the picture you §aw, Bunni. Tiny ayoomfa-krorli§ or §something,' Pipple suggested. Like Humphrey she preferred to believe her own eyes than my fanciful tale.

'Maybe they will use *tiny magic* to squash us very small like tiny krorlis,' Sixpence suggested. 'Then we could go inside the hard shiny chirrit to Brittin. Yay for Brittin!'

'It'§ po§§ible,' Pipple nodded sagely, 'We do know that ayoomfa§ have a very powerful mujaji whi§ch can make all kind§ of thing§ §mall enough to fit in the magic window.'

'Run away. It's best,' Choklit said.

'Yes, well on careful consideration he's quite right,' Humphrey said, 'I see no alternative. We must make a Big Runaway. We will stay in our house. We must never allow ourselves to be captured, put in boxes, made tiny like krorlis, or stuffed inside a chirrit. Be always on your guard and be prepared for capture at any time of day or night.'

Operation Runaway made us all look stupid. Every time an ayoomfa passed by - often on a perfectly innocent journey to make shufa in the little washing room - we would all flee as fast as we could, scrabbling to beat each other to the safety of the outdoors through our little door within a door. The ayoomfas must have thought we were very foolish. We all lost face several times a day and would try to conceal our embarrassment by stopping our panicked flight in our tracks and washing diligently. By the end of each day we were spotlessly clean and our tongues ached. The Woon boys were by this time growing yowlis and sometimes it slipped their minds that they were no longer tikki puriks. One such time Choklit-Butch was so desperate to get through the little door within a door and run away that he tried to force himself through it at the same time as his brother Sixpence with the result that they both got stuck in the door for a while. Choklit-Butch set up a desperate howling which inevitably caused Daddi to come see what all the fuss was about. When he saw the two Woon boys stuck in the door with Choklit-Butch's hind paws paddling frantically but ineffectively skidding and slipping on the hard shiny of the floor, Daddi laughed uproariously and took the opportunity to tickle Choklit-Butch's tail while he was helpless and unable to escape. In panic Choklit-Butch squirted him with *brown stink juice* from his shufa hole which caused Daddi to immediately cease laughing and go away to wash and change all his body coverings. He was very cross.

Pipple's participation in Operation Runaway was limited because she didn't really do running. She employed Khat Stealth Knowledge to move along in a kind of silent, phluffi glide that drew little attention to her passing. Another reason for her lack of fervour for Operation Runaway was that she grew a kind of pimple on her eyelid that was not unlike my famous nose pimple. This concerned the ayoomfas greatly and Pipple was bundled off to the whitecoati several times. In the end the whitecoati stole Pipple's eye, much like he'd stolen Humphrey's and the Woon boys' seedballs. Tabithat save us from these thieving creatures!

Pipple, however, wasn't overly distressed about the theft of her eye.

'At lea§t my eye doe§n't hurt anymore,' she said. 'It wa§ getting §o §ore I couldn't keep it open for long anyway. I remember Gruf Bakerloo had only one eye and he managed ju§t §plendidly.' For a few pads of days she was apt to bump into things, but she soon adapted to her changed circumstances and carried on gliding around in a stealthy, phluffi manner as if nothing had happened.

After a moon of us all darting about like nervous blue-head cackacks while no ayoomfarolê made the slightest attempt to make Capture on any of us, we came to the conclusion that the anticipated mutiny of our servants was no longer imminent, and we relaxed and reassumed our normal unstressed pace of life.

Having forgotten about Operation Runaway Humphrey resumed his normal duties as a Godfather, and set about teaching the Woon boys to hunt, fight, make unpleasant wailing noises, mark territory with wizz and various other things considered important to yowlis. To explain the art of hunting he took them outside. Then he went into the long grush and caught a tikki squee as a teaching aid which he carried back to the boys in his mouth and released in front of them. He'd been careful not to damage it too much and the tikki squee sat for a moment looking dazed and unhappy, before it started to totter off hoping desperately against hope that these were nice cats that only ate vejtibils.

'Now catch it and kill it like I explained to you, by biting it on the neck and holding it in the bite until it's stopped breathing,' Humphrey instructed. With instinct and the added benefit of Butch's vast experience, Choklit proved to be an adept pupil, for he immediately seized the hapless squee and summarily bit its head right off in one great chomp. Then before anyone could stop him, he gulped the rest of the squee down his gullet, scarcely bothering to chew it at all. Humphrey was not pleased and scolded him severely.

'NoNoNo! That's not what I told you to do, you greedy little cat! I wanted to teach you several important things, but you just gobbled the squee down almost whole before I had a chance! Shame on you, Choklit!' But Choklit just sat there, licking his lips and blinking impassively.

'Now listen carefully, boys: When the squee is dead - and only when it is dead - you may begin to eat it. Not before. To eat any creature live - except a bizzum - is a very bad thing and is only done by slinkis. It's against Khat Lore.'

Choklit burped suddenly and looked somewhat unsettled.

Sixpence asked, 'Uncle HuffPuff, why is it alright to eat a live bizzum but not a live squee?'

'Khat Lore doesn't say why, but we must always trust Khat Lore. Now pay attention: there is no one correct way you should eat a squee but it is vitally important to take out the *blibble*. . .'

'Oooooh I feel sick,' Choklit moaned, 'I think I'm going to make bloik-bloik. . .'

'Yes, well I'm not surprised,' Humphrey said.

Choklit began to heave and make a horrible squawking sound like those huge water-chirrits do when they're calling for a mate, with his eyes crossed like some demented creature, and before long he'd retched up the chewed remains of the squee. He sat looking unhappily at it, uncertain whether to try eat it again or ignore it.

'I was just about to tell you that if you eat the blibble, you *will* be sick. But I guess you wanted to find this out for yourself.'

'What's a blibble, Uncle HuffPuff?' asked Sixpence. Choklit continued to simply sit and stare queasily at the vomited squee.

'All food animals have a blibble inside them. It's a green-grey thing about the size of your little nose and it tastes bitter and absolutely horrible if you happen to bite into it. It will always make you bloik-bloik if you swallow it, so I strongly advise to always rip it out and cast it aside. I will show it to you but as you can see I need a new squee - I can't use this one anymore, Choklit has ruined it. You boys please wait here for me and I'll go hunt down another one.' Humphrey ambled off into the long grush, sighing in exasperation.

After the time of two naps he returned with another tikki squee.

'Sixpence, this one's for you,' he said, 'I want you to kill it like I told you, but that's all. Don't do anything else.' Humphrey placed the live squee down in front of Sixpence and it started to move towards him. Sixpence became most alarmed and covered his eyes with his little paws.

'Oooh - eee! I forgot what to do!' he cried in panic, 'Oooh - aah it's coming closer! Help me, Uncle HuffPuff!'

'Don't be such a phraidy cat!' Choklit said scornfully.

'Yes come on, Sixpence, it's only a squee and it can't hurt you. Cats should not be afraid of squees. NoNoNo. It's against the spirit of Khat Lore. Now catch it in your paws and kill it by biting it on the neck - it's very easy. Don't bite it head right off like Choklit did; that's totally unnecessary.'

'Sorry, Uncle HuffPuff, but I can't stand it. See how it's looking at me with it's tikki eyes! I just can't bring myself to hurt it.'

'By Tabithat, you boys really are a useless pair of cats! Totally useless, both of you. Oh, YesYesYes. I don't know what you youngsters are coming to nowadays, I really don't. What's so difficult about catching a squee? Now watch and I'll show you one more time.' With that, Humphrey swatted the squee down with a massive forepaw and grabbed it around the neck in his powerful jaws.

Choklit watched in interest with his head cocked to one side and licked his lips.

'Oooh - eee!' wailed Sixpence in dismay, and he ran away.

'Hey hey hee hee. He ran away from a squee! Phraidy cat phraid. . .'

'Shut up, Chocolate! Sixpence, come back here at once! I am your Godfather and these lessons are compulsory. YesYesYes! It's no good hiding behind that bush, I know you are there. Just because you can't see me it doesn't mean that I can't see you.'

Sixpence slowly poked his head around the bush and walked reluctantly back to his lesson.

'Sorry, Uncle HuffPuff,' Sixpence muttered, eyes downcast in embarrassment. He'd lost a lot of face.

'You'll never be Hero of the House,' Choklit smirked unkindly.

'Leave him alone, Choklit. You have an unfair advantage. Remember you weren't always Hero of the House and it wasn't long ago we were all laughing and singing at you running away from *POWDER!*'

Sixpence gingerly walked up to the squee, shut his eyes tight and grabbed it around the neck.

'Sixpence, I have killed this squee already, so you don't have to kill it again. It's dead already and it won't get any more dead. What you have to do now is tear it open and take out the blibble.' Sixpence looked as if the mere idea was going to cause him to make bloik-bloik and he swallowed nervously.

'But Uncle HuffPuff, maybe it's not dead. Maybe it's only pretending to be dead and it might really be alive. Then I'd be disrespecting Khat Lore. P'raps if we leave it alone now and come back tomorrow. . .'

Choklit could contain himself any longer. Here was a delicious freshly killed squee about to go to waste just because his stupid brother was too much of a phraidy cat to get his paws bloodied tearing it open. Before anyone could stop him, Choklit darted forward, seized the squee in his mouth and ran away with it.

'NoNoNo, this is too much!' Humphrey lamented, 'You two boys are something else, really! I don't know which of you is worse. Go ask Auntie Pipple to teach you to hunt.' And he turned around and shambled back inside the house, shaking his head in despair.

*****

CHAPTER SEVENTEEN:
Cats that fly

When it happened it took us all by complete surprise. Capture! We all thought the ayoomfas had abandoned their foolish whim of taking us to Brittin in an error plain. Neither of them had even spoken of it in my presence - let alone in front of the four living cats they could see - for several moons. Most days they just waffled on with their usual interminable drivel about work and peppers and criminals and how the khouncile and something called the *guvvamint* were both full of scumbags.

It happened in the early afternoon when all my friends were having a well deserved sleep inside the house, out of the hot summer sun. Daddi picked up Humphrey, as he often did in order to play with him or cuddle him. Humphrey gave a sleepy grumble as he usually did when so disturbed, but saw nothing amiss. The next thing he knew Daddi had carried him into the stinkiroli room and put him inside a big box he'd never seen before. Pipple was already inside, fast asleep. And within a few blinks of an eye the innocently dozing Woon boys had also been captured and put inside another box. The boxes were big and comfortable with windows covered by fence. They smelled new and clean and we could tell they had not had cats inside them before. Each contained two beds, a bowl of plokkits and a bowl of water. There was enough space for a cat to pace around in little circles, which Humphrey immediately and anxiously began to do. A strange ayoomfa woman with a small stinkiroli had sneaked in with these boxes whilst my friends had been asleep in the heat of the day and it was clear that the woman was about to load the boxes into her stinkiroli and take them Tabithat knows where. She was evidently a conniving party to this wicked Capture and Box conspiracy. Mummi and Daddi were clearly riddled with guilt over their disgraceful behaviour and were sadly crooning their goodbyes and apologies to each of my friends in turn. Sixpence was afraid and making little squeaks of fear, but Choklit-Butch seemed to be peacefully resigned to his situation.

'What are they saying? What are they saying! Where are we going? HeyHeyHey?' Humphrey urged me to translate the ayoomfaspeaks. He was pacing around the box in great frustration.

'Mummi says not to be frightened. . .' I started to explain.

'That's easy for her to say - she's not been captured in a box!'

'Mummi don't leeeave meeeow!!!' Sixpence wailed.

'. . .Mummi says she's sorry that she put you in a box, but you're going away to a new home and she and Daddi will come there soon. You're going on an error plain to some place called *Kworren Teen*, which is in Brittin. It will be exciting, she says.

'Daddi says he loves you all and will give you all big Huggitty-Bumpity and Full Encapsulation of Head when he sees you again soon after you get to Kworren Teen. He says you must be good cats and not bite or scratch anybody. Mummi says she has to go now or else she will cry.'

'Mummi, pleeease don't leeeave us!' wailed little Sixpence, 'There's room in my box for you - look, I'll sit in the corner like this. Come with us, Mummi. Please.'

'Don't worry my puriks. I'll come with you,' I said, and I placed myself in the box between Sixpence and Choklit. Now Mummi was crying. Daddi held her in big huggity.

'§§§shu§§shh, you boy§! I'm trying to §leep here,' Pipple protested.

'How can you sleep at a time like this? When. . when . .when we are in such peril!' Humphrey snapped irritably and clipped her on the ear.

As the stranger's stinkiroli trundled up the dusty path towards Choklit's *ROAD!*, we had our last view of our fine house in Midrand, with its memories of Phat Balune and Butch. With all its many trees and long grush and exciting hunting places. Mummi and Daddi stood outside waving to us and we gazed longingly at them until we couldn't see them anymore.

We tried asking the woman in the stinkiroli what was going on and where we were being taken, but not surprisingly she didn't understand any Khat and simply crooned silly lullabies at us in an endeavour to dupe us into sleeping quietly. Humphrey was not going to sleep quietly.

'Hey You! Hey Missus Capture! Where you taking us? You can't do this, you know. NoNoNo! We are Citizens of a House and we got rights. YesYesYes, for sure. What do you think you doing, HeyHeyHey?' He continued this angry tirade for a long time, occasionally asking me to translate what Missus Capture was saying or singing. 'What's she saying now, Bunny? HeyHeyHey? What's she saying?'

'She says nobody's going to harm us and everything will be alright,' I translated.

'Bah! Meeeeowl!' Humphrey snarled, 'What about the harm to our dignity? What about our loss of face being captured? Bet she didn't figure on that, NoNoNo! Hey, Mrs. Capture if you stick your softclaws anywhere near this box I swear I'll bite them and drag you right through these little holes in the fence thing, big as you are! Meeeoooowoowwwwl!' He shouted, ending with a particularly loud growl.

'She's now singing an ayoomfa song about cats being in a cradle,' I told Humphrey.

'What's a cradle, for Tabithat's sake?'

'The song doesn't say. It may be a name for one of these big boxes. But the underlying theme of it is of peace and quiet and everything being okay, so I don't think it's a bad thing. Oh, that song's stopped now. She's singing a song to help little ayoomfa puriks go to sleep.'

'For Tabithat's sake! Do you see any ayoomfa puriks here? No. Because there aren't any. So she's either stupid, blind, or both. Yeeeoooowwwl!'

'Mummi and Daddi promised they would see us soon and take us to a new house, and they've always been good to us. I see no reason not to believe them. Just take it easy and stop ripping all your fur out like that.'

After a while Humphrey realised the futility of expending such an effort making a big fuss and he settled down to a long drink of water. He had shouted himself almost hoarse and could barely croak out another word. Pipple was still asleep and Sixpence had cried himself to sleep quietly. Butch had been asleep but he suddenly woke up and cocked his head to one side quizzically, then began to look extremely fearful.

'I can hear the screaming wind,' he said, 'Wake up, Sixpence, it's the screaming wind. We must run away! Now!' Sixpence woke up.

'Yes, I can hear it too,' Sixpence said, 'But we can't run away, there's been Capture and we're in a box.'

I didn't want panic to spread, so I said as calmly as I could, 'Don't be afraid, my boys, it's not the screaming wind. It's the noise made by error plains. I've been out on the roof of the stinkiroli and I can see we're getting close to what I think is an eating and drinking place for error plains. They are all gathered around a big building that is many, many, many times the size of our house and which has what I think are feeding things sticking out of it. The error plains seem to be lapping at these tubes. I suppose they get very thirsty going up in the sky. After all, chirrits get thirsty and they drink lots of water - I've seen them. I've even caught them when they were busy drinking at My Grandad's Chirrit Rock'

'Yes, but what's that noise?' Sixpence asked.

'The error plains that are moving make a noise like the screaming wind. It must be their digestion. I think error plain mujaji must be very similar to screaming wind mujaji, with a big sack inside that gets full of *smort* and has to be emptied every so often. Maybe you'll travel inside the smort bag of the error plain?' I realised after I'd said it that that was a particularly stupid thing to say if I wanted to keep my friends from becoming alarmed. I hastily told them I was only jesting and allayed what could have become complete screaming hysteria in four cats.

The stinkiroli came to a halt in front of a building, and Missus Capture opened the back of it and lifted out the two boxes containing my companions. She placed them on a kind of push-roli thing that she pushed into the building. I sat on top of Humphrey and Pipple's box so I could see what was happening and relay both facts and speculations to my friends inside the boxes.

'They're busy with peppers now. Lots of peppers. There are other boxes here, just like the ones you are in. And there's an enormous brown guelph here of the kind that ayoomfas ride on and which they call a *hors* or a *dong-key*.' I've never been clear on the difference between them and to me they look much the same. 'This dong-kee,' I continued, 'has a much bigger box than yours all to itself, and it doesn't seem too worried about anything.'

'Well, it could stomp the ayoomfas into the ground if it really wanted, and it isn't doing this, which means we'll probably be alright. Unless. . . Unless . . . What does a dong-kee eat, Bunny?'

I saw quickly where this was going. 'Grush,' I said, 'They eat mainly grush. Lots and lots of grush. And some *vejtibils*. No meat at all. I have seen this myself. Don't worry, HuffPuff, the dong-kee won't eat you.'

At that moment a whitecoati appeared. He was not our whitecoati from Midrand. He made speaks with Missus Capture about peppers and then began to open the box with Humphrey inside.

'NoNoNo!' Humphrey protested, 'My seedballs have already been stolen! And those of my two Woon Godcats in the other box. Also Pipple's eye and Bunny's nose Pimple and. . . there's really nothing worthwhile left to steal here. Please go away and leave us alone. . .'

I told Humphrey to be calm and not to fight the whitecoati, and he reluctantly complied. The whitecoati was very gentle and carefully studied him all over. After making some markings on a pepper with a marking stick, he took out his thorn thing and gave Humphrey a little prick with it. Humphrey seemed to relax tremendously after that. By the time the whitecoati had repeated his inspection of the Woon boys, Humphrey was looking most benign and peaceful.

The whitecoati examined Pipple - whom he had to wake up - but he didn't give her a prick with his thorn like he'd done to Humphrey and the Woons. Then he wandered off to discuss peppers with the other ayoomfas.

Humphrey began to sing, very woozily:

> *Peppers, peppers, everywhere*
> *Makes me want to curse and swear*
> *I'd rather catch a binigaus*
> *And eat it up inside the house. . .*

I had to stop this before it caused a problem and I urgently hushed Humphrey who reluctantly stopped singing and sat quietly and foolishly with his tongue sticking out. But now the Woon boys had also started to sing. It was all I could do to keep them quiet.

For several long naps the ayoomfas abandoned us in that room along with the dong-kee and some other cats and grufs. Once it was fully dark outside an ayoomfa woman who we'd not seen before, arrived and together with the whitecoati we'd seen earlier, they lifted our boxes onto one of the push-roli things and rolled us outside. I sat on top of Humphrey's box and gave commentary, to all who would listen, although I suspect most of my friends were feeling too dozy and foolish to pay any attention to me.

'We're outside now, as you can smell from the cool air. There's a funny smell about; it's a bit like the smell you sometimes smell underneath a stinkiroli, but it's sharper and sweeter. And you can be grateful you're inside your boxes - it's quite frightening out here and I've half a mind to come inside with you. . .'

'Come inside, chick chick - Inside with us choom choom,' Chocolate sang sleepily.

'Quiet, Butch! Listen and learn! This is amazing! The error plains are like huge chirrits made out of hard shiny stuff. So big, I think even our house in Midrand - which as you all know is immensely huge - might fit inside these error plains! There are glorp of them out here, all making screaming wind or big whistle. There are ayoomfas everywhere, scurrying about underneath them like squees, doing things to the error plains with what look like magic rain slinkis. . .'

'Slinki slinki choom choom, chikka chukka. . .' Sixpence was also singing now. I was too amazed at what I was seeing to bother with my woozy companions.

'It looks like we're headed for an error plain which is making big whistle out a little hole high up at the back, probably its shufa hole. There's a kind of hill that leads to a big door on the side of the error plain and we seem to be headed for that. Some ayoomfas are pulling the dong-kee along in its dong-kee box with a small yellow stinkiroli. Higher up than this door there's a long box thing that goes all the way from the side of the building to the side of the error plain.'

When I saw this thing earlier I thought the error plains got their food through it, but there was a window in the side of it and I spotted ayoomfas walking inside. It's a kind of passage they can walk in so they don't have to walk on the ground amongst the error plains, dodging the various yellow rumbleroli things that trundle back and forth.

'Down with box, down with capture . . . Yikkety yukkety choom choom. . .'

'Quiet Humphrey!'

Before long we were inside the error plain which had a flat lid and a flat floor but round walls. From above there came the sounds of great scuffling, thumping sounds like those made by ayoomfas and I went up through the lid to see what was happening. Above us was a long room with glorp chairs and most of them had ayoomfas sitting in them, tied down with those flat black slinkis of the kind you see inside a stinkiroli and which the clumsy ayoomfas need to stop them falling out of their seats. Other ayoomfas were milling about lifting boxes and bags, bumping into each other and getting annoyed.

Back in the room below the whitecoati and his lady friend tied the two boxes to a shelf using more of the flat black slinkis. The dong-kee box was placed a few cat's lengths away from us and secured in place with flat black slinkis as well as a number of fat sticks made of hard shiny. The ayoomfas busied themselves with more peppers and then some of them left and shut the door of the error plain. The whitecoati and his lady friend stayed inside with us. They sat on some seats and tied themselves to them with more of the flat slinkis. Before long the screaming wind began and it was very loud and frightening. And something odd happened to the air, which felt thin like it was being sucked away and which made Pipple sneeze wetly. Maybe I'd been right when I'd jested that the error plain was nothing more than a big screaming wind, and we were all inside it's bag. But there was little point in alarming my friends with this revelation.

Despite all the noise it was making the error plain was moving very slowly on the ground. I went outside and sat right on the very top of it where I had a splendid view of everything around us. In a while we had trundled away from the other error plains and the building and the scurrying ayoomfas were all far away. We rolled along an enormous black road much wider than Choklit's ROAD! and with many stripes and markings, surrounded by nothing but grush and a few small trees as far as I could see. It seemed a painfully slow and inefficient means of travel and I feared the journey to Brittin would take many moons. Even Mummi's red *paddlefoot-roli* could go faster than this and it had only two rounds, whereas the error plain had many sticks of fat black rounds underneath it. I was just about to return inside to tell my friends of all this when the error plain suddenly snorted and began to make the most frightening, ear-shattering roaring I'd ever heard – many times louder than the digestion of Daddi's blue stinkiroli. And it surged forward and began to race along the big black road, faster and faster with a great rumbling on the road below. The woo-woo was immensely strong and would easily have blown away an ayoomfa or even a big guelph like a hors as if it were nothing more than a leaf. Fortunately it just blew through my tiny Phirish body; I was aware of it but did not feel a thing. Just when I could see the end of the big black road in front of us, the front of the error plain started to point up into the sky and within the time of a wink or two the rumbling on the road suddenly stopped and the whole error plain was lifted into the air! We were flying in the sky, just like a big chirrit! I could see many small ayoomfas and houses and stinkirolis on the ground. They looked about the size of squees and small enough for a cat to swipe them away with one flick of their paw. It's always been a mystery to me why things get smaller when they go far away, but there is absolutely no doubt that they do. It was ever so. I wonder what it must feel like to get smaller like that? I suppose the ayoomfas don't mind because they know they'll get bigger again when they come back. I'll have to ask Tabithat about this some day.

I went back inside the error plain's screaming wind bag and told my friends of what I'd seen. Woozy as they were, they were truly amazed to be told they were flying in the sky inside a big shiny chirrit. The dong-kee seemed most disturbed and was making a loud snorting noise. I decided I would try to comfort it.

'Hello, Dong-kee. My name is Khat Bunni. Don't be afraid - everything will be just fine. What's your name?' But far from comforting it, this seemed to infuriate the dong-kee, which began snorting, sneezing and stamping its feet in anger.

'How. . .how dare you call me a dong-kee! I am a purebred stallion, possibly the fastest horse in all the land. I am an elite, efficient, perfectly groomed creature of speed and grace. And you call me a dong-kee? A dong-kee! I'd really like to stamp on you, you ignorant furball vomiter!'

'I'm sorry, Hors. . .uh, I didn't catch your name. I really meant no offense. I always thought a hors and a dong-kee were much the same - big guelphs that eat grush and which ayoomfas sometimes ride on.' But this only seemed to inflame him further and I saw no point in continuing the conversation if the hors was determined to be offensive, so I turned my back on him and resumed exploring our surroundings.

At the very front of the error plain was a room where two ayoomfa men were sitting all by themselves. Everywhere there was stuff just like the stuff I'd seen at Daddi's work. Flashing magic suns, tikki sticks that were pulled or flicked or pushed, little rounds that were spun round and round and others that had had flashing mujaji markings come and go on them. There was a round thing like a magic window but it didn't have sensible pictures on it and I suspect its magic was broken. Its picture was nothing more than green line from the middle to the outside of the round that swept around and around. Sometimes you could see it swept up little bits of green stuff but mostly it just swept round and round pointlessly. I decided this must be the place of work for the two men here, because a woman came and brought them kofi now and again and it's well known that ayoomfas cannot do work unless they have kofi. These men were somehow connected with the error plain, although what exactly it was they did I couldn't fathom, nor why they should want to do whatever it was they did up here in the sky. But they did have a nice window in front of them through which they could see exactly where the error plain was taking us.

Behind the men at work was the big room in which the glorpness of ayoomfas were now all tied down to their seats and most of them were eating some unappetizing looking shmoo kukri from tiny boxes which had been given to them by their captors. Beneath this was the room with my friends and the hors, and next to it was another room that was filled with a seemingly endless pile of boxes and bags and boxes and more bags, all filled with various articles and coverings which I presumed belonged to the ayoomfas above. It never ceases to astonish me how much stuff ayoomfas feel obliged to take with them wherever they go anywhere. How can they enjoy life to the full when they encumber themselves like this? It must be like having a big stone tied to one's tail.

Further along there were other little roomis full of noisy, smelly, hot mujaji things that moved about and made a noise like a gruf or buzzed like bizzums, and a special roomi where all the error plain's fat black rounds were kept when it was in the sky and didn't need them. The rounds were quite hot from rumbling along the black path. Right at the back of the error plain were two roomis each with a shufa bowl, but it wasn't one of the magic ones like Mummi and Daddi had at Midrand, with the special water that was always there. It wasn't even white and had smelly blue water which suddenly disappeared with a great sucking noise. I went below the floor and found a great big round drum where all the blue water and the ayoomfa shufa were stored. I would have thought they would want to be rid of their shufa and would throw it out into the sky rather than keep it, but ayoomfas are strange creatures at the best of times.

Daddi's blue stinkiroli had one digestion, but this error plain had four *screaming wind digestions*. Each of them was bigger than the whole of Daddi's blue stinkiroli. They were outside the error plain, underneath some flat boards, which is just as well because they each had a roaring fire inside, they made a fearful noise and a hot woo-woo came out the back. It would have been unwise to put them inside the error plain for they would have caused a big disturbance, maybe a fire as well. I wisely kept well away from the screaming wind digestions, and simply watched them through a window.

It is well known that I am an immensely wise and intelligent cat, but even I could not establish what made this error plain fly in the sky. When a chirrit flies it is easy to see that it does this by flapping its arms - we cats call them wings - up and down, to beat down the air. To fly you must beat down the air, this much is obvious, but the hard shiny boards that the error plain had instead of wings did not flap up and down. There was nothing at all I could see which was beating down the air and the four big screaming wind digestions outside seemed to do nothing but create noise, woo-woo, and bad smells.

Humphrey had reluctantly accepted his predicament and to pass the time was telling anyone who was interested - which was no one, really - things that Mrs. Malaprop had told him.

'Mrs. Malaprop is a very wise ayoomfa woman. She told me I was a handsome tabby, probably the most handsome in the world.'

'Only probably, Uncle HuffPuff?' Sixpence asked. He was slowly getting wise to Humphrey's tall tales but he still liked to play along.

'Of course, Mrs. Malaprop didn't know *all* the tabbies in the world, so she couldn't really say for sure. She knew all the tabbies that came to her house though.'

'How many was that, Uncle HuffPuff?'

'Only me. But Mrs. Malaprop explained to me once that ayoomfas have a special numbers knowledge and do not need to actually *see* all the tabbies to know things about them.'

'How does that work, Uncle HuffPuff?'

'Quite simple, my boy. Mrs. Malaprop explained it to us like this: Suppose you see a flock of big chirrits flying your way. Suppose you see the first one has wings. .'

'All chirrits have wings!' Sixpence observed. 'That is why they are chirrits.'

'YesYesYes, Sixpence, I know, but suppose you didn't know that. Now if you look at the first chirrit as it flies past and you see it has wings, you might wonder if they all have wings.'

Pipple had woken up and was shaking her head sadly.

'I know they have wings, they're chirrits.' Sixpence insisted.

'Yes Yes Yes, but suppose you didn't know that and you were wondering about it. Mrs. Malaprop says . . .'

'But all chirrits have wings, Uncle HuffPuff,' Sixpence said. 'I've known that since I was a tikki purik. Why do ayoomfas have to make such a big deal in figuring out what all animals know to be so? Even my brother Choklit knows that chirrits all have wings and he's not very smart at all. Although he is a Hero of the House,' he added hastily as Choklit began to look outraged.

'Humphrey, I think Mrs. Malaprop was taking you for a fool and she simply filled your head with all this nonsense so you'd keep bringing her hopits,' I said. Did she teach you *anything* even remotely useful in all the time you spent visiting her?'

'Mrs. Malaprop gave me quality knowledge for each hopit I caught,' he insisted. 'She told me about square roots.'

'I've never seen a square root!' I said in scornful disbelief, 'All the roots I've seen have been kind of round, rough and hairy. How about you Pipple? Sixpence, Choklit, anyone ever seen any square roots?'

'No.'

'See, Humphrey. Either ayoomfas are all far more stupid than we thought, or Mrs. Malaprop was simply fooling you.'

Humphrey buried his face in his paws in despair at our lack of faith and shook his head.

I was intrigued as to how Mrs. Malaprop managed to communicate all this esoteric drivel to Humphrey. It had occurred to me that Humphrey might have simply conjured up her and all her supposed wisdom from his imagination.

'I know you don't understand ayoomfa-speak, Humphrey. Did Mrs. Malaprop speak Khat to you?' I asked.

'Yes and no. Mainly no. But also a bit yes.'

'Meaning what, exactly?'

'Um, she gave me quality knowledge straight into my head.'

'I see,' I said, although I didn't really see.

At one point in the night the error plain became very bumpy. I went outside to see what was happening but could find nothing amiss. We were still high in the sky, so high that I couldn't see what was below us, and it was dark. All I could see was the moon, the stars and four hot fires that burned in the error plain's digestions. The air outside was so very, very cold, and there seemed to be so little of it that it would have been difficult to breathe. I knew that a living cat outside here would have been killed in a few winks and blown off the error plain to fall a long way onto whatever horridness lay below. I went back inside the error plain which was filled with much thicker air and which was comfortably warm.

'What's going on out there?' Humphrey asked. Why all the bumpity bumpity?'

'The air outside is very bumpity,' I replied, feeling a bit silly.

'Air can't be bumpity, §illy!' said Pipple, shaking her phluffi head with the perfectly straight line down the middle where the orange met the black. 'Air i§ alway§ §shmoo and §oftah.'

'Yes, utter nonsense!' Humphrey said scornfully, 'At least Mrs Malaprop never taught me nonsense like that! Bumpity air indeed! Next thing you'll tell me that the error plain has rounds which roll on the air.'

'It does have rounds but they've been put away now. It only rolls on them when it's on the ground.'

'How doe§ it §tay in the air,' Pipple asked.

'Uh, I don't know. I couldn't see anything obvious holding it up,' I confessed sheepishly.

'See! You're a stupid Phirish. Yes! Mrs Malaprop would know how it stays in the air, for sure! Yes Yes Yes!'

The rest of the night wore on in much the same way.

Some sleeps later I went outside again to look at the sunrise, which was truly beautiful. We were flying higher than the clouds and the sun was higher still and shining on the top of the clouds making them look like a fine fluffy wubbis. But close up they looked more like smoke. I shall ask Tabithat all about flying one day.

I sensed the error plain was sinking lower all the time and the four digestions sounded like they were getting quieter and we were slowing down. After a while I could see the tiny houses and stinkirolis again and before long various things started to happen. The sticks with the fat black rounds woke up and came out of their roomi where they'd spent the night. Other things started making grinding and gnashing noises and the error plain began to go down quite steeply. I must confess I was a bit afraid for my friends for it seemed at first the error plain was set to smash into the ground and kill everyone inside, including Hors Horrible. But then I saw a long black path with stripes and markings laid out on the ground, much like the one the error plain had rumbled on before we'd risen into the sky, and after a great shaking and bumpity-slippety and sideways-rockity the error plain lowered itself onto the great black road and began to rumble along. The four digestions started to make such a great noise I really thought they were about to burst, but then they quietened down and after a nap or two's trundling on the ground we had come to a halt in a place which looked exactly like the one we'd left from.

'Flying is simple,' Humphrey said loudly, puffing out his chest in bravado, 'Of course I wasn't frightened at all, you know.'

'Must have been the hors that came into your box in the night and made wizz then,' I said.

*****

CHAPTER EIGHTEEN:
Kworren Teen

Once we were on the ground again events unfurled backwards for us. We were taken out of the error plain on a pushroli, kept waiting in a building for half a day while ayoomfas fussed about with peppers. There were more ayoomfas and more peppers involved than there had been during the Sowf Efrika phase of our journey. Clearly pepper play was very important for ayoomfas in Brittin.

Two whitecoatis examined my friends from head to tail, seemingly obsessed about something called *ray-bees* that they eventually conceded we hadn't got inside us. I had heard Mummi and Daddi discussing these ray-bees with the whitecoati in Midrand. Midrand whitecoati told Mummi and Daddi that the last time anyone had seen any ray-bees in Midrand had been before he was born, but that the whitecoatis in Brittin were fixated with ray-bees.

Our first impressions of Brittin were mixed. We were obviously pleased to be safely out of the error plain, but when we had left Sowf Efrika it had been warm and sunny, and Brittin was anything but warm and sunny. It was cold and wet. Winter in Sowf Efrika had been cold and dry. Whatever this was in Brittin was cold and wet. Everything was cold and wet. Even the air was cold and wet. I learned later that it was always cold and wet in Brittin and one could tell winter from summer because winter was much colder and wet than summer. And it was so noisy! Everywhere you looked there were ayoomfas and stinkirolis. The ayoomfas spoke the same speaks as Mummi and Daddi, but it sounded different somehow; perhaps the wet air had changed their voices? However, all the ayoomfas we encountered were kind and polite to us and were clearly fond of all cats. They fed us good food and the whitecoati even said 'sorry, my boy' when he pushed a shiny stick into Humphrey's shufa hole, something for which our Midrand whitecoati had never apologised. Humphrey swore at him nonetheless.

Eventually we were taken away in a stinkiroli with another Missus Capture who twittered nonsensically to us like a chirrit for the whole journey. Looking out the fence side of their boxes through the front window of the stinkiroli my friends could see big open lands dotted with trees and houses and with grush greener than they had ever seen in Midrand. But on the other paw some places we passed had very little green grush at all, just identical houses packed right on top of each other, surrounded by fat-trees, and with any space between them occupied by glorp stinkirolis and fat ayoomfa ladies pushing their ayoomfapuriks in enormous sitzrolis with glorp rounds.

After about half a day in the stinkiroli we eventually stopped; not a moment too soon for Missus Capture's continuous twittering was beginning to drive me crazy. Had I not been a Phirish I would have leaped up on her shoulder and bitten her nose. Furthermore, Humphrey was starting to nag me about when he would get the cackack carcass I had rather rashly promised he would get in return for behaving acceptably on the error plain, and the Woon boys were getting restless as only youngsters can. Pipple was still happily asleep, making soft sleepi-rumble and dribbling slightly into her white bib fur.

Kworren Teen was a huge shock to all of us. It was a low, flat construction in the middle of open lands of green grush, with no trees and only an occasional bush to break the monotony of the landscape. Overhead a number of fat strings of the invisible mujaji fire were carried by a row of huge constructions that looked like dead trees. A long line of them came from farther away than we could see, and as the mujaji strings swayed overhead between the dead trees they crackled and buzzed with the power of their invisible magic fire. On the horizon there were mountains, but they were unlike any I'd ever seen before - completely black with no grush or trees growing on them at all. And they were smoking as if the whole mountainside was on fire! Some fat-trees near them had pipes sticking out of them which gave off clouds of dirty smoke which smelled bad even from far away, and which made much of the sky above Kworren Teen a sickly yellow-grey colour. Every now and again a big fire would erupt with a great roar out of one of the fat-tree pipes. From the low building outside which we had stopped came the sound of many grufs - all shouting their anger and frustration - and I realised that Kworrren Teen very closely resembled the description of the Hell that we'd been raised to fear. The same Hell Tabithat claimed didn't exist. My companions - even Pipple who had eventually woken up - were all in silent shock and sadly I had no news or explanation that could possibly comfort them and allay their darkest suspicions that Mummi and Daddi hated them so much they had sent them to Hell.

Tabithat owed me an explanation and I didn't care if he was busy or not - I focussed my Phirish mind and sought him out.

'Oh Lord Tabithat, why have Mummi and Daddi sent my friends to Hell?'

A great rumble filled the air and flowing patterns of coloured cloud enveloped me. I could not see Tabithat at all this time.

'I've told you before, Little Wargi, there is no Hell,' Tabithat said, somewhat peevishly.

'Lord, with all possible respect, my friends in the real world would disagree. The place they are in closely matches all the descriptions they've heard of Hell from many sources.'

'It's not Hell, Little Wargi. It's just one of several awful, bleak places in northern industrial Brittin. They only seem like Hell.'

'But why have Mummi and Daddi sent them there?'

'They had no choice. Your companions have to spend six moons in Kworren Teen before the Brittin whitecoatis will allow them go live in their new house. While they are at Kworren Teen the whitecoatis will watch them to see if they get ray bees. It's important pepper play for the ayoomfas, little Wargi. I wouldn't squander your valuable cat thoughts on it. The important thing you need to tell your friends is that they will have to stay in Kworren Teen for six moons, and that it's not Hell, even if it sometimes seems like it. Tell them also that Mummi and Daddi love them dearly and will come and visit then quite often over the next few moons. Now if that's all I'd like to get back to washing my extraordinarily fluffy and magnificently holy striped tail.'

With that thought Tabithat was gone in the blink of an eye.

Kworren Teen was a prison. Nothing more, nothing less. Humphrey and Pipple were put in one room and the Woon boys in another room next to it. The rooms had fence on all sides but were fortunately big enough to run around and play games in. My friends could see and smell the grush outside, but they couldn't touch it.

Six moons is a very long time to spend locked up inside two fence rooms and every opportunity for contact with the outside world was eagerly awaited. Every morning shortly after sunrise an ayoomfa woman came bearing bowls of food and water for everyone. Humphrey asked this ayoomfa the same insistent questions every day.

'Is my Daddi coming to take me home today, Missus Morning Food? HeyHeyHey? Is he? Is he?' The ayoomfa woman couldn't understand Khat and usually responded as best she could by picking Humphrey up and giving him chukkachin, which always helped to soothe him. Missus Morning Food then carefully left the room and went next door to feed the Woon boys. Sixpence always greeted her with tremendous enthusiasm, but then Sixpence was becoming a very vocal cat and relished every opportunity to speak and be picked up. For a few days Missus Morning Food tried to pick up Choklit-Butch, but he always trotted away just out of her reach.

'Me run away,' he said to her, blinking impassively, 'It's best.'

After a week or two she gave up trying.

In the afternoons it was a young ayoomfa man who brought the food and he liked to pick Pipple up and stroke her. Humphrey pointedly ignored him, Sixpence chattered to him and Choklit ran away. Humphrey scornfully maintained the man was a phraidy man who only felt safe when picking up gentle old lady cats. To prove this to us one day he waited until the young man had picked up Pipple and then went up to him, looked him straight in the eye and snarled loudly, fiercely, and at length. The young man wasted no time in putting Pipple down and he beat a hasty retreat from the room. Sixpence and Chocolate had been watching through the fence between the rooms as this display unfolded and were seriously amused.

'You see, you see' said Humphrey, strutting around in pride, 'Phraidy man. Like I said.'

This was enough to cause the Woon boys to launch into a chant: 'Let's all bite the phraidy man - Chunka chunka chomp chomp'

About once every two paw's pads or so days we had a visit from two ayoomfa ladies, one of whom was a whitecoati. The other one seemed to tag along mainly to carry peppers for the whitecoati. These visits were eagerly awaited by my friends. The whitecoati picked up everyone - including Choklit-Butch who always tried to run away but was inevitably caught in the end - and examined them from head to tail in search of ray bees. But the lady with the peppers invariably carried a bag of especially delicious treats and she would give each of my friends several of these as a reward once the ordeal was over. These two ladies became known as Missus Whitecoati and Missus Treats.

To while away the long, bleak moons we had endless discussions on weighty and difficult questions, including my favorite about how things get smaller as they get farther away.

'That's all a load of nonsense!' said Humphrey. *I* certainly don't get smaller as I get further away from you and I'll prove it to you. First I'll come sit up close to you like this, and I'll put my forepaws on the fence here. See how each paw covers four of the holis in the fence?'

'Yes, I see.'

'Good, now watch as I walk away from you. . .'

'You're getting smaller. . .'

'So *you* say. But now at the other side of this room, I put my forepaws on the fence again, and see: each paw still covers four of the holis in the fence. So you're wrong. I haven't got smaller at all. I'm still a large, magnificent tabby cat like I always was.' He smiled conceitedly.

'No, No, HuffPuff, the fence has also got smaller. I can see that clearly.' Humphrey was not convinced.

'Sixpence, Choklit, your paws are about the same size as each others,' he said. 'Sixpence, you come here by me and measure your paw with the holis in the fence. Choklit, you go over there to where your Auntie Bunni is and measure your paw using the holis in the fence where she is.'

Sixpence and Choklit-Butch eagerly embarked on this investigative measurement.

'How many holis, Sixpence?'

'Three, Uncle HuffPuff.'

'How many holis Choklit?'

'Three, Uncle HuffPuff.'

'There, you see, Bunni! Things *do not* get smaller as they get further away. Using clever tabby reasoning knowledge I have proved this beyond any doubt.'

I still trusted what I saw with my own dead eyes, although I had to admit that Humphrey's demonstration was very convincing.

'Let's ask Pipple,' I said, knowing that she was firmly in my camp. 'Pipple, do things get smaller as they get further away?'

'Ye§, it'§ ab§olutely true,' she splattered.

'But you've just seen me prove it's nonsense!' Humphrey railed.

'I §aw what you did, but perhap§ there wa§ §ome §§leight of paw. I can prove it'§ true by u§e of Phluffi Logic experiment. It'§ a powerful knowledg§e from Tortoi§eshell Tradit§ion which i§ u§ed to §olve intere§ting problem§ like thi§. HuffPuff, put one of your forepaw§ in front of your fac§e.'

'But then I'll fall down.'

'Not if you §it down or lie on the ground, §illy!'

Humphrey sighed, sat down and put his big forepaw over his face.

'Tell me what you §ee.'

'Nothing. My paw is covering my eyes.'

'Don't cover your eye§ completely, you fooli§h tabby. Move your paw a bit away so you can at lea§t §ee all of it.'

'Like this?'

'Ex§actly. Now keep your paw there and look pa§t it to the fenc§e. Count the holi§ in the fenc§e to §ee how big your paw i§.'

Humphrey did this. 'It's six holis from top to bottom.'

'§plendid! Now §tay where you are and move your paw away from you in a §traight line a§ far a§ you can reac§h. Then count the holi'§ again to §ee how big it i§ now.'

'It's four holis from top to bottom,' Humphrey said, frowning.

'§ee! Bunni i§ prec§ic§ely right. Your paw get§§ §maller a§ it get§ further away! Everything el§e doe§, al§o! All proved by §imple Phluffi Logic ex§periment from Tortoi§es§hell Tradit§ion.'

Humphrey was most perplexed about this and not a little worried. 'Does this mean the rest of me is getting bigger? Do I look like a squee with foolish tiny little forepaws?'

'Phluffi Logic doe§n't §ay,' Pipple said and glided away, her work done.

Humphrey spent the next few naps squinting at his paws from various positions but was unable to contradict the evidence which was literally before his eyes.

'My forepaw doesn't feel like it's getting any smaller,' he muttered to himself in denial.

For the Woon brothers the time spent in Kworren Teen was educational. They had unrestricted access to a captive Godcat in the person of Humphrey, who found himself inundated on a daily basis with questions on a wide variety of subjects. Many of these questions he was able to answer truthfully and honestly because he knew the answers from either experience or Khat Lore. The rest he simply made up in order not to lose face.

'Uncle HuffPuff, why do cats have so many names and what do they mean?' asked Sixpence. Usually it was Sixpence who asked the questions; Choklit-Butch did not share his older brother's enormous thirst for knowledge.

'All cats have a *secret name*, known only to themselves and the Khat Khouncile that gave it to them. If they forget the secret name, or it becomes known to others, they have to go to the nearest Khat Khouncile to be issued with another.'

'Ye§, that happened to me onc§e,' Pipple added, nodding knowingly. 'You mu§t be e§pec§§ially §ecret about your §pecial §ecret name or el§e you could find your§elf in §eriou§ di§gra§e like I did!'

'YesYes, thank you Pipple,' Humphrey said, wiping his face with his paw, 'You Woon boys have not yet been issued with secret names. Back in Midrand we were boycotting the Khat Khouncile because it was corrupt and useless. It's sad, but most Khat Khounciles seem to end up that way. However, there is a way around this. YesYes! *Tabby Lore* says that if you can't find a Khat Khouncile to issue you with a secret name, you can make up a secret name yourself and tell it to Poyk in a dream. As your Godcat and a handsome tabby myself, I could declare you both honorary tabbies for a day so you can comply with Tabby Lore and make up your secret names.'

'Thank you uncle HuffPuff. What about the other kinds of names?' Sixpence blinked earnestly in his eagerness to learn.

'Every cat also has a *street name*. The street name is the name by which you are known to cats on the street who are not part of your household. Street names are chosen to project yourself as you want other cats to see you. Yowlis always choose names that suggest how tough and fearless they are.'

'What's your street name, Uncle HuffPuff?'

'RipperClaws.'

'Gosh! That's a *very* fierce name, Uncle HuffPuff,' Sixpence said, wide-eyed in awe.

Humphrey bared his teeth momentarily to appear suitably savage and continued.

'You can make up your own street name to be anything you want, but if you ever come across another yowli with the same street name, Khat Lore says you have to fight him until one of you gives up the name. To the death if necessary.'

'I'd like to be called Little Dancing Feet,' Sixpence announced. Choklit-Butch snorted in derision and Humphrey said, somewhat scornfully, 'Well you certainly won't have to fight many yowlis for that name.'

'Good.' Sixpence smiled in satisfaction.

'Then there is the *house name* that we call each other, as friends and fellow Citizens of a House. Usually the Chief Cat of the House - often a magnificent tabby like me - decides what they are. Your house names are Sixpence and Choklit, which I gave to you when you were tikki puriks.'

'But those are the *ayoomfa names* given to them by Mummi and Daddi.' I said. 'You didn't give them their house names.'

Humphrey was embarrassed. He suddenly found a bit of grease on his striped chest fur and started to wash this intently while he deliberated his response. 'I gave them the names first - the ayoomfas must simply have copied them.'

'But how could the ayoomfas know what these names were when they don't speak Khat?' I asked. I set about laying a cunning trap for him so that he would lose much face as a braggart and speaker of foolish gloats.

'Ayoomfas are fiendishly clever. If they can make sunshine in the night and make tiny magic so that little people dance around in the magic window, finding out the house names of two Woon cats that live with them should be as easy as falling asleep. Anyway, it's not important. Now if you've quite finished with these rude interruptions, Bunni, I'd like to continue my lesson.'

'Please don't upset Uncle HuffPuff, Bunni,' Sixpence pleaded earnestly, 'He's getting cross and he might bite us or stop the lesson. . .'

I had lost face. This would not do and I searched for anything I could think of to even the score. I said, 'By the way, HuffPuff, did you know that Daddi says you have a tail like a lamprey?'

'My Daddi knows full well I have a beautiful tail. Oh Yes Yes Yes! Not as fat and fluffy as Pipple's tail, I do concede, but a beautiful tail nonetheless. What's a lamprey?'

'Uh. . .' Now it was my turn to find a bit of spiritual grease to lick off my spiritual fur. My plan had backfired and I had lost even more face. I decided to go sit further away with my back turned towards Humphrey and pointedly ignore him while still listening carefully in case I found an opening for retaliation.

'As I was saying, my boys,' Humphrey said with renewed confidence, 'your house names are Sixpence and Choklit. Mine is HuffPuff and Pipple's was Spinach but the ayoomfas renamed her Timeshare and somehow everyone now calls her Pipple.

'Finally, there are a cat's *ayoomfa names*. These are the names that ayoomfas bestow on us. The names may change in time, and names may come and names may go. It's a great honour for us to have many ayoomfa names, for it means that the ayoomfas think a lot of us and hold us in great affection, as is only right. For example, the names I've heard Mummi and Daddi call Choklit are Choklit, Butch, Bosephus, Large, Simply Large, Largely Simple, Palindromic Cat, Black Panther, Bobble, Mister Shreddit, RunAway, Le Gouffre, and El Sick up.'

Choklit-Butch beamed with pleasure and licked his lips.

'Wow! They must love Choklit very much,' Sixpence said, and then he began to look downcast. Does this mean they love Choklit more than me?' He looked so sad I thought he might be going to cry and so I intervened once again.

'Not at all, little Sixpence. They love you greatly, as much if not more than Choklit.' Choklit glowered darkly at this and shook his head.

'I've heard them call you Sixpence, Bibble, Six-D, Sixness of D, Poppit, Poppitoon, Smudge, Big D, Squeak, Little Pie, and many more.'

Sixpence looked sceptical. He began to count carefully on his paws but gave up after a while.

'I'm sure I heard Uncle HuffPuff say more names for Choklit than you said for me, Auntie Bunni,' he said.

Choklit-Butch nodded and grinned smugly.

'Yes but many of Choklit's names suggest how foolish he is, whereas all your names suggest only how lovely you are.' I couldn't do better than that or I would make myself sick. Sixpence looked as if he would burst with joy.

Choklit's smug smile changed instantly to a dark glower again, and he got up and sat down again with his back towards us. He made a big stink of air shufa.

'What are your ayoomfa names, Auntie Bunni?' Sixpence asked.

'I was usually called Bunni. But also HopAway, Rocket88, Mad Monk, White Cat, Bird Murderer, Siamese Phool or Earth Mother.'

'Do all of these names say that you were lovely, Auntie Bunni?'

'Uh. . . not exactly. . .'

'Do any of them say how foolish you were, Auntie Bunni?' Humphrey asked, mimicking Sixpence's young voice.

'Uh. . Well, I suppose so. . .'

'Which ones, Auntie Bunni?' asked the real Sixpence.

I could feel my face slipping away like rainwater sinking into parched ground.

'All of them,' I muttered.

Some days it's best not to talk to anyone.

*****

CHAPTER NINETEEN:
The Missing Ayoomfas

After spending two moons with my friends in Kworren Teen I decided to go see how Mummi and Daddi were getting on back in Sowf Efrika. My poor friends had taken the best part of three days to get from Midrand to Kworren Teen in a variety of noisy, shaking, ayoomfa transport contraptions, but as a Phirish I was able to make the return journey instantly through thought space in less time than it would have taken Humphrey to lick his forepaw. I suppose it counts as one of the perks of being dead.

To my dismay I found our Midrand house empty and Mummi and Daddi nowhere to be seen. All their ayoomfa constructions and articles were also gone. Only dust and emptiness remained, along with the echo of so many memories of happy times spent there with my ayoomfa assistants and my many feline friends. So much sunshine, so many fire festivals, so much laughter. Then I found the house wasn't totally deserted. In the upstairs sleeping room I discovered a big ayoomfa lady with yellow head fur whom I recognised as one of Mummi's friends. She was singing to herself while painting the walls a bright pink, in fact the same colour exactly as Humphrey's wizzlepizzle when it gets excited. I was quite concerned about Mummi's reaction to this, but much, much more concerned over her present whereabouts. It's all very well being able to think yourself around from place to place in an instant, but if you don't know where someone is, you don't know where to think yourself to. I decided to visit MyGranni in the hopes that she could shed some light on the whereabouts of Mummi and Daddi.

MyGranni was in her little house where I'd last seen her and she was delighted at my arrival. Although she could see me and speak to me, I couldn't speak to her. Intentionally or not, Tabithat had made a half-job of my communication abilities and it was very frustrating. MyGranni was under the impression that I already knew where Mummi and Daddi were and expected I'd already been to see them. I grew highly agitated because I was getting no closer to finding them. MyGranni sensed my distress and invited me to sit on her lap and curl up on her bed at night, all of which was a great comfort to me. I decided to spend a paw or two's days with her, listening and watching everything that happened, until I heard or saw some clue that would lead me to my Mummi and Daddi.

MyGranni spent a lot of time talking into her *magic speakstick*. This is one of the more curious ayoomfa magics, and one which the female ayoomfas seem to like using for long times - even whole sleeps at a time. Ayoomfas speak into it as if they are speaking to another ayoomfa, as if that ayoomfa were right there in the room with them. They hold the speaking stick next to their head and they can hear the sound of other ayoomfas speaking to them from inside it. If a cat has sharp ears and is not too far away from the speaking stick when it's being used, it is possible to hear the other ayoomfa speaking with tikki voice from inside it. I have examined the magic speakstick from all sides, and even used my Phirish powers to look inside of it, but I cannot find any place where a real creature - not even a feeble puny ayoomfa that's been shrunk by *tiny magic* - can get inside of it. Most magic speaking sticks are tied to the wall of a house with a string of invisible mujaji fire, but some ayoomfas are so devoted to their speaksticks that they have special ones that aren't tied to anything and which they carry around with them wherever they go, like a disease.

I followed the mujaji fire string of MyGranni's speakstick into the wall and saw that it went under the ground outside and into a big green box in which there were glorp upon glorp other mujaji fire strings coming and going in all directions. But no creatures other than krorlis were hiding in this box and krorlis can't speak - they just work, work, work all the time, the foolish creatures.

Now it's well known from Khat Lore that trying to speak to a creature that's not present is as about as much use as speaking to the sky, or to a hole in the ground. So I can only assume that the ayoomfas do *practice speaks* with the magic speakstick to make themselves feel better. In a way it's not unlike the magic window, which shows all manner of things happening in the house which aren't really happening in the house. Ayoomfas thrive on all this make-believe. It's almost as important to them as pepper play. Sometimes the ayoomfa will start using the magic speakstick by lifting it off its bed and then using their softclaws to fiddle around with it before speaking at it. At other times the magic speakstick first draws their attention by making a dreadful screeching noise like a *shreeka-shreeka* bizzum and it either carries on making this noise until the ayoomfa picks it up and speaks at it, or after a long time it simply gets hoarse and shuts up. All sensible creatures would ignore it when it shrieks, put paws over their ears, or better still, run away, but few ayoomfas appear to have the intelligence to do this. It's a strident noise which causes the ayoomfas to respond with great urgency, no matter what they are doing. To an ayoomfa nothing takes precedence over the insistent shrieking of their magic speakstick. Even if they are busy eating or making shufa on the shufa bowl, if the magic speakstick shrieks at them they will stop whatever they are doing and go make practice speaks into it. In fact I once told Humphrey that if he ever mastered the mysteries of the magic speakstick, he could use it to devise a scheme to ensure we were properly fed on demand.

MyGranni was in the winter of her life and I could tell from her radiance that her strength was beginning to fade. It is well known that this happens but ayoomfas invariably wish to defy the ways of nature and fight them, as if they are not part of Tabithat's world. This only makes life much harder for them. MyGranni was no exception and she wasted many naps of valuable sun basking time struggling to do silly tasks that her body found difficult and her mind ought to have told her weren't worth worrying about. She cleaned things that didn't need cleaning, counted stuff that didn't need counting, and tied up all manner of ayoomfa articles with little pieces of green string. Had I been alive I would have played with the string to amuse her; she always used to enjoy playing with me when I was in my prime and we lived near the fat trees in Vietnam with MyGrandad and Young Man. But all I could do as a Phirish was watch her struggle on needlessly with pointless toil.

Sometimes the sisters of Daddi would come and visit MyGranni and they would make ayoomfa speaks for many, many naps, even a whole sleep or two. One of them - the big one - had a cat she lived with called Milkhi-Baa. From all accounts Milkhi-Baa was similar to Phat Balune in appearance and disposition, and was greatly cherished as an important Citizen of her House. The other daughter of MyGranni - the smaller one - sadly did not have a cat companion and instead had a huge gruf and a chirrit with a yellow head. She sometimes brought the chirrit with the yellow head in a fence-box to see MyGranni and when it got excited the chirrit would shriek hysterically like a magic speaking stick. The shrieking would continue unabated until either MyGranni or her daughter would cover the chirrit's fence box with a wubbis to trick it into going to sleep. MyGranni was clearly very fond of this chirrit with the yellow head, despite the unpleasant racket it made. The daughter with the chirrit would have undoubtedly benefitted from having a cat to guide her through life but I think with the big gruf and the noisy chirrit there were too many obstacles to peaceful sleep for a cat to be a happy Citizen of that House.

I started by listening intently to these speaks between MyGranni and her daughters with a view to finding out how I could get to see my Mummi and Daddi, but I learned very little, for nearly all of the speaks were just nonsense about silly ayoomfa things. I did at least discover that Mummi and Daddi were alive and well and living in a place called Fifield, which was somewhere in Brittin but I knew not where. They were apparently missing us cats and planned to visit us in Kworren Teen, but I knew not when.

Daddi had found a new work as a Mujaji Lord in a place that had something to do with how ayoomfas and other things get into the magic window. Mummi had also found a new work which she did at home and which was again making markings on peppers. The magic window I can understand, but Mummi's work is difficult to fathom for nothing moves nor speaks and therefore even a foolish cat like Choklit-Butch would know that it isn't real. But never mind, if it makes her happy she might as well do it. Much as I liked staying with MyGranni my only hope to be reunited with Mummi and Daddi was to go back to my companions in Kworren Teen and wait there for them to come visit. If I missed them I might lose them forever.

We were truly delighted to see Mummi and Daddi again. They arrived early one afternoon in a stinkiroli that I hadn't seen before and which was the colour of rotting fruit. Humphrey was nearly wizzing himself with excitement and he darted back and forth between Daddi's hind legs, rubbing himself against them and gushing up a torrent of speaks.

'YesYesYesYesYes! Oh Daddi! I love you Daddi! Yay for Daddi! I'm pleased you've come to take us home Daddi. GoodGoodGood - we've been here two moons already.'

I tried to tell Humphrey that Mummi and Daddi were only visiting us and that he wasn't leaving Kworren Teen just yet but he dismissed my suggestion as preposterous.

'Nonsense, Bunni! Anyone can see that Daddi's come to take us all home now. Daddi, shall I lead the way? Let's go now Daddi, there's no point in hanging around here. Come this way. Come, let's go. Let's go, let's go, let's go.'

Mummi and Daddi had brought delicious treats for all of my friends and spent quality time playing with them with an assortment of new toys they had brought. Amongst these was a very splendid thin, crispy leaf as long as two cats and it made an exciting swishing action that Choklit and Sixpence found irresistible. Mummi had them chasing around in circles after this crispy leaf until the two boys were totally exhausted and panting and had to lie down for a nap. There were also other toys of the kind ayoomfas make especially for cats. These usually have silly tinkling balls on them and they smell very exciting for a few days but then become lifeless and boring. What ayoomfas don't seem to understand is that we really like them to play *with* us - I learned later that this kind of play with an ayoomfa is called *inter-actiff*. It can be performed using whatever simple toy is handy - a long leaf, a string, a dead squee; even plokkits make nice toys.

Daddi lavished great affection on Humphrey, giving him Face, Full Encapsulation of Head, Chukkachin, Chukkacheek, and Skweezycat. He'd made up a new one, too, called Huggity-Bumpity, but Humphrey was impatient to get home.

'ComeComeCome Daddi, you can do this all later. Stop shaking me about now and let's go home. Come, this way - stop messing about. Let's go, let's go, let's go.'

Pipple was similarly eager to leave. She said to Mummi, 'Thi§ plac§e §tink§, Mummi! Over there there'§ black hill§ with fire in them that §tink§. And it'§ §o very cold - my poor pad§ ache in the morning§. You §houldn't have left u§ here in thi§ §tinki pri§on - it's an ab§olute di§grac§e. It'§ all your fault, Mummi. You mu§t take u§ home at onc§e!'

The hurt and indignation felt by my friends when the ayoomfas left without taking them along was terrible to behold, but I could see that Mummi and Daddi were equally upset. I tried to explain to my furious feline friends that Mummi and Daddi truly wanted to take us home, but other ayoomfas wouldn't let them.

'NoNoNo! There's no excuse! Daddi should get his bangstick and make these other ayoomfas die of big bangfright!' Humphrey snarled indignantly. 'It's an outrage, it is! YesYesYes! I will bite the next ayoomfa that comes in here to feed us! I will bite one of their silly pink claws right off! Just you wait and see if I don't.'

'Don't do that, or they won't feed you,' I tried to placate him, knowing what great store he placed in food. After a bit more grumbling he went and sat by the fence and gave a long sigh of defeat. Pipple simply turned her back on me and glided away.

'Thi§ i§ all your §tupid fault, Bunni!' She splattered indignantly under her breath and for four days she sulked and refused to speak to anyone. Sixpence wailed plaintively for a long time after Mummi and Daddi left, but the Woon brothers were young and adaptable and soon distracted themselves with a sibling squabble.

The second visit from Mummi and Daddi didn't cause any celebration. Humphrey started by deliberately ignoring them because he felt betrayed and deceived. He said it wasn't even worth the effort to be nice to them because they'd just leave us all in Kworren Teen again. It was all he could do not to hiss and spit at them. But he couldn't stay angry for too long. Daddi picked him up and gave him Tickletum and Skweezycat and he had no choice but to burst into a loud happi-rumble. Sixpence and Choklit were as effusive and joyful as they'd been on the previous visit, but Pipple sulked and wouldn't even acknowledge any visitors. It took a lot of Chukkacheek and Top of Head before Pipple stopped pretending that she didn't have the faintest idea who her visitors were. Then sadly, Mummi and Daddi again left without us.

I spend some time teaching Sixpence to count. He was an ideal pupil, since he fully believed everything I told him and in between lessons he diligently did the exercises I gave him. I'd already taught Choklit-Butch to count years before when he was Butch and his participation in the lessons I gave to Sixpence was limited, rather like his understanding.

Choklit-Butch said, 'Auntie Bunni, I didn't do the exercise because something is definitely wrong here.' He held his paw up close to my face. 'Here's my paw, see. There are four pads in it; I've counted them over and over again. One, two, three, four. Only if I look right down here on my forearm before where my paw starts, do I see another pad. It's not really a proper pad, and I don't even know what it's for, but I count it anyway. So I have five pads on my forepaw. There is no way there are six - I have looked everywhere and I am very sure about this. Yet you say this is how we count, with six pads on a paw?'

'Yes, quite right! The wise elders who created Khat Lore said that for counting purposes there are six, even if there *aren't really* six. They did this to make counting easier for us.'

'Easier? It's not easier at all? It's much more difficult because you look at your paw and you say to yourself, one, two, three, four, and five . . . and then what? What do you say then? There's no pad for six. What then? What are you supposed to do?'

'The elders did this on purpose,' I explained, 'to discourage us from counting on our paws and to encourage us to rather count in our heads like clever creatures.'

'But that's nonsense, Bunni! There are no pads in our heads at all, so counting in our heads is quite impossible.'

Choklit-Butch was equally unhappy about measurement of size according to Khat Lore, which I explained to the brothers Woon one cold day - in fact I think it was the day the strange white powder fell from the sky and covered everything as far as one could see.

'Cats need a way to tell each other how big or small something is, or how far away something is. It's always a good idea to use something that's there for all to see, like holis in a fence, but sometimes there are no fence holis to be seen and sometimes there's nothing useful around at all. When this happens we make use of things that all cats will know well, namely the cat and the tree. Now we all know roughly how long a cat is, so we can imagine cats standing head to tail in a long line to help us measure. As an exercise, how far is it from one end of this prison to the other? Sixpence?'

Sixpence screwed his eyes tightly shut and mouthed counting for a long time. Eventually he said, 'I can imagine three paws' pads of cats standing in a line from one side to another.'

'That seems rather a lot, Sixpence? I wouldn't have said there were more than two paws' cats.'

'My cats were tikki puriks, Auntie Bunni.'

'You are supposed to think of big cats like Uncle HuffPuff.'

'I tried, Auntie Bunni, I did. But none came. Only tikki puriks came.'

'Never mind. Well done. Choklit, how many cats?'

Choklit-Butch looked most distressed. 'I can't count them,' he complained, rubbing his eyes with his paw. 'The cats in my head won't stand still in a line. They're milling about and playing and fighting and I can't count them.'

There was little I could do about the small size or bad behaviour of the cats inside the Woons' heads, so I decided to continue regardless.

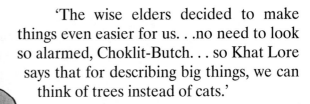

'The wise elders decided to make things even easier for us. . .no need to look so alarmed, Choklit-Butch. . .so Khat Lore says that for describing big things, we can think of trees instead of cats.'

'How many cats make up a tree, Auntie Bunni?' Sixpence asked. He was really quick to learn.

'Six.'

'But that's a small tree,' Sixpence observed, 'Maybe it's far away from us so it's become small. But there are big trees as well, Auntie Bunni, I've seen them. What about big trees?'

'Don't worry about big trees,' I said impatiently, 'You must train yourself to see small trees in your head.'

'My head is still full of cats,' Choklit-Butch complained, 'I can't think how to make them go away.'

I decided I'd had enough of trying to teach Choklit-Butch anything. He simply could not *think in ideas* like Sixpence and me. Sixpence seemed quite comfortable with this way of counting and measuring so clearly it wasn't just me who was exceptionally clever.

When the third visit by Mummi and Daddi took place two moons later, Humphrey didn't even bother to do more than slightly open one yellow eye when they came into the prison. He was still half asleep when he found himself scooped up and deposited in the same fencebox he knew by smell as the one in which he had often been taken to the Midrand Whitecoati.

'WhatWhatWhat is going on? HeyHeyHey?' he blustered indignantly.

'It looks like you're going home,' I said. 'Everyone's been put in a fencebox now and the ayoomfas are looking at peppers and making markings on them. This might take a nap or two - you know how seriously they take pepper play here in Brittin.'

But in only a few winks the fenceboxes containing my four friends were put on the back seat of the rotting-fruit-coloured stinkiroli I'd seen Mummi and Daddi arrive in, and I discovered it had a nice wide shelf at the back for me to lie on, to observe our surroundings and oversee my companions.

Mummi and Daddi got in the front seats of the fruit stinkiroli and the next thing we knew we were rolling along a big road with our beloved ayoomfarolês singing to us as we headed to our new home.

*****

CHAPTER TWENTY:
Ray bees and Essex

'Not now! No time now! NoNoNo! BusyBusyBusy!' Humphrey snapped when I opened my mouth to ask him a question. He was finding his first few days in the new house very stressful.

'So much for a Chief Cat to do,' he muttered darkly. 'So little time. Always BusyBusyBusy'.

In this he was quite right. There were many roomis and boxes and dark corners to inspect and carefully sniff. Mummi and Daddi had to be supervised so they didn't do anything foolish. And there was a whole new garden outside which had to be carefully marked as our territory. And who knew what lay beyond those fences? Humphrey would have to find out by doing a thorough perimeter inspection along all the fences to check for grufs, big guelphs that kick, angry ayoomfas with magic water slinkis, hazardous ayoomfa constructions or other potential dangers to him and his fellow Citizens of the New House. Beyond these fences were also new hunting grounds that had to be identified, tested, and any questions of their ownership resolved through the time-honoured negotiation of lengthy yowling followed by tooth and claw.

Quite high up on Humphrey's list of chores was the important mission of identifying a suitable shufa ground for us. The First Claws of Khat Shufa Lore tells us that for reasons of cleanliness a shufa ground must not be located within the boundaries of the cats' own house. And obviously one shouldn't establish a shufa ground within the borders of another cat's house, for this is just rude and so is forbidden by Khat Shufa Lore. The most attractive place for a shufa ground is around a house in which there are no cats or grufs, but whose ayoomfas have set up rows of flowers and coloured plants surrounded by soft soil that has been carefully turned. It's thought that the ayoomfas without cats set up these colourful plants to lure cats in the hopes that some will honour them by taking up residence in their house. Of course this never happens because of the First Claws of Khat Shufa Lore, but most cats are too polite to pointedly disappoint the lonely ayoomfas and so humour them by using their lures. Another good place for a shufa ground is around a house in which there is one tikki gruf but no cats, as force of cat claw can always be brought against the gruf if it waxes uncooperative or cheeky. Shufa Lore cautions us that this strategy only works if there is only one gruf and it is very tikki.

Pipple and the Woon boys left all this stressful toil to Humphrey and spent their days grubbing in the garden, sniffing the bushes and trees and chasing bizzums. Our new house was much smaller than the house in Midrand and Mummi and Daddi had great difficulty finding places to put all the glorp upon glorp of ayoomfa articles that they'd somehow brought all the way from Sowf Efrika. They spent a lot of time looking for places to put things until Daddi discovered there was a big dark room up in the lid of the house where he could put things that didn't need to be in the light.

The garden of our new house was full of plants that were very green and juicy and looked as if they ate very well, unlike the plants we had had in Midrand which usually seemed hungry, dusty and thirsty, except for a few days after the rains. The healthy plants in our Brittin garden hid a great glorpness of krorlis and bizzums in the damp darkness under them, including several types of bizzum we had not come across before. In Midrand we had been well acquainted with the small striped stinging bizzums that Humphrey said were honorary tabbies and which the ayoomfas called *bees* and treated with a great wariness. But the bees we saw in Brittin were truly enormous! They had bodies the size of a cat's nose and with their wings out they were easily as big as a paw. And they had beautiful stripes that left Humphrey seriously in awe. He said he thought these might be the *ray bees* the whitecoatis at Kworren Teen were always banging on about. Sixpence simply couldn't resist catching one of these Brittin bees to inspect it more closely. These huge bees buzzed slowly around the coloured plants and flowers, in no great hurry and frequently blundering into things rather like ayoomfas do when they've lapped too much happi-water. Sixpence was an expert bizzum catcher and he easily fished one of these slow and clumsy Brittin bees as it rumbled past him. The bee didn't seem to mind this very much and it obligingly walked around and around on the ground while Sixpence inspected it intently from every side. He even knocked it upside down to see what it looked like underneath. After a while he decided to eat it to see what it tasted like, and his efforts to lick it up the dozy bee eventually goaded it into action and it crawled up onto his nose and stung him before buzzing away as if nothing had happened. Sixpence squeaked in anger and pain and rubbed his nose furiously with his paw.

'You see how dangerous ray bees can be!' Humphrey chastised him earnestly. 'The ayoomfas in Brittin know this and are very sensible to stop more of them coming here than are here already.'

'So that's why they kept us in Kworren Teen. . .' Everything began to fall into place for me and I eagerly explained it to my friends. 'The whitecoatis kept us in Kworren Teen in case there were ray bee eggs inside us that might have hatched into ray bees!'

'I hate these horrid ray bees!' Sixpence shouted angrily. 'Worst of all it didn't die after it stung me - it simply flew away while I was rubbing my poor nose in pain! I thought all bees died if they stung something?'

'Fly away. It's best,' Choklit contributed.

'Ray bees are indestructible and cannot be killed by any creature, only by fire - that's why they are so dangerous,' Humphrey opined severely. 'Ayoomfas have to use big magic fire slinkis to stop great swarms of ray bees from going on a stinging rampage and taking over the whole world.' Sixpence looked very alarmed and his eyes grew wide and round.

'How do you know that, HuffPuff?' I asked. 'Or did you just make it all up so that you'd sound wise and knowledgeable to the Woon boys?'

'It's not impossible. . .' he said defensively, sheepishly washing the fur on his chest, 'It was you that said the eggs. . .'

'Yes, yes, I know that! But there's absolutely no reason to think some ray bees will bring on the end of the world. Really, HuffPuff, sometimes you're full of shufa! Sixpence, please don't be frightened by what Uncle HuffPuff says - he's just being silly. Ray bees will probably not sting us if we don't bother them.'

'But it did sting me, Aunty Bunni. Stung me terrible sore on my nose leather!'

'Yes but you tried to eat it.'

'Eat plokkits, it's best.' Choklit advised. 'We don't know where they come from but we know they don't sting you'.

We'd seen a huge slob of a cat hanging around a house on the other side of what was evidently a stinkiroli road made of hard black sticky, although luckily very few stinkirolis seemed to use it. This cat was a kind of blue-grey in colour and it was easily as big as Humphrey. We weren't interested in it at all and so paid it no heed, but it looked as if this great big cat was taking a special interest in us. This was bound to cause a problem - you knew this just by looking at the mutinous scowl on it's fat grey face and the fact that it spend a good deal of its time just sitting outside its house staring at us. To stare is rude - it's well known from Khat Lore. But the fat grey cat's rudeness knew no bounds. When it sat staring at us from across the road it was tolerable - just - but after a moon or so it became emboldened and crossed the road and sat staring malevolently at us from just outside the boundaries that Humphrey had so carefully marked around our house. One afternoon when it was doing this, Sixpence pattered up to it and in his usual sociable manner said,

'Hello, big grey cat. My name is Sixpence, what's your name?'

The grey cat responded by clouting Sixpence over the head and said gruffly,

'My name's Essex Innit. And don't speak to me unless I speak to you first, you phraidy phairy cat!'

This sent Sixpence scurrying back inside where he reported these events to Humphrey.

'. . .and he called me a phraidy phairy khat, Uncle HuffPuff! He was right there outside the stinkiroli room, Uncle HuffPuff.'

Humphrey went to look for the big grey cat but it had cautiously retreated back across the road and was sitting inside its house, sneering at us from behind a big window. Humphrey was not a cat with confrontational nature, but he felt it appropriate to let this grey thug know that he wouldn't stand for intrusion, so he spent some time pacing up and down outside our house, displaying his powerful striped body to good advantage. Then he spent the rest of the day sitting outside the front door of our house staring back at Essex Innit.

'If you ever see that Essex Innit cat it on our territory, you must call me at once,' Humphrey told Sixpence, Choklit and Pipple, 'don't try to speak to it or chase it away, just call me. One day when you're bigger I will teach you boys how to fight.'

Pipple was Essex Innit's next victim. She liked to grub around the plants outside the front of the house, dreaming peacefully amongst the flowers and the bizzums, and one day when she was doing this she looked up and saw Essex Innit standing right in front of her. It was too late to retreat without losing face, so she smiled and sweetly said, 'Hello, Essex' and tried to walk past him. Essex responded by biting her tail, which made her squeal and sent her running inside the house with no consideration of the loss of face. Essex Innit's behaviour was against Khat Lore. A yowli is not permitted to attack an old cat, especially a queen. Old cats of must be left in peace and always treated with respect and deference. It is our way.

'I will take care of this,' said Humphrey angrily, and he stalked across the road to where Essex Innit was sitting on a fence, looking smug.

'Hey you, fat grey cat. . .'

'You talking to me?' sneered Essex.

'You are Essex Innit?'

'Yeah, s'right. What about it?'

'Well I wanted to give you this!' said Humphrey and fiercely attacked him, taking him completely by surprise and knocking him off his fence into the bushes. This was most unusual, for normal Khat strategy is for a yowli to stare at their opponent for several minutes before wailing is commenced and then at least three naps worth of wailing is undertaken before actual physical force is used. Essex Innit was so taken by surprise that all he could think of was to run away inside his house, where he sat nursing his bruised pride and plotting revenge.

And so it came to pass a few days later that Essex came over and ambushed Humphrey from behind while he was making wizz. Humphrey was an extraordinarily brave cat, as I've mentioned before, and he stood his ground and fought furiously. Essex was a big yowli and he put up a good fight, managing to sink his teeth into Humphrey several times, but he'd not grown up on the streets like Humphrey nor earned his stripes fighting the wicked Grondus. He had the sense to realise that in the long term he'd likely be beaten, and it would serve him better to run back home and return to fight another day. The Woon boys and Pipple had been watching all this and cheering Humphrey on from the safety of the house and they saw Essex off with a barrage of derisory chants.

'Look, what's that running away . . .'

'Is it a squee? Is it a slinki?'

'No, it's a phraidy cat called Essex Innit.'

'Phraidy phraidy phraidy cat run away and don't come back . . .'

But Essex did come back. Again and again. And despite suffering serious injuries himself, he managed to wound Humphrey on several occasions so that Mummi and Daddi had to take him to the whitecoati.

'This is nothing,' Humphrey bragged as he returned one day from a whitecoati visit with part of his chest fur having been stolen, 'Essex will be *living* at his whitecoati's by now. Won't even be worth the trouble for him to come back home. Might just as well stay there and be stolen away bit by bit until he's nothing more than an insides-only cat.' Evidently the Brittin whitecoati also had a picture of an insides-only cat. It must be something all whitecoatis have.

Essex returned from the whitecoati looking most foolish. The whitecoati must have been on Humphrey's side, for he had devised a clever punishment for Essex, and he'd sent him home with his head stuck inside a strange white bowl. Essex couldn't see very well with this construction around his head and he kept largely to himself for a moon or so, spending all his energy trying unsuccessfully to remove the white bowl from his head, and plotting vengeance on us.

This sequence of events repeated several times and both yowlis became very battered. It was not unusual to see one or the other - or both - of them limping around with their head in a white bowl, or their paw wrapped up in softah, or parts of their fur stolen and wounds held together with some the whitecoati's pesky little black strings. At least none of them had to walk around with their tails in a hard white pipe as did poor Harvey some years later as a result of Sixpence's violent phase.

Still Essex came back. And every time Humphrey fought him off. I'd seen my Daddi making speaks with Daddi Innit at the whitecoati's and they both agreed that Essex's fighting with Humphrey had to be stopped. So Mummi and Daddi became involved in the fights and declared a *water war* on Essex. They did their best to chase him away whenever they saw him, but ayoomfas' reactions are so slow that by the time they'd got themselves ready with the magic rain slinki or a bowl of water, Essex was long gone. He thought this was terribly funny and he would tease my Daddi by sitting just out of reach where the magic rain slinki wasn't long enough to go. Daddi would end up simply making magic rain on the flowers and plants while Essex sat out of harm's way, chuckling to himself. I thought this very risky, as it is not wise to make war with the ayoomfas because they have very powerful magic and they can defeat any cat, given enough time.

And so it was that my Daddi, the great Mujaji Lord, employed clever and fiendish magic to make great water war against Essex and assist Humphrey in his valiant defense of our house. One of these magics was the powerful *surprise rain* magic. The surprise rain magic was a special stick that Daddi pushed into the ground in the middle of the grass. It had a long rain slinki attached to it, and some magic that Daddi could work from inside the house.

In due course Essex swaggered across the road to come see what it was Daddi had left stuck in the grass. It seemed to be doing nothing. Essex went up to it and sniffed it all over, deciding it was merely another foolish ayoomfa artifact and not an item of any consequence. He had just turned away to amble off home when Daddi made a tikki magic from inside the house and the stick in the lawn suddenly came alive and gave forth a great splattering rain in all directions, thoroughly soaking Essex, who ran home with major loss of face. One would think that he'd learned his lesson at the hands of the surprise rain magic, but he was a very stubborn and a very stupid cat, and in less than a moon he returned, his face regained, seeking to bully us or fight with Humphrey. But both Daddi and Humphrey were lying in wait for him, this time assisted by another of Daddi's clever magics, the *roli rainslinki*. By this time Essex knew exactly where he was safe from Daddi's usual rain slinki, and he'd contrive to remain just out of reach so Daddi couldn't wet him. His favorite spot was in a corner by our stinkiroli room, which was out of reach of the rain slinki but tauntingly still well in our territory. But he reckoned without the roli rainslinki, which has a big round with slinki on it and when the round spins the slinki just keeps coming endlessly. The slinki has a clever magic stick on the end of it that Daddi can use to make any kind of rain: from no rain at all to big rain, little rain, sideways rain, flat rain like a wall, and even misty rain like water smoke. The roli rainslinki can reach anywhere, and it easily reached Essex Innit in the corner that he thought was safe. He sat glaring at Daddi, defying him to make rain reach him. So Daddi did. With his magic stick he suddenly made angry hard rain, so strong that it kept Essex pushed up in his corner and he couldn't run away. Daddi showed no mercy, the hard rain just kept on coming until Essex looked like a fat squee that had drowned. We applauded this attack with cheers and taunts.

'Yay for Daddi! Wet him, wet him, wet him! Drown him in rain! Don't let him get away,' Humphrey urged.

After a good long rain Daddi decided that Essex had had enough and he moved the hard rain in a way that swept Essex out of his corner and away. Right to where Humphrey, emboldened by Daddi's presence, attacked him savagely. Essex was in no condition to defend himself and Humphrey gave him the thrashing of his life, so much so that Daddi had to come break them up with more rain from the roli rain slinki. Essex escaped and ran across the road towards his home. But Humphrey followed him, determined to settle this matter once and for all. And Daddi followed them both with the roli-rain slinki that goes anywhere, and he gave Essex another good soaking on his home ground, right outside his own door within a door. For one moment I thought that Daddi was going to make rain right *inside* Essex's house!

Essex never came on our side of the road again.

The food we were given in Brittin was broadly similar to that we ate in Sowf Efrika, but some of the special treats were missing. Daddi's delicious shmoo cheese that tasted of *pink sea slinkis* and which had nice lidda and potta proved impossible to get and we gave up hoping for it after a few moons. On the other hand Daddi would sometimes come back at sunset with a big brown bag of ayoomfa food which had a colourful marking on it. On closer inspection we saw that the marking on this bag was exactly the same as the marking on Humphrey's head - the marking he proudly said was unique to tabby cats and which other lesser cats did not have. So much for tabby exclusivity. The food inside the bag was the usual rubbish that ayoomfas like to scoff - a round of some meat and some cheese decorated with plant matter, drenched in sickly pink slime and heated with fire to remove what little goodness it might once have had. This abomination was stuck between two round softah things that the ayoomfas called *buns* and which tasted of nothing at all and are only really good eating for chirrits, squees and krorlis. Notwithstanding the shortcomings of this stuff, Humphrey made a big thing about it and called it *Tabby Food* because of the marking on the bag. On the few occasions Daddi came home with one of these Tabby Food bags, Humphrey would nearly go berserk and clamour for tidbits as if he were starving and it was truly delicious food. Not normally a very vocal cat to the ayoomfas, he would gurgle and trill and rumble and squeak like a tikki purik until Daddi capitulated and gave him a piece of the Tabby Food. And when he was given some he would eat it with tremendous relish - even bits of the tasteless plant matter drenched in pink slime. Also in the Tabby Food bag was a smaller bag filled with some of the little plant matter sticks that the ayoomfas call *chips* and Humphrey would obligingly eat several of these as well, commenting to all of us how delicious they were while trying hard not to gag.

What we didn't know at that time was that Capture was set to be an ever-present threat for the rest of our days. When we were at Midrand and Mummi and Daddi took it upon themselves to go away for some days, we always had Uncle Wessel and Auntie Gretha come stay with us to make up for the loss of our serving staff. We would still punish Mummi and Daddi when they returned, by deliberately ignoring them for a day or two to show that we cared so little that we hadn't even noticed that they were back. Humphrey wasn't very good at this could seldom hold out a stony attitude for more than a few hours, then his excitement would get the better of him.

'Yay!! DaddiDaddiDaddi!' he'd shout and he'd nearly throw himself at Daddi's feet and writhe around and make loud happi-rumble and fawn about like a silly gruf. We all loved Uncle Wessel and Auntie Gretha very much, and as I recall it was Uncle Wessel who several times took me to the whitecoati when I was sick and about to die.

None of this happened in Brittin. There was no Uncle Wessel or Auntie Gretha, but Mummi and Daddi still insisted on going away now and then. I could not understand this at all. If they loved us properly they would not want to be parted from us and would never go away. Or they would take us with them, but we'd probably get bored and want to come home within a few naps so it would be simpler for them to not go away in the first place. Whenever Mummi and Daddi were about to go away we would be taken by surprise and captured - usually as we were innocently eating our breakfast - and taken in fence-boxes in the stinkiroli, loudly shouting our displeasure, to various prisons where a variety of scowling and bloated ayoomfa ladies kept us in cold cages and fed us inferior fare. It wasn't until some winters later when we stayed at our beloved Auntie Sue that prison ceased to be an unpleasant experience and although we never, ever would admit it, we rather enjoyed our stays at Auntie Sue and returned home fat, sleek and contented.

We would all try and predict when Capture was imminent by watching for little telltale signs from our ayoomfas. Little things could give the game away - things like them packing their body covering softahs in boxes put on the bed; Daddi making hiss-hiss on the black rounds of the stinkiroli with his *hissing air slinki*; Mummi spending more time than usual on the magic speaking stick; and hushed speaks between them. Humphrey had a number of what he called 'fail proof plans' for predicting Capture but ayoomfas can be very sly creatures and despite our best efforts and Humphrey's plans, we never managed to accurately predict and pre-empt capture. Although Capture was an outrage out of our control, it was less loss of face than to falsely predict Capture and go shooting off up a tree like a crazy cat frightened of its own tail, with the ayoomfas laughing at us.

The day would dawn like any other day, and Daddi would stumble out of his ayoomfawumpus to go feed us and make tea for Mummi and himself. He would do exactly the same things as he did on every other day, so that there was nothing to remotely suggest anything was different or suspicious about Capture Day. Tea would be made in the rumbling potta, our food would be prepared and neatly chopped up the way we like it, and Daddi would carefully place our four bowls down in a row. On an ordinary day he would then go away, but on Capture Day Daddi would quick as a flash sit down right in front of our little door within a door so we couldn't go outside. He'd then call out to Mummi to begin rounding us up. Unbeknownst to us, while Daddi had been bashing things around and making the noises he did every other day, Mummi had been sneakily making Capture preparations and fence boxes suddenly appeared from nowhere. The reactions of my friends to Capture varied tremendously. Humphrey knew better than to dash about and hide away, and he simply continued with his breakfast until it was finished. Then, seeing the Woon boys had fled, he ate their breakfast, too, and if Pipple had already wandered off, he ate hers as well. When he'd cleared all the bowls, he simply sat and fatly waited to be captured. Pipple's reaction was to quietly glide away and sit quietly in some obscure place in the hopes that everyone would forget about her. Choklit figured if he couldn't see the ayoomfas, they couldn't see him, so he usually pattered off to hide on the ayoomfawumpus, under the softahs, where the ayoomfas found him immediately because he made a big bump in the softah and it was quite obvious there was something under it.

Sixpence, however, became totally hysterical on every single Capture day. He would run away and take refuge in some place where Mummi would have to grovel down on the floor and move all kinds of heavy ayoomfa constructions out the way in order to laboriously extract him from his hiding place. During this extraction, Sixpence invariably worked himself up into such a fearfully panting state of anxiety that he made accident-wizz all over Mummi. Mummi was always very kind about this and to avoid further embarrassment to Sixpence she pretended not to notice she was drenched in wizz, even though the most insensitive nose could detect the smell from two trees away. And when it was so bad that such deniability wasn't an option, Mummi would kindly claim that it wasn't his fault at all, and she had made the accident-wizz herself.

*****

CHAPTER TWENTY ONE:
Sixpence's Fish

Distractions lead to Capture and so it happened again that we again found ourselves mewling in dismay inside fence-boxes in the back of Daddi's rotting-fruit-coloured stinkiroli, headed, we suspected, for another stay in prison while the selfish ayoomfas went off somewhere without us. No doubt we'd find ourselves under the watchful eye of yet another rotund, disgruntled old ayoomfa hag that smelled of cooked vejtibils. No doubt in yet another cold, damp, cheerless place amid muddy fields peppered with large heaps of shufa carelessly dropped by big guelphs. No doubt in the company of many other miserable cats and endlessly yammering grufs. And indeed it was so.

Of course we were pleased when the ayoomfas returned some days later to take us back home, but this pleasure soon turned to alarm when it became clear we were not being returned home, for the journey was far too long. What inconvenience and disruption they had in mind for us we could only wait and see. After the time of a good sleep we arrived at a house set with a few others in pleasant surroundings at the foot of some wooded mountains. Once inside and released from our fenceboxes we soon recognised various ayoomfa articles which had been inside our last home but which had mysteriously disappeared one by one. We hadn't given this much thought at the time, as it's of no concern to us what ayoomfas do with their silly toys, but in hindsight we should have treated the disappearances of these articles as suspicious for they were clearly also a sign of impending Capture.

Humphrey immediately started to explore this new house, sniffing every corner of every room and every roomi and climbing up and down the bumpity hill that joined the Down House to the Up House. The ayoomfas had provided us with a door within a door but they'd played a trick on us and it was closed shut and wouldn't open, no matter how hard Humphrey pushed it with his big, strong head. As a further prank they smeared our clean paws with some horrible yellow shmoo that we'd sometimes seen them eat. Perhaps they intended to amuse themselves by watching us lose face making fools of ourselves sliding around on the hard shiny floor? But we'd had a stressful morning and really weren't in the mood for providing them with amusement, so we all trotted up the bumpity hill and gathered on Mummi's and Daddi's big ayoomfawumpus which we found in one of the rooms in the Up House. Luckily we were able to get most of the yellow shmoo off our paws by walking around on the white softahs of the ayoomfawumpus, and by the time Mummi and Daddi found us our paws were clean again and we were all fast asleep together on the ayoomfawumpus in a big heap of cat.

After a few nights Mummi and Daddi tired of their pranks and we discovered that the door within a door would open and close like it should. My companions all climbed through it to see what the new outside had to offer. The new outside was called Ox-Fid-Shuh, according to the ayoomfas. I'd already been outside, of course, but saw no reason to spoil the fun of their discovery. Like the last house, this one also had houses on either side and a small road in front of it. But the new outside seemed quieter and there were very few stinkirolis and even fewer ayoomfas around. We could see wooded mountains quite close by and unlike our last house, this one was in one of those places where you can see for a very long way and the sky looks big like it was in Midrand. There were cats living in many of the surrounding houses but they were all phraidy and none of them posed the least threat to us. So much so that when young Sixpence went across the road to politely greet a cat that looked a bit like himself, it immediately went scuttling inside it's house in fear.

At the back of out house in the middle of our garden was a place of water that the ayoomfas called a *pond*. It had rustling reeds and other interesting plants both in it and around it and to our great intrigue there were three fish swimming about in it. Quite big fish - each about the size of the dead ones that the ayoomfas bring home to burn and eat. These ones were the colour of the sunset and very shiny, like enormous *gulpas*, and one could see them clearly even though the water in the pond was muddy. I learned from listening to the ayoomfas speaking that the fish were called Harry, Frank and Louis, and that the ayoomfas were displeased at finding them there and intended to make Capture on them and take them somewhere else. Sixpence was mesmerised by the fish and spent every morning outside by the edge of the pond intently watching them swim lazily about, his eyes big and round. We originally assumed that Mummi and Daddi had been specially cultivating Frank, Harry and Louis with the intention of someday eating them, and that in accordance with the Second Claws of Khat Lore, we should not interfere in this activity. The Second Claws states that it is unmannered for one cat to steal the food animals of another. And for the purposes of Khat Lore, *ayoomfarolês* are declared honorary cats.

In the light of the revelation that the fish were not food animals of the ayoomfas, Humphrey gave Sixpence permission to catch and eat one if he could. Humphrey himself couldn't spare the time from his duties as Chief Cat, Pipple had found an orange bush to doze under and wasn't interested, Choklit-Butch was usually out hunting squees and chirrits in the many fields that lay within walking distance of our new house, and I was dead and so couldn't catch them anyway. So Sixpence spent day after day at the edge of the pond, gazing wide-eyed in rapture at the fish, chattering his teeth noisily at them and stretching ever further over the water. Every now and then when one of the fish approached close to the edge, Sixpence would put his paw out and smack the water above it, and the fish would then dart into the safety afforded by the reeds in the middle of the pond, and stay there for the rest of the day. Sixpence became very frustrated and asked me to help him.

'Auntie Bunni, you can go under the water without getting wet and through the ground without getting sand in your fur?'

'Yes, I can. Why do you ask?'

'The fish I'm after - the one called Frank - never comes close enough for me to catch it and it's making me very cross. I was hoping you'd be able to help me. . .'

'But Sixpence, my boy, you don't even like hunting. Why now do you suddenly want to catch a fish?'

'It's only the killing part and the tearing open that I don't like, because I don't like blood. The chasing and catching part is quite fun.'

'So what would you do with the fish if you did catch it?'

'I'd throw it back in the water and catch it again tomorrow, Auntie Bunni.'

'But that's a waste of a food animal. Khat Lore says that it's bad to waste a food animal when so many cats all over the world are starving. Claws Five, I think it is.'

Sixpence looked crestfallen, and then his face lit up.

'I know what I'll do! I'll catch the fish and then take it inside and give it to Mummi. She can do all the horrible blood things to it and then feed it to us in our bowls when it's all ready.'

'I don't know if Mummi will think this a good plan. It's always been my experience that the ayoomfas are remarkably ungrateful for the presents we bring them. I think it makes them embarrassed because it so blatantly demonstrates that our hunting skills are superior to their own.'

But Sixpence would hear no objection.

'Mummi loves me,' he said. 'Mummi will fix my fish for me.'

Well what harm could it do? And I'd never chased a fish in the water before so it could be quite exciting - being dead can be terribly boring and one is forever searching for interesting diversions. I agreed to participate in Sixpence's plan, which he'd clearly been plotting for several days. I would go into the water and herd the fish called Frank towards the edge of the pond where Sixpence was waiting for it and would scoop it out of the water with his agile paws. It had to be Frank, for Sixpence didn't want to catch Louis for some reason, and Harry was too big for him to catch anyway.

The water in the pond wasn't really that deep, a big gruf could stand on the bottom and still have his head above the water, but it was muddy and dirty and smelly. The pond might have been nice when it was new, but the ayoomfas who had been in the house before Mummi and Daddi hadn't kept it clean, and the water was so dirty that as I walked through it on the muddy bottom, I struggled to see more than a cat's length ahead of me. I felt very sorry for Harry, Frank and Louis living in this fetid mess, and would rather have been doing almost anything other than trudging underwater along the bottom of a murky pond trying to scare fish, but I had promised Sixpence. After a long time blundering about in the murky gloom I almost collided with the three slinkis, who had found a small oasis of cleanish water close to the surface in the middle of the pond, surrounded by a protective border of reeds. I'd forgotten to ask Sixpence which one was Frank, but I assumed he would know, so decided it was safest to chase all of them together. Also, I wasn't too sure how to scare a fish but as it turned out the mere spectre of a cat right there in the water next to them was sufficient to scare them witless and all three of them darted away, with me in hot pursuit, growling and hissing and looking as frightening as I could as I paddled myself under the water. Frank and his friends proved most uncooperative and I was forced to chase them all three times around the pond before they had the good sense to allow themselves to be herded closer towards the edge where Sixpence was waiting.

Then there was a great splash, which I assumed was Sixpence catching Frank. But Frank, Louis and Harry had disappeared and it was Sixpence who was before me in the water, splashing and thrashing about as he struggled to swim to the edge. After a short while he managed to make land and clamber out of the pond, shivering in the cold and looking more like a squee than a cat.

'What happened?' I asked. But Sixpence burst into tears and went running back to the house, calling for help.

'Mummi, Mummi, I fell in the water!' he cried as he threw his sopping body through the little door within a door, 'Mummi, it was horrible and stinky!' he mewled. Fortunately, it wasn't a day of work and Mummi was at hand with a pink *softah* to rub him dry and provide comfort and solace on lap. Sixpence felt very sorry for himself and continued his lament of how horrible and stinky it was for many days thereafter. Choklit and Humphrey were both highly amused at the events of the day, and not a little disparaging.

'So much for your special name of Little Dancing Feet,' Humphrey teased, 'Maybe you should change it to *Water Guelph.*'

'Swim away. It's best,' said Choklit-Butch, and trotted off to have a snack of plokkits.

Mummi and Daddi took it upon themselves to catch Harry, Frank and Louis. This was truly an amusing spectacle of ayoomfa ineptitude at its best. Realising they stood little chance of catching the fish in any honest and direct manner, they resorted to cunning ayoomfa trickery. I sat with all four of my companions outside the house and watched with interest as the tableau unfolded. Both ayoomfas donned long coverings made of soft green *bouncy* over their hind legs and these green things kept out the water so that they could walk around in the pond without getting wet and muddy.

'That's a clever thing,' Humphrey observed, 'Perhaps Sixpence should get himself some of those bouncy green coverings for his paws. . .'

'It was *horrible*,' Sixpence muttered darkly, '. . .and *stinky*.'

'So you've said, my boy. Many, many times.' sighed Humphrey.

'Fish should swim away today. It's best,' Choklit-Butch said seriously.

Using a variety of specially fabricated ayoomfa sticks Mummi and Daddi managed to cut down and remove all the reeds and plants in the pond, so they could walk around in the filthy water unobstructed. This looked like it could be interesting, so we all moved closer and sat in a neat row just on the edge of the grass, watching the ayoomfas as they clumsily thrashed about in the pond.

Then they obtained from inside the house a number of cheerfully coloured drums and laboriously filled these with stinking water from the pond and emptied it out on the grass. It was very hard work for them and they puffed and panted and muttered darkly as they toiled. Their breath made clouds of white water-smoke as they sloshed around in the stinky water under the low and feeble sun of a winter's afternoon. I really cannot understand how creatures that have water magic so powerful that it can make a great waterfall come rampaging from nowhere into a shufa bowl and then simply disappear back into nowhere again, have to resort to such pathetically crude methods to empty a pond!

After a while there was only a small pool of fetid muddy water in one corner of the pond and Daddi was able to scoop Frank, then Louis into one of the coloured bins. Fish Capture! Meanwhile Mummi had filled another of the bins with clean water from the magic water that came out the wall and Daddi dumped Frank and Louis into this clean water where at least they could breathe properly and see where they were swimming. Big Harry proved more elusive and it was only when scowling and grumbling, Daddi had got down in the mud himself and cornered Harry in one last remaining tiny puddle and Harry was flapping about helplessly in the mud, that he finally surrendered to Fish Capture.

'What will they do with the fis§h?' Pipple asked.

'They'd make good eating,' Humphrey said, licking his lips. 'Especially that big one they call Harry. He gave Daddi a lot of trouble and I should think Daddi should have him for supper tonight.'

'Maybe they'll save some for us,' Choklit said hopefully.

'Those fish deserve to be eaten. It was their fault that I fell in the water. It was *horrible*! And *stinky*!' Sixpence reminded us all yet again.

'Be quiet, boy!' snapped Humphrey.

Daddi carried the drum of water which housed Harry, Frank and Louis to his rotting-fruit-coloured stinkiroli, and with Mummi holding the bin carefully so no water would be spilled, they rolled away. It being too late for my curiosity to kill me now, I went along with them, resolved to see what fate lay ahead for the three fish. After a few naps the stinkiroli stopped in the road outside a most interesting place indeed. Outside this place were arranged several wooden gruf-houses and bags of gruf food, and a big festively coloured chirrit in a fence box which hung from the roof squawked a few words of ayoomfa speak to ayoomfas as they passed by. Inside the building was a great glorpness of fascinating things: Everywhere I looked food animals were in fence boxes. Big white chirrits with yellow heads like the one of MyGranni's daughter sat preening themselves, small green chirrits squabbled and chattered, delicious looking squee-like creatures ran around and around endlessly on round things, and fish of every size and shape swam around in window-like boxes of water and special ponds. In one corner of this busy room a number of ayoomfa puriks stood admiring some hopits snuffling in their dry grass, while another group of tikki ayoomfas marveled at a meal-sized slinki that sat on a tree branch and changed himself from one colour to another in an attempt to render itself invisible. Stupid slinki! Capture has happened already - it's too late to hide. Piled everywhere were sack upon sack of plokkits for cats and grufs, bags of seed for chirrits, toys for cats, toys for chirrits, and big bone things made of red *bouncy* on which the stupid grufs can practice their drooling and slavering. There were schnoogli wumpus beds of many shapes and sizes for cats and grufs, more wooden gruf-houses, an assortment of fence-boxes of the kind used for Capture, and too many other things for a tikki Phirish to comprehend at one time.

I concluded the place was some kind of emporium where ayoomfas could exchange toys and food animals for their cats and grufs. Daddi spoke to one of the ayoomfas in this place, and they emptied Harry, Frank and Louis from their grubby drum into a kind of wooden pond in which there were plants growing and a little stream that tinkled over some grey rocks and became a tikki waterfall. The wooden pond already had several other sunset coloured giant gulpa fish swimming around in it, one of which was huge - nearly as big as Sixpence. This was the new home of Frank, Louis and Harry.

Despite the many opportunities to delight their cats with presents, Mummi and Daddi came back empty handed. Empty handed! I told my friends where they'd been and what had happened.

'You mean they gave away three perfectly succulent fish? In exchange for what? A tasty brown squee running on a round thing? A couple of crunchy green chirrits, perhaps?'

'No, nothing.'

'Not even a sack of plokkits? Not a delectable strip of treat meat? You mean absolutely nothing? Paws empty, mouth empty, belly empty nothing?' Humphrey was speechless.

'Yes, that kind of nothing,' I confirmed sadly.'

'These ayoomfas of ours are really useless!' he fumed, and stalked off. 'Sometimes I don't know why we bother to help them.'

It grew very cold that winter and we were astonished when a glorpness of white powder fell from the sky. We had seen this white powder from afar while in Kworren Teen, but having it underfoot everywhere was a new experience for my friends. The white powder was soft and cold and lay on the ground as deep as a cat's legs. Cats with dangling, fluffy underbelly *lollijubber* like Pipple and Humphrey had to suck in their breath as they walked outside to make wizz, otherwise their bellies would drag in the white powder and become frozen. As the only queen in my household, Pipple had to make wizz standing up like a Tom, to avoid her bottom freezing. She couldn't quite master the technique and ended up with the stream of wizz running hotly down her fluffy hind legs. Humphrey found this enormously amusing and pranced around her squirting his wizz far and high to show her what a skillful wizzing yowli he was. But even a yowli has to sit down to make shufa and the white powder caused us a lot of bother. It was necessary to scrape enough of it away to be able to sit comfortably on the earth below and this intensive digging in the white powder made forepaws very cold indeed. Pipple and Sixpence, who had light pink pads, found that they suddenly had very red pads.

The ayoomfas had a special name for the white powder - they called it *snow*. It seemed to excite them tremendously and many of them went outside their houses and began throwing the snow at each other. Mummi began piling great quantities of it into a big heap that she spent a long time shaping so that it looked like a cat. But it wasn't a real cat, just another of those ridiculous ayoomfa make-believe constructions. Everyone knows that cats do not have eyes made of stones and whiskers made of grass. Mummi could have used her time and energies more fruitfully sitting inside in the warm house with all her real cats on her lap.

The following spring Pipple became unwell. She was by this time quite an old cat and had splashed her way through nearly three paw's pads of winters. She decided one day that she was going to die and told us this.

'My time ha§ come to die. I'm going to §it under my orang§e bus§h and wait for Tabi§that to come take me away.'

There wasn't much we could say about this and simply watched as she glided into the garden and installed herself under her favorite orange bush, the morning sun playing patterns on her face as she blinked her one eye. The day wore on and sunset came. Pipple got up and went inside.

'Tabi§that didn't come today,' she said, very disappointed.

'Perhaps you're not going to die after all?' I suggested.

'No, I'm ready to die. Tabi§that may come tomorrow.'

After two days of Pipple not eating her food and staying outside all day, Mummi and Daddi became suspicious that something was wrong with her. They made Capture on Pipple and took her to the whitecoati. Of course I went along as observer. Whitecoati poked and prodded Pipple, he kneaded and squeezed her all over, he stuck the shiny stick up her shufa hole, he listened to her belly with his ear slinkis, he looked inside her mouth, and he shook his head sadly. The gist of the ayoomfa discourse that followed was that Pipple was very old and lots of things inside her were tired and worn out. Whitecoati used a pointing stick to show Mummi and Daddi on his big picture of the Insides Only Cat where these tired and worn out things were.

I'd not noticed any sudden changes in Pipple's radiance but it occurred to me later that compared to that of my other friends, her whole radiance had dimmed, and it had done so very gradually, as autumn fades to winter. It had happened so slowly I hadn't noticed it happening.

'What'§ he §aying, Bunni?' Pipple asked.

'He says you're going to die unless the ayoomfas can manage to get you to eat.'

'But eating i§ pointle§§ becau§e I'm going to die,' Pipple slobbered stubbornly. 'Thi§ i§ §imple Phluffi Logic. The §tupid whitecoati i§ ju§t wai§ting everybody'§ time.'

Pipple was brought back home and the ayoomfas did their best to feed her as she lay in her bed on the pink wubbis MyGranni had given her. They put a small dollop of very shmoo kukri on a tikki ayoomfa eating stick and tried to push it into her mouth, but Pipple was having none of this. She steadfastly kept her mouth tightly shut and the ayoomfas merely succeeded in smearing kukri all over her white muzzle and whiskers. Following instructions from the whitecoati, Daddi found a magic way to squeeze Pipple's mouth open a bit so that Mummi could quickly push in some of the kukri but this also didn't work. Pipple merely spat it out again when they were not watching. Pipple's life force was fading fast and she no longer had the strength to walk outside to her orange bush. She was most vexed about this.

'I want to die in the §un§shine!' she shouted. Not in thi§ cold, dark ayoomfa hou§e. Tabi§that'§ not ex§pecting me here and he won't find me, don't you §§seee!' She lurched out of her bed and stumbled towards the little door within a door, but when she got there she didn't have the energy to make the little jump through it, and collapsed onto the floor, shouting angrily at the world. Even Mummi and Daddi - simple ayoomfarolês - could not fail to understand Pipple's wishes. They picked her up, took her outside and placed her down gently under the overhang of her favourite orange bush in the exact position they had seen her spend so many days, with the dappled sunshine on her face. Humphrey came outside too, trying to be helpful.

'Pipple, old girl, you must hurry up and die,' he said seriously. 'If you haven't died before sunset the ayoomfas will worry about you dying in the cold and they'll take you back inside for the night.'

And wouldn't you know it, he was quite right. The ayoomfas took her back inside and placed her basket right next to their big ayoomfawumpus in the Up House. Mummi used Pipple's pink wubbis to wrap her up into a sosij role, like she had done for me when I was near death after being attacked by the gruf. And they took her outside again the next morning after one more fruitless attempt to make her eat.

At high sun on the second day Tabithat found Pipple by her orange bush and lifted her spirit away. The ayoomfas were heartbroken and my family of cats weren't far behind them. Pipple had been a soft soothing, smoothing presence in all their lives and in my afterlife. I hoped Tabithat would have her bed ready.

*****

CHAPTER TWENTY TWO:
Humphrey's Legacy

Only a few moons after Pipple went to Tabithat, Daddi became unwell. His radiance showed a yellowing around his chest and I noticed he was becoming very angry and red in the face at everybody and everything, more so than usual. I thought it would be wise for him to go to the whitecoati. When I told Humphrey this he became every distressed and did not want to let Daddi out of his sight. Whenever Daddi sat down or lay down, Humphrey would climb up his chest so he could nuzzle Daddi's face with his big striped head. He simply would not leave Daddi alone. I was expecting Daddi to think him a pest and chase him away, but Daddi knew he was unwell and he welcomed Humphrey's presence. Humphrey said this was called *partial tabby comfort* and it was one of two kinds of tabby comfort. The other kind, called *total tabby comfort,* was more comprehensive and involved fully covering the subject in tabby cats all making happi-rumble at the same time. But Humphrey said he could not find enough tabby cats in our area to do total tabby comfort, as the only other tabby living nearby was Sylvester, whom Humphrey said was a complete nincompoop incapable of reliably following simple instructions. Humphrey hoped that partial tabby comfort would make Daddi well again, but it wasn't enough. One night Daddi woke up in the middle of the night feeling very bad indeed and he woke Mummi to tell her about this. Mummi spent some time comforting herself on the magic speaking stick and sometime after that a *wee-woo flashroli* appeared outside our house, making a most dreadful noise that sounded something like a yowling contest between Wicked Grondus and Essex Innit. The wee-woo flashroli was a white box stinkiroli, with lots of magic blue suns on top which danced around and around in a fascinating way and woke up all the cats in the street. And so horrible was the noise it made that Choklit-Butch got right into the big ayoomfawumpus and burrowed his way down under the softahs until all that could be seen was a bump.

'If I can't see them, they can't see me,' he repeated his comforting mantra over and over again. Sixpence sat by the window, staring intently at the wee-woo flashroli outside, his eyes big and round. Thankfully the dreadful noise was choked off after a short while and two ayoomfas in bright yellow coverings - a man and a woman - emerged from the front doors of the wee-woo flashroli and went round to the back, where they opened a big door and took out a *roli-board*. They carried the roli-board into our house and Humphrey ran excitedly around and in between their feet, trying to marshal them.

'This way! This way!' he chattered urgently. The ayoomfas picked up Daddi and put him on the roli-board. Some discussion then followed on where they were going to take him. Mummi suggested the name of a place, but the wee-woo flashroli woman told Mummi that there were 'no beds available' at this place. I had a moment of panic that this was one of Tabithat's places, and that Daddi was going to die, for I know from experience that Tabithat has great trouble finding beds. It's the Maine Coons in Facilities, he says. The stupid Coons can't be trusted to do anything right. And they're so cheeky. But I digress; with much nodding of heads the wee-woo flashroli ayoomfas decided to take Daddi to another place, hopefully one where there was a special whitecoati who understood how ayoomfas work inside and maybe had a picture of an insides-only ayoomfa to remind him where things were. Daddi was carried outside on the roli-board and put inside the wee-woo flashroli. Then the ayoomfas shut the big back door, climbed inside the front part and the wee-woo flashroli rolled away, shrieking its terrible noise. Two of the cats from across the road had woken up and they came over to ask Humphrey what all the excitement was about.

'It's nothing to do with you bums. Go back to bed before I tear your heads off !' he snarled ferociously, sending them scuttling back inside their houses.

Mummi was very unhappy and Humphrey determined to transfer the benefits of the partial tabby comfort to her, which I could see she appreciated.

Daddi was away at the whitecoati for about two paws' pads of days. One morning Mummi brought him home and I could see that his radiance was much stronger and that the yellow patch in his chest had gone. He didn't go to work for another couple of paws' pads of days, during which Humphrey lavished him with partial tabby comfort. Daddi responded well to this and was soon back to his normal state and able to properly fulfill his duty to feed and entertain us.

Humphrey adopted a strange habit of playing toms and queens with Choklit-Butch. He would sit on top of Choklit-Butch, holding him by the ruff of the neck and making fruka-fruka actions with his pink wizzlepizzle sticking out. I'd not seen this before, maybe it's a tabby thing. Humphrey had being doing it a lot lately, much to the tremendous amusement of the ayoomfarolês, who would laugh so much they couldn't stand on their hind legs and had to sit down. Choklit seemed fairly resigned to his role in this strange game and although he may have wanted to run away, he made no attempt to do so. Not that he would have got far, for Humphrey had him very firmly pinned down.

'Shame on you Humphrey!' I told Humphrey one day when he was playing his strange tabby game with Choklit, 'You're taking unfair advantage of poor Choklit because he's not very bright.'

'Yeeesssss!' said Humphrey.

Khat Lore doesn't say anything about such acts so I though it wisest not to interfere further.

Also around this time, Humphrey began taking Sixpence away for long times, for 'special skills training by Reverend Spooner' he claimed.

'Who is Reverend Spooner? What happened to Mrs. Malaprop,' I quizzed him.

'Mrs. Malaprop lived near our old house in Sowf Efrika, far away. And the type of training the boy needs now is altogether different. You need not concern yourself with it, Bunni. I am your Chief Cat and as always, I have everything under complete control.'

This served only to further intrigue me, so one day I followed them from a discrete distance making full use of *Phirish Phollowing Knowledge* to see what they got up to with the Reverend Spooner. But there was no Reverend Spooner. What Sixpence and Humphrey did was fight. Sixpence, of all cats, fighting! Sixpence with his dainty dancing feet and theatrical whiskers! It became clear after watching this performance for a while that Humphrey was teaching him to fight - and apparently making a fairly good job of it, for Sixpence was giving him quite a pasting!

When they returned I asked Sixpence casually, 'So what did the Reverend Spooner teach you today, Sixpence?'

'Uh…this and that, Aunty Bunni. This and that,' he answered nonchalantly. Humphrey, too, was casually evasive, 'Reverend Spooner is a good teacher,' he said.

Sixpence's training continued for several moons. It was obviously proving very successful and increasingly, Humphrey was starting to look a bit battered on their return.

'What happened to you?' I asked him one day, 'You look as if you've been in a fight.'

'No, no, no! I fell in a hole in Spooner's back garden,' he said.

'Are you alright, HuffPuff? I've noticed lately that your radiance seems to be a bit dimmer than it normally is,' I asked.

'Fah! Nonsense! I'm as strong as Poyk and getting stronger every day!' he boasted. Just a bit tired because I had to scrabble out of a hole. I think I'll go lie down and rest now.'

Humphrey's excuses became more and more fanciful as time went by and he became progressively more battered. A couple of good ones I remember: *We were on our way home from Spooner's and I was attacked by a swarm of ray-bees which overwhelmed me. . .* and . . . *Part of the lid of the Reverend's house fell down on my head. . .* and then the most imaginative of all: *A tikki guelph in a tikki rumbleroli rode into me.* This one I definitely couldn't accept at face value.

'Is this true, Sixpence?' I asked.

'Yes, of course Aunty Bunni. I saw it all happen with my own eyes.' He nodded furiously.

'What sort of guelph was it?'

'Uh. . You know, just an ordinary tikki guelph. Like you see in the woods,'

'And it was in a tikki rumbleroli?'

'Uh yes. . ' Sixpence said, slightly hesitantly, 'A red one.'

'Also like you see in the woods,' Humphrey added.

'I've never, ever seen a tikki red rumbleroli in the woods,' I challenged.

Humphrey shrugged in disinterest. It clearly wasn't his problem that I hadn't been in the right place at the right time.

'Sixpence, what do you think a tikki red rumbleroli would be doing in the woods,' I persisted.

'I could only speculate, Aunty Bunni.'

'Probably delivering *rumbloid*,' supplied Humphrey.

And it got worse and worse!! According to Humphrey, tikki guelphs that lived in holes in the trees in the woods could not make happi-rumble by themselves like cats do, and if these hole-dweller guelphs wanted to make happi-rumble, they had to first lap up a fluid called rumbloid. Rumbloid could only be obtained from rumbloid wells in a hot, sandy, faraway place called Rumbloon. And rumbloid from Rumbloon was delivered to hole dwellers in the woods by tikki guelphs in small red rumblerolis. . .

It must have taken even the fanciful Humphrey a paws' pads of days to concoct this intricate web of nonsense! In the end I gave up and left them with their secret still secure.

'I have something important to say to you all,' Humphrey said one morning, a few days after coming out with the ludicrous tale of the rumbloid, 'You too, Bunni. This concerns everyone. Let's all meet in the outside room which has floor but no walls or lid.'

'I'm dead. You don't have any jurisdiction over me,' I told him. No cat, alive or dead, likes being told what to do.

'Yes Yes Yes, I know that. Bunni, *please* come listen to what I have to say.'

I had nothing better to do than humour Humphrey, so I went along to sit in the sunshine in the room with floor but no walls or lid, where the Woon Boys were already waiting for their Chief Cat to address them.

Humphrey said, 'I've got you all together to tell you that I am very sick and going to die.' Choklit looked mortified, although Sixpence was not as shocked as I would have expected him to be. Humphrey continued, 'Poisons I got from fighting the wicked Grondus have been hiding inside me for several winters and have now awakened. They are destroying me from within.'

'Maybe it's kid-nees,' suggested Choklit-Butch, seriously.

'But you are a young cat,' I said, 'You've seen only eight winters - it's not as if you're finished and worn out like Pipple or me. Surely the whitecoati will be able to do something?'

'These are very powerful poisons which the wicked Grondus created in Hell and I doubt the whitecoati's magic is a match for them. Now, as I am your Chief Cat, it falls upon me to appoint a successor.'

Everyone's eyes turned to me. 'Don't look at me!' I protested. 'I can't be Chief Cat, I'm dead.'

'NoNoNo, that wasn't my plan,' Humphrey said. 'Obviously it must be one of the Woon boys.' Hearing this, Choklit-Butch beamed and turned his face sideways so the sun would reflect off his magnificent hunting whiskers. To further emphasise his splendid physique he began ostentatiously washing one of his huge hunting forepaws.

After a long pause Humphrey said, 'I've decided that Sixpence will be Chief Cat.'

'Thank you Uncle HuffPuff!' Sixpence said.

Choklit looked appalled and stopped washing his paw. 'But . .b. . .but he can't even hunt!' he protested, 'He's Mummi's baby with his little dancing feet and theatrical whiskers. And he's chubby! Look at me, I've got powerful hunting forepaws, magnificent hunting whiskers and I'm fit and strong. . .'

'And what would you do if evil Essex Innit tried to invade your house?' Humphrey asked him.

'Run away! It's best.' Choklit said with no hesitation at all.

'Exactly. And that's no good, Choklit. It's a jungle out there. A Chief Cat must be fearless and be able to fight off any threat. You can't just run away. NoNoNo'

Choklit looked chastened   'Since when is Sixpence such a fearless fighter?' he asked resentfully.

'Since I trained him. With a little help from the Reverend Spooner,' he said, winking at me.

'Not forgetting swarms of killer ray-bees and a tikki red rumbleroli full of rumbloid. . .'

'YesYesYes, them, too. Choklit, my boy, I know you are in fine shape, and a truly magnificent hunter, but a Chief Cat needs to be more than that. A Chief Cat needs to have a brave heart, and above all, be very, very smart. Sixpence is truly a clever cat, and you're, well. . . how can I say . . .'

'Completely stupid,' Sixpence supplied for him. Choklit-Butch looked indignant and started to protest, but before he could say anything, Sixpence had pounced on him, held him down, and whumped him repeatedly on the head, causing a chunk of black fur to waft over and fall at my feet. 'I am now Chief Cat and these dancing feet will help you remember that!' he said firmly. Then he sat down again next to me and began washing his paws, leaving us all astonished and Choklit-Butch somewhat worse for wear.

'By Tabithat! Did you teach him how to do that, Humphrey?' I was quite impressed.

'Well, uh, . . .a bit of yes. And also a bit of no. Now listen, my time is nearly up. Much as I would like to, I can no longer be your Chief Cat. Everyone, it's been a pleasure. Sixpence, you are in charge of this house as of now. You know what to do, so do it well. Now I'm going to make partial tabby comfort with my Daddi.'

'But Daddi's not sick anymore,' I said.

'YesYesYes, I know that, Bunni. This time it's for me,' replied Humphrey, and walked away.

*****

CHAPTER TWENTY THREE:
The Reign of Sixpence

Humphrey would be remembered fondly by everyone, especially his Daddi, with which he had spent so much time imbibing in partial tabby comfort. Little Sixpence was very aware of the big paw prints that his Uncle HuffPuff had left for him to follow as Chief Cat of the house in Ox-Fid-Shuh.

A Chief Cat must be ready for anything at any time and to show surprise is a great loss of face which could result in the Chief losing the confidence of other Citizens of the House. Rather unfairly I thought, Tabithat saw fit to test Sixpence's preparedness by devising a myriad of outlandish events with which to confront him. The first of these was an enormous chirrit the likes of which none of us had ever seen. It was coloured deep orange and its head was decorated with a fascinating variety of red and white and green shiny bits like some festive article one might expect to find in Tabithat's house. And it was big, very big. It came out the sky and settled in the back garden and began scoffing the seed and other unpalatable white softah that Mummi kindly strew around to attract little chirrits for us to catch and eat. Sixpence was sitting gazing out the window in the Up House with his Mummi when it arrived, His eyes became round like saucers and he began chattering through his teeth at the big chirrit. Mummi thought this was amusing and I learned that this gaudy chirrit was what the ayoomfas called a *fezzint*.

'D. .don't panic, Mummi. I'll go ch. .chase it away,' Sixpence stammered nervously in Khat, then trotted down the bumpity hill and outside to bravely defend his domain against this new and unknown evil. Once outside he saw that the fezzint appeared considerably bigger than it had been when viewed from the window of the Up House, and it was quite a bit bigger than him. Sixpence twitched his theatrical whiskers and swallowed nervously as he approached it. His dancing feet suddenly felt very small.

'Hey you there - big chirrit with the red head! This is my house! G. .go away!'

The fezzint just looked at him. 'Cuuuurrrrrkkk,' it said defiantly, and resumed pecking for food. This angered Sixpence and anger boosted his courage. A Chief Cat could not be seen to be defied by a trespassing chirrit with a red head, and he would have no face left at all if he didn't resolve this properly.

'If you don't go away right now I will come and bite your silly red head off,' he warned the fezzint by chattering his teeth furiously in the traditional manner understood by all cat-fearing chirrits. Seeing him approach the fezzint decided that it should take some action. But it couldn't decide what action to take. First it ran a few steps away from him. Then it saw that this would lead it into a corner of the garden where it would be trapped, so it changed its mind and turned around and ran straight towards Sixpence. No good! It tried to run towards the left, but saw that that would lead it into the stinkiroli road, so it changed its flustered mind and darted off to the right. And then indecision struck again and the whole cycle repeated, with the agitated fezzint shrieking in distress and Sixpence watching in wonder as the huge chirrit seemed set to implode itself in a fit of frenzied dithering. Eventually it seemed to remember it could fly and with a great beating of wings and a loud *cuuuurrrrk* it clumsily flapped itself into the air and flew off towards the road, not far from the ground. Sixpence watched in amazement as the stupid fezzint flew straight into the front of a passing stinkiroli, whereupon it exploded in a great cloud of feathers and fell to the ground in a very dead heap. Boomaskwasha! The stinkiroli stopped, a man got out of it, inspected the front of the stinkiroli, picked up the lifeless fezzint and put it down on the side of the road, then got back into the stinkiroli which rolled away again.

'Gosh! Did I do all that?' Sixpence asked aloud, amazed at the great power he now wielded. He wandered over to the dead pheasant and sniffed it over very carefully. The foolish ayoomfa in the stinkiroli had killed then simply abandoned this valuable food animal, against all the sage teachings of Khat Lore. Sixpence decided he would drag the fezzint back inside the house to show Choklit and Mummi what a huge chirrit he, Chief Cat Sixpence, had caught and killed all by himself. Straining with effort and puffing with exhaustion, he managed to get it as far as the back door of the house, only to find he simply didn't have the strength to lift it up and heave it through the little door within a door. This was just as well, for as a wise Phirish I could see that the fezzint was in any case clearly too big to pass through our little door within a door. Sixpence was forced to leave his fezzint outside the house and content himself with a big, colourful feather which he brought inside and gave to Mummi amid a great outburst of self-congratulatory trilling.

'You've nothing to fear now, Mummi,' he said. 'Chief Cat Sixpence has effortlessly defeated this dangerous intruder and will confidently deal with anything else that comes along.' Humphrey had evidently taught him this kind of conceited patter. Maybe all creatures feel the need to speak in this pompous way once they've been given a modicum of authority?

Mummi was delighted with her fezzint feather and put it in a special kind of round box she sometimes put on top of her head-fur. Choklit-Butch, Mummi and Daddi were all decidedly impressed at the size of Sixpence's kill, and Sixpence wallowed in all this admiration and gained much face. Daddi initially had some doubts that Sixpence had killed the chirrit, but Mummi staunchly defended him and told Daddi that she had seen the fezzint in the garden, she had seen Sixpence run outside to take issue with it, and the next thing she saw the fezzint lying dead outside the back door. It had to have been Sixpence that killed the fezzint. Daddi reluctantly accepted this version of events. I promised Sixpence that I would keep his secret.

Tabithat must have been very chirrit-focused at that time, for not long after the fezzint incident, we had a visit from some other massive chirrits. These ones were very much like the common grey chirrits that used to gather in huge numbers at Chirrit Rock back in Vietnam, and for eating one of which I was punished by MyGrandad's magic rain slinki. But the three that Tabithat sent to us in Ox-Fid-Shuh were bigger, much bigger, nearly the size of a small cackack and they were so fat they could barely flap themselves off the ground. These chirrits were what the ayoomfas called *pidjins*. As an expert on these and most other things, I would hazard that it would take a very big and skilled hunting cat to catch one of these fat pidjins. Humphrey would have managed, and possibly Choklit-Butch, but definitely not Sixpence with his little dancing feet and theatrical whiskers. Sixpence, however, thought otherwise. He believed sincerely that he had sent the fezzint to it's death through his magic powers as Chief Cat, and that he could now accomplish virtually anything. The arrogant pidjins made no move to flee as Sixpence stalked them, creeping low on the ground as he had seen done by his brother Choklit, while all the time trying to keep his soft white belly fur above the wet grush by sticking his bottom up in the air. He looked thoroughly ridiculous. Even Mummi, who was quietly observing this spectacle from inside the house, could not help from laughing. The fat pidjins reasoned that this small, chubby, and apparently demented, cat couldn't possibly pose any threat to them and they paid him no heed as they greedily gobbled up the chirrit food that Mummi had scattered around. And so it was that Sixpence was able to walk right amongst the pidjins unnoticed and grab hold of one of them in his paws. It wasn't easy, for the pidjin was so fat that Sixpence couldn't properly clamp his jaws around its lower neck like he had seen done by his Uncle HuffPuff and his brother Choklit. He managed to strain his mouth open wide enough to get a tentative purchase on the chirrit and then shuffled awkwardly back to the house, waddling unsteadily with the big pidjin in his mouth. Surprisingly, it made very little effort to struggle, being either resigned to its fate or confident that Sixpence would sooner or later come to his senses and let it go. Sixpence was overjoyed. Now at last he was a Great Hunter like his brother Choklit! And it had all been so easy. He could barely wait to take his big chirrit to Mummi so she could prepare it for him. He would tell her all about it, how he had stalked it so quietly that it hadn't even noticed him creep up right next to it. How he had been fearless and brave and captured it. How he had determinedly brought it back to the house with all the odds stacked against him. He looked around to see who all had witnessed his triumph; Unfortunately Choklit-Butch was out hunting somewhere and nowhere to be seen, but Mummi had seen it all and she had come outside, I thought probably to stop Sixpence bringing the pidgin inside more than to congratulate him.

When he saw his Mummi come to greet him in his finest hour, Sixpence could no longer contain himself.

'Look Mummi! Look what I caught! I caught this big chirrit. . .' he began to chatter excitedly. Needless to say, the moment he opened his mouth to speak, the fat pidgin took the opportunity to escape. With a great beating of wings it flew up onto the fence and apparently none the worse for wear, it sat preening its feathers where Sixpence had slobbered on them. Sixpence was aghast. In the blink of an eye his finest hour had turned into his worst nightmare and he was left embarrassed and humiliated.

Mummi tried to stifle her laughter to avoid further humiliating him, but in this she failed utterly. And now Daddi had come outside too, and both ayoomfarolês were chortling merrily. Sixpence was devastated. How could he possibly justify his allowing the fat pidgin to escape? His self-esteem was shattered and his face. . .his face was all lost. He began washing his chest, very slowly and very carefully, and thought of ways he could regain his lost face. Mummi probably felt a bit guilty that she'd laughed at Sixpence, and realising how embarrassed he must have felt, she scooped him up in her forepaws and took him inside the house to comfort him.

'It was the right thing to do, to let it go, Mummi. It would have made Choklit feel inadequate as a hunter,' Sixpence told her, 'As Chief Cat I have to consider the feelings of others in my household.'

Mummi, who could not understand Khat, simply patted him on the head and made soothing sounds as she smiled to herself.

'I suppose you'd like me to forget about this, too?' I asked Sixpence. He looked shamefaced at me and nodded.

Tabithat became bored of sending us chirrits, and some moons after the escape of Sixpence's pidgin he sent us the most extraordinary guelph any of us had ever seen. It was quite tikki, smaller than Sixpence's pidgin, and it had four short legs on which it slowly trundled along close to the ground. It was a uniform grey brown colour and was covered everywhere except its face and legs with long hard spikys. I learned later from listening to Mummi and Daddi speak about it that this tikki guelph was not uncommon in Brittin, and that the ayoomfa name for it was *hej-hog*. I learned further that it was a very wise guelph indeed, as it was in the habit of sleeping for the whole winter. But that spring when Sixpence came across the hej-hog while he was grubbing in the garden, he knew none of this, and at first he thought it was a piece of old dead log. He reached out one of his little dancing paws to gently touch it, and got a nasty surprise when it pricked him with its sharp spikys. This was indeed a strange spiky log, he thought, and he sat watching it and contemplating its significance. When the spiky log suddenly got up and began to walk towards him, Sixpence got a big fright and jumped into the air on all fours. The spiky log also got a big fright and it stopped walking and curled up into a round spiky ball. Sixpence sat watching it intently, fascinated, his eyes like big round moons. After a long time the spiky ball uncurled again into a spiky log and decided Sixpence did not constitute a hazard. Sixpence watched, totally absorbed as it ambled along about its business. He went up to it and gently touched his nose against its nose, which startled them both and caused the hej-hog to roll up into a ball again and Sixpence to jump up in the air. Undeterred, he sat down next to the hej-hog and waited, watching it in fascination and pondering to himself. Maybe he, Chief Cat Sixpence, had discovered an entirely new kind of guelph that no cat had ever seen before? Maybe he'd be remembered in Khat Lore as the cat who invented this kind of guelph? Like Poyk was remembered in Tabby Lore for inventing the hopit and the binigaus for other cats to hunt?

All this activity drew the attention of Choklit, who sauntered over to see what all the fuss was about.

'Is our brave and fearless Chief Cat trying to hunt again?' he asked, 'I saw you jump high in the air and thought you might need some help from a *real* hunter. Like myself, for example, with my fine hunting whiskers. Show your brother what it is this time that you're trying to catch and your brother will take care of it for you,' Choklit sighed in mock exasperation.

Sixpence nodded toward where the hej-hog lay curled up in a spiky ball. 'Be careful, Choklit,' he cautioned, 'I don't know what it is or what it can do. I touched it and it stung me a quite bit, so be careful, it may hurt you.'

'Nonsense! I am a proper hunter with great fat hunting paws. This is simply a dead spiky log, I'll simply whack it out of the way if it frightens you...'

'No, it's not a log, Choklit. It's a tikki guelph. I saw it get up and walk about earlier. If you just sit still and watch it quietly for a while it might get up and walk about again.'

Choklit looked highly sceptical. He said, 'Then I'll just give it a mighty whack with my great fat hunting forepaw in any case and if you're right then it will wake up and then I can chase it. And if it's just an old spiky dead log like I think it is then it'll stay an old spiky dead log.'

'I wouldn't hit it if I were you, Choklit. It...'

'Meeeooowwwrrrlll!!!' Choklit emitted a piercing shriek of pain as he thumped the hej-hog with all his might. 'My paw! That. . .that. . monstrous thing hurt my beautiful fat hunting paw!'

Choklit sat glaring at the hej-hog while licking his wounded paw.

'You see, Choklit, this is why Uncle HuffPuff made me Chief Cat and not you,' Sixpence said smugly. 'It's all very well that you're an awesome hunter of squees and chirrits, but you're not *wise*. A chief cat needs to be wise. Very wise. I told you to be careful and you took no notice and now this tikki guelph has hurt you. Yet when Daddi wants to pick you up to give you Chukkachin, you run away like he's going to kill you? You are not wise, Choklit, you are very foolish. Now I think it's best that you should run away now - or at least hobble away - and leave me in peace to study this amazing guelph.'

*****

Humphrey's teaching Sixpence to fight had some unforeseen consequences. For a relatively small cat with tiny dancing feet and theatrical whiskers, he was utterly fearless and would take on any opponent, and usually manage to beat them into cowering submission with negligible injury to himself. His fighting prowess allowed him to expand the territory he inherited from Humphrey to include several houses around us which either had no cats, or were owned by nervous cats who nodded respectfully, stepped back a pace or two, and cast their eyes to the ground as Sixpence sauntered past them. For example, in the house next to ours there lived a timid little tabby queen named Pitstop who was so afraid of Sixpence that she was frightened to venture outside into her own garden to make wizz! She waited one morning until she was sure Sixpence was away and then came to me to and ask if I could have a word with him. Sixpence grudgingly agreed to leave her alone provided she was prepared to acknowledge in principle that her garden was his garden.

When Sixpence learned from me of the difficulties Tabithat was having with his Maine Coons in Facilities, he seemed to take it as a personal insult and became angry and vengeful. Some distance away from our house, on the fringe of Sixpence's empire, lived a pair of Maine Coons in a house with two very thin and phraidy ayoomfa females who gasped in alarm and waved their forepaws about at almost everything that happened. They spent much time tittering like chirrits and brushing their sulky looking Maine Coons, who were, needless to add, of very similar disposition to their ayoomfa servants. Sixpence held the view that these Coons needed to be punished for the wrongdoings of Maine Coons everywhere and he took to invading their house during the night and eating all their food.

'You can't just come in here and eat our food!' one of them protested indignantly. This one went by the ayoomfa name of Aphelion. His brother was called Perihelion.

'I just did,' Sixpence said, his mouth full of the delicate shmoo kukri that the willowy ayoomfa ladies had carefully set out for their distinguished aristocats.

'This is outrageous! It's *our* house! It's *our* little door within a door! And it's *our* food!'

'I am Chief Cat of all Ox-Fid-Shuh and everything here is mine,' Sixpence stated simply, as he licked up the last of the kukri. Coon Perihelion went up to him and gave him an effete smack on the head, saying 'No! It's our food!'. This was unwise, for Sixpence turned around and mercilessly attacked him and would not let up until he'd beaten Coon Perihelion into simpering submission in a corner. Meanwhile, Coon Aphelion ran away and set up a terrible frightened howling from the safety of another room, with the intention of waking the willowy ayoomfa ladies and summoning their assistance. Sixpence decided it was an opportune time to go home and he unhurriedly exited through the little door within a door and trotted home, his belly full.

This routine was repeated every few nights. In the middle of the night Sixpence would climb through their little door within a door and jump right into their basket, which was conveniently placed near the door and the food, so the Maine Coons wouldn't have to walk more than the length of a cat to either their food or their bed. It mattered not to Sixpence that the Maine Coons may be sleeping in their basket when he jumped into it.

'Get out!' he demanded gruffly, 'Chief Cat of Ox-Fid-Shuh is here.' And unless the Maine Coons complied immediately and fled from their own home through their little door within a door, Sixpence would beat them up and chase them out. Then he would proceed to eat their food. All of it. Even if he wasn't hungry at all. After two or three times, Aphelion and Perihelion knew what was expected of them and if they happened to see him striding purposely towards their house, they fled outside and sat in their garden until he had gone.

Mummi noticed that Sixpence seemed to be getting fat. And the willowy ladies noticed that their precious Maine Coons seemed to be getting thin and appeared very nervous all the time. Suspecting that Sixpence might be stealing someone's food, Mummi fitted both him and his brother Choklit with a *collar*. A collar is what the ayoomfas call a ring of brightly coloured softah that they fit around the neck of a cat. It's very, very difficult to get rid of it. Sometimes the collar has a little round with ayoomfa markings on it, and sometimes also a wicked shiny ball that makes a silly jangling sound as the condemned cat walks about. The jangling ball serves no constructive purpose, in fact it scares the chirrits away and interferes with hunting. There is not much that brings about such a loss of face for a cat than to have a collar put around their neck. Sixpence and Choklit-Butch were furious and for several days they were too embarrassed to venture far from the house for fear that someone might laugh at them.

Choklit-Butch was always very active during the night and he would play furiously for hours on the special scratching log that Daddi had installed for him, so that the wicked jangling ball jangled most of the night and kept Daddi awake. After a few days Daddi took the wicked jangling balls away. This was some progress. More progress was made one night when the Chief Cat of all Ox-Fid-Shuh went on a mission to steal food from the Maine Coons and beat them up. As he was leaving through their little door within a door, his collar happened to hook on something and came off. Sixpence was pleased.

But he was far from pleased when the two willowy ladies came to his house with the collar and remonstrated with Mummi. I listened in on what followed. Amid much fluttering of forepaws and anxious gushing the phraidy ladies explained that Sixpence had been invading their house and terrorising their Maine Coons, which they said were very *valuable,* whatever that means. They knew it was Sixpence because of the markings Mummi had made on his collar, which they had found in their Maine Coons' water bowl. Mummi was very apologetic, but this didn't seem to satisfy the two phraidy ladies and they babbled on and on. Then Daddi came home and the two phraidy ladies started all over again. Several times they repeated how *valuable* the Maine Coons were. Daddi quickly lost patience with them and he told them that there was nothing he or Mummi could do about this problem. He told them that the Maine Coons were each much bigger than Sixpence and should learn to defend themselves against intruders like all proper cats do. He added that Sixpence and Choklit were also very *valuable.* After that the phraidy ladies went away, gushing and shaking their heads. Mummi refitted Sixpence with his hated collar.

Not all cats took Sixpence's invasions lying down meekly. Across the road from the Maine Coons was a house on a kind of hill which the ayoomfas call an embankment. The embankment was a most desirable place for a cat, as it had grush and bushes and small trees to hide amongst and squees and slinkis to chase, maybe even a binigaus or two. And it was an excellent shufa ground. It was like a little piece of Midrand right there in Ox-Fid-Shuh and Sixpence wanted it very much for his empire. Unfortunately for him, the embankment belonged to the cat who lived in the house on top of it. This was Harvey, a Woon very similar in appearance to Sixpence, but a bit bigger and a bit older. Harvey had white smudges on *both* cheeks, and he was not at all phraidy.

'What do you think you're doing here? This is my embankment!'

'I'm Chief Cat of all Ox-Fid-Shuh and everything here is mine,' Sixpence gave his stock reply and continued grubbing around, confident that Harvey had heard of him and would melt away and leave him be. Instead, Harvey attacked him and caught off guard, Sixpence was given a right pasting. The Chief Cat of all Ox-Fid-Shuh tottered home with much face lost and went straight to his Mummi for comfort and solace. In the days that followed, Sixpence decided he would not accept this defeat and he went back to the embankment where he found Harvey making shufa, blissfully unaware of his presence. Sixpence attacked him and they fought noisily and furiously. Harvey was easily a match for Sixpence and with shrieking and hissing and growling and shouting the fight went on for a long time with no clear victor emerging. Harvey's Mummi came out of the house and broke them up. Harvey and Sixpence both tottered off resentfully, licking their wounds.

Sixpence would not accept that he couldn't have Harvey's embankment and he returned time after time to do battle. These conflicts invariably had to be broken up by Harvey's Mummi wielding a magic rain slinki. On one occasion Sixpence lost his collar during the fight, and this led to Harvey's Mummi paying a visit to our house. But Harvey's Mummi seemed to be a sensible kind of ayoomfa lady, unlike the Maine Coons' phraidy babbling Mummies. Mummi obtained for Sixpence a number of new toys and she spent more time playing with him, but Sixpence was very focused and it was several moons of further battle with Harvey before he finally abandoned his crusade.

The whitecoati in Ox-Fid-Shuh was a kind and caring ayoomfa fellow whom we got to know as Uncle Joe, even though he wasn't related to us at all and he wasn't even a cat. We had cause to go see him quite a lot when Chief Cat Sixpence was fighting for his empire and conquest of Harvey's embankment. As usual at the whitecoati's we had to first wait in a room with other ayoomfas, all of whom had cats or grufs or chirrits which needed Uncle Joe's healing mujaji. We often saw Harvey with his Mummi at Uncle Joe's after Harvey and Sixpence had been fighting. The wounds were often quite serious and on one occasion we saw Harvey with his whole tail wrapped up in a white softah. Apparently Sixpence had bitten it nearly in half. Sometimes Daddi also came along to Uncle Joe's and he would always quietly ask Uncle Joe whether Sixpence or Harvey had fared better in the fight. Having been coached by Humphrey, Sixpence was often marginally victorious, and this seemed to please Daddi very much. When they got home from the Whitecoati Daddi would shower Sixpence with praise and give him much Chukkachin and Top-Of-Head as well as numerous treats. Once he even gave him a brand new schnoogli wumpus with a lovely dangling round toy inside it - that was the time Harvey had had his tail all wrapped up. Mummi was not at all pleased by this and she told Daddi that he was not being helpful and that he should not encourage Sixpence to be a *bad cat*. She said that all male creatures are stupid, always have been, and always will be.

Our Mummi and Harvey's Mummi were not at all pleased about the fighting and the resulting visits to Uncle Joe and they spoke at length about what bad cats were Sixpence and Harvey. Especially Sixpence. They thought he was most dreadfully naughty to invade the embankment and fight with Harvey, but they admitted they weren't that concerned about his terrorising the Maine Coons and eating their food. Indeed, Harvey's Mummi confessed quietly that she'd once or twice seen Harvey returning from the Maine Coons' house licking his lips and looking extremely smug and satisfied and she suspected he was doing exactly the same as Sixpence. At the end of a long ayoomfa speaks the two Mummies concluded there was really very little they could do about it, as Sixpence was in charge in our house and Harvey was in charge in his house. The two Mummies decided that they would let Uncle Joe Whitecoati make Sixpence, Choklit and Harvey clever invisible and silent collars that could only be detected with a special ayoomfa magic stick. This would save face for the two Mummies over collars that inexplicably came to be found in the Maine Coons' house, and so protect the privacy of Sixpence and Harvey, who could henceforth pillage and terrorise them with impunity. Woons Two. Coons Nil.

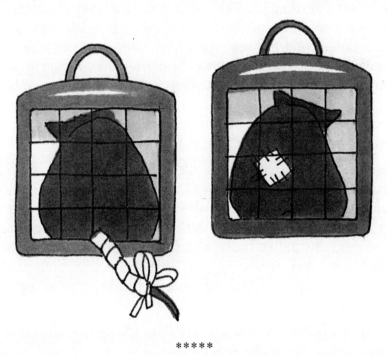

*****

CHAPTER TWENTY FOUR:
Lookkit wha'got inm'm'ouf!'

I suspect that Sixpence's persecution of the Maine Coons Aphelion and Perihelion may have been as a result of a visit I had from Tabithat at around that time. On this occasion Tabithat made himself felt by making a woo-woo of endless roundness which blew me around and around and up into the sky. As I was blown ever higher the day sky grew darker into night sky and I could see stars and the moon. It was very quiet and peaceful. I could feel Tabithat gently stroking the top of my head with his huge - and very holy - paws. I set up a timid happi-rumble in respectful appreciation of His attentions.

'Little Wargi, how are you doing?' the deep voice boomed.

Surely the great omnipotent Tabithat hadn't brought me all the way up here to make small talk? In any case I would have expected that being omnipotent, he would fully know how I was and would not need to ask. Nevertheless, I did not wish to criticize Tabithat lest he turned me into a bizzum.

'So-so, My Lord. I have good days and bad days. I can assure my Lord that it would be a very good day indeed if my Lord had news that my bed was ready in my Lord's house and that my Phirish days were over.'

'Ah yes, your bed. You'll remember that I gave it to your friend Balune when she came to me unexpectedly. . .'

Well? Well? Where is it? When can I go to it? It was very difficult keeping calm and respectful. 'Yes, Lord,' I said.

'Balune won't be needing it for a while because she's been chosen for Phirish Duty. Cats in my house can be called on at any time for Phirish Duty, as you well know.'

'Does this mean I can come home to my original bed, my Lord?'

'No. You are still on Phirish Duty. Balune is now on Phirish duty, too. I have an important Special Project which requires two Phirish of the highest calibre. Balune will be joining you soon.'

'And what of my bed , Lord?'

'You seem very concerned about your bed, little Wargi. Health and Safety have finally approved your brand new Phello's Bed and Facilities are holding it safely in storage. Even At this time we don't have a shortage of beds – your friend Butch was so productive in my workshop that indeed we have a glut of beds - so both you and Balune can rest assured that your beds will not be given away.'

'Thank you, my Lord. It's just that I don't really trust those Main Coons of yours in Facilities. Who knows what they might do with my bed. . .'

'I understand how you feel about the Maine Coons,' Tabithat said wearily. 'I've tried several times to get rid of them and replace them with hardworking, honest Moggies, but they are civil servants and I can't fire them. My holy paws are tied. To make matters worse they've barricaded themselves up there in Facilities and they run it like their own personal fiefdom, preening themselves conceitedly and biting and scratching any other cat who comes near.'

'Surely, all cats in My Lord's house are bound to obey my Lord and do my Lord's Phluffi Will?'

'Yes, but they do it so slowly and so ineptly, keeping just short of what it takes for me to be able to dismiss them. But fear not, I have a plan.'

'I'll wager it's a magnificently clever and cunning plan, My Lord.' It wouldn't do any harm for me to be obsequious at this time, I felt.

'Yes it is. I plan to create a completely new department called something that's so vague and ambiguous that nobody, least of all the Maine Coons - who aren't known to be the sharpest claws on the paw - will understand what it does. I thought *Phluffi Projects* would be a suitable name. The new department will be staffed by fierce ginger street tabbies and managed by bright-eyed black and white Woons. It will gradually take on the functions of Facilities and usurp their workload. I'll appear to suddenly discover this duplication one day and then be perfectly justified in amalgamating the Maine Coons into Phluffi Projects where they can spend the rest of eternity guarding smelly fish bones on my refuse tip under the watchful eyes of the ginger tabbies. Then sometime later I'll restructure Phluffi Projects and call them Facilities again.'

This was indeed a plan befitting of the Great Tabithat. I'd certainly feel more confident if my bed were under the care of ginger tabbies than a bunch of conceited, lazy and incompetent Coons.

'What is the nature of my Lord's Special Project that involves Balune and myself'

'You don't need to know that yet. Someone from Phluffi Projects will give you the details when the time comes.'

The woo-woo of endless roundness began again, except this time it was spinning in the opposite direction and it sucked me downwards rather than blew me upwards. Sometime later I was deposited outside my house in Ox-Fid-Shuh, shaken, and somewhat dizzy. This was what it must feel like being a spinnelly, a corner krorli or a leaf that had been sucked up inside the ayoomfas' Screaming Wind. No wonder Choklit-Butch was so terrified of the Screaming Wind and always ran away.

*****

In the middle of the winter season most of the ayoomfas in Brittin held an elaborate festival that they took very seriously indeed. They prepared obsessively for this festival even though it seemed to cause them a great deal of stress. Of all the things ayoomfas did, the Festival of the Dead Tree was perhaps the most ludicrous. The focus of the festival was a dead tree which ayoomfas would drag into their house and festoon with numerous shinies and tiny winking magic stars. Some ayoomfas even went as far as to adorn the outside of their houses with strings of coloured magic suns and winking magic stars.During the moon preceding the festival, ayoomfas would acquire a stock of silly articles, which they would wrap up in colourful peppers and leave by the dead tree. On the day of the festival other ayoomfas would come to the house and they would all wax excited about these articles and pretend they had no idea how they got there. They would rip all the peppers off the articles and pretend to be surprised and delighted with them. For cats this was an excellent occasion for play amongst the crinkly coloured peppers and shiny strings, with the understood goal of the game being to rip all the peppers to shreds and pull the strings of shiny winking stars from the dead tree and run away with them. Later in the festival day the ayoomfas would make a great feast of an enormous chirrit, easily the size of a gruf, and so big that it would barely fit through the door of the *burning box* in the food room. As usual, the idiots removed all the delectable parts from inside the big chirrit and hid them in the Gone Box, while contenting themselves with eating the bland outer meats, accompanied by a load of the usual sort of burned vejtibil rubbish they like to consume.

During the great feast ayoomfas would put coloured peppers on their head fur, drink enormous quantities of happi-water and play with coloured bangsticks that made a frightful noise when pulled apart. After the feast they would spend time bickering amongst themselves until nearly sunset when the visiting ayoomfas would go away. The following day was spent cleaning up all the mess. Many of the articles that had been wrapped in coloured peppers and which had so excited the ayoomfas on the festival day, seemed no longer to appeal to them, and they put them in the Gone Box.

The Festival of the Dead Tree was the same every year in every house along our road, with no variation. Ayoomfas did the same things with the dead tree, ate the same uninspiring parts of the big chirrit, made the same horrible noises with the coloured bangsticks, and over imbibed the happi-water, winter after winter. I checked inside every house along our road and it was always the same. The neighbourhood cats soon bored with the unvarying monotony of Festival of the Dead Tree - which the ayoomfas called *Krismis* - and groups of disinterested cats congregated at the edge of one of the nearby fields to bemoan the monotonous stupidity of their servants and avoid the atmosphere of frenzied disturbance that the festival brought to their homes.

Sixpence and Choklit-Butch were seldom at home during the Festival of the Dead Tree, for Mummi and Daddi often chose to go away at that time. This meant Capture! Mummi and Daddi were great Lords of Capture and none of the cats in our house ever managed to escape. In Ox-Fid-Shuh my captured companions were taken to an unusually nice prison run by a friendly ayoomfarolê lady called Auntie Sue who was greatly respected and loved by all cats who knew her. Over the bitter winter nights she kept the cats in her prison snug in cosy bedrooms with magic warm softahs. During the day each cat had their own outside fence room, where there was space to frolic and play with the toys provided, and luxuriate in the winter sun when it occasionally showed itself. Auntie Sue spoke to all her cats during the day and played with them often. There was a cheerful atmosphere and the food was tasty and plentiful. In the outside fence rooms cats could talk to each other and sniff noses through the holis in the fence. Sixpence and Choklit-Butch made numerous friends while in Auntie Sue's prison - tabbies, Woons, white cats, grey cats, and ginger brown cats from all around Ox-Fid-Shuh spent Krismis with Auntie Sue. There was even once a family of Maine Coons there, but they were very conceited and refused to speak to any other cats. Apart from these and one or two other disgruntled individuals there was good cheer among the cats at Auntie Sue's. So much so that at times Sixpence and Choklit-Butch forgot they were in a prison and were even reluctant to go home when Mummi and Daddi came to fetch them. The knowledge that they were destined for a few days at Auntie Sue's made Capture quite bearable, but to show this would entail great loss of face, so they continued to act betrayed and badly done by during Capture, with all the frightened mewling and unhappy moaning that this entailed.

In Ox-Fid-Shuh Choklit-Butch had ample opportunities to develop his already fine hunting skills. Close to our house were many fields where ayoomfas were growing the tall grasses. In summer these grasses would grow big seeds on them and this seems to have been a signal for the ayoomfas to cut them all down. An ugly green stinky roaring monster from Hell - easily as big as our house - would be brought to rumble back and forth across the fields, cutting down the tall grasses in its path, rolling them up into rounds, covering the rounds in black shiny like the bags for the Gone Box, and spitting them out behind it like plokkits of shufa. It never seemed to tire and would roar back and forth across the fields through day and night without rest until all the grasses had been cut down. The arrival of the ugly roaring monster from Hell was a big event in Ox-Fid-Shuh, for it came carried atop an enormous *floor-rumbleroli* which rumbled down the road towards the fields and was followed by a pack of excited young ayoomfa disciples who watched in fascination as the green monster was lifted off the floor-rumbleroli and onto the fields of the tall grasses. A team of men spent the best part of the day fussing around it and toying with its digestion before it was coaxed into life and began its horrible roaring and munching up of all that lay before it. A wise cat - and even a not-very-wise cat like Choklit-Butch - would know better than to venture into the fields when the green roaring monster from Hell was around, for it could easily gobble up a cat without blinking. One or two of the phraidy cats across our road told me tales of some of their unfortunate friends who had been cut down and gobbled up by the green roaring monster from Hell. I can only think they must have been exceptionally stupid cats, for the monster from Hell spent only a few days each summer on the fields, leaving the rest of the year safe for cats to hunt the rich bounty of squee that lived in the long grasses. Choklit-Butch was duly circumspect when the green roaring monster from Hell was around, and he hid under the big ayoomfawumpus where he couldn't see it, and where, according to his philosophy, it couldn't see him either.

In spring and summer scarcely a day would go by without Choklit-Butch catching a squee or a chirrit or a binigaus in the fields of the tall grasses. One would see him striding purposely towards the fields in the morning and he'd be gone for much of the day, returning only to eat his supper when he heard Daddi calling him. Then he'd be off again, returning in the middle of the night with his prey. He would have to wait until both Mummi and Daddi were soundly asleep in their ayoomfawumpus before bringing his freshly killed food animal into the house, for if they saw him bring something inside they became very jealous of his catch and would shout and clap their forepaws together and chase him out the little door within a door. While Choklit's great hunting prowess made the ayoomfas feel inadequate, it made him swell with pride and he'd want to make sure that Chief Cat Sixpence was around to witness his magnificent accomplishment. He'd come into the house in the middle of the night and try attract Sixpence's attention by making an ugly keening sound while still holding the prey firmly in his jaws.

'Look't me,' he'd wail in an ugly manner, 'Lookkit wha'got inm'm'ouf! Look't me!' Sometimes this would wake Daddi, who would then go crashing and thundering about in the dark, knocking things over while trying to chase Choklit outside. Choklit gave him a terrible runaround and would duck and dive and slink and hide in dark corners, all the time firmly holding his precious food animal. Nothing would make him go outside until Sixpence had witnessed the latest hunting success. But Sixpence wasn't interested at all and would remain fast asleep in his schnoogli wumpus or on the big ayoomfawumpus with Mummi and Daddi.

After this happened night after night Daddi begat a great ayoomfa cleverness which he used to get Choklit outside. He simply picked up Sixpence, wherever he happened to be innocently sleeping, and shoveled him outside through the little door within a door. Realising that the Chief Cat of all Ox-Fid-Shuh and some of Bucks was now outside, resentfully and sleepily blinking in the moonlight, Choklit would immediately go outside himself.

'Look't me! Lookkit wha'got inm'm'ouf!'

'Yes, yes, yes,' Sixpence would yawn. 'Very nice, Choklit. Now eat it up so I can safely go back to bed.'

Sometimes Choklit would do this. Other times he would stay for ages outside playing with his dead food animal, tossing it high in the air and running furiously after it as it came down again. Sixpence was expected to watch and admire this play fest and could not safely return inside until Choklit was seen to be systematically crunching up his food animal to eat. Any premature withdrawal by Sixpence would see Choklit follow him back inside the house after a few minutes, squee in mouth, searching for him with the ugly and unmistakable 'Look't me! Lookkit wha'got inm'm'ouf!'

Choklit-Butch had a habit of gulping down whatever he ate with such haste that it was barely chewed at all, like a slinki eats. This put a great strain on his digestion and significantly increased the chances of his making bloik-bloik. Mummi and Daddi really did not like bloik-bloik at all. Day or night, the instant they became aware of it they would furiously set about removing it by rubbing and scratching and using all manner of softahs and brushes and stinking white stuff which came out of a spitting tin, all the time muttering angrily about it. The bloik-bloik sites were then covered for a few days with white peppers that the ayoomfas inspected periodically and which we were not allowed to play with. All this bloik-bloik removal stuff smelled much worse than the bloik-bloik to me, but evidently the ayoomfas didn't share my view, and they accumulated a veritable arsenal of special brushes, hairyback cleaning softahs, spitting cans, and numerous bottles and drums of frothing stink, to deal with bloik-bloik. Fortunately for them, Choklit-Butch always gave very loud and clear-cut audible warning of impending bloik-bloik with a tragic and wet-sounding "Gurrlwooikk gurrlwooikk" sound that Mummi and Daddi soon learned to recognise. It would wake them and send them crashing about in the dark, trying to find Choklit and chase him outside before he could make too much bloik-bloik on the floor softahs. Mostly this merely succeeded in distributing the bloik-bloik so that it formed an intermittent trail all the way from the original site to where Choklit-Butch, staring stupidly cross-eyed while heaving and retching pitifully, was finally shoved through the little door within a door. All this compounded Sixpence's nightly disturbances and ruined his sleep, so as Chief Cat he introduced a rule: Any cat who had eaten a food animal outside during the night was not permitted inside the house until dawn. However, enforcing this rule required constant vigilance which in practice cost Sixpence more sleep than before, so he settled for simply beating up Choklit the next morning if there was evidence that he'd transgressed.

*****

CHAPTER TWENTY-FIVE:
A Tail of Two Phirish

Phat Balune suddenly appeared one morning while we were sunning ourselves outside the house in the Only Floor room. She made a very splendid Phirish, as Tabithat - bless his generosity - had adorned her with festive highlights in her fur which changed colours like one of those strange slinkis and she shimmered with great spectral beauty when she moved. She must have found Tabithat's House very agreeable from a culinary perspective, for she'd grown larger than ever and was at least twice my size. Her fluffy tail was now easily as wide as my whole body and when she flicked it, it left a trail of little sparkling stars in its wake. Balune was indeed a most magnificent and powerful Phirish and I felt almost embarrassed in my common plainness.

'Just like the old days, Little Old Lady,' Balune said, 'The Midrand Phirish team: Me, you and Butch.'

'Not strictly speaking true, Balune, Choklit-Butch is not a Phirish. He's *reconstituted.*'

'Reconstituted?'

'Yes Tabithat told me that I shouldn't bust my head trying to understand it. And I haven't. Never mind that, let me introduce you to everyone.'

The Butch in Choklit-Butch was delighted to see Balune again and told her that she was more beautiful than ever, to which she replied that she knew this and it was why she now called herself *The Magnificent Balune* and we were welcome, and it was inferred, expected, to call her this.

Sixpence asked me who my 'sparkly dead friend' was and when I told him he introduced himself as 'Chief Cat Sixpence of nearly all Ox-Fid-Shuh'.

'I'm in charge, you know,' he said, proudly. Ever loquacious, he seized the opportunity to tell The Magnificent Balune that he had defeated an army of Maine Coons, that he was the inventor of the hej-hog and that he had killed a fezzint by merely thinking about it. Balune raised an eyebrow and expressed disinterest.

'The tedious affairs of you mortal cats do not concern me,' she said haughtily, and gave a great swish of her great iridescent tail. 'I'm here as a consultant for Tabithat on an important assignment. . .'

'About which we presently know nothing at all,' I interrupted tersely, ' and while we're guests in his house, we at least need to show Chief Cat Sixpence the respect he's due by Khat Lore. As I'm sure you know well, of course. Believe me, you don't want to make him cross, you really don't.'

I could not have this ostentatious mobile light show being disrespectful to my family.

'Uh, yes, of course, Bunni. Quite so. Quite so.' Balune looked a bit embarrassed and began washing her sparkly tail. The illuminated parts sizzled as she licked them.

A few days later we got wind of our assignment when we were paid a visit by Rambaxy, a mortal messenger from Tabithat's newly formed Phluffi Projects division. Rambaxy was a medium sized striped cat of a kind I hadn't seen before. She was quite a pretty young queen with brown tabby colours, but she wasn't a proper tabby as many of her stripes were more like blotches and spots. I learned later that she called herself a Bengal.

Rambaxy thought she could simply wander uninvited into Sixpence's House to talk to us. Sixpence had established himself as undisputed leader in his fiefdom of Ox-Fid-Shuh, and he relied heavily on his reputation to implement security. On the night of Rambaxy's trespass, he was literally caught napping. He was soundly asleep in his schnoogli wumpus and Rambaxy was able to walk into the house completely unchallenged. She had a token nibble of Sixpence's food, a slurp of his water, and then she climbed the bumpity hill to the Up House to where Balune and I were looking out the big window and watching the night sky in anticipation of messages of grand instruction from Tabithat. Choklit-Butch was not asleep and he saw Rambaxy saunter casually up the bumpity hill. He was appalled at this flagrant breach of security and immediately woke Sixpence, Chief Cat of the House.

'Sixpence! Wake up! Wake up! There's an intruder in the house!'

Sixpence woke up and performed an amazing transformation. One moment he was a sleepy Mummi's cuddle cat, and the next he was the dreaded Chief Cat of all Ox-Fid-Shuh, and some of Bucks, fierce custodian of Uncle Humphrey's legacy and Terror of the Coons. Choklit began to trot away.

'And just where do you think you're going?' The Terror of the Coons demanded.

'I thought I'd run away. It's best. . .'

'No, you can't run away now. I may need you to help me.'

'Aw Sixpence, I'm a hunter not a fighter. It really is best if I run away. . .'

'No! Absolutely not! You will not run away! You're coming with me and that's an order from the Chief Cat of all Ox-Fid-Shuh.'

Sixpence with a reluctant Choklit in tow crawled stealthily up the bumpity hill to where Rambaxy had just identified herself to Balune and me and was about to give us a crucial message from Phluffi Projects. But her words were drowned out by a yowling and snarling from Sixpence, the likes I'd never heard before. I even began to have certain sympathy for the Maine Coons.

'Eeeyyowwwwwwwooorrrlll! Who in Tabithat's name are you and what are you doing in my House?'

'I'm Rambaxy, from Phluffi Projects and . . .'

'I don't want any! Get out of my house! '

Choklit-Butch said, 'Hello, Rambaxy. I'm Choklit and this is my brother Sixpence. We live here and. . .'

'Be quiet, you stupid cat!' Sixpence snapped at him. The menacing yowling resumed and Sixpence advanced closer. Rambaxy cautiously retreated to the top of a small tay-bill in a corner of the room and began a defensive yowling of her own.'

'Meeeeooowwwwurll' she cried, 'I'm only a messenger with a message for Bunni!'

'Eeeyyowwwwwwwooorrrlll!' snarled Sixpence, 'Get out of my house!'

'I'm really sorry about this,' said Choklit-Butch, 'I wanted to run away, but he wouldn't let me. . .' Sixpence told him again to shut up and cuffed him sharply over the head, causing him to fall over. I felt I had to intervene.

'Listen, you boys. . .'

'Rrooowwwwwooorrrlll! Get out of my house!' This was followed by a fit of explosive spitting of the kind I was so good at in my stupid days. For such a small cat, Sixpence really was quite terrifying to behold when he was in attack mode. No wonder Coons Aphelion and Perihelion ran away when they saw him coming. He didn't have the muscle of Humphrey and so relied much more on psychological intimidation, which served him well for most of the phraidy domesticated cats he came across in Ox-Fid-Shuh. Whether he'd have held his own against the likes of the wicked Grondus or Essex Innit is doubtful, but he'd have certainly given it his best shot.

'Meeeeooooooooooowwwwl. . . Eeeeeeeooooooooowwwwwwwourrrll. . .'

'Weeeoooooooooooooooooorrrll. . .'

'Sixpence! This is my guest, for Tabithat's sake!' I shouted at the top of my voice. Even Phat Balune was quite alarmed and went to stand behind Sixpence where Choklit was failing dismally at pretending to pretending to be fierce and aggressive.

'Is he always like this?' she asked Choklit.

'Often. Yes. I wanted to run away,' he said sadly. 'It would have been best.'

'Yes, I think it probably would have been.'

The cacophony created by Sixpence and the cowering Rambaxy woke Mummi and Daddi who were very alarmed to see a strange cat in the house in the middle of the night. Much of their alarm was for Rambaxy's safety as they thought that Sixpence was on the verge of attacking her. Khat Lore, however, strongly discourages male on female violence, unless it is necessary to make fruka-fruka, and Sixpence had little interest in fruka-fruka since his seedballs had been stolen by the whitecoati. He would only have set upon her as a last resort. But Mummi didn't know any of this and - very foolishly - tried to befriend Rambaxy with a view to a rescuing her through Capture. In fear and panic, Rambaxy bit Mummi's soft pink forepaw and made it bleed.

This was a gross outrage and quite unforgiveable! Khat Lore is quite clear on this: You simply cannot invade another cat's house, attack the housekeeping staff and expect to get away with it. So everyone attacked Rambaxy, even Choklit-Butch. She bolted from her high corner refuge and tore down the bumpity hill towards the little door within a door, hotly pursued by the madly shrieking Chief Yowli of all Ox-Fid-Shuh and his timid assistant Choklit-Butch, a pair of furiously spitting Phirish, and two clumsy, blundering ayoomfas carrying an assortment of defensive softahs in one forepaw and various offensive stick things in the other. Rambaxy ran up a tree on the other side of the road. Sixpence and Choklit didn't bother to pursue her beyond the little door within a door and simply went back to bed, since Mummi and Daddi had adequately taken care of the intruder. Balune and I followed Rambaxy up her tree.

'All I wanted to do was give you a message from the Phluffi Projects Division!' she cried.

'You bit my Mummi,' I said angrily.

'And you violated Khat Lore in our house!' added a furious Balune.

'But I thought she was going to make Capture on me. . .'

'Yes, yes, I know she was' snapped Balune, 'She is a Great Lord of Capture, but by Tabithat, you bit *our* ayoomfarolê servant while you were in *our* house. Humphrey would have killed you for that. Now tell us what you want and be gone.'

'Tabithat says to tell you that you have but one task to complete before you can both go back to your beds in His House.'

'And what is this task?'

'You have to make your Daddi tell your story to the entire world.'

Balune and I looked at each other in amazement. How in the world did Tabithat expect us to do this? We can't be seen by most ayoomfas. I can understand their talk but I can't talk back to them and neither Balune nor I could make any sense of the markings they spent so much time studying in noose peppers and on the kom-pewter. What they did with it remained a mystery, and not one with anywhere sufficient interest content for me to pursue. This was an impossible assignment! I couldn't help wondering whether it was merely Tabithat's way of keeping me in Phirish limbo forever.

'That's it then,' I said to Balune as we walked back home. 'I guess we'll be Phirish forever.'

'Don't be defeatist, Bunni. You must trust Tabithat. I've been a Citizen of His House for a long time and I know he'd never ask us to do anything that's not possible. There is a way. We just have to find it.'

I decided to go with Balune and visit MyGranni, who, unlike most other ayoomfas, had at least been able to see me. Perhaps she'd have some suggestion on how we might accomplish our assignment. Since Balune had died she hadn't been to see MyGranni, and she didn't know how to get there. Of course I could get there by just thinking of the place, and I instructed her to think of being close to me at all times. If her attention wandered and she got lost it wasn't too serious. She could always think of Ox-Fid-Shuh and get back home.

MyGranni was not in good condition at all. She had a sickness that was eating away her strength day by day and she was very weak and miserable. She would be going to Tabithat soon, I thought. It was clearly the highlight of her day when she saw us suddenly appear on her ayoomfawumpus.

'My dearest Bunni! And Princess, too!' she said with great joy, 'You've both come to visit me.'

One of MyGranni's daughters was present, but she was Phirish-impervious and clearly thought MyGranni was seeing and talking to things that weren't there. Realising this, MyGranni became argumentative and insisted that her two favourite cats had appeared as spirits and were sitting on her ayoomfawumpus. She became very angry with her daughter for doubting our presence and told her to go away and come back another day when she could see properly. A great exchange of affection between MyGranni and us then took place for a considerable time, during which Balune and I found we could communicate with MyGranni, albeit in a very slow, and frustrating way. If I held a clear mental picture of something or someone, I could evidently share this with her, for she would speak of it to us. But to try get across in a series of thought pictures that Tabithat had asked us to make Daddi tell our story proved too difficult. I thought of Daddi and she understood that. I thought of me and Balune and Butch she understood that, too. And she recognised Midrand, Harvard, Vietnam, and even Ox-Fid-Shuh, although she'd never been to Ox-Fid-Shuh. Or Bucks.

'This isn't working,' said Balune. 'She just thinks we're telling her a story'

MyGranni was getting very enthusiastic about all the memories that we were feeding her, but the communication couldn't support the subtleties that we needed to convey. Then she picked up her magic speaking stick and pushed on its pads with her softclaws. She spoke into it as if she was speaking to the Young Man, my Daddi. Obviously she wasn't really speaking to My Daddi - as I've explained before the magic speaking stick creates these illusions - but I let her pretend that she was.

'Do you know who has come to visit me?' she asked the speaking stick. 'Bunni and Princess are sitting right here with me on my bed. We're having a pleasant afternoon together thinking about all the days gone by.'

There was a pause and the speaking stick made some noises.

'No I don't want to see the doctor!,' MyGranni said testily. 'I've had a lifetime of doctors and their tinkering! I'm quite alright just sitting here with my cats! What's the matter with you, boy!'

More noises from the speaking stick.

'I don't need any more rest. All I ever do is rest and where does it get me? Just makes me tired, it does. So to Hell with rest! I'm spending today happily reliving memories of times gone by with my dear cats. What a fabulous story they'd have to tell if only they could speak! You should tell their story instead of wasting your time filling the world with yet more electronic rubbish. Balune's got bigger than ever before and she's full of sparkling lights. As I speak they're both jumping up and down excitedly on my bed.'

I didn't know what *electronic rubbish* was but gathered it was something my Daddi, the once Young Man, spent his time doing at work as a Great Lord of Mujaji. MyGranni's advice seemed very sound, but I doubted whether Daddi would follow it. Like most male ayoomfas, Daddi does not respond well to advice and does not like being told what to do, but I hoped he'd give MyGranni's idea some thought at least. Tabithat's task was still far from complete.

MyGranni had tired herself with all the excitement and very wisely decided to take a nap. Balune and I explored her little house while she slept. So many little things I recognized from Vietnam and Harvard were there. Here and there on the walls were some pictures of cats in once familiar surroundings.

'That's you, Bunni' Balune said, referring to a startled looking cat in one of the pictures.

'Nonsense!' I scoffed. 'That cat looks cynical and suspicious. Can't possibly be me.'

'It's definitely you,' insisted Balune. 'Look, you can clearly see your nose pimple that caused you so much trouble.'

'Mmmm, well maybe I was in pain at the time. And see, here's one of you lying on the big eating surface at Midrand. . .'

'That's not me. That's a very fat cat with tangled fur. Not at all beautiful like me.'

'It's you. See the three-coloured patch on your head. It can only be you.'

'Ummmm. I'm sure these pictures don't accurately represent what's in the world. For one thing, they're flat. Look at me, do I look flat like that?'

'No, you are very round indeed. Definitely not flat.' The ayoomfa picture magic is most clearly defective. These cats don't look anything like us.'

'But there's one of Butch which is actually quite good. It looks just like him.'

'How do the ayoomfas know which cat is which if the pictures are so bad?' Balune asked.

'These ones have ayoomfa markings underneath the pictures. Perhaps these are the markings for our names?' An idea occurred to me. Of course it was a good idea, as most of my ideas are. I said to Balune, 'Do you think you can remember the markings underneath these pictures?'

'Probably. What good will that do? We know who we are. It's the ayoomfas who're likely to get confused because of their bad picture magic.'

'Humour me. We're going to try something. Think of the markings and don't forget them. I'll try remembering them, too. Now let's go back to MyGranni.'

'*My* Granni.'

'Yes, yes. While we're with *our* Granni you must think hard of the markings underneath this picture of Butch but don't think of Butch himself - just the markings under the picture.'

MyGranni was asleep, and she stirred as we jumped on her ayoomfawumpus. We sat there, both gazing at her and both thinking as hard was we could of the markings underneath the picture of Butch.

'This is hard work,' said Balune, 'concentrating on these silly shapes and squiggles.'

'Quiet!' She's waking up.' MyGranni blinked and opened her eyes

'Butch. .?' she asked, puzzled.

We spent a few more days with MyGranni, working hard every day to remember the markings for our names. MyGranni was aware of this effort, for she said to us one afternoon, 'You cats are always thinking of yourselves. It's no wonder some people say you are selfish creatures.'

Back in Ox-Fid-Shuh we told Sixpence and Choklit-Butch of our visit to MyGranni and related proudly that the trip had left us both even cleverer than we were before, since we now knew how to make the ayoomfa markings for our names.

Sixpence, however, was sceptical. 'I can't see how this will help send a message to Daddi. You know how to make a message but none of us can hold an ayoomfa marking stick in our paws. Not even I, Chief Cat of nearly all Ox-Fid-Shuh, can do this. Despite being blunt and useless for really important work like hunting, fighting and covering up shufa in the sand, the softclaws of the ayoomfas are very suited for grasping fiddly things like sticks.'

'Then we shan't use an ayoomfa marking stick. We will find another way.' Balune said sulkily.

Choklit-Butch was lying lazily on his side, casually playing with some plokkits that had escaped his bowl and found their way onto the floor. 'Plokkits is best,' he said.

'You stupid cat!' Sixpence snapped at him.

'No wait, Sixpence, maybe he's got an idea. None of us have any ideas at present. Choklit, how can plokkits help us?'

'I can make plokkits pictures. It's best.'

'You stup. .'

'Shut up, Sixpence! Could you show us how to do this, Choklit?'

While we watched, Choklit-Butch scooped some plokkits out of his bowl onto the floor, and began meticulously arranging them one by one with his paw. It was a slow process and Sixpence began to grow very bored and yawned, but I urged him not to disturb Choklit while he was busy. After a long time, Choklit moved his last plokkit into position.

'And now?' Sixpence asked tetchily.

'A box,' said Choklit-Butch proudly. A box of plokkits.'

Choklit had arranged the plokkits carefully into the shape of a box, and had put some plokkits inside the box, too. Balune and I looked at each other and smiled.

'Tabithat will certainly reward you for this great cleverness, Choklit-Butch,' I told him. 'You are a top quality cat.'

'Clever? Top quality? Choklit? Give me strength!' sighed Chief Cat Sixpence and padded off in disgust.

On the first night we'd scheduled to make our messages with plokkits, we had to cancel the task.

'Can't make plokkit pictures tonight,' Choklit said simply.

'Why not?'

'Not enough plokkits. I was hungry and ate most of them.'

We had arranged that Sixpence would sacrifice his supper of shmoo kukri to Choklit, thereby leaving plenty of plokkits available for making messages. But Sixpence was very greedy and had eaten not only his own supper but Choklit's as well, leaving nothing but plokkits for Choklit to eat.

'You greedy little cat!' I scolded Sixpence. But he merely blinked at me and said, 'A Chief Cat needs his strength. . .' before waddling off to go sleep in his shnoogliwumpus.

After a few abortive attempts we got lucky and commenced our message building late at night after Mummi and Daddi were safely sleep. The bowl of plokkits was almost untouched as Choklit had been hunting at dusk and had caught a chirrit, so he wasn't hungry. We decided on my name for the message, as creating the markings with plokkits was very time consuming and my name was the shortest. Also, I was the most important of all the cats involved. From memory, Balune and I coached Choklit-Butch on the shape of the ayoomfa runes and directed him on how to carefully form the trail of plokkits into these shapes. Considering what fat hunting forepaws he had, it was quite impressive to watch him using them for such a delicate task. We made the message quite big - with the runes each as big as one of the patterned squares of slippery stuff from which the floor was made. By dawn our task was done and we were all very tired. Choklit, the plokkit sculptor, was very hungry and suggested we eat some of the plokkits that he'd so carefully pushed into position on the grounds that nobody would notice the difference, but Balune and I strictly forbade it.

Daddi came to feed us just after dawn, as usual. He thundered down the bumpity hill grumbling deeply to himself about all kinds of things: the dark and the work and the khouncile and the man in the house next door and some things called banks, which he said were corrupt. Daddi always made a lot of grumbles until he'd had his tea, which seemed to make him much happier. He staggered woozily into the food room where Sixpence and Choklit-Butch were sitting neatly by their bowls, eagerly awaiting breakfast, and he saw the message we had made. For a moment I thought we had killed him with Big Fright, but then he said,

'B-U-N-N-I? It says Bunni! Who did this? Did one of you boys do this?' I translated this astonished outburst for the boys.

Choklit trilled at him in delight and rubbed up against his hind legs. Sixpence just glared and shouted at Daddi, 'C'mon, C'mon, don't just stand there gawking! Give us our breakfast!'

But Daddi rushed up the bumpity hill to the Up House and woke Mummi, who came with him down to the food room, sleepily rubbing her eyes and grumbling about not being asleep. Mummi was tremendously impressed with our message.

'This is a *mirikil*,' she said. 'And a sign. These cats are trying to tell us something.'

Sixpence was hungry. 'Yes, yes, of course it's a sign. Now get a move on and make our breakfast,' he yelled at her in angry Khat. The ayoomfas didn't understand the words but the intent was unmistakable.

Daddi made breakfast for Sixpence and Choklit while Mummi made tea, then they sat gazing in wonder at the message while they drank their tea. Daddi went up the bumpity hill again and came back with his little box of big flash magic which he pointed at our message. It made a bright flash and then through some clever ayoomfa mujaji it made a picture of the message on a tiny magic window on the back of the box. Mummi and Daddi sat there for a long, long, time making ayoomfa speaks about the mysterious message. After a time Choklit-Butch thought the plokkits message must surely have served its purpose and we went around and systematically scoffed it all up.

In case there were to be further communications Daddi made sure there was an abundant supply of plokkits. The communal plokkits bowl was filled to overflowing with a great glorp of plokkits and Sixpence was somewhat riled that the food which was in the greatest abundance was not his favorite. He'd never been a great eater of plokkits which is probably why he'd become tubby on a diet of shmoo kukri. The ayoomfas always tried to mix plokkits with the shmoo kukri to give the Woon boys something to crunch and exercise their teeth, but Sixpence had an amazing ability to sift through the mix and eat the shmoo kukri while leaving the plokkits behind. He developed this selectivity even further when presented with chunks of shmoo kukri in gravy or jelly, and would eat all the gravy while leaving the chunks untouched.

Mummi and Daddi spent some time watching us to see if we would make any more messages that day but of course we didn't. It would lose Choklit and Sixpence great face if they performed the messaging trick in front of an audience, so they simply sat there blinking serenely at the ayoomfas until they went away. But late that night when we were certain the ayoomfas were soundly asleep, great works were done with plokkits and the next morning Daddi came down to feed us and found another message.

'B-U-T-C-H ! ?' he said, looking at the message. We were very proud of our handiwork. This time Mummi wanted to call someone from the noose peppers to witness what she said was another *mirikil,* but Daddi persuaded her that it was a private mirikil between the cats and themselves and he didn't want other ayoomfas tramping around in our house.

On the third day when Daddi saw the message which read B-A-L-U-N-E he was so amazed he had to sit down and compose himself before he could do anything. The Woon boys had to wait for their breakfast because Daddi went to the magic speaking stick and made pretend speaks with MyGranni, which lasted a long time.

'Do you think it will work?' Balune asked me a few days later. We'd not repeated the messages in case we overloaded the ayoomfas with too much information which would diminish the significance of our messages. Also we didn't know any other ayoomfa words.

'Who can say? Ayoomfas are such stupid animals. I sometimes wonder whether Tabithat will ever let me see my bed again. What's Daddi doing now?'

'He's sitting in front of his kom-pewter. Gazing at the kom-pewter magic window. Sometimes he laughs and then he hits the little pads on the flat box in front of it with his softclaws.'

'He's probably doing something silly.'

Markings appeared on the kom-pewter's magic window.

It was an outrage! An absolute spitting, hissing outrage! We had been kidnapped from Harvard ...

*** THE END ***